Praise for
SUSAN JOHNSON

"Her romances have strong, intelligent heroines,
hard, iron-willed men, plenty of sexual tension and
sensuality and lots of accurate history. Anyone who
can put all that in a book is one of the best!"
—*Romantic Times*

"No one . . . can write such rousing love stories
while bringing in so much accurate historical detail.
Of course, no one can write such rousing love stories,
period."—*Rendezvous*

"Susan Johnson writes an extremely gripping story.
. . . With her knowledge of the period and her
exquisite sensual scenes, she is an exceptional
writer."—*Affaire de Coeur*

"Susan Johnson's descriptive talents are legendary and
well-deserved."—*Heartland Critiques*

"Fascinating . . . The author's style is a pleasure to
read."—*Los Angeles Herald Examiner*

A TOUCH OF SIN

Susan Johnson

BANTAM BOOKS

New York Toronto London Sydney Auckland

A TOUCH OF SIN

A Bantam Book / March 1999

ISBN 0-553-57865-0

Bantam Books are published by Bantam Books, a division of Random House,
Inc. Its trademark, consisting of the words "Bantam Books" and the portrayal
of a rooster, is Registered in U.S. Patent and Trademark Office and in other
countries. Marca Registrada. Bantam Books, 1540 Broadway, New York, New
York 10036.

PRINTED IN THE UNITED STATES OF AMERICA

OPM   10 9 8 7 6 5 4 3 2 1

Dear Reader,

I want to take this opportunity to thank everyone who's written to me recently. I very much enjoy hearing how my stories bring pleasure to readers. As a devout romantic, I subscribe to the optimistic hope for love and happiness and aspire in some small way in my writing to demonstrate that those longings can be realized. And my characters, undaunted, self-reliant, cynical at times—as well as cheerfully roseate—give evidence that those hopes and dreams can prosper. In A TOUCH OF SIN, Pasha and Trixi offer their own special observations on the delights and complications of desire, passion, and love. I hope they bring a smile to your day.

Best wishes,

Susan Johnson

A TOUCH OF SIN

1

A country house outside Paris
March 1825

"Odile's much too young and vulnerable since Guillaume's death," Teo Duras noted. Her gaze lifted from the letter declaring their daughter's newfound love, and distress filled her eyes. "And Langelier's twenty years older."

Her husband turned back from the view of the Seine outside the window, his expression grim. "Worse yet, he cheats at cards."

"I don't know if I should mention Langelier has a mistress tucked away in the Marais," their son casually declared, shifting his long legs draped over the arm of the couch into a more comfortable sprawl. His lack of sleep last night was beginning to catch up with him. "Dilly should look beyond his suave charm and his dramatic propensity to quote Goethe."

"You know how important her poetry is to her," Teo murmured, a worry line drawing her delicate brows together. "The man's completely turned her head."

"Let's hope that's all the blackguard's done," Andre Duras growled, his tall form silhouetted against the twilight sky. "I don't trust his predatory instincts."

"Particularly with a beautiful young widow." Pasha's voice was softly sardonic.

1

"More pertinently, a rich young widow," Duras crisply remarked. "Perhaps it's time to make a call on him."

"I'll join you," Pasha cheerfully offered, undraping his legs and pulling himself up into a seated position. Running his fingers through his wild black hair, he lazily stretched. "I hear he's good with a rapier," he murmured with a gleam in his eyes. "Why don't I stand you second, Papa, or you could second me. That should put an end to his pursuit of Dilly."

"For heaven's sake," Teo exclaimed. "Nothing so drastic is required. You men could just talk to him, couldn't you? I'm sure Odile is the merest flirtation for him."

Pasha knew better; he knew Philippe Langelier. They gambled at the same clubs and met occasionally at the same demi-rep entertainments, like the one last night. And the man needed money. "I'm sure a talk will suffice," he said, not wishing to alarm his mother. "If you want, Papa, I think I know where to find him now."

"Don't wait up," Duras said to Teo, walking over to kiss her good-bye.

"I won't," she replied, rising from her chair. "But I'll sleep more peacefully in Paris," she significantly added.

Duras knew better than to argue when he heard that tone of voice, but he was firm on one point. "You can't see Langelier."

"Very well," Teo grumbled. "I suppose men have all that manly talk that might soil my ears."

Duras glanced at his son, who smiled. "We're going to scare him to death, Mama. It won't be a pretty sight."

"As long as you're not violent. Although I dare say,"

Teo went on, her mouth curved into a smile, "a small scare might just do the trick."

It turned out slightly different.

When father and son walked through the opened door of Langelier's apartment, they discovered he'd been murdered by someone more disgruntled than they. While his beautiful mistress stood naked on his bed, his still-warm body lay in a spreading pool of blood.

"A man with an ax did that—just moments ago," she calmly said, brushing aside a honey-colored curl from her forehead. "And I can't move with all that blood." Apparently she was less concerned with her nudity or her lover's demise than wetting her feet. "Would you lift me down?"

Pasha was more than willing; she was utterly gorgeous.

"Thank you," she softly said, her lush violet eyes lifted to his as he set her down in the adjacent room. "I don't know what I'm going to do."

No thought was required, no hesitation or reflection. "Perhaps I could help," Pasha pleasantly said.

"I'd be ever so grateful." Intent on escaping Langelier's apartment with all speed, Beatrix Grosvenor smiled up at the handsome young man regarding her with interest.

"It might be advantageous to leave before the authorities arrive," Duras suggested, returning from a swift survey of the apartment.

"Would you like my coat?" Pasha's inquiry was overtly polite, as if there was a sudden chill in the air.

"I'll dress quickly." She held up her hand, fingers spread. "Five minutes." And turning away, she disappeared into Langelier's dressing room.

Pulling out her small portmanteau, she quickly found the key for the armoire in Langelier's coat pocket

and began gathering her few garments. She worked
feverishly, focused only on her task at hand, not allowing her mind to dwell on the swift and bloody justice dispensed on her jailer. Still partially in shock, she
repressed the hideous murder, Langelier's screams, the
chill calm of his assassin, necessity mobilizing her, her
survival instinct taking over. Clothes . . . money
. . . her few belongings . . . The words echoed
through her mind repeatedly, urgently, a litany of liberation and deliverance after four long weeks in custody.

Hastily dressing once she was packed, she then began
her search for funds, hoping to find any money Langelier might have secreted. Although she wasn't unduly
optimistic, for Langelier had been losing heavily at
cards. Softly swearing under her breath, she rummaged
through drawer after drawer, becoming increasingly
frantic with her lack of success, desperate for passage
money home.

She silently cursed Langelier's treachery and her own
naivete that had allowed him to take advantage of her.
Lesson learned, she hotly reflected, moving to another
bureau, jerking open another drawer. She'd never be so
gullible again. Several minutes later, her face sweat-
sheened, her heart pumping as though she'd run ten
miles, she'd discovered Langelier's entire cache, hidden
beneath his soiled cravats. Five hundred francs. She almost burst into tears. It was nowhere near enough to
see her home to England.

Could she ask these strangers for a loan? she briefly
wondered, but as quickly decided against exposing her
vulnerability. After her experience with Langelier, who
had virtually kept her prisoner, she viewed all Parisian
males with suspicion. Drawing in a steadying breath,
she straightened the folds of her skirt. As if it mattered
how one looked when one was alone and destitute, she

reflected, smiling faintly at her automatic responses. Although actually, she thought with the same un-flinchingly pragmatic resolve that had allowed her to survive Langelier's incarceration, under her current cir-cumstances, perhaps it *did* matter how she looked.

A quick glance in the mirror assured her she was presentable. She bit her lips to brighten their color, practiced an artful, ingratiating smile, and debated briefly the options available her—the merits of truth or fiction. And then setting her smile in place, she picked up her portmanteau and pushed open the dressing room door. She would do what she had to do to get back home.

"Let me help you with that." Pasha reached for her valise, wondering for a moment if Langelier had taken up with an out-of-work governess. Her gray silk gown was so démodé no self-respecting courtesan would be seen in it.

"We'll use the back staircase." Duras indicated the direction with a nod of his head. "No need to call attention to ourselves."

"Langelier had any number of enemies," Beatrix of-fered. "He slept with a loaded pistol under his pillow. So the list of suspects will be long." She spoke matter-of-factly, her voice in her ears curiously strange, as though she were observing an actress on a distant stage.

"He owed several people money," Pasha added. "Some of them unsavory."

"The man who killed him tonight had the look of a thug."

"You're fortunate he didn't harm you."

"He was very professional. His orders didn't include a woman, he said after he'd split Langelier's skull with his ax. I was extremely grateful."

And I as well, Pasha selfishly thought.

"I'm surprised Langelier lived as long as he did,"

Duras declared, holding the door to the stairway open, his statement plainspoken. After years of fighting France's wars, he was familiar with the sight of death. "Give the lady your hand on these stairs," he said to his son. "I'll see that nothing incriminating was left in the apartment and be right down."

Their carriage was luxurious, Beatrix noted when they reached the curb, the driver immaculate in bottle green livery. They were obviously men of means. Now if she could manage to acquire only a very minute portion of that wealth, she could buy passage to Calais and then home.

After handing her into the carriage, Pasha tossed her valise to the driver and then leaned in through the open door. "I'm sending the carriage around the corner, so it's less conspicuous. Will you be all right alone for a few minutes?"

"Yes, of course," Beatrix replied, her thoughts totally concentrated on escape, her mind already racing before he'd closed the door. Might there be money somewhere in the carriage? Could she be so fortunate after months of misfortune? The moment the carriage began moving, she started searching the interior.

Pasha found her thus when he returned, on her knees, opening one of the compartments under the seat. "Could I help?" he pleasantly inquired, not surprised by the lady's behavior. Any mistress of Langelier would be duplicitous.

"I was looking for a wrap against the evening chill," Beatrix dissembled.

"Allow me." Pasha shrugged out of his coat and handed it to her.

Reseating herself as gracefully as possible under the awkward circumstances, Beatrix settled the silk-lined coat over her shoulders and, a moment later, felt the added warmth of his body as he seated himself beside her. She had no room to move within the narrow confines of the carriage, not with his muscular thigh against hers, his silk-shirted arm pressed into hers, his masculinity overwhelming. He was a very large man. And when his father—the resemblance was clear—took his seat opposite them, the dimensions of the interior seemed to shrink further, the sense of male power intense.

"I hope Dilly isn't too upset." Pasha spoke to his father in a cryptic undertone as the carriage began to move.

"I'll talk to Berri about having some of her work published. A diversion, as it were."

"She likes Berri."

"And he's more suitable than . . ." Duras's mouth turned down in a transient grimace. "Although that's no longer our concern. Are you going—"

"To my house. Mansel knows."

The driver had already been given orders and as the men spoke to each other in undertones Beatrix surveyed the streets they traversed, careful to take note of her surroundings. If she were successful in securing her passage money she might have to leave precipitously and she needed to know her whereabouts.

After crossing the Seine near Notre-Dame, they traveled west along the left bank for only a short distance before coming to a gated terrace overlooking the river.

Pasha had his hand on the door latch before the carriage had completely come to rest. "You should be safe from inquiries here," he cordially said to Beatrix, opening the door. Jumping down, he turned to offer her his hand and, after a polite au revoir to his father, he helped her descend.

The driver carried Beatrix's valise up the flagstone path to the front entrance and placed it near the door. The scent of lilac perfumed the air as Pasha escorted her through the informal garden fronting the river. How wonderful the lilac smelled, she wanted to say, but more serious matters—like having escaped death at an assassin's hands—distracted her thoughts from such trivial pronouncements. Alert to every possibility in her desperate need for funds, she was waiting to see what opportunities might arise.

Pasha, on the other hand, was considering only what pleasant diversions this lush beauty would offer him tonight. Since she was obviously making her own way in the world, he was more than willing to reward her for entertaining him instead of Langelier for a day or two.

Her reserve intrigued him; she'd barely spoken since they left Langelier's apartment. He was equally intrigued by her modest appearance, her voluptuous form disguised by the plainness of her gown. But he knew what lay hidden beneath the tailored gray silk and he was looking forward to seeing that glorious body again.

As they approached the entrance, a servant opened the door and candlelight spilled out into the spring night.

A gracious host, Pasha turned to her. "Would you like something to eat?"

Yes, ten courses and champagne, Beatrix thought. The derelict state of Langelier's fortune and pantry had offered scant sustenance the month past, but she didn't intend to stay long enough to eat so she said instead, "No, thank you. I recently dined."

"We won't be requiring anything, Hippolyte," Pasha said to the servant. "Take the lady's valise to my apartments."

The servant complied without expression. Apparently this young man had brought women to his home before, Beatrix decided, surveying the splendid entrance hall with the dispassion that seemed to have descended upon her at the murder scene.

"Do you like Richelieu's taste?"

She turned to find Pasha watching her, a half-smile on his lips. "It's very grand."

"It should be. He spent a fortune."

"And with good results. Do I detect Vianne's hand in the stuccoes?" The actress voice echoed in her ears— her new mysterious alter ego. And if she'd not been so distracted by her need to return home with all speed, she might have come undone at the stranger within.

"Very astute." Pasha surveyed her with curiosity. How many courtesans knew of Vianne's work? "Where did Langelier find you?" he mildly asked.

"At a barrister's office."

His brows rose. "Doing what?"

"Conducting business," she said with dramatic simplicity. Molière would have been proud.

His smile appeared. "Ah."

She didn't bother to disabuse him of his interpretation; the less he knew of her the better. More importantly, more pertinently, the dispassionate persona directing her actions considered that anyone living in this magnificent home surely had money lying about. Now to find it—and quickly. "Could I refresh myself somewhere," she politely inquired, "and change into something more comfortable?"

"Certainly. Hippolyte took your valise to my suite. Make yourself at home and I'll see to a bottle or two of champagne."

"How kind of you," she replied as though they were discussing the possibility of meeting for tea.

The conversation turned on details of interest in the interior decor as they ascended a long flight of marble stairs and traversed a lengthy hall carpeted in Aubusson and draped in Gobelin. All the while her mind was

involved in a different interior musing: How far was
the nearest coaching station? Would they accept an
objet d'art in payment for her fare? Would this wealthy
young man attempt to stop her from leaving? That was
a worrisome thought. At the end of the corridor, she
was escorted into a suite of rooms opulent enough for a
prince of the blood. "My dressing room is right
through that door," Pasha noted, gesturing toward an
inlaid door across the huge room. "Take your time."

"Thank you so much . . ." She hesitated, his name
unknown to her.

"Pasha Duras," he offered with a bow.

Even in her short sojourn in Paris, she'd heard the
name; Langelier had spoken of him. He was a very
wealthy young man from a prominent family. Although these surroundings certainly gave one a clue as
well.

"Does Mademoiselle have a name?" he gently
prompted.

Her gaze didn't meet his for a moment and then she
said, "Simone Croy."

She spoke French with a faint English accent; she
was no more Simone Croy than he was king of the
gypsies, but he smiled and said, "I'm very pleased to
meet you, my dear Simone."

He watched her with a kind of distracted attention
as she moved toward his dressing room, his gaze taking
in her graceful form, his mind questioning the oddities
in her behavior. She had a refined air about her that set
her apart from the ladies of the demimonde, although
he couldn't quite decide what it was that gave him
pause. Her slight accent of course, but it was more than
that. Her natural restraint, perhaps—not generally a
quality in the ladies of her class. Or maybe it was her
brief pause before lying to him about her name. Most

courtesans were more sophisticated in the art of deception.

Was she new at her trade?

And genuinely shy?

He asked himself that same question a short time later when she'd not yet emerged from the dressing room. Although he wouldn't have expected shyness in Langelier's mistress. Nor was she shy, he discovered brief moments later when he opened his dressing room door to find the chamber empty. A swift survey of the room revealed the lady's true occupation.

The small money box he kept for petty cash in his bureau was empty on a chair. And the pretty, self-styled Simone had disappeared along with her portmanteau.

She wouldn't know the second-floor corridors as well as he, he calmly thought, striding back through his sitting room, nor would she find the latch on the front gate a simple device to operate. A remnant of Richelieu's penchant for mechanical contrivances, he'd kept it as a conversation piece. The back entrance was relatively inaccessible so he needn't worry about her finding that. But he ran down the corridor, took the stairs in leaping bounds, and exited the house through the library doors, well shielded by shrubbery. His view of the front gate brought a faint smile to his lips.

Moments later, he softly said, "That's a tricky latch."

She twirled around at the sound of his voice and stood rigid against the twined metal, her hands clenched at her sides. "It's not what you think." Her mind had suddenly gone blank, as though too much had occurred in too short a time, as though no further disaster could be assimilated.

"You're a clever little baggage," Pasha drawled. "Did Langelier teach you that ploy?"

"You don't understand. I despised him—everything about him."

Pasha's brows rose slightly. "Now I'm wondering if you killed him . . . but you were too pristine in all that blood. Perhaps you *had* him killed."

"I most certainly did not." It was her own voice once again; his accusation was so jarring the actress had fled.

Her vehemence was well done, he thought. She was an accomplished little performer. "And I'm supposed to believe you?" he lazily inquired.

"It's the truth." Each word was clipped; her eyes seemed to blaze in the darkness.

"As is the ten thousand francs you stole from me." His temper showed for a moment as well.

She had the grace—or, more likely, the intelligence—to look remorseful. "I can explain."

"Why don't you explain to me inside," he said, a quiet restraint in his voice.

"No. I can't . . . I have to go. I can't possibly stay . . ."

His dark eyes widened briefly. "What makes you think you have a choice?"

"If you try to stop me, I'll scream for help." She wouldn't allow herself to walk blindly into another trap.

"And should someone actually appear in the middle of the night," Pasha softly said, "I'll tell them that you just stole ten thousand francs from me."

"I didn't know I'd taken so much," she quickly retorted, not in atonement but in vindication. "All I need is two thousand. You can have the rest back."

"You should have waited. In the morning I would have given you *five* thousand."

"No . . . I couldn't. I mean—I couldn't stay. You don't understand."

"Explain it to me later," he coolly said. She didn't

seem apologetic about taking his money; he was mildly intrigued at such brazenness. But he was more intent on having the beautiful mademoiselle in his bed to-night, and that took precedence over any degree of curiosity. He reached down to pick up her valise.

Pushing his hand away, she snatched up her belongings.

Nursing his smarting fingers, he gazed at her with a cool regard. "And here I was looking forward to a quiet evening at home," he murmured with a sardonic smile. "Now I'm going to have to exert myself."

"Don't touch me," she warned.

He gave her marks for rash courage. "But I want to."

"You can't." Terror-stricken, she felt her heart thudding in her chest.

"No one's said that to me in a very long time," he observed in almost a whisper, advancing on her.

"I'll bargain with you," she blurted out, trying to melt into the metal gate.

"We'll bargain with each other." He grasped the ornate ironwork on either side of her head and leaned into her body.

"No, no, I didn't mean that," she cried, dropping her valise, then pressing her palms against his chest, pushing, trying to hold him back.

But a second later she felt his powerful body hard against hers.

"Now you tell me what you want," he murmured, "and I'll tell you what *I* want."

"No . . . please. You're wrong about this." She pushed against his unyielding weight. "Incredibly wrong."

"*Au contraire,* this feels very right," he whispered, moving his lower body in a slow, tantalizing rhythm.

His erection was enormous, hot against her body. She should feel affront or rage at the indignity, at the disrespect, at the assumption she was Langelier's mistress, but she felt instead an unwelcome, provocative, sharply physical response deep in the pit of her stomach, and as he leaned down to touch her lips with his, she struggled to dismiss the sudden flare of pleasure streaking through her senses. Pummeling his chest, she frantically cried, "No," into the soft warmth of his mouth.

His hands shifted to clasp hers, to still their movement, and she fought to resist the intoxicating sensations she hadn't experienced for years. This was impossible, this couldn't be happening to her, she thought, horrified and appalled at her body's shameful response. In an urgent rush of guilt and self-pity, she thrust her entire weight against Pasha, kicking out violently.

He swung away at the stinging pain, standing beyond the range of her feet. "You're going to leave bruises, darling," he softly said.

"I'm not your darling." But her breathing had altered. She was flushed, trembling.

Pasha recognized female arousal to a nicety after years of standing stud to all the Parisian belles, and the mademoiselle's body was available, he knew, whether she cared to admit it or not. He lifted his hands in a calming gesture. "I have no intention of hurting you."

"This is frightfully disturbing," she whispered.

She was huddled against his garden gate like some lost urchin, and suddenly struck by her vulnerability, he said as one would to a frightened child, "Would you like to come inside where it's warm and have something to eat?"

When she looked up at him, the moon framed her golden hair in a radiant nimbus, drenching her in a startling innocence. Her eyes were huge in the light, all her uncertainties mirrored in their depths. She didn't answer for a very long time, and then softly said, "I *am* hungry."

"Come then," he offered. "Have something to eat."

"Just that," she cautioned.

"No one's going to make you do anything you don't want to do." He had a conscience, rare in men of his class.

"I still need some of your money." She had given in to weariness and taken a leap of faith, but she had to make her position clear. The events of the past few moments were too unsettling to allow anything but pragmatic considerations of the future.

"I understand."

"I could pay you back . . . eventually."

"If you wish." He shrugged. "A couple thousand francs isn't of great issue. Would you like me to carry your valise or would you prefer carrying it?" He grinned. "Or we could leave it here for a convenient exit later."

He hadn't seen her smile before. He was dazzled.

"Usually men who live in houses like this are less selfless."

"I know. They're my friends. Although don't think me a saint," he clarified. "You'd be wrong."

"Understood, Monsieur Duras."

"Pasha."

She didn't reply for a lengthy moment and then she said, "Pasha," so sweetly, he had to remind himself he *had* a conscience.

As it turned out, he carried her valise into the house but she stopped him from returning it to his apartments. "I'd prefer the dining room," she said.

There were choices of dining rooms in the house Richelieu had built and he allowed her to choose one even while his first instinct was to take her directly to the small breakfast room at the back of the house.

They must have been soul mates in some other universe because she preferred the breakfast room, too. Because of the birds and butterflies painted on the walls, she told him. Because of the soft cushions on the window seat, he thought, and the seclusion from the rest of the house.

Pasha's chef was wakened along with his staff, and the mademoiselle indicated her preferences in food. Simple fare as it turned out, so in order to bring a smile to his chef's face, Pasha ordered his special strawberry soufflé.[1] "And champagne," he added, "if Mademoiselle agrees."

Ensconced in a down-cushioned *fauteuil* near a small fire that had been set in the grate to take the chill from the room, the candlelight lending a magical realism to the birds and butterflies on the painted walls, Mademoiselle smiled and nodded her agreement.

A smile like that prognosticated well for their future friendship, Pasha decided, moving toward her.

The servants had withdrawn, the firelight lent an added enchantment to the mademoiselle's considerable charms, and peace had been restored. The evening should prove gratifying. "It's cold for May, isn't it," he pleasantly said, dropping into the chair opposite her.

"I want to explain about the money." She ignored his politesse, new resolve in her voice, her sense of self restored in the tranquil ambiance of Pasha's household. "I'm not what you think I am."

"Your name isn't Simone Croy," he replied with a smile.

"No."

"And?"

"I'm not sure I wish to divulge my name."

"Suit yourself."

His tone was too suave, too understanding. "You may not believe me anyway, you're saying."

"I'm saying, Mademoiselle, you can tell me as little or as much as you wish. Nothing more."

"Because you're not really interested," she gently countered.

"Don't take offense so easily. We're not all like Langelier."

"He kept me against my will."

Pasha's gaze sharpened. "You were a prisoner?"

"His hostage," she bitterly replied.

"For what purpose?" Her story was bizarre even for Langelier.

She hesitated briefly, not sure how much of her life she cared to expose.

"For money obviously, knowing Langelier," Pasha interposed.

"Of course for money." Aversion vibrated in her voice.

"He was more of a cad than I realized," Pasha murmured, half to himself. "Did he have other women working for him?"

"No!" Shock registered on her face. "You misunderstand! I was never his mistress. He simply wanted my son's inheritance."

"He's a relative?" Sleeping with a niece was a bit of an outré relationship even for Langelier. Despite her avowal, he found it difficult to believe she wasn't his mistress, unclothed as she had been.

She sighed, looked away for a moment before facing his gaze once again. "It's all very personal."

"But then we had a uniquely personal meeting. And I'm not easily shocked."

She turned cherry red under his amused scrutiny. "He kept my clothes locked away in his armoire."

"Really," he murmured. "Always?"

"No, no, not like that," she hastily replied, reading

the innuendo in his tone. "I had my dressing gown to wear."

"Not when I saw you." Softly put, it was more a statement than a challenge.

But she felt the need to explain for her own peace of mind. "I was going to sleep when Langelier ran into my room trying to escape his executioner."

"Really." That musing conjecture again.

"Yes, really," she staunchly affirmed. "I *hated* him. Like others, apparently." She shut her eyes briefly to close out the stark, bloody vision of that awful scene, resisting the memories, not wanting to ever relive those terrifying moments. "He told me he had a wife and family, that I could stay with them while the lawyer worked on my case," she went on with a small weariness, the weeks under his custody like a nightmare. "I should have known better."

How trusting, Pasha thought, like a young school-girl on her first sightseeing trip to Paris. She was remarkably naive.

"I was *never* his lover." She shuddered minutely at the thought. "In fact, I bargained away part of my inheritance in order to retain my respect."

"You're a virgin?" He gazed at her from under his dark lashes, faint disbelief in his tone. Her impetuous arousal short moments ago suggested something else.

Her blush deepened, her discomfort obvious. "I have a son," she quietly declared.

Of course. She'd said that, which explained why she didn't have the responses of a virgin. "So this is your husband's inheritance Langelier was trying to appropriate?"

"No."

He masked his surprise. "I see."

"The inheritance is in controversy."

"The father's family is resisting." A common response with a love child.

She nodded. "I'm a widow."

So she'd been married, but not to her son's father. Again, not a particularly rare circumstance. "My sister was recently widowed," he politely remarked, his speculation left unsaid. "I'm sorry."

"Don't be. My husband was a spineless drunkard."

"I see," he said again, mildly astonished. The lady was full of surprises, Pasha mused, and unconventional to all appearances. A pleasant thought.

"I would have preferred not telling you all this, but under the circumstances . . ."

"Your explanation clarifies things immensely," he said with a polished charm. "And rest assured, your disclosures will be kept in the closest confidence. I can't imagine—"

"I have a confession."

His gaze took on a sharpness as he anticipated a more realistic account of her relationship with Langelier. She was so flamboyantly female, he found her story of a virginal captivity difficult to believe.

"I'm glad Langelier's dead," she said, clearly uncomfortable. "I know I shouldn't be . . . but I am. I felt in a way as though the murderer was an avenging angel come to save me." Her violet eyes held a note of entreaty. "Do you think me mad?"

"No, of course not. Langelier was long overdue for an avenging angel."

"He wouldn't have let me go, you know. With each passing day I'd become more certain," she quietly declared. "I'm not mystical by nature, but I feel a profound sense of divine intervention with . . . first Langelier's"—she took a small breath—"death . . . and then your sudden appearance. Like a savior."

"Nothing so sanctified," Pasha protested with a faint

smile. "We were on an avenging mission as well. My sister had fallen under Langelier's spell and my father and I were going to suggest he find some other prey."

"I'm so pleased you came," she simply said, "regardless the reason. And I appreciate all you've done for me."

"My pleasure," Pasha murmured. "You could hardly be left out in—"

A servant entered with the champagne.

"Just leave it, Jules." Pasha rose from his chair to take the ice bucket. "We can manage. Ah, the reserve bottles." He gave his majordomo a nod of gratitude. "You'll like this—" He looked up from placing the container on a table, the door closing with a faint click as he gazed at her. "What *is* your name?"

"Beatrix."

He paused in his manipulation of the cork. "You don't look like a Beatrix."

"This is what a Beatrix looks like." She smiled at his objection. "My family called me Trixi."

"There. I knew you had to have another name. You're a perfect Trixi."

"Pasha suits you."

It was her first personal remark. He was encouraged. "My maternal grandparents were Russian."

"How wonderfully exotic. My family is stolidly from Kent. Or were," she softly corrected. She still forgot that her family was gone—at times like this when her thoughts were in disarray, when she wasn't at home to be reminded of their absence.

"My family is in Paris at the moment. You met my father tonight." He handed her a glass of champagne. "To future success on all your ventures," he offered, lifting his glass to hers.

"I've rather given up on my ventures," she said with

a rueful smile, lifting her glass. "But I'm looking forward to going home to my son."

They talked idly then of children. Pasha had four younger siblings, he told her, the youngest fifteen. Trixi's son was four and precocious, she said. She smiled when she spoke of him, of his favorite activities and his love for his pony. They shared memories of their childhood ponies for a time and he discovered small revealing bits of her background. An only child of a country gentleman, the Honorable Beatrix Grosvenor had spent an idyllic youth in Kent. She never mentioned her husband or the father of her son, however, and he had no intention of asking her. When they touched briefly on the money she needed for her return to England, she apologized for deceiving him.

"Keep the money," he said. "Buy something for Chris."

"You're too kind." She felt warmed by the fire, by the wine, by her host's convivial benevolence. By her liberation from Langelier. As for the money, she'd think about that later.

She laughed at something he said shortly after and he was charmed. Her smile was warm, expansive as she lounged back in her chair; her eyes held his for a glittering moment.

It must be the wine, she thought, startled at the sudden rush of desire.

I'll unbutton the small pearl buttons at her prim collar first, he thought, watching the flush rise on her beautiful face. Very slowly, and then . . .

"Isn't the fire absolutely wonderful," she suddenly said, shaken by her unexpected feelings, by Pasha Duras's dark, heated gaze. "So pleasant on a cool evening. It reminds me of home . . . not this room of course," she nervously went on, "considering Richelieu's no-expense-spared approach, but the quiet and warmth and—Wherever do you get *applewood* in the midst of the city?"

"I'm not sure." Gratified by her agitation, her heightened blush, he watched her twist her fingers in her lap. "Would you like me to ask Jules?"

"Oh, no . . . really, that's not at all necessary. I only meant—that is— *Must* you look at me like that?"

"You're very beautiful." He smiled faintly. "I'm enthralled." Was she truly so innocent? Or was Langelier's lush hostage more skilled than most at playing the ingenue? Such bountiful femaleness and artlessness seemed incongruous.

"You said we were just eating."

He hadn't, of course. He'd been very careful not to say that. "The food should be here soon." Was she actually trembling? His voice was gentle when he said, "Let me add a bit more champagne to your glass."

"No."

But her sharp refusal ended in a wavering vibrato, he noticed as he leaned forward to pour a small portion into her glass and she didn't move to stop him. "Champagne helps just about anything," he soothingly said.

She clenched her fingers tightly against the overwhelming urge to reach out and touch him. His body was disconcertingly close, his virility overpowering: the startling width of his shoulders beneath the fine silk of his shirt; the flexed muscles of his thighs when he half rose from his chair; the raw strength of his large hands grasping the bottle and her glass. "You have to sit down," she said, taut and low.

His gaze briefly raked her, his expression shuttered, and then, with a small deferential inclination of his head, he set her filled glass down and dropped back into the chair.

It seemed suddenly as though they were alone in the universe, the last two people on earth. Quiet expectation strummed in the air. Blatantly male, dark as the devil, sinfully handsome, he exuded brute power and lust on a primal level, as unbridled desire burned in his heavy-lidded eyes. And long-forgotten memories of sensual pleasure, of vaunting need stirred within her.

His nostrils flared as if he could scent her willingness.

"How long must we wait"—her voice caught—"for the food?"

"It won't be long now," he murmured, his large form utterly still, a sensual undertone to his innocuous words.

Bolting upright, Beatrix leaped from her chair, knocking over her glass in her desperate need to escape. Champagne dashed across the carpet, the shimmering flash flame gold against the firelight.

Leaning forward, Pasha picked up the stemware and placed it back on the table, but his gaze followed her as she paced the perimeter of the small room. Returning a few moments later, she stood behind her chair, as if shielding herself from temptation. Gripping the upholstered back, she crushed the moss green needlepoint, her fingers white with the intensity of her emotions. "I don't want you," she said. "I don't want this. I have no intention of being seduced tonight. Do I make myself clear?"

"Perfectly."

"Good." A clipped, firm utterance.

Very good indeed, he mused; her desire was almost palpable. "Let me ring for Jules and see what's keeping supper."

Tense and agitated, she stood unmoving as he walked to the bell-pull, her mind in turmoil, shame flooding her senses. How could she respond to him with such inexplicable wantonness when she'd only just met him under the most bizarre circumstances? How

was it possible that his stark maleness drew her so
when the last thing on her mind should be sexual longing? How could she be so perverse after being witness
only short hours ago to a brutal murder?

Turning back to her, Pasha pleasantly said, "Please
. . . sit down. Would you be more comfortable if
Jules remained in the room when he returns?"

How worldly he was, seemingly immune to the tumult and agitation convulsing her mind, Beatrix
thought.

"Whatever you decide is perfectly fine," Pasha went
on when she failed to respond.

"Langelier rather eroded my faith in men," she finally said, unable to verbalize the entire complex disorder of her thoughts.

"I understand." Pasha poured himself another glass
of champagne. "Here's to speedy oblivion of unhappy
memories." As he raised the glass to her, a soft knock
sounded on the door, and swiftly downing the contents
of the glass, he bid the individual enter.

Jules arrived bearing food and trailed by a multitude
of other servants who proceeded to set a table with fine
linen and silver, crystal and flowers. A nearby sideboard
was soon laden with a variety of savory dishes, the
lady's choices along with several enticing delicacies Pasha's chef decided were de rigueur for a late-night supper à deux—oysters, chocolate cream, a magnificent
gâteau Pithiviers, scrambled eggs with creamed aspara-
gus, molded pears, a syllabub for the lady, iced curaçao
for Pasha, and a score more entrées and delicacies.

It had been so long since she'd seen such sumptuous
fare, Beatrix found herself salivating. How she would
have liked Chris to keep her company at such a feast.
Their own household had been frugally run for so many
years, she'd forgotten such splendor.

"Please, Madame," she heard Pasha say with an emphasis she realized was that of repetition. Refocusing her gaze, she found him standing at her side, his arm held out.

"Forgive me." She placed her hand on his arm, another temptation being offered her by this man notorious for his personal allure. "The food is quite glorious."

"Michelet will be pleased," Pasha replied, escorting her to the table. "Jules, offer the lady's compliments to the chef." Helping her into a chair, he signaled to the servants with a brief nod of his head and sat down opposite her.

Each dish was offered her and depending on Beatrix's response, Pasha had the item left on the table or returned to the sideboard. So long bereft of pleasure, she found herself seduced by the most basic human needs—food, companionship, personal kindness. But at the twentieth dish presented, overwhelmed by the multitude of items, she said, "Please, stop. There's too much."

Pasha glanced at Jules, a silent message in his gaze, and within moments Jules had directed the servants from the room. The vanished bustle and activity left a hushed silence in its wake. She looked up from the lobster before her, beautifully presented atop a bed of saffron rice and truffles, and apprehension flickered briefly in her eyes. For a second Pasha considered asking the lady again whether she required a chaperone. The impulse passed as quickly; he wasn't quite so self-sacrificing.

Smiling over the rim of his wine glass, he said, "Lobster is one of Michelet's specialties. He's originally from Marseilles. Do you like it?"

The simple phrases seemed to put her at ease; the fear vanished from her eyes. "Yes, very much, thank you."

"He prides himself on his sauces. A mark of an accomplished chef, I've found."

"Papa used to say as much." She allowed herself to relax. Pasha was enchantingly amiable. Marveling at the degree of his charm, she set aside the last of her apprehensions. "Papa took to cooking himself when our finances no longer allowed for a multitude of servants. I've fond memories of our kitchen at Burleigh."

"Do you cook then?" He'd never had the opportunity to ask that question of a lady.

"Occasionally when Mrs. Orde's arthritis is bothering her. You smile. Is that so strange?"

He was picturing any of the noble ladies he bedded with a soup ladle in their hand. Repressing his smile with difficulty as the Comtesse Dreux with her taste for role-playing came to mind, he said, "It is, in my bachelor world—granted, a very narrow venue. You must enjoy the informality of your life."

"Do you work at all?" she asked, her gaze suddenly pointed.

"My mother has gold mines and my father a shipping line. I've been known to participate in those businesses." He was in fact a highly motivated participant and a strong factor in their profitability. "Is that better?" he lightly teased.

"Yes, actually it is. Men without purpose are a plague on society," she added with a touch of bitterness, memories of her husband's wastrel drunkenness unpleasantly recalled.

"You speak from experience?"

"I do indeed. Please pass me the *pommes* Anna, if you would."

Apparently the subject was closed, he decided, passing her the golden, buttery potato cake. "Save room for the strawberry soufflé," he suggested, courteously moving to less personal conversation, "or Michelet will pout for days."

"Gladly. I see Chantilly cream as well," she added with a smile, wishing to dismiss any reflections concerning her husband—a habit of long standing. "Do you eat strawberry soufflé or is it a delicacy for ladies only?"

"I eat just about anything."

"But not tonight," she noted, glancing at his empty plate.

"I haven't slept much the last few days. Fatigue takes away my appetite."

"Don't let me keep you up."

His libido was keeping him up at the moment, his appetite of another kind. "I don't need much sleep. And I enjoy your company."

She set her flatware down and he wondered if he'd somehow spoken amiss. Leaning back in her chair, she said, "I want to thank you. It's been a month since I haven't been afraid—or hungry. Since I was able to dismiss fear from my thoughts. You're very kind."

"I'm sorry someone didn't know of your plight earlier."

"*I'm* sorry I was so naive as to accept Langelier's offer of aid." Leaning forward, she once more took up her knife and fork. "It won't happen again."

"It was unfortunate you had to meet Langelier when you first came to Paris. Might I offer my family's help with your inheritance?"

She shook her head. "A month of captivity in Langelier's apartment gave me ample time to think. I decided it had been a gross mistake to petition for my son's inheritance. Christopher is quite content with our life in Kent." She shook her head again. "At least I'm firm on that point now. We'll manage as we have in the past. The Clo"—she caught herself in time—"Christopher's father's family can rest easy."

"Why don't I see you to the coast," Pasha offered, shocked to hear himself utter the words.

"Thank you, but you needn't." Her smile was gracious.

Relieved and simultaneously guilt-ridden to be saved from his errant impulse, he said, "Let me at least arrange for some funds for you."

She looked up from the serving of compote d'abricots she'd spooned on her plate. "Whatever for?"

"As an apology for Langelier's abuse."

"Are you a relative?" Her gaze held his for a moment and then she said, "You needn't be Langelier's conscience. The two thousand francs is sufficient. That at least is possible to repay."

"Since I've plenty of money and you don't, why not accept a small loan?"

"That I could never repay."

He *had* a conscience, he realized, because the method of repayment that immediately came to mind went unspoken. "Perhaps you'll marry again. Call it a long-term loan."

"Pour me some more champagne, Pasha, and that will be quite enough. I can't take your loans."

He liked that she'd said his name with a captivating warmth in her voice; he liked that she enjoyed his champagne. And her resistance to his offer of money could be overcome, he knew. In his experience, women always accepted his gifts.

He did eat as it turned out, coaxed by Trixi to try some of Michelet's stuffed mushrooms. And he shared some of her soufflé when she offered him spoonfuls, necessitating a closer proximity than the length of the table allowed. He pulled up a chair nearer hers, and they diminished Michelet's bouffant concoction in playful intimacy, first she feeding him and then he her.

"I'm full," she said at last, at ease, leaning back in her chair and exhaling a great sigh. "How glorious a feeling . . ."

What a glorious sight, he thought. Her hair was a mass of spun gold in the candlelight, tendrils tumbling from her upswept coiffure, her pale skin flushed a delicate pink, her lush bosom raised high as she arched her back and stretched. "There's nothing more you'd like then?"

She smiled—a winsome, half-seductive smile he'd not seen before. "However often I've tried to dismiss the inexcusable sensation in the hour past," she murmured, "I find myself wanting to say . . . perhaps"— her voice dropped to a whisper—"one thing."

His pulse rate soared.

"I'd be more than pleased to oblige you," he quietly said.

Her direct gaze held his for a moment. "I know."

"And?"

"I'm still"—her brows rose the faintest distance, the extent of her desire scandalous—"debating."

"I see."

"Perhaps it's the champagne." She looked for some reason such urgent desire spurred her senses. She'd already blamed the food, the firelight, her fatigue, his blatant sexuality, the shock she'd sustained at Langelier's.

"Perhaps." Polite, obliging, he smiled.

"You're not helping," she charged, restless under her unusual, sharp-set urges.

"You want an excuse?" He slid lower in his chair and gazed up at her from under his long lashes. "You're asking the wrong person." His libido flamed bright in his eyes.

She grasped the chair arms to steady herself against her own inexplicable susceptibility. How intoxicating he was, tautly muscled beneath his lounging pose, honed to a fine pitch despite his languid sprawl, ready and waiting.

He seemed carnal lust personified and she found herself wanting to make love to him—a scandalous thought. Her feelings were so intense and pervasive she wondered at her sanity. How would it feel to be engulfed by his potent virility and strength, touch his strong, corded neck, run her palms over the swelling muscles of his shoulders, slide her hands down his lean torso . . . and lower, where his mesmerizing arousal stretched the fine black wool of his trousers?

Her gaze lingered and he saw the longing in her eyes. "Let me give you what you want," he said, his voice hushed and low.

His erection swelled at such lascivious words, and a corresponding heat spiraled downward within her, melted between her legs, the damning wetness answer to his query. She inhaled deeply, and on the merest wisp of breath because she couldn't stop the words no matter what conscience or propriety demanded, she said, "Just this once before I go." She looked away, clearly discomposed. But when her gaze returned to his and she spoke again, her voice was stronger. "I feel as though I'll die if I don't touch you, if you don't touch me."

"I'd be pleased to touch you anywhere you wish," he murmured, an inherent politeness in his offer of sexual satisfaction.

"You can't *come* in me." An exacting fiat no matter her breathlessness.

He raised his eyebrows, contemplating her. "Orders?"

Flushed, acutely agitated by his raw sensuality, she

maintained enough control over her emotions to reply, "Yes, orders."

His sudden grin was boyish and unabashedly impudent. "Sounds fine to me." He quickly surveyed the room. "Would you prefer a bed?"

Clearly tense, she shook her head.

"Then let me suggest the window seat. The stars are out."

"How romantic." But a fine edge colored her trembling voice.

"It is actually. You'll be surprised." Aware of her discomfort, he gently noted, "I'm not in a hurry. Take your time."

A sudden flicker of awareness showed in her eyes. "This may be a mistake." Hastily pushing back from the table, she jumped up and stepped away.

He didn't move to check her withdrawal. She was skittish, high-strung, unable to completely acknowledge the extent of her sexual longing. He was patently aroused by such virtue.

"I don't make a practice of doing this," she said, standing stiffly upright a safe distance away.

"I know."

"I'm not a harlot."

"I know. You're Beatrix Grosvenor from Kent."

"I'm not sure what's come over me. After—everything that happened tonight," she fastidiously said.

Less squeamish about the loss of Langelier's kind, Pasha pointedly asked, "How long has it been since you've slept with a man?"

"Too long, obviously." Sarcasm touched her voice.

"That's what I was thinking. How long has it been?"

"Two years."

A libidinous jolt brought him upright in his chair. "That's a long time," he breathed, unable to fathom two years of unsated desire.

"It suddenly seems like a long time."

"We'll have to remedy that."

"So I shouldn't be overly disturbed by—"

"Anything," he said with discreet emphasis. "Particularly sweet lust."

"And if I am?"

"Don't be. It's pleasure, pure and simple."

"How easy you make it sound."

"It is, darling. Forget about propriety. Indulge yourself."

"I should simply assuage my carnal desires?" Disconcerted she could even contemplate such licentiousness with this stranger, she fully expected to be struck dead by a bolt of lightning.

"Why not? I offer that assuagement worry-free," he gently said. "Guaranteed." Never a man of mystical propensities, he knew better than to contemplate retribution from other than worldly sources. And even those were generally within his power to curtail.

"How can you offer guarantees?"

Did she realize she'd capitulated in asking that question? he wondered. But he knew better than to force the pace. "Considering your son you mean."

"Yes."

"This is only one night." His brows rose in query. "Or was the other one—"

"No, no, of course not."

"In any case I'm very dependable."

A small silence fell, the sound of the wind outside suddenly audible.

"I'm sorry," she said at last, never having found herself in so compromising a position before where no impulse beyond desire impelled her. No excuse or rationale, no extenuating circumstances offered solace. "You must find this annoying."

"Not in the least." Pasha recognized that she needed

a modicum of persuasion to appease the moral strictures assailing her conscience. "Let me show you the stars at least," he suggested, uncoiling from his chair. "That should be safe enough." He plucked a bottle of champagne from the ice bucket before moving away from the table.

"This is all very confusing."

"That's fine. It doesn't matter," he soothed, his voice comforting, cordial. "Come," he went on, holding his hand out to her. "Sit with me and we'll see if Orion is visible tonight."

She should refuse, she knew; decorum and convention demanded it. Despite her son, she was a woman of conscience. But Pasha was so very close and tempting, and the strange, powerful pulsing within her seemed not to respond to any normal restraints. For a woman who'd known only two men in her life—the first a monster, the second, a friend—she questioned her sanity when she was so flooded with ravenous need, overpowered by the sheer physical presence of the man holding his hand out to her and offering her the stars.

Her hand seemed to come up of its own accord. Their fingers brushed, met, and his hand closed gently around hers, warming her, the delicious sensation shimmering through her body like liquid light.

"How small your hand is." He pulled her to her feet, raising her hand to his mouth, bending his head to brush her knuckles lightly with his lips.

"*You're* very large," she whispered, a frisson of ambiguity in her words, her violet eyes flickering downward, plainspoken in their need.

"I won't hurt you," he softly said. "I'll be very careful."

Her knees went suddenly weak. She felt light-headed at such a dizzying prospect.

Catching her in midfall, Pasha righted her, the champagne bottle cool on her back.

"This is impossible." She was shocked by her giddy, delirious response. But he was holding her tightly against his powerful body, his erection flagrant between them, and intemperate longing put the lie to her words.

"Kiss me," he whispered.

"No." A last breathless act of untainted innocence. But she lifted her face to his.

And her eyes mirrored a passion he'd seen a thousand times before.

His mouth closed over hers, drawing in her breathless sigh. Impatient, Pasha began counting down from one hundred by threes because a lady of such uncertainties would require wooing. And that called for unprecedented restraint in his current rapacious mood. But he'd reached only eighty-eight when Trixi began kissing him back; and drawing her to the window seat, he eased them both down, she atop him.

"The stars *are* out for you tonight." He glanced up, setting the bottle on the windowsill. "And Orion is on guard," he added, his breath warm on her mouth.

"Will he guard me from my salacious urges?"

"If you want," Pasha kindly replied, his hands warm at the base of her spine.

She raised her head and gazed out the windows at the brilliant starlit sky. When she looked at him again, she was smiling. "You must think me an adolescent with all my uncertainties."

"Virtuous perhaps," he gently remarked. "Never adolescent." Her plump breasts and curved hips were too voluptuous for youth, her heated responses those of an alluring woman.

"I don't know how to do very much," she apologized. "If you're expecting an accomplished lover."

"I have no expectations save those of pleasure."

"Tell me if you want something," she hesitantly murmured, her arms propped on his chest, her expression tentative.

He chuckled. "You don't have to perform for me."

"Good," she replied, grinning, "considering my inexperience."

That inexperience intrigued him. A widow with a love child wouldn't ordinarily be considered inexperienced. And for a man who prided himself on the sophistication of his amorous partners, he found himself curiously excited by the prospect of her innocence. He slid a finger over the appliquéd lace on her gown. "Let's take this dress off first. I've been thinking about it for a very long time."

"While I've found you irresistible for a very long time," she breathed. "How do you do it?"

"Do what?" His smile was angelic, the hush of his voice perfumed lust.

"Make me feel this way," she whispered, touching his fingers as he gently unbuttoned her bodice.

"The stars are out tonight," he teased. "I take no responsibility."

"It's the stars then making me feverish. And not this?" Pushing herself upright, she sat across his legs, ran her fingers over the bulge in his trousers, his erection hot under her hand—the tantalizing lure and focus of her intoxication.

He started counting again, not sure who was more inexperienced tonight. He'd never felt this way, almost out of control, adolescent again, breath held as she touched him, like the first time when he was fourteen and his mama's maid lured him into her bed. "Maybe the stars are making both of us feverish. I wouldn't do that if I were you," he said on a caught breath as she molded her hand over the wool-covered length of his penis.

"Do this?" Her fingers closed hard over him.

Jerking her hand away, he inhaled harshly. "Don't." Sex wasn't going to be a game exclusive of emotion tonight.

Hitching up her skirt, crushing the silk above her thighs, she whispered, "Please . . ." when she'd never in her life begged for sex. "Please . . ."

He was already unbuttoning his trousers, discarding any further notion of wooing. This lush, pleading woman was so hot, she was about to come with or without him.

That realization made him consider the question of her innocence with a certain degree of cynicism.

He'd know soon enough, he decided, sliding the last button free. Drawing his erection out, he said, "Here you go," in a newly cynical tone. Suddenly testy at having been taken in by a very adept actress, he forced his arousal upright and brusquely murmured, "It's all yours."

Even in the dim light, he could see the heated blush rise to her cheeks. Her lashes dropped, shielding her gaze; and biting her lower lip, she shivered, tears slipping from her downcast eyes.

Instantly contrite even as a perverse gratification inundated his senses, he whispered, "Lord, don't cry," and reached up to brush away her tears with his shirt cuffs.

"I'm sorry," she breathed, humiliated by her gaucherie and worse, her ravenous need. "I don't know what to do."

"Look at me." He touched her chin and when her liquid gaze met his, he said very low, "*I'm* the one who should be sorry. And you don't have to *do* anything.

Here . . . come here," he whispered, patting his shoulder. "Lie with me."

"I don't know if I can."

"If you can wait, you mean?"

She nodded, her golden hair loosened, pale tendrils falling on her shoulders, her bodice partially undone, her full breasts visible above the skewed neckline of her chemise, her bare thighs hot on his.

"Do you want your gown off first?"

A flame-hot rush of pleasure streaked through her body, anticipation so tautly felt it seemed as though she'd explode if she moved.

"Let's just slide this skirt away instead." Her skin was like silk under his fingers as he adjusted the skirt, his palms heated on her flesh. She was visibly trembling beneath his hands.

He lightly stroked the crisp blond hair at the apex of her spread thighs, slid his fingers down her drenched cleft in the gentlest of motions, slipped a finger inside her hot passage the merest fraction, an incipient, casual prelude, and she instantly climaxed, whimpering, sobbing, tears spilling down her cheeks.

Drawing her down, he held her close until her sobs quieted, until the feverish tempest within her had stilled, until her breathing calmed, and then he murmured with the kindness that distinguished him from the other men she'd known, "Two years is a very long time."

His simple words eased her shame, lightened the confusion in her mind. All the ambiguity of modesty and morality became less intimidating when one considered the merely physical.

Looking up at him, she touched his cheek. "How gracious you are."

"Pleasure is pleasure," he genially noted. "It's not a liability."

Mortified at her precipitous orgasm, she whispered, "What must you think of me. I hardly know you."

"Then again, I'm looking forward to getting to know you."

The throbbing between her legs resumed as if her body automatically responded to the insinuation in his voice. "I don't know what's come over me. It's as though I've jettisoned all scruple."

"You worry too much," he serenely said, idly stroking her back.

"I should just enjoy this." Lying in the crook of his arm, she touched his erection, poised and ready.

"Hold that thought," he teasingly murmured.

"Who will ever know?"

"Who indeed? And the next time you come I guarantee it'll be much better."

"You can guarantee that?"

"Oh, yes."

"Because you're stud to half of Paris?"

"Only half?" he laughingly replied.

"I should take advantage then of your talents."

"Why not? You'll like it."

"So sure." A playful gleam shone in her eyes.

He grinned, then slid a finger down her wet cleft. "I don't think it'll be much of a problem bringing you to orgasm a dozen more times tonight."

She sat upright, naivete in her astonished gaze. "A dozen?" she said, her voice shaking.

"Should we get started?" He smiled in the moonlight, a teasing, playful smile. "Or should we do something else instead while you're in Paris?"

She didn't answer, couldn't answer so bold a question.

"Should I tell you?"

He lay sprawled before her, temptation in a white silk shirt and undone trousers, his arms thrown over his head, his powerful body hers for the asking. And more than anything she desired him. "I want your clothes off," she impetuously said, allowing her fevered longings expression, understanding she couldn't rationalize her feelings away no matter how much she talked. "I find myself very susceptible to your sexual allure."

Her words made him smile although he carefully masked his response; how polite she was, as though she were expressing her admiration for a bonnet or teapot. "Then you know how I feel," he graciously replied. "Let me help with that." He eased her fingers away from the neckcloth she was muddling into a tighter knot. "Watch now . . . for next time."

His words sent a thrill coursing through her, although no future existed for them. But she was beyond reason at the moment, beyond all but the most elemental feelings of impassioned urgency.

He undressed her swiftly, familiar with the drill; then she undressed him with no finesse and he wondered how inexperienced or selfish her lovers had been to leave her so unsure.

Since she was filled with moral trepidation, he resolved to make love to her the first time in the most conventional of ways, determined not to frighten her away, determined to see that her orgasm was sublime.

He gently spread her legs as she lay beneath the moonlight and starlight and eased himself over her. He kissed her, only kissed her for a very long time, on her eager mouth, on the tender dip behind her ear, on the warm pulse of her throat, on her downy brows and lashes, on her bare shoulders, then lower, where her breast met the tender undercurve of her arm, and when her breathing had changed from languorous sighs to a feverish panting, he kissed her on her taut, aching nipples.

She cried out, the exquisite pleasure infusing her

senses, melting downward to the torrid core of her body, and clutching at him, she implored him for more.

"Soon," he murmured, his mouth closing over her nipple again.

Her hips rose as though she could lure him inside with the dewy heat between her legs, with the sensuous rhythm of her hips and the pressure of her mons.

"What a sweet, hot little pussy," he whispered.

Her second orgasm washed over her, his lascivious words the hair-trigger to her vaunting urgency.

Short seconds later, orgasmic but not sated, still throbbing, liquid with wanting, she whispered, "I'll hate you soon."

"We can't have that. We'll have to give you what you want."

She plunged her fingers into his long, flowing hair and grabbing handsful, pulled his face close. "Don't play with me anymore, Monsieur Duras." Her voice sounded shockingly fierce in her ears.

He smiled, pleased to see all her hesitancy disappear, leaving hot-blooded passion in its wake. "At your service, Lady Grosvenor."

She felt as though she'd split apart with aching need. "Pasha, please," she softly cried.

He obliged her, entering her very slowly at first, his enormous size stretching her by degrees while she gasped, whimpered, nearly fainted from the pleasure. And once he was completely submerged, he lay quiescent inside her, her soft, blissful moans warm on his shoulder. He moved after a time with circumspect attention to his rhythm, neither too deep at first nor hurried, until her body absorbed him more easily, until she clung to him, her arms laced around his neck and heatedly demanded more. He gave her what she wished then and before long she was transported, thrilled, bold in the throes of an exaltation that ravished her mind and body and virgin spirit.

Her arousal building, she fought against his withdrawal stroke, intent on sustaining the exquisite ecstasy. He liked the new air of command she'd acquired; docile women had never appealed. Although he'd known her as a woman of passion since her instant response at Richelieu's gate.

And she was unabashedly crying out for the indulgence of his downstroke—again.

His lower body swung forward, his engorged length stretching her, thrusting deeper and deeper into her sleek, hot interior until he reached the mouth of her womb where he held himself stationary for a long moment, felt her shudder beneath him.

She moaned, her hands firm on his back as he began withdrawing. "No, no, no . . ."

But he knew better and seconds later when he sank back inside her, glided, slid, forced his rampant erection to the very depths of her honeyed passage, she sighed in rapture, in thanksgiving, smiled up at him, languid-eyed, gratified. "You're wonderfully, fearfully large."

"You like it, do you?" A rhetorical question, delivered with a smile in his husky voice. He'd known since adolescence what women liked.

"This must be heaven," she breathed as he moved in a delicate, slow rhythm inside her.

"Very near." He penetrated that last small distance more where tingling anticipation met beatific expectation. And she screamed that time into the quiet firelit room.

She forgot all but the immediacy of sensation in the next blissful interval, sweetly orgasmic three times more in rapid succession, and when Pasha considered she'd been sufficiently indulged for the moment, he allowed himself to climax, withdrawing at the last to come on her belly.

"Thank you for remembering," she murmured some moments later, watching him wipe his semen from her stomach.

"Someone has to," he said with a half-smile, tossing his damp shirt on the floor.

Still incapable of moving in the afterglow of orgasmic bliss, she whispered, "You've bewitched me, my body, my senses . . ."

Seated beside her prostrate form, his carnal passions still on full alert, he was sensitive to his own degree of bewitchment. "Are you in the mood for a bed yet?" He brushed her damp curls back from her temples, hoping she was because he was.

"Ummm . . ."

"That sounds like a yes." Leaning forward, he kissed her until she purred.

"You make me feel tingly and ravenous again," she breathed, her eyes heavy-lidded. "Are you as good in bed?"

He chuckled. "Wait and see." Kissing the tip of her nose, he rose from the window seat and moved toward the table. "I'll bring a bottle of champagne with us."

How incredibly large he was, she mused, gazing at him, all lithe grace beneath the obvious power, the rhythm of his gait the perfect meld of muscle, sinew, bone. His skin was bronzed, not tanned, inherently dark, his heavy black hair brushing his shoulders, overlong for current fashion.

His physique could have been the classic ideal, so faultless its proportions, each element perfection—each foot and strong ankle in exquisite relation to the length of his calf, that in turn in elegant ratio to his powerful thigh, the symmetry of shoulder width to tapered hip consummate beauty, his lean, hard musculature neither massive nor effete, but sleek and fit. His height drew her eye; he dwarfed most men. And then he turned around, a champagne bottle in his hand, and the most splendid of all his splendid assets stopped her breath.

His erection—perhaps insatiable if its still-roused state was any indication—rose from the luxuriant black curls at his crotch, reared upward, its swollen, gleaming crest brushing his navel, the pulsing veins further augmenting its size.

"Ready?" he murmured.

Had a woman ever said no to that query and vision? she briefly thought.

"I'll carry you," he added when she didn't respond, not unfamiliar with her reaction.

"Like this? Without . . . clothes?"

"Everyone's sleeping."

"They can't be." A sizable establishment such as his with a master who kept late hours had a staff at the ready.

"Shut your eyes."

"Let me find my gown." She quickly sat up, surveying the environs of the windowseat.

"You won't see any servants," he amicably declared, lifting her into his arms. "Put your head on my shoulder."

"But they'll see me," she protested.

"My servants know better than to look."

"How convenient. For your orgies, I suppose."

"I don't participate in orgies," he retorted, walking toward the door. At least not at home, he reflected, leaning forward slightly to press the door latch with his fingertips.

The corridor was ablaze with gaslight. "Oh, my God," Trixi softly exclaimed and, taking his advice, she shut her eyes.

He strode swiftly through the main corridors, turning twice before he reached the staircase.

Peeking through her lashes as he began ascending the grand marble stairs, she was gratified to see no servants. Unaware of Pasha's faint nod, she didn't notice the footman at the top of the stairs melt into the shadows, no more than she'd caught sight of the servants on the main floor scurry out of sight.

Arriving at his bedroom suite a few moments later, Pasha shut the door and brushed her forehead with a kiss. "You can open your eyes. We've reached safe haven."

"Lord, you're rash," she teasingly admonished.

"Maybe we're both rash," he silkily drawled.

She blushed.

"Don't blush. I *like* women with nerve."

"Then dare I say, *I* like your superb sexual expertise."

"Dare anything you wish, Lady Grosvenor." Grinning, he placed her on his baroque, canopied bed. "We're quite alone."

He offered her license and a blissful freedom she'd not experienced for a very long time—since her indulgent parents had died and she'd become the ward of despicable relatives. It felt as though he'd given her a lush, wonderful gift, a lavish reward for the recent misery of her life. "Come closer then, if I may dare anything. I want to touch you." Her voice turned velvety. "You're very splendid, you know."

He glanced at the clock on the mantel, charmed by her sensual appetite, wondering how long she'd want what he wanted, gauging the possible duration of this exquisite paradise.

"Do you have another engagement?"

"Do I look like a fool?"

"Well, then?" she purred.

He had no intention of declining; she was as gloriously enticing as the amorous Venus of myth.

Much later when they'd both fully explored the
world of touch, he with finesse, she with ingenue inspi-
ration, Trixi first noticed the mirror overhead, a frag-
ment visible beneath the shirred brocade canopy. "Do
you bring women here often?" she asked, lying beneath
Pasha, her gaze on the glimmer visible in one corner.

"No." It was only a marginal lie; he rarely brought
women to his home.

She didn't believe him for a minute. "Why do you
need a mirror, then?"

"I was waiting for you," he playfully replied, rolling
off her.

"How sweet, Monsieur Duras." She rolled back on
top of him. "Show me how it works."

"In a minute. Let me catch my breath."

"I suppose I'm like this because it's been two years,"
Trixi whispered, licking a path across his chin. "I'm
sorry."

"I'm not complaining, darling." His grin flashed. "I
just mean, literally, I have to catch my breath. Count
to sixty, poppet, then we'll undrape the mirror and see
what you think of it."

She was genuinely delighted with the mirror, like a
child with a new toy, and asking numerous questions,
she examined the handiwork and detail of the apparatus. Captivated and entranced, she admired herself and
him and then them in a variety of postures, her naive
excitement charming to a man of jaded tastes.

They were both laughing at the end and, leaning
close, she held his face between her hands. "You're so
much fun," she whispered, nibbling at his mouth.

He smiled broadly under her nipping bites, her artless joy unutterably refreshing. "We try."

"You're the very best, Pasha, darling. I feel like putting notches in your bedposts, you're so fabulous. Was that ten or twelve?"

He didn't count. He never counted, not out to set records. He stretched his arms above his head, lying spread-eagle beneath her. "You decide, and I'll try to keep up."

"Can I give you orders?" A purr, a giggle, then she ran her tongue over his teeth. When she gazed at him wide-eyed, he couldn't help but laugh at her playful, expectant expression.

"Within reason," he said, humoring her.

"Meaning?"

"I'll let you know when you've gone too far."

She did.

And he did, shocking her momentarily by bodily lifting her away and growling, "Don't bite."

"I'm sorry, I'm sorry," she instantly whispered. "Did I hurt you?"

"I'll survive." A faint scowl accompanied his gruff retort.

"I'm so very glad." She smiled sweetly. "You can give me orders if you wish," she contritely added, a seductive undertone vibrating through her words.

His gaze came up. "And you'll comply?"

"Of course."

It was a game, pure and simple, hot-blooded and feverish, intoxicating, heedless of all but sensational passion.

Unforgettable even for a man of excess.

2

"I want the Englishwoman found," a tall, grim-faced man asserted, tapping his fist into his palm, his eyes the unforgiving color of ice. Surveying his companions at breakfast, Jerome Clouard added in a low growl, "We can't have her going to Clouet."

"We've a watch at the solicitor's office and at the judge's," a smaller man bearing a familial resemblance quickly affirmed. "Another at the coaching station for Calais, three more covering the routes north. The neighboring police prefects are all under observation." His gaze came up from his coddled egg. "Also, Langelier's man tells me she was without friends in the city, so—"

"It sounds as though you're rid of Madame Grosvenor," a younger version of the two men interposed. "Sit down, Jerome, and relax. She's gladly gone from the city. I'll bet a thousand francs on it."

"If you had a thousand francs, Victor," Jerome rebuked.

"Do us all a favor and eat. A rasher or two of bacon might mitigate your rudeness," Victor retorted. Disparaging remarks about his gambling habit were all too familiar.

"I recommend the coffee this morning," Phillipe, the man eating his egg, blandly remarked, his spoon arrested just short of his mouth. "And the sweetbreads with mushrooms are particularly fine. Is there any news concerning Langelier's murderer?" he casually inquired, clearly not as agitated as his brother.

"Some Balkan rabble from the looks of it," Jerome replied, sitting down at the breakfast table, a faint frown still creasing his forehead. "The murder weapon was found in the gutter," he went on, reaching for the coffee. "A Macedonian ax blade, the prefect said."

"A paid killer, then," Phillipe said through a mouthful of egg.

Jerome nodded.

"Hired by one of Langelier's numerous enemies." Victor Clouard gambled in the same clubs.

"Creditors, you mean," the older man corrected his younger brother. "The man owed everyone."

Victor looked up from his brioche. "He won on occasion."

"Not from you I hope."

"Would I tell you if he had?" Victor coolly countered. "Although you weren't supplying him with enough money to play high."

"*Au contraire.* We paid him a substantial sum to keep Theodore's paramour captive."

"I never understood that," Victor noted, disgust evident in his tone. "Holding her prisoner. Why not buy off the judge instead?"

"The woman's petition had been scheduled for Clouet's jurisdiction. The risk was too great."

"The boy *is* Theo's son," Victor maintained.

"Perhaps." Phillipe's jowls quivered with the same indignation he'd exhibited when he'd first heard the news of Christopher's birth. "A woman like that—who knows?"

"Theo adored her and his son. If she could have divorced, he would have married her. Surely you know that."

Jerome's eyes snapped with affront. "Are you defending her?"

"There's no need to defend her," Victor replied. "Theo's will was quite specific."[2]

"Our nephew was a wild, bohemian artist without morals," Jerome irritably declared, cutting his bacon into precise lengths. "Hardly the kind of person likely to make a practical decision about his life."

"Some would debate your view." Victor had never understood the paradox between Jerome's righteous propriety and his unprincipled malevolence.

"Theodore died at thirty-two from debauch and excess. Any *proper* person would understand the unbalanced state of his mind."

"He died of a horseracing accident, not excess."

"Because his racers were as wild as he."

"A shame Clouet won't interpret the law to suit your bias," Victor sardonically noted. "The man's integrity must be disturbing."

"Clouet may no longer be a problem now that the Englishwoman has disappeared. And should she reappear—"

"All likely locations are being watched," Phillipe interjected. "The Grosvenors are being apprised of her escape as well," he went on with a self-satisfied smile. "If she returns there, we'll be notified."

"I'm surprised you didn't have her done away with like Langelier," Victor remarked, his gaze jaundiced.

"We're businessmen," Jerome replied, reaching for the sweetbreads. "Nothing more. Not murderers."

"If she happens to starve to death though, that's acceptable."

"Since when did you become a pillar of sensibility, Victor? If I recall, the young woman with child you left in Rouen was rather low on funds."

"I was very young. And I hadn't lived with her for

two years, for God's sake. *And* if you must know, the allowance I send her is generous."

"So you don't spend every last sou at the gaming tables. I commend you," Jerome mocked.

"Theo meant for the boy to have his inheritance. You know that, of course."

"How fortunate for us then that you haven't yet reached the age for *your* inheritance."

"Seven hundred days and counting," Victor countered, his voice chill.

"Thankfully, Papa understood your propensity for cards, or you would have gone through your fortune by now."

"Thankfully, I only need appear here on infrequent occasions to collect my stipend. I wish you good day, brothers," Victor coolly said, rising from his chair. "May your greed bring you all the happiness you deserve."

"Kindly try to last til the next disbursement, Victor," Jerome said in a deprecating murmur. "I dislike your moneylenders at my door."

"I'll allow you the last word." Victor was already moving across the room.

"Then kindly do so," Jerome sourly noted.

But the youngest Clouard was gone, exiting without a backward glance.

"He's incorrigible," Jerome muttered.

"Like Theodore."

"Not precisely. Victor has no talent."

"But fewer vices."

"Yes," Jerome gruffly agreed. "Considerably fewer. And if we have the good fortune to be rid of the Englishwoman, the last of Theodore's vices will be eliminated."

"The police are on the outlook for her as well."

"So I've been told. But I don't have much faith in Tulard's efficiency. We'll keep our staff on alert for the rest of the week."

"Until the hearing has passed."

"Yes, until then."

3

The sun was already up when Pasha rolled over in bed and discovered he was alone.

Instantly alert, he surveyed the room. Had she managed to slip away again?

Softly swearing at his days without sleep that had finally overcome him, he swung his long legs over the side of the bed and came to his feet. He had no intention of letting Trixi Grosvenor walk out of his life—at least, not yet. Already debating the most likely route she'd take to the Calais station, he swiftly crossed the large room and shoved the dressing room door open with the flat of his hand.

"I was going to wake you before I left."

Arrested on the threshold, he blinked against the sun shining through the bank of windows. "Would you have now?" he murmured, taking in her packed valise and traveling clothes.

"Yes, of course. I had an absolutely wonderful time."

He was taken aback. Her response was amiable, courteous—like that of a convivial dinner partner.

"Don't look so shocked. I take it you're not usually thanked."

Standing nude in the doorway, he slowly smiled. "Not precisely in that way. You're very polite."

"And you're a very remarkable man—sensational,

actually. I shall *always* remember last night with gratitude and fondness."

"As will I, *chouchou.*" He stretched with an unstudied
grace, every sleek muscle momentarily in high relief.
"But there's no need to leave so soon, is there?"

"I must," she said, picking up her gloves, finding it
difficult to remain focused on her priorities, pressing as
they were, with such unalloyed male virility before her.

"I'd rather you didn't."

Her body went rigid. "Don't, Pasha." Knowing his
strength, she wondered nervously how well she knew
him after all. "Don't do this to me, or even think it.
Just move away from the door."

"Rest easy, darling," he said, stepping into the
room. "I don't intend to detain you against your will."
Walking to a nearby wardrobe, he opened the mirrored
door, took out a patterned green dressing robe, and
slipped it on.

"You understood I wasn't staying." She quickly
snapped the locks on her portmanteau. "I've been gone
too long. I want to return home as quickly as possible."

"Why don't you show me Kent?"

She turned to him. "Just like that?"

He shrugged. "Why not? England in the spring has
its charms. And I haven't had enough of you."

Nor she of him, she thought with a frisson of longing. He stood in his sumptuous Japanese silk robe like
some barbarian prince transported to Richelieu's ornate
dressing room, his powerful masculinity striking
against the delicate fabric, his long black hair gleaming
in the morning sun, his exotic bronzed skin the heri-
tage of ancestors beyond the Urals, his sensual, tilted
eyes so compelling she felt a spiking heat race through
her veins. But she couldn't so casually oblige him when
her life was circumscribed by parochial, parish values,
by the presence of powerful, hostile neighbors. She

didn't have the advantage of his princely fortune and its concomitant freedoms. "I'm sorry," she gently said, "but circumstances in my life won't allow me to bring you home with me."

"We could stay in London if you prefer."

She gazed at him, mild affront in the arch of her brow. "You must always get what you want."

"Just about always."

The audacity of great wealth, beauty, and charm, she thought. "I may find that offensive."

"I'm sorry. I should have lied," he casually said, unabashed. "I thought you enjoyed yourself last night."

"Of course I did." The word enjoy was much too abstemious for the extent of her enthusiasm. "But that's not reason enough."

"Yes, it is," he simply said.

"For men like you perhaps."

He had no intention of arguing the finer points of gender roles. "You could show me the sights *beyond* Burleigh House," he pleasantly remarked.

"And you could show me what you know, I suppose." Her voice was sardonic.

He grinned. "If you'd like."

"Such smugness."

"How can it hurt to have company at your house?"

"Because I have dangerous neighbors there. Grosvenors who don't like me. And servants and villagers who gossip, and a son."

"No problem. I'll be scrupulously prudent in public." His voice drifted into a lower register. "I'd very much like to touch you again."

She shook her head, knowing her responsibilities. "It's not possible, Pasha."

"How many times did you come last night?" he asked, his voice like velvet.

And her body opened as if his query were a lush password to her deepest longing.

"Everything doesn't have to have a reason in this world," he whispered. "I can give you pleasure on any terms you want."

"Don't say that," she breathed, a blush rising on her cheeks.

"I'll make love to you wherever you want, whenever you want," he murmured. "In the dark of night, behind locked doors, anywhere you feel safe . . ."

Feverish need overwhelmed her, a vaulting rush of pleasure coursed through her body. Prey to all the carnal temptations he so lushly offered, she heard herself say as if reason had departed her mind, as if such an answer could be given without lengthy deliberation, "If you come with me, you must consent to my terms—completely."

"Completely," Pasha instantly agreed.

"You can't touch me in front of Christopher or even allude to any intimacy. I mean it absolutely, absolutely."

"Of course not." The barouche, he thought, would bring them to the coast faster.

"And you can't stay long." As if she would be protected from her wanton longing with defined boundaries.

"You set the time limit," he replied, assured of his skills as a lover.

"And you must *never* look at me like that in public," she declared, reading the shameless message in his eyes.

"In public I shall treat you like a monk."

She couldn't help but laugh. "Are you capable of such a role?"

"Well, there are monks and there are monks," he murmured, amusement in his gaze.

"I'll need more assurance than that, Monsieur Duras," she briskly noted, simultaneously playful and assertive.

"I'll be brutally distant if necessary." He was careful to respond with respect. "No one will suspect a thing."

She exhaled a small sigh. "I find myself wanting you to come with me very much. Too much," she gently added. "And I shouldn't."

"The neighbors won't suspect a thing, nor the servants or Chris," he promised. "My word on it."

"I wasn't thinking of that."

"Ah . . . society's rules you mean."

She nodded.

Recognizing her struggle with conformity, he came to her and, drawing her into his arms, held her close, his embrace comforting, passionless, offering her the bulwark of his strength and confidence against her uncertainties. How good it felt after so many lonely years, she thought, his strong body warm against hers, his venturesome soul like a ray of sunshine in her life. Dare she allow herself more time to savor the delights he offered, the blissful sexual gratification, his genial companionship? Could she afford the price his company in Kent might exact?

"We should buy Chris some toys before we leave," Pasha murmured.

"No, please, I'd rather you didn't."

He took note she'd said no to the toys, not him. "How can a few toys hurt?" he coaxed. "Think of Chris. Every child like presents."

He struck a nerve with his simple assertion. Her inability to buy her son the luxuries of life greatly distressed her. "I don't know," she murmured, hesitant to be more beholden than she already was.

"We'll buy just one or two," Pasha gently argued.

"You shouldn't."

Aware of the new ambiguity in her tone, Pasha said, "Does Chris have some favorite storybook?"

"Oh, Pasha." Her eyes suddenly filled with tears. "I've been poor for so long."

"More reason yet, sweetheart," he soothed. "I've plenty of money. Accepting a gift doesn't lessen you, and it would give me great pleasure." The pleasure she'd given him last night was worth a princely sum. Had she not so many scruples, he would have said as much. "Say yes now," he cajoled, "and make me happy."

Telling herself to put this in some kind of perspective—she wasn't selling her soul, she was giving pleasure to her son—she smiled, a tentative, wet-eyed smile. "Chris would adore it. Thank you."

"Perfect. And then we'll buy some clothes for you, too," he softly added, touching her cheek with the back of his hand.

She shook her head. "No, please, I don't need anything."

"Chris first," he whispered, bending to drop a light kiss on her nose. "And then yours," he asserted in his single-minded Pasha Duras mode. "You deserve it."

Pasha's packing was accomplished with lightning speed by a host of servants, and the toy store on the rue du faubourg St.-Honoré was all abustle when they arrived there a scant half hour later. The manager greeted them at the door, his cravat precisely folded, his hair sleek and glistening.

"It's an honor, sir, to have received your message," he said. "Forgive our disorganized state this early in the morning. The rest of our staff will arrive shortly. In the meantime, it would be my pleasure to help you select some gifts for—"

"Lady Grosvenor's son," Pasha supplied.

"Enchanted, madame, to be of assistance. How old is your boy?" He took care to school his features to a courteous blankness. Although if Pasha Duras was taking interest in a young child, he assumed the boy's paternity wasn't in question.

"Christopher is four." She smiled up at Pasha, grateful for his kindness to her son. "He's going to be thrilled."

"Perhaps you could suggest some toys, darling, so M. Aumont can direct us."

"Toy soldiers, I think. He likes them immensely. Just a few, Pasha. Really."

"We've already had this discussion," he murmured near her ear. The carriage ride over had been devoted to her objections and his assurances that he could well afford a few toys for Christopher. "And I *wish* to do this," he quietly added.

"Toy soldiers then, Monsieur Aumont," she said with a winsome smile, knowing the joy such presents would bring.

Pasha bought two entire armies, hushing Trixi's protest by playfully threatening to kiss her before M. Aumont if she persisted in her opposition. He bought a large rocking horse, too, and a mechanical dancing bear. Firmly grasping Trixi's hand, he walked through the store selecting games and musical instruments, balls and hoops, dress-up clothes and stuffed animals until, finished shopping at last, he had enough playthings to fill a second carriage hastily summoned from his stables.

Trixi took increasing issue with his casual largesse as the shopping spree progressed.

The shop manager was ecstatic.

And Pasha found himself curiously delighted to be in a toy shop after so many years.

"There now," he cheerfully said a short time later,

helping Trixi into his carriage. "I think Chris should find some of that to his liking." Seating himself, he smiled at her pouty face. "And thank you for your cooperation."

"I *dislike* being dragooned," she bristled. "You put me in a very awkward position."

"Don't fuss over a few francs," he calmly replied.

She scowled. "A few *thousand,* you mean. It's a debt I can never repay."

"Your company is payment enough." He was astonished by her opposition to gifts—a novelty in terms of the women in his life.

"Like a whore, you mean."

"No, not like that," he quickly retorted, capturing her hands. "Look, I didn't mean to offend you." He tightened his grip as she struggled to escape his hold. "Do you want me to take them all back?" A touch of bewilderment showed in his eyes. "I will, if your reputation is at stake, if these toys for your son are some damnable stumbling block. But, darling, understand, please, I respect and adore you and no one saw us save Aumont, who knows better than to gossip."

"You're putting me in the role of courtesan."

"No one would ever mistake you for a courtesan, *chouchou.*" His smile was suddenly teasing. "Especially in that démodé gray gown with the schoolgirl lace collar. Courtesans prefer more striking attire. And Aumont knows the difference, believe me."

"So he would have considered us friends? No more?"

"Only friends," Pasha lied.

"Truly? That's all?"

He nodded and smiled. "Truly. Friends . . . a family friend, a relative perhaps. A man and woman can shop for toys without any implied sexual overtones."

"This is all very unfamiliar to me," she said with a sigh. "I've lived too long outside society. Oh, dear," she abruptly exclaimed, his comments on dress suddenly recalled. "I hope my shabbiness didn't embarrass you." Démodé gowns would be out of place in Pasha's princely world.

"Rest assured, darling, you're stunning in any gown." He touched a golden tendril curling on her temple. "I was merely pointing out the differences in dress between you and a courtesan."

"You take them shopping I suppose," she said, her curiosity overriding boundaries.

"No." He perjured himself without a qualm. "Although I'd enjoy buying you a gown if you'd agree."

"I'd be too uncomfortable. Toys were awkward enough, a gown would be too personal."

"Maybe we could come to some agreement," he suggested, intent on having his way.

Perceptive, she said, "You have your way, you mean."

His gaze was innocent. "I was thinking more of a compromise."

Making a small moue, she considered his beneficence for a moment. "I don't think so," she finally said, not able to disregard the moral liabilities.

"You'd look very lovely in ribbons and lace." His gaze trailed slowly over her body. "Something frothy and feminine . . ."

"Please, Pasha . . ." she breathed, drawing as far away as possible within the narrow confines of the carriage, his heated gaze disturbingly close.

"Perhaps violet silk to match your eyes."

And the tantalizing image of a gown in violet silk teased her senses. How long had it been, she wistfully thought, since she'd had a fashionable new gown? Since she'd had any new gown? Her entire wardrobe consisted of altered garments from her mother's closets. How disastrous would it be to her peace of mind to

accept such a gift from him? Would the pleasure of a
new dress seriously jeopardize her honor? Although after last night, perhaps issues of virtue were no longer
completely pertinent. No one in Paris actually knew
her, she rationalized, dazzled by the lure of something
pretty and frivolous after years of wearing hand-me-
downs. And a lady's frock for a man of Pasha's wealth
was a mere bauble. While she debated, the notion of
violet silk became increasingly tempting. "Would you
think me scandalously greedy and grasping if I decided
to accept your offer?" she finally asked, finding it impossible to dismiss the idea of a glamorous new gown
from her mind. "I could pay you back in a year or so
when my stables have improved."

"You're the least greedy person I've met," Pasha replied with genuine sincerity. Jewels were the preferred
female gift in his experience. "And if you wish, you can
pay me back when your stables are more lucrative."
Sensible of her equivocal feelings, pleased with her conclusion, he tactfully, swiftly shifted the conversation to
something less fraught with angst.

He asked her about her journey to Paris the previous
month and listened with interest as she spoke of the
rough seas in the Channel and the odd mix of travelers
in her coach from Calais. Commiserating with her on
the state of the roads, he suggested they journey farther
north this time to avoid Amiens. He'd sent instructions
for his yacht to be brought up from Le Havre, he mentioned, at which point she excitedly asked a score of
questions. She'd sailed with her father when she'd been
young, Trixi told him.

"Just small sloops out of Dover," she explained.
"Nothing so grand as yours." By the time they'd exchanged several sailing stories, Pasha's carriage had
come to rest before a small shop on a quiet tree-lined
street.

"I'm not sure I can actually go through with this, violet silk or not," Trixi murmured, gazing through the carriage window at the gilded facade. She glanced back at Pasha. "They're probably not open this early, anyway."

Having sent a note to Mme. Ormand as they were packing, he knew better. "I think someone should be available to help us. It's almost nine-thirty. And there's no need to be anxious. We'll simply find a dress for you and be on our way."

"The shop looks terribly elegant," Trixi nervously remarked.

"Mme. Ormand has a stylish flair, I've heard." An understatement from the dressmaker's premier customer.

"I need some reassurance," Trixi murmured, intimidated by the possibility of rebuff or censure.

"She's a dressmaker, not royalty. Relax, darling," Pasha soothed.

Taking a deep breath, Trixi straightened a wrinkle from the skirt of her gown. "This dress *is* out of fashion, isn't it?"

"Not unduly, darling," Pasha mollified. "Mme. Ormand will appreciate its fine quality. Lyons silk, isn't it?"

Her brows rose at such expertise in a man. "How can you tell?"

"I've two sisters. One learns. Now give me your hand and we'll see what fripperies we can find on short notice." At Trixi's continued hesitation, he smiled his encouragement. "There's nothing to be frightened of. I'll protect you."

"I don't *want* your protection."

"Forgive me. I didn't mean to imply anything discreditable. Would you prefer being a family guest from England?"

She smiled. "I'd be more comfortable with that fiction."

"You've already met my father," Pasha conceded, "so it's truthful enough." He held out his hand and after a last indecisive moment, Trixi took it. "You'll be just fine." Gratified she'd been persuaded, he leaned close and lightly kissed her. "Now, let's find you something pretty."

Mme. Ormand's greeting was urbane and tactful. One would have never known she and Pasha were on a first-name basis.

"Welcome, monsieur, and—" She hesitated diplomatically, query in her gaze.

"Mme. Duras," Pasha supplied, with a small bow, quickly improvising when given such an ideal opening. "My wife is in need of a new gown, something we can take with us. We're about to leave Paris."

"Certainly. I'm sure we can find something," Mme. Ormand replied, astonished at the young woman's unfashionable gown. Not Pasha's usual style. And Mme. *Duras*? How *very* interesting for a man who valued his independence. Although the young beauty had turned rosy pink when he referred to her as his wife. What a delicious little scenario, when no one in Paris thought Pasha Duras had a romantic bone in his body. The dressmaker's mouth curved into an artful smile. This visit should prove delectable. "Would Mme. Duras care for tea?" she pleasantly inquired.

Pasha glanced at Trixi and at her small nod, he answered, "Yes, please."

The tall, stately woman who dressed the most fashionable ladies in society and the demimonde concealed her surprise at such deference from a man who generally treated women with a casual disregard. Not that he wasn't generous; he had spent a fortune with her. But he'd never appeared in this solicitous role. The young lady must be exceptional in bed. Motioning gracefully with her hand, she said, "Perhaps one of our private rooms would suit your wife."

"Thank you, yes," Pasha agreed. Holding out his arm to Trixi, he murmured low, "You're doing beautifully."

Overhearing Pasha's hushed words, Mme. Ormand reassessed the sumptuous blond woman. Was she truly an innocent? And if so, where had Pasha found her in his profligate world?

The private room was even more elegant than the reception area, the sense of luxury profound. The ceiling was draped in gold tissue, the walls covered in aquamarine silk, the carpet awash in pale yellow roses, the whole perfumed with the heady scent of jasmine. The delicate rococo furniture was scaled to feminine proportions with the exception of an oversize sofa in tasseled, fringed brocade the color of a muted sunset. Trixi could almost envision harem houris lounging on its sumptuous cushions.

Interrupting her musing, Mme. Ormand offered her a small pamphlet. "We have these gowns ready as models for our patrons. Might I suggest number six as particularly fine with your coloring. And we have additional sketches for your perusal," she went on, indicating a pile of watercolor pages on a nearby table. "Milk or lemon with your tea?"

At Trixi's answer, she bowed herself out of the room to arrange the showing.

"This is overwhelming," Trixi murmured, leafing through the score of sketches spread over the table, each gown lavishly designed, only a few suitable for day wear.

"Just pick the ones you like."

"They're all gorgeous."

"Better yet. Any in violet?" Pasha lazily inquired.

"I don't see any." Trixi glanced through the small pamphlet now. Looking up, she smiled at Pasha. "But this is a lovely experience, gown or no. I've never seen anything like this room. Is it supposed to resemble a harem or is my imagination overactive?"

"Looks like a harem to me," Pasha returned, smiling faintly.

"That sofa seems to fit you." She took in his lounging form sprawled across its length.

It did, he knew from previous visits; it actually fit two very nicely, but he only said, "That other furniture would break if I sat on it."

"I suppose men aren't frequent visitors here."

That need for omission again since Mme. Ormand catered to women who required rich men to keep them, whether in or out of marriage. "This room does have the look of a woman's boudoir."

"Something you're familiar with?" Trixi noted with a mischievous grin.

"I suppose as a bachelor I've seen one or two."

"I feel very wicked, being here with you."

"How nice," he said, smiling. "Should I lock the door?"

"Don't you dare," she quickly retorted. "I was just teasing."

"It wouldn't take long . . . as I recall," he softly said. "Or are you more restrained in daylight?"

"Hush," she insisted, blushing. "Someone might hear."

"I could lock the door, you know. No one would interfere."

"No, good God, no. Don't move." She nervously straightened the pile of sketches on the table before her. "I couldn't bear the thought of everyone's eyes on us as we left. You're much too licentious and—"

"Shameless?" he finished with a grin.

"Yes, exactly. I warn you, Pasha," she quickly went on as he shifted, "I'll scream if you get up from that sofa."

"That would draw a crowd."

"I'll leave."

"In that case, I'll behave." He wanted her to have some new gowns.

And he *did* behave, his conduct so out of character, Mme. Ormand scrutinized him with a searching gaze on more than one occasion. Familiar with his normal insouciance, the young modistes carrying in the gowns cast smiling glances his way, but received no response. His attention was solely on the woman he'd brought with him at an ungodly early hour, and they wondered what hold she had over him that he was so devoted to her interests.

While Mme. Ormand described each gown to Trixi, Pasha listened attentively, occasionally offering his suggestions, always deferring to her judgment. He even drank tea. Unprecedented to date. And if someone had asked him why he was behaving as he was, he wouldn't have had an answer.

But he wished to.

It gave him pleasure to see the muted glow in Trixi's eyes, the excited animation as she surveyed the beautiful gowns.

"What do you think of this navy silk?" she asked him, delicately stroking the lace-trimmed collar of the day dress.

"I like it," he pleasantly said. "You could go calling in that, or see the vicar."

"Do you have vicars?" Her voice was teasing.

"I don't think so, but I'm afraid I'm no authority," he amiably replied. "Do we have vicars, Madame Ormand?"

"Only the English do, sir."

"You'll have to introduce me to one, dear," he playfully murmured.

Trixi blushed furiously.

And everyone's gaze flickered next to him, waiting for his reaction. "Forgive me, darling," he said, genuinely contrite. "I didn't mean to embarrass you." How different she was, he thought, from all the frivolous, mannered ladies in his life.

Several observers' mouths were actually agape at that point.

Pasha Duras wasn't one to appease.

"I think I know what I want now," Trixi quickly said, a sudden need to escape all these avid spectators overwhelming.

"Then we're ready, Madame Ormand," Pasha declared, promptly rising from the sofa.

"I'll take the navy silk." Trixi's voice was tight with constraint.

"And the yellow pongee, the green riding habit, both the morning gowns, and three or four others you think suitable," Pasha briskly said to the dressmaker, curtailing Trixi's argument with a shake of his head. "As soon as possible," he charged.

"Yes, sir, it will take only a few minutes," Mme. Ormand replied. Ordering her minions from the room with a brisk sweep of her hands, she followed the group out.

As soon as the door shut behind the dressmaker, Trixi took issue with Pasha. "You're *not* buying all those dresses."

"Why don't we discuss it later," Pasha murmured, casting a glance in the direction of a young modiste still folding gowns.

"Very well, *later*," Trixi said in a heated whisper, "but discuss it we *will*."

"Pasha, help me!" The cry exploded into the hushed, silk-hung room.

Swinging around, Trixi stood transfixed, her gaze on the pretty, dark-haired modiste dashing across the room. Throwing herself at Pasha, the woman wildly exclaimed, "Please, Pasha, I'm desperate!" She clutched at his arms, her eyes wet with tears. "You said . . . you'd . . . help me . . . if I ever needed help! You said you would," she sobbed.

Speaking to the woman in an undertone, Pasha tried to calm her.

"You know her!" Trixi blurted out, all the feminine giggles and whispers, the sidelong glances from Mme. Ormond's minions suddenly crystal clear. "You know *all* these people here!"

Pasha's head lifted. "I can explain."

"Don't bother," she snapped, outraged by the subterfuge. "I'm not in the mood for any more of your duplicity." Everyone knew, she furiously thought, everyone in the entire establishment. "I hope you were all amused by this charade," she rapped out, stung by the deceit. "I didn't realize I was playing to such a knowing audience. If you'll excuse me now," she said, her voice suddenly ice cold. "You look as though you're busy."

Pasha's dark brows instantly came together in a scowl. "It's not what you think."

"I don't care what it is, Pasha. I didn't even know you yesterday, so none of this really matters." Angered, embarrassed, hurt, reminded afresh of the treachery of men, all she wanted to do was get as far away as possible.

"Pasha, please!" the modiste interposed, wailing afresh, tears pouring from her eyes, her petite form draped in a half-swoon against Pasha's tall, powerful body. "You have to do something right now or I'll die!"

The lurid vision struck Trixi with ominous foreboding—a cast-off lover, grief-stricken and in distress—a presage of her own future if she stayed with Pasha. Men of his ilk never offered more than transient pleasure, and while she'd understood that, she'd rashly chosen to overlook the bitter consequences. Turning from the appalling scene, she dashed from the room, the young woman's laments following her, ringing in her ears.

Deceit, lies, deceit, lies, everywhere in Paris—everywhere she turned in Paris. Deceit, lies—the litany cycled through her mind as she ran through the reception rooms without a care for the employees' startled looks. Jerking open the glass-paned door, she fled into the cool morning air, wanting only to forget the hideous, wretched scene, the crying woman, Pasha's disgusting involvement.

Swiftly moving toward the carriage, she lifted the cover on the luggage compartment, pulled out her valise and, ignoring the driver's anxious queries, raced away.

She'd recognized from the beginning that Pasha's style of man—handsome, wealthy, prodigal—was without conscience, for all his charm. She should have known better than to become involved, she reflected, hindsight always keen and clear. Run, run, it's not too late, her inner voice urged. Run, run . . . run.

The streets in the affluent arrondissement surrounding Mme. Ormand's shop were quiet at that hour of the morning, the inhabitants of the opulent homes not yet about their activities of the day.

Putting distance between herself and the shop as quickly as possible, she hoped Pasha might consider himself well rid of another troublesome woman and not follow her. Pray that were true, she thought, hastening past the fenced and gated properties lining the street.

But short minutes later, Pasha's shout echoed down the boulevard and, fear gripping her, she glanced over her shoulder. He was running hard, his dark hair streaming out behind him, his great strides fleet, like a coursing animal after its prey.

An involuntary cry burst from her lips.

How could she possibly outrun him?

Her heavy valise struck her leg with every step as if to remind her of her physical limitations, her lungs were already burning from her exertions, and the street stretched limitless before her. She desperately needed concealment if she had any hope of escape. With her pulse beating in her ears, her breath rasping in her throat, she scanned the street ahead.

The morning sun shone brightly through the canopy of leaves, dappled light glowing in dancing patterns on the pavement before her, the brilliant spring morning unmindful of her wild, headlong flight. Forcing herself to pick up speed despite her flagging energy, she covered the next half block in record time, the gated mansions providently giving way at that point to elegant town houses. Perhaps an alley or mews might offer her refuge now, she thought, urging herself on, and with her lungs laboring painfully, moments later, a narrow break in the elegant facades appeared. Swerving sharply to her left, she raced into a cool, shaded corridor, the sun abruptly eclipsed by the buildings, shadow engulfing her, and she felt a small hope. Panting, her valise dragging on her arm, she sprinted with the last vestiges of energy, searching the rear elevations for some sanctuary. Dare she knock on some stranger's door? Would she be in more or less danger? Panicked, near exhaustion, she came upon a small portal left slightly ajar, and offering up a prayer of thanks, she slipped inside.

Quietly closing the door, she found herself in a diminutive courtyard, her heart pounding in her chest, her face sweat-sheened. Hoping one of the rear entrances was unlocked, she hurriedly tried one, then another without success. Frantically, she pulled on a third door that suddenly gave way when she turned the latch and, with a gasp of relief, she leaped into a dim hallway. Her lungs heaving, she dropped her portmanteau and collapsed against the wall. Alert to danger, though, she gazed down the corridor leading into the house, listening. But only muffled noises were audible, the faint sounds apparently above stairs; blessed silence enveloped her. After a protracted interval her breathing calmed and her eyes became accustomed enough to the dark to recognize she was in a servants' hallway, with work garments neatly arranged on wall hooks, heavy boots lined up beneath them.

Feeling momentarily secure, she remained in her rustic asylum for some time longer, ever vigilant to intruders. But no one disturbed her and after a lengthy time—sufficient she hoped for Pasha to have given up his pursuit—she ventured a peek outside.

The courtyard remained deserted. Encouraged, she cautiously made her way across the worn paving stones, stopping at the doorway to the alley. Slowly opening the small painted door, she peered out. Not a sign of life met her gaze and, relieved, she adjusted her grip on her valise and stepped over the threshold.

"I thought you may have fallen asleep in there," a familiar voice drawled.

Swiveling around to her right, she gazed in the direction of the languid sound.

Pushing away from the wall, Pasha walked from the deepest shadows, his formidable size looming larger in the obscured light, his dark hair darker, his eyes shaded, only the white of his cravat a touch of brilliance in the gloom.

"How did you find me?" she exclaimed, peevish and fretful.

"Your scent." His smile flashed. "I'd remember it anywhere."

She softly swore.

"And the front entrance is securely locked, so I only had to wait. You shouldn't have run," he quietly added.

"Women never run from you, I suppose," she tartly noted.

One shoulder lifted marginally.

"I'm not like all the others, Pasha," she adamantly declared, deeply frustrated at having been discovered, resentful of his unruffled calm. "You're wasting your time."

"Let me be the judge of that."

"What of the sobbing lady? Have you discarded her so soon?" Each word was heavy with reproach.

"I wouldn't do that." He moved toward her. "Give me your valise."

Hastily retreating, she swung her valise aside.

Lifting his hands in a gesture of conciliation, he said in a mild, forbearing tone, as though she were a recalcitrant child, "At least listen to me."

"You needn't explain your bereaved lovers to me." Angry, affronted, she'd never forget the distasteful image of the pleading woman swooning in Pasha's arms.

"The woman at Mme. Ormand's is in love with one of my friends, *not me*," he softly emphasized. "Her name is Marie Sanserre and she'd just received word of her lover's capture by the Turks. So she was *understandably* distrait. Gustave's in prison in Greece. Would you like more details?"

"Really, Pasha, I don't need details or an explanation. None of this is necessary. I hardly know you." If this woman, Marie, didn't happen to be his lover, surely there were dozens more who were. Why would she wish to be added to the list of Pasha's discarded paramours?

His brows rose, his voice took on a sardonic intonation. "You know other men better?"

"Don't bait me, Pasha. You know what I mean. There's no point in continuing this discussion. I wish to leave Paris alone, I don't wish to travel with you. My only objective at the moment is to return to my son."

"Hear me out first."

"Do I have a choice with you blocking my path?"

"Certainly, you have a choice," he cordially returned, but he didn't move. "I want you to understand my relationship with Marie is purely platonic."

Could he read her mind?

"And I'd never leave a woman crying or unhappy."

An understatement of vast proportions.

"I've sent Marie to my solicitor's, where Charles will see to Gustave's release. With sufficient money one can be paroled from a Turkish prison; my funds are at her disposal. Tell me when you've heard enough to reassure yourself. I could go on and explain Gustave and Marie's relationship if you wish. Gustave's family tends to judges and prelates who don't approve of either Marie or Gustave's life. We've all been friends for years."

"This all sounds very sympathetic and helpful," Trixi interjected, "but that woman looked like more than a friend to me. I'm not sure I believe you." Although she questioned her good sense that she was even allowing this debate, that it made any difference whether Marie was a friend or lover.

"Go to my solicitors," Pasha suggested. "Talk to Marie yourself." If he wasn't so intent on having Trixi back—the impulse overrode all others—Pasha might have questioned his unprecedented efforts to mollify a woman.

"There's still the charade at Mme. Ormand's," Trixi reminded him, bristling at the disagreeable memory, at the thought of everyone knowing her status in Pasha's life.

"I was just trying to save you discomfort. And admit it—until Marie appeared, you were enjoying yourself."

While he might be right, she still wasn't in a cordial enough mood to complacently agree. "Should that exonerate you?"

"You seemed so nervous over a damned dressmaker, I felt you might be more at ease." He shrugged. "But I'm sorry. I shouldn't have done it." He smiled faintly. "You have my permission to chastise me all the way to the coast if it will alleviate your anger."

Submission from Pasha Duras held momentary appeal. But, moody still and plagued with doubt, she countered, "I'm supposed to just ignore what happened?"

"Yes, please. It was all a mistake . . . and I'm sorry," he softly added. He couldn't let her go yet, for no reason that made sense.

She should reply with an emphatic refusal regardless his justification and regret. Anyone with good judgment would.

A small silence fell.

Two children came running into the alley, their voices shrill with laughter.

Shattering the hushed stillness.

As if released by the noise, Pasha advanced toward her and reached for her valise. "Neither one of us knows why we're doing this. I haven't been to England in years."

"And I've never even talked to a man I didn't know

before," she admitted, recognizing how inexplicable her actions were.

"Lucky for me, then." Heartened by her admission, he took her valise from her hand and drawing her near, moved back against the wall, making room for the children to pass.

With his strong body warm against hers, she gazed up at him, her mouth lifting in a tentative smile. "Perhaps I'm lucky as well."

"Friends?" His voice was velvety and very close.

"Slightly more, I'd say."

"Sensationally more, my dear, sweet Trixi." He bent to lightly kiss her cheek. "Let me show you the Channel from the *Peregrine*'s deck."

She softly sighed. "You make it very easy to say yes."

"That's my plan. You tell me what you want and I'll deliver."

"No wonder you have lovers by the score."

"That's not why," he wickedly murmured. "But I'm on my best behavior with you so you won't bolt again."

She took a deep breath, realizing she was back to her original reservations. All the liabilities of his visit had returned. "I shouldn't be doing this."

"Consider it a holiday," he cheerfully offered.

"From my dull and uneventful life."

"From both our lives," Pasha suggested, their relationship as odd to him as it was to her. Easily bored, he rarely stayed with women for any duration, yet he was contemplating an extended journey to Kent.

Chris *would* love the toys, Trixi thought, her son's happiness the strongest of motives. And to be bluntly honest, moral and ethical considerations aside, she found herself loath to give up Pasha's enchanting company. She was being offered unalloyed pleasure after years of unhappiness and the temptation to accept was overpowering.

"Say yes," he whispered.

Still plagued by a thousand doubts, she hesitated.

"The *Peregrine* is swift," he cajoled. "I'll have you home in three days." His gaze took on a mischievous glint. "And the company's better than on the packet boats."

She laughed. "A superior argument, Monsieur Duras. I'm finding merit in your view."

"Thank you." The promise of assent in her words pleased him. "May I see you home, Lady Grosvenor?" he inquired as a young boy might, all deference and courtesy.

"If it were only myself, I could be easily persuaded, but I have to consider—"

His mouth stifled her misgivings, his lips warm on hers, his kiss lush with promise, heated, tantalizing, offering roseate hope. And sweet, sweet, beyond their memories of sweetness.

But when they'd walked back to the carriage and were about to enter it, Trixi declared with unreserved directness, "While I've agreed to have you come with me, I want to see your solicitor first."

Pasha looked startled for only a second. "Gladly."

"You understand, I can't allow myself to be so foolish again," she said, taking his offered hand to mount the step, "or trusting."

"Fair enough."

"And," she declared a moment later, a determined light in her eyes as he seated himself beside her, "we still have to discuss those gowns."

"At your leisure," Pasha said with a small smile; the gowns were already packed away on his carriage.

"After the solicitor."

"That would be fine." She was back. He was content.

·   ·   ·

Charles Doudeau was young, handsome, and brilliant. His Norman ancestors manifested themselves in his fair coloring and startling size—some long-ago Viking blood still running true. But within minutes his diplomatic and legal expertise outshone his pleasing physical attributes, and in brief minutes more, Trixi came to understand that Pasha and his solicitor were friends as well as business associates.

Marie, considerably more composed since her discussion with Charles, offered her apologies to Trixi.

"Pasha told me of your terrible misfortune. Please, no apologies are necessary," Trixi assured her with a warm smile.

"Pasha was ready to strangle me for chasing you away," Marie remarked, casting a sidelong glance at Pasha.

Charles looked amused.

Given his dark, devilish looks, Pasha had the rare capacity to look angelic. "Not quite that," he pleasantly dissented. "Now, Charles, I presume you've assured Marie of Gustave's release," he declared, not inclined to publicly discuss his feelings for Lady Grosvenor.

"As much as possible, given the information we have. As I mentioned earlier apropos diplomatic relations with Turkey," he went on, "there are no unconditional guarantees, although with Guilleminot on our side, all should go smoothly. I'll have a message sent to the ambassador this afternoon." He handed Pasha a map. "Gustave's exact location is still uncertain, although he was last heard of at Patras. As you know, the various levels of bureaucracy have to be bribed. That could take some time, but not more than a fortnight. Then, barring treason or espionage charges, we should be able to negotiate a price for Gustave's release. Exchanges are commonplace enough." He directed a reassuring smile at Marie. "With luck, Gustave should be back in Paris within the month."

"Do we know how he was captured?" Pasha inquired, surveying the map.

The young solicitor shrugged. "Marie received word through friends in Rome, so we don't know how reliable the information. He was with Deligeorgis's brigade when the Turks ambushed them."

"When?"

"Two or three weeks ago."

Pasha frowned. He'd been to Greece twice since the war for independence began in 1821. A man could die very easily in a Turkish prison in much less time than two weeks. "You can do this now?" The question was in the nature of a command.

"All it takes is money, *mon ami*," Charles affably replied, leaning back in his chair.

"Time is a factor," Pasha cryptically noted, setting the map down.

"Guilleminot owes me several favors. Word should reach him in Constantinople within ten days."

"Use one of our ships."

"Done."

"I may be out of the city for a time, but I'll leave my direction should you need to communicate with me."

Charles's expression was cordial. "I should be able to handle this without you."

"I can't thank you enough, Pasha," Marie said with heartfelt emotion. "I didn't know where to turn, with Gustave's family estranged from him and with my own circumstances so—"

"Thank me when Gustave's back," Pasha graciously interposed. "We'll go out to Argenteuil for a weekend and do nothing."

"Like last summer." The remembrance made her smile.

"This time we'll really teach you how to sail."

"I'm not sure that's possible."

Pasha grinned. "We'll stay til you learn." Coming to his feet, Pasha leaned across Charles's desk to shake his hand. "You'll see that Marie gets home?" At Charles's nod, Pasha turned to offer his hand to Trixi. "We have a considerable distance to cover yet today." His explanation was directed at Charles and Marie. "So we'll bid you adieu. Lady Grosvenor wishes to return home posthaste."

And after the required politesse and good-byes, they left the solicitor's office and, in short order, Paris.

4

At the first post stop outside the city, Pasha said, "If you wish to reach Kent in three days, we should travel straight through."

"You don't mind?"

"Not at all."

"Then I'd like that," she happily replied. Now that she was actually on her way home, Trixi felt as though she couldn't reach Burleigh House fast enough.

They drove at top speed, changing horses at every post stop in record time, Pasha's grooms and drivers a precision team with harness and tack. Pasha drank to pass the time and while Trixi declined that style of travel, she marveled at his capacity for wine.

"Do you mind?" he said, aware of her studied gaze when he broached his third bottle.

"No, well . . . I . . . no, of course not," she finished, a small tension in her voice.

"There's not much else to do," he casually remarked. "And don't be alarmed. I'm never difficult until my eighth bottle."

She suddenly went pale.

"This *is* bothering you isn't it?" He twirled the bottle between his hands.

"I don't know you very well," she said, her voice tight.

"Liquor affects me very little, if that's what you're

worrying about. And I *never* become difficult because of this." He nodded at the bottle.

"I'm sorry. It's just that . . . well . . . my husband was a problem when he drank. I'm afraid my response was automatic."

"Would you prefer I not drink?" A novel thought for a man who spent his leisure time in various forms of carousal. An incredulous offer, any of his friends would opine.

"That's not necessary," Trixi murmured. "I mean . . . I'm sure there's nothing to cause me concern." Her faint smile was apologetic. "A little amnesia would be helpful here."

"A touch of oblivion?" he queried, offering her the bottle.

"Not just yet." Pasha Duras was *not* her husband, she told herself; the comparison was ludicrous.

As if reading her mind, Pasha said, smiling, "I promise to behave."

And he did, remaining the perfect gentleman despite the number of bottles he consumed, conversing with an effortless charm, entertaining her with stories of his family and edited ones of his life, asking her questions that were neither too personal nor too curious.

After returning to the carriage following a quick luncheon at a post stop, astonished at his continuing self-control and genial forbearance, she said, "You are *amazingly* well mannered. If I didn't know better I'd say you're androgynous." His conversation over their meal, like those in the carriage, had been well bred, gallant, unremittingly courteous.

"I'm simply counting the hours, darling. I know you're in a hurry. I can wait."

"I didn't know libertines had such control," she remarked. He looked very beautiful sprawled in the seat opposite her, his neckcloth undone, his dark hair tousled, his marvelous eyes sultry beneath their half-lowered lids.

"This libertine does." An act of enormous discipline.

"So I've noticed."

"Would you like to stop somewhere? I'm more than willing," he tendered. And with gratification, he watched her hesitate that small fraction of time.

"I can't," she finally said.

He knew how eager she was to reach home. "We *could* make ourselves comfortable here," he gently offered, recognizing that intrinsic longing in her voice.

"Here?" she said with some astonishment and he realized she'd led a very sheltered life.

"Here," he softly repeated. "We've still ten hours until Calais."

"Ten hours . . ." Her voice drifted off, a wisp of heat in its undertone.

"No one would disturb us if I closed the curtains."

She felt a sudden shimmer of lust, as if the delicious possibilities had traveled from her brain to her pulsing tissue instantly. "No one?"

"Not a soul," he murmured, reaching for a shade pull.

She watched each descending shade close out the glow of the setting sun, a tingling anticipation heating her senses, the throbbing between her legs increasing as each window was veiled. "We won't be disturbed even at the next post stop?"

"Not even there."

"We'll have complete privacy?" Her voice held the smallest dubious edge.

"Complete," he pleasantly affirmed. His servants were well trained. "Would you like some wine now?"

"I don't think so." She could see evidence of his erection in the stretching of the fine fawn-colored wool of his trousers, and she found her entire attention drawn to the tempting sight.

Aware of her gaze, he said, "Something else then?"

"If you don't mind," she whispered, shaken by the immediacy of her need.

"Lord, no." His voice was husky. "I've been waiting all day." Putting aside his bottle, he leaned forward, lifted her from her seat in a flutter of silk skirts, and settled her across his knees. "I thought you'd never ask." Playing the gentleman had been arduous. "Now then," he whispered, his breath warm on her ear, "we should undo the front of this gown."

He slipped a pearl button free while she shivered, prey to a powerful surge of lust—immediate and disconcerting. A novice to voluptuous self-gratification, she struggled to maintain some control over her sensibilities, wondering, how could she so wantonly crave this man? Making love in a carriage within earshot of others reeked of dissipation and debauch. "Maybe we shouldn't," she started to say but then another button came loose and Pasha slid his fingers down the deep valley between her breasts, a small proprietary gesture that vividly brought to mind all his flagrantly proprietary license of the night past. And she quivered inside at that lush remembrance.

"You'll be more comfortable with this gown off." He pulled the remaining buttons free, opening the front of her dress. "More fuckable."

His words, basely carnal, smacked of casual sexual conquest, and rather than taking offense at the coarseness as any self-respecting lady would, she felt the pulsing between her legs accelerate, her craving immune to respectability. Obsessed, corrupted by what he could make her feel, she responded to his graphic authority, turned liquid inside, melted, as if making herself ready to service him.

"We both know how much you like it." Sure of what he was doing to her, he recognized the change in her breathing, the flush rising up her throat. Shifting her position, he lifted and turned her so she was straddling his lap, making her even more available, his conspicuous erection pressed into her bottom so they were half-conjoined. Throbbing with desire, she moved against him, squirmed into his irresistible hardness.

"How did you ever last two years?" he whispered, sliding her dress from her shoulders and arms.

Her violet eyes, sultry, heated, held his. "I was waiting for you."

"How nice." His gaze drifted downward as he lifted her skirt away, exposing her pink thighs and golden mons. "I'll take care of you," he whispered, stroking her pale hair.

She trembled at the lush promise in his voice, at the delicate contact of his hand, shuddered as his middle finger glided over her sleek, wet labia, then slipped inside.

Slivers of light gleamed on the borders of the shades, the setting sun insinuating itself into the carriage interior in a diffused glow, illuminating the carnal heat in Trixi's eyes, gilding her pale flesh, burnishing the silken curls flat against Pasha's palm.

"I like that you were waiting for me," he breathed, sliding his finger deeper, adding a second one, forcing his hand upward, stroking her slick tissue with such deftness she held her breath against the agonizing rapture. Whimpering, she writhed into the movement of his hand, wanting him to come inside her and do all the things that only he could do. Overwhelmed with desire, she fumbled for the buttons on his trousers, found one, stripped it open, then another and another, her needs as scorching as their traveling speed, the quicksilver rhythm of the swaying carriage adjunct to her fevered urgency.

"No more foreplay?" he said, amused. He slid his fingers free.

"Do you mind?" Lustful and uncoquettish, she gazed at him.

"Do I mind fucking you?" He looked amused again. "What do you think?"

"I think you'd fuck anyone anywhere, but I happen to be here now." Her boldness even shocked her. This must be what came of having Pasha Duras's overt sexuality in close proximity—it made one brazen. But he only looked mildly shocked; he'd probably heard that before. On second thought he didn't look shocked so much as interested.

"You're like a virgin let out of a convent for the first time." His voice was husky, languid with heat, as though he fancied being the gatekeeper at that convent gate.

"And I need what you do to me." She felt virginal, unsure, terrifyingly aware she wanted him much more than she should.

"Then we must see if we can put this"—he drew his erection out—"in here," he softly added, stroking her pale pubic hair.

He seemed larger, more intimidating; she'd forgotten how big he was. He was terrifyingly aroused. And she wondered if reason had disappeared from her consciousness that she was willing to have that threatening penis inside her.

He slid his hand down her thigh as if he could read her mind and he knew she needed gentling. Maybe he'd done that before too; maybe he always had to when women saw him unclothed.

She shivered at his touch, her body betraying her as

it always did with him, a sexual frisson quivering down her spine.

"I won't hurt you."

He misunderstood; he made her lose her mind and reason and every shred of decency, she thought, but he didn't hurt her. On the contrary, Pasha Duras knew how to refine pleasure to opulent dimensions.

A man of sexual finesse, he held her with gentleness, his hands spanning her waist, first raising her to her knees then easing her downward with infinite care. He guided himself into place, allowing her to sink down slowly on his engorged length and the violent pulsing between her legs became the unerring, single focus of her world.

"You're perfect," he breathed, fully absorbed, every nerve in his body hypersensitive. "We fit"—he flexed his hips upward—"perfectly."

"Stay then." Her sigh drifted into the golden light, ecstasy inundating her senses.

"I'll be staying." At least until he no longer wished to feel this dizzying, hot rut, he thought, lifting her slowly. Not a reasonable assumption at the moment. "You're damned enticing," he said, velvety and low.

"It's you." Or some blissful magic spell, she thought, languidly descending down his rigid length.

"It's us," he corrected, his experience legion and unspiritual, this ferocious lust particular to a violet-eyed blonde from Kent. Forcing her hips down, he held her firmly in place, his sex buried in her, not letting her move for a long, sensational time so she felt him with every pulsing breath. "I'll keep you filled with cock until Calais," he whispered.

A tantalizing vision of paradise if she didn't die of ecstasy long before. Her ravenous desire was so sharp-set and urgent, she was trembling in his arms. Driving upward, he forced himself deeper with a slow, inexorable pressure that burned white-hot in the throbbing, avaricious core of her body and in her brain and brought her after a mindless interval, breathless, panting, whimpering to a long, hovering, half-fainting climax.

"You do like sex, don't you?" Pasha whispered afterward, gently cradling her in his arms.

"I . . . never knew . . . I did." Still breathless, she smiled into his shoulder.

She'd make a delectable mistress, he thought—always ravenous and eager. The prospect of having her waiting in a love nest somewhere almost made him consider taking on the unprecedented role of protector. Almost.

Lifting her head, she gazed at him with an artless smile. "Thank you very much," she sweetly murmured, "for showing me. I'm very grateful."

"I'm grateful Calais is still hours away."

"I may not last," she playfully noted, trailing a finger down the dark skin of his throat.

"I have a feeling you will." And he should know, she thought as he slipped her chemise straps down her forearms, wondering if there was some esoteric gauge of sexuality familiar only to hard core libertines.

Immune to such philosophical uncertainties, Pasha had the straps of her chemise looped through his fingers and he was observing her large breasts bobbing above and beneath the delicate linen undergarment with idle curiosity. "Do you ever wear a corset?"

"I outgrew them a long time ago." Her voice caught at the last, a lurch of the carriage forcing his erection bewitchingly higher.

"We'll have to buy you some when we get to England." He eased the fine linen down, exposing her breasts, the soft flesh vibrating with the pitch and roll of the carriage. Cradling their heavy weight in his palms, he gently lifted them into pale mounds. "If we had some corsets made for you, these magnificent breasts would be more showy. You could wear your corsets for me at night when everyone's sleeping. Or perhaps I'll make you wear them in the daytime under your country gowns," he quietly went on, squeezing her plump breasts so they swelled even higher. "Everyone will wonder why your breasts are so ostentatious, but they won't dare ask. And when no one's looking, I'll touch your nipples so they'll stand out pert and stiff and you'll have to cover them with your arms and hide them or people will know you're ready for sex. Like now," he added, his voice silken. "You're slippery wet again . . . Lift up for me—show me how much you want my cock."

Obedient to his commands, addicted to his sexual allure, she rose to her knees, her breasts conveniently rising near Pasha's mouth. "Maybe we should see if we can make you wetter," he whispered, "so you'll take me more easily, so I won't hurt you. Don't move, now," he ordered, drawing a nipple between his lips, gently biting the tip. Holding her captive with his mouth and hands, he sucked and nibbled until her nipples were swollen and thick and the color had changed from pink to red. Until the tips were so sensitive the tactile pressure of his mouth made her whimper.

What he was doing to her breasts she could feel between her thighs, the cause and effect so profound she squirmed and writhed on the swollen crest of his erection, trying to move downward, searching for satisfaction.

"I could just suck on you until you come," he murmured, his hands hard on her waist.

"Not if you want to survive," she breathed, her eyes wild with wanting.

He pretended not to understand. "Are you talking about fucking me to death?"

"It's a possibility," she whispered.

His brows flickered upward briefly. "Now there's a challenge."

"Please, Pasha," she said on a caught breath. "I don't have your steely nerves."

"You haven't had the practice," he indulgently remarked. "But then I haven't seen such chaste longing for a very long time." Probably never, he reflected, considering the style of his amorous entertainments. Sympathetic to her plight, at heart a gracious lover, he took pity on her, released his hands from her waist, and glided back into her hot, soaked cleft.

Unspeakably grateful, she put her arms around his neck and nuzzled his throat, offering her thanks, touching him with her tongue, tasting him, feeling as though she was meant to be filled by him. Impaled on his full length, she felt gloriously defined by sex, exalted by sex, stupefied, overflowing with sex, rising and falling, raising and lowering her body, voluptuously gorged, filled.

With his hands on her hips, Pasha guided, disciplined the rhythm, the extent and depth of thrust, how far she was allowed to descend, deliberately orchestrating the intoxicating flux and flow. Her deep cleavage flared wide on the downstrokes, converging on the ascent; her pleasure was expressed in a low, throaty purr.

"Tight, but not too tight." He forced himself deeper, his breath a warm ripple on her cheek. "The perfect pussy."

His words floated through the lustful haze and pungent heat and she lifted her lashes, his eyes surprisingly close as she drifted back into reality, his gaze dispassionate as though he were quite separate from his hard cock inside her. She was dying for him and he was letting her fuck him. A shocking thrill tore through her. It was depraved and shameful that she should want him so, more so because he knew it.

"Are you enjoying your ride?" His voice was hushed, a knowing undertone to his words. "You're almost there again, aren't you?" Neither question required an answer, nor was she capable of one for he'd tightened his grip on her hips as he spoke, and holding her, he shoved upward with such force, she felt herself stretch wide, fiercely wide.

And drenched and pulsing, she heard her orgasmic scream rise into the shaded interior of the carriage.

She collapsed on Pasha's shoulder, clinging to him while he held her gently, their bodies swaying with the motion of the carriage. Moments later, roused from her lethargy, she whispered, "No . . . no more," and began to lift herself away.

"Are you sure?" Pasha stroked her back, holding her lightly in place on his erection. "Umm . . . now that's nice." He moved in a small, succinct way, a blissful way that made her feel faint.

And she was no longer sure about anything.

"Let me show you something," he said, smiling. "Tell me what you think."

The heat inside her rekindled as he shifted slightly beneath her, burned degrees hotter if possible, frightened her with its intensity, as though she were mindless to all but an abject sexual craving.

"Don't do that," she protested, trying to pull away, some remnant of self still operating beneath the sensual deluge.

"This?" He slid deeper, glided along every shuddering susceptible nerve in her vagina, invoking an inarticulate whimpering need that made her forget all but her distended, pulsating core, the splendid flux and flow of Pasha's thick, hard penis. She dissolved around him, helpless against the opulent, swelling desire.

The carriage lurched, slowed. Her fitful gaze came up, anxious, uncertain. "Don't worry," he murmured, sustaining the lush rhythm, kissing her half-parted lips.

Seconds later, raised voices signaled the approach of a post stop and a moment of panic showed in her eyes. But she was already beginning to crest and it was too late, the tidal wave of sensation impossible to curb or deter, the swelling tumult irrepressible. Her orgasmic cry reverberated as the carriage came to a rest.

"Everyone heard," Trixi whispered several moments later, nervously pulling her bodice up to cover her bare breasts, as though those outside could see as well.

"Don't do that," he abruptly said, pulling her gown back down. "These are much too luscious to hide."

"Pasha, no," she protested, her horrified gaze flicking from window to window.

"The shades are down, darling. Relax." He eased the gray silk from her fingers. "I still haven't had my turn."

"Pasha, not here!" she said in a panic. But even as she uttered the words, a perverse excitement rippled through her senses.

He read the flush on her cheeks and the twinge of shameful terror in her eyes. "Does the danger excite you?"

"Don't say that."

"I'm sure the post boys would love hearing you again, or seeing you." A wolfish smile appeared. "But I'm too selfish. These are for my eyes only," he whispered, tweaking her distended nipples. "*You're* mine." He slid his hands beneath her skirt, cupping her bottom, his fingers slipping over the verges of her drenched vulva stretched around his erection. "Tell me

you're mine," he murmured, astonished by his possessive impulse, disconcerted. "Because I intend to fuck
you all the way to the coast," he added, clarifying his
sense of possession into recognizable motive. "Beginning . . . let's see where we are." Freeing one hand,
he pulled the shade back enough to glance out, his wet
fingers leaving stains on the silk.

A hot, sticky imprint, a memento of her passage
through his life, she thought, gazing at the blemished
silk, wondering how many other women craved him
the way she did.

"Beginning at the Coq d'Or," he drawled, dropping
the shade back in place, familiar with all the post stops
to the coast. "How appropriate," he said, half smiling,
"with you liking cock so much."

She should say no, she didn't, when he looked at her
like that with such wicked, carnal assessment, but she
couldn't when he looked at her like that. When his
eyes told her he knew how shamelessly she liked *his*
cock inside her.

"You can hardly wait for more, can you?" His fingers
stroked her lavish breasts. "Luckily, we still have hours.
Look." He lightly flicked her nipples with his thumbs.
"They must have heard. They've swollen larger. With
hours to go, you'll be sore by the time we reach Calais.
I'll be sore." His appetite for her was as insatiable, a
disturbing thought for a man who had always reached
the point of indifference quickly.

"Let's get rid of this dress." His voice took on a hard
edge when he considered his unwanted compulsions. "I
want you naked."

"You as well," she replied languorously, still suf-
fused with postcoital mellowness. "If you're not afraid
of getting cold."

Amusement returned to his gaze. "I don't anticipate
being cold."

"You *feel* hot," she said, very, very softly, moving her hips in a slow, serpentine undulation that brought a smile to both their faces.

"And you feel really fuckable," he whispered, putting aside disquieting thoughts in favor of more pleasant activities.

The journey to Calais turned into a sexual marathon, one of discovery and indulgence, excitement and urgency, sweetly virginal at times for them both, all hot haste and enthusiasm at other times—until shortly after the moon came up. "We have to stop," Pasha said. "I need food or you're going to complain."

"What makes you think I'd complain?"

He cast her a droll look. "Let's just say I have this feeling you can be a shade demanding."

"In that case, stop by all means," she cheerfully acceded. "But you just go in. I'm lazy. I couldn't possibly go anywhere looking like this anyway." Illuminated by moonlight shining through the carriage shades, she lay nude on the opposite seat, her hair loose on her shoulders, her clothes in disarray on the floor.

"Why not?" he inquired. "If you're tired, I'll carry you in."

"Lord, Pasha, that's all I need. As if I wouldn't appear improper enough with a crumpled gown and disheveled hair."

"You look fabulous," he disagreed, relishing his view. "Now if we can find some decent food, life will be bloody near perfect."

"A hairdresser and a lady's maid for my gown would add to that perfection."

"Do you want me to find you some servants?"

"No, no—really, I don't." She could tell he was quite willing to do just that, which would only embarrass her further. She wished she had his contempt for public opinion.

But he eventually prevailed upon her to accompany him inside, helping her put her hair and gown to rights with sweet intent if not competence. But it required a high-handed arrogance to stare down those who gazed at them when they walked through the public rooms to their private dining parlor.

Warm water and a mirror were procured in their private parlor, together with a substantial meal. Sometime later, thoroughly refreshed and nourished, the young couple returned to their carriage.

After assisting Trixi in, Pasha took a half-step back and glanced up at his driver, Mansel, who sat at the ready, waiting for orders. "We won't be stopping again, save for changing horses. Is that clear?"

"Yes, sir." Mansel understood his master wasn't to be disturbed.

"We should reach Calais by morning?"

"Before dawn, more likely."

Pasha smiled and entered the carriage. At the snap of the door shutting, Mansel cracked his whip and the horses broke into a canter.

They reached Calais in the early morning and found the *Peregrine* only recently docked. Pasha's captain had unfurled all sail to bring the yacht up to Calais in record time. Pasha's message had been clear—all speed was required.

Pasha carried Trixi aboard. Sated, replete with pleasure after the long hours to Calais, she made no protest even when he tucked her into his berth in his stateroom. "Sleep, darling," he murmured, kissing her flushed cheek. "I'll join you once we're out into the Channel."

"You're much too nice."

"And you're too damned delectable," he softly replied, knowing he could have her a hundred times more and not have enough. Mildly unnerved by such need, he swiftly left the stateroom, putting distance between her and his lust.

The cool sea air brought a modicum of reason back to his brain, and on deck he was able to view his obsession more dispassionately. She was a strikingly beautiful woman with a fresh innocence that tempted his jaded soul. And, he reflected with a faint smile, she possessed a lush, extravagant sexuality—both flagrant and startlingly unaffected. He'd be a fool not to enjoy his holiday with her. And when it was over, he'd return to Paris. That was simple enough. There was no need to justify every nuance of sensation.

But despite his attempt at a rationale, he found himself wanting her again, only minutes later, with a covetous urgency that caused him considerable misgiving, and he forced himself to remain on deck until the *Peregrine* was well out into the Channel. He went belowdecks, though, shortly after and slipped into his berth beside her and slipped into her body as well and gratified his inexplicable need.

She welcomed him with an addictive fervor she could no more understand than control. She'd given up trying to comprehend her startling sexual need for him long before they reached Calais. Reason had proved useless, no convoluted explanation sufficed to fathom the degree of her response. Pleasure alone impelled her, and she allowed herself to simply savor the feeling.

The sea air, tantalizing and pungent, enveloped them, the isolation of Pasha's small stateroom enfolded them; they felt a kind of deep, contented togetherness separate from their passion.

"It's because I'm going home," Trixi said, her voice winsome, her smile enchanting.

And the man who would have scoffed at the word enchantment two days ago wondered if one of his mother's shamans had cast a spell over him.

They stayed at anchor offshore England that night, waiting for dawn before docking. At sunrise, they stood on deck together, watching the white cliffs of Dover turn from pink to tangerine to gold, contentment warming their souls.

Pasha had never experienced this degree of satisfaction, his life since adulthood devoted to more feverish degrees of sensation.

Like a prisoner recently allowed her freedom after years of emotional deprivation, Trixi only savored the joy.

That rare bliss, unique to both their lives, forged an uncommon bond between them, and a sweet affinity quite separate from lust pervaded their senses.

At quayside, Pasha helped with the complexities of transferring his carriage to land, working the block and tackle with a deft touch, swinging the large conveyance over the side and setting it down so delicately the springs barely bounced. The green lacquered barouche glistened under the pale sun, oddly out of place on the docks stacked high with cargo, like a dazzling objet d'art amidst swine. While his men harnessed hired horses and packed the dray wagon engaged to carry their luggage and most of Chris's toys, Pasha made arrangements for his men at a local inn.

Seated in the parlor with a cup of tea, Trixi observed another side of the man who had charmed her so. Brisk and efficient, he paid the drayman and the stableman, talked to the harbormaster about the *Peregrine*'s berth, and gave orders concerning the rooms and meals for his crew, his manner authoritative yet cordial, his English without accent. He offered his hand to everyone in parting, so unusual a gesture from a gentleman, the locals were momentarily startled. But, beaming, they all shook his hand, his name now not only a byword for generosity—he'd tipped everyone a princely sum—but for courtesy as well.

"The crew's arranged for," he said, walking over to the table to join Trixi. "And the landlady is bringing us some breakfast. A little of everything I told her, if that's all right with you?"

"I haven't eaten so well in years," Trixi replied, smiling.

"I haven't *enjoyed* myself so well in years. It must be kismet," he added with a grin, dropping into a chair in a comfortable sprawl.

"Food and lust you mean," she teased.

His brows arched, amusement twinkled in his eyes. "Always a good combination."

"The tastes of a Parisian libertine, no doubt."

"Do you think so? English rakes don't eat?"

"We'll have to ask when next we see one."

His eyes narrowed minutely. "I'd just as soon you not see any."

"Are we jealous?" she playfully inquired.

"Oddly, yes."

"How nice." His brusque reply warmed her heart.

"And very strange," he said with a tangible perplexity. "Perhaps I'm hungry," he mused, masculine logic at work. "Actually, I *am* hungry." Subtleties of emotion rarely occupied his interest for long. "Ah, there's my coffee," he exclaimed as a maid entered the room carrying a tray.

Within the hour, well fed and refreshed, they were away from Dover on the road to London, and a scant hour later, they were turning onto the country byway that would lead to Burleigh House.

"You must think me a ninny, always filled with doubts and uncertainties," Trixi said, as the familiar landscape rolled by the carriage windows, "but in my parish everyone knows everyone and when you appear in our midst, questions will be asked."

"I'm a cousin on your mother's side." Pasha indulgently repeated the story rehearsed countless times already. "The Teeside Ripons sent one of theirs off to France, where she married, and two generations later, voilà. Pasha Duras. And I shan't embarrass you," he assured her again. "My word on it."

"You'll be particularly careful of propriety around Chris?" she posed, as though they'd not discussed it numberless times before.

"I promise." His voice was grave; he understood her concern.

"I hope I don't stammer too much when I introduce you to the staff."

"You needn't answer—but how did you manage when Christopher's father was with you?" She seemed so abjectly nervous it seemed as if he were the only man to visit Burleigh House.

When she didn't reply, he immediately offered his apologies.

"You needn't apologize," she said at last. "You have a right to know." Her voice was so low he had to strain to hear. She bit at her lower lip before she finally said, "Actually, Christopher's father was staying with my husband's family."

It took effort to keep his voice neutral. "Where was your husband?"

"His family had put him in an asylum by then."

"I'm sorry."

She looked momentarily distracted and then uncomfortable, a small grimace evidence of her unease. "I could never feel sorry for a man completely lacking in humanity, although God knows I tried."

He knew brutal men like that. "Were you married long?" he gently asked, sympathy in his gaze.

"Five years."

"That's a long time."

"Hellishly long."

"How miserable for you," he kindly said.

"Yes," she murmured, forcibly suppressing the wash of cruel memory. "But the Grosvenors wanted my land and nothing else mattered."

"No family member intervened?"

"My parents were gone. My two uncles, who were trustees of my father's estate, compelled me to marry George. The Grosvenors are very influential in Kent."

"Good God," Pasha softly exclaimed. "Compelled?" He knew arranged marriages were common enough; his mother's first marriage, in fact, had been inflicted on her, but that was long ago, before he was born, and the concept was remote to a man disinterested in matrimony.

"It's over now," Trixi said, with such constraint he knew it would never be completely over for her. "And thank God, I'm no longer beholden to the Grosvenors."

"The land?"

Her smile was tight. "The marriage settlement was very specific—they took my land. Since I was seventeen, my uncle signed for me."

"Very convenient."

"Very. Now I intend to change the subject because it's much too nice a spring day to dwell on the past. You now know all the sordid facts relating to my life," she sardonically murmured, "and if you still choose to stay in my company, we shall soon be within view of Burleigh House."

"I very much choose." Pasha gently stroked the back of her hand. "As for sordid," he added with a half-smile, "I'm afraid my scandals have far outstripped yours. So it's rather if you choose to stay with me."

"For no sane reason in the world," she said, "I do."

"In my experience, sanity is much overrated." Leaning over, he kissed her rosy cheek.

He was like a vivifying tonic in her life, she joyously thought, all sweetness, good cheer, sumptuous, unbridled passion—stark contrast to the grim reality she'd faced for so long. "I'm very glad you came with me." Reaching up, she touched the firm line of his jaw, drew her finger down its graceful curve. "Very glad."

"You couldn't keep me away." He arrested her finger with his, nudging it upward to his mouth where he gently nibbled on it.

Her violet eyes took on a glowing warmth at his profoundly erotic tenderness. Taking his face between her hands, thanking the panoply of gods for their favor in giving him to her, she said, "Do you believe in miracles?"

"Oh, yes," he whispered, this flagrantly pagan man.

And for a brief, fleeting moment, the spring morning vanished from their consciousness, the pounding hooves and swaying carriage faded away, the rhythm, cadence, pulse of the universe stopped.

Pasha broke the silence first, his sangfroid disciplined, his avoidance of emotion ingrained. "What toy do you think Chris will like best?"

Trixi mustered her composure with effort, half breathless still. "His British army." She managed a shaky smile. "I'll never be able to sufficiently repay you for the happiness those toys will bring."

"I'm sure I can think of one or two ways." The melody of the taiga sang in his rich voice; his dark eyes were redolent of the East.

"You must behave," Trixi warned, fearful of his bold gaze.

"Certainly."

"I mean it." Although her voice suddenly trembled.

"Absolutely."

"Your word," she nervously declared. "You gave me your word."

"I won't come within a foot of you in public." A promise sure to tax his self-control.

"Oh, dear God." She wanted him and as desperately did *not* want him, every nerve in her body shakily on edge, his proximity alone arousing. "I don't know if I dare look at you . . . when others are around."

"Of course you can." Taking her hands in his, he firmly said, "Look at me."

Her lashes fluttered for a moment and then her gaze met his. "Everything will be fine," he assured her, his voice restrained, as were his urgent desires. "You'll be a wonderful hostess and I'll be discreet and endeavor not to be too French since the English find French affectations annoying. Additionally, I'll help entertain Christopher because with young brothers myself, I'm very good at playing their games."

"I thought you knew only amorous games," she lightly said, feeling more collected after his comforting words.

"I'm versatile." His smile was shameless.

"How versatile?" she purred.

"You'll get your chance to find out tonight when everyone is safely asleep."

"I'm thinking perhaps . . . an early bedtime." Her eyes gleamed with mischief.

"Or even a nap this afternoon," he lazily enticed. "Think about it."

When the carriage drove up, Christopher exploded out of the front door of Burleigh House like an unleashed dynamo, his nursemaid racing behind.

"Mama, Mama, Mama!" the four-year-old screamed, flying across the raked gravel, his arms opened wide.

Jumping out of the carriage before it had completely

come to a stop, Trixi dropped to her knees and caught her exuberant son in her arms. Hugging him tightly, she cried, tears of happiness streaming down her cheeks, the feel of his sturdy little body so familiar, so precious, the scent of him crowding her with sweet memory.

She was home.

But four-year-olds defy holding and within seconds he was squirming in her arms. "What did you bring me?" he cried, breaking free, dancing from foot to foot, his dark curls bouncing, his eyes alight. "Katy saw the carriage, I knew it was you, I told her it was you. See, Katy, it *was* Mama!"

Coming to her feet, Trixi greeted her small household, who stood just outside the door of the Jacobean cottage. Mrs. Orde, plump and rosy, welcomed her home first, then young Jane, who helped Katy, gave her a blushing curtsey. "We're all so pleased you've returned," Kate Milhouse said, her face wreathed in smiles. And old Will, who'd been part of her father's generation, doffed his cap and in his gruff manner said, "Reckon all's well now, my lady, seein' you're back."

"Where I intend to stay," Trixi replied with feeling. "I was away too—" Her words were cut short by her son, impatient with adult courtesies, and grabbing her hand, he tugged hard. "Mama! Merrycat has kittens! Daisy has puppies! And you have to see them right now!" Dragging on her arm, he urged her forward. "Merrycat's kittens are all black and white and speckly and the puppies are teeny, teeny tiny. Come see, Mama! Right *now*!"

"Just a minute, darling," Trixi murmured. "There's someone—"

The carriage springs creaked at that moment, a small sound in the bright morning air but arresting, and all eyes swung around to gaze at the tall, dark stranger descending from the stylish barouche.

He looked very un-English, although his tailoring was fashionably English, understated and plain, black jacket, cream waistcoat, buckskin riding pants, and Hessians. His long hair curled on the white linen at his neck, its color so black and gleaming, it momentarily drew the eye. Until he raised his head and gazed at them with his mystical, oblique eyes.

"Hello," he said, and when he smiled they all understood why their lady had brought him home.

"Are you from China?" Chris piped up, his eyes wide with curiosity.

"Not quite," Pasha said, a faint smile twitching his mouth. "Have you heard of Siberia?"

Chris shook his head.

Pasha squatted to be at eye level with the young boy and held out a small ivory charm. "Here's something from Siberia. It's snowy there. This was part of a walrus tusk."

Chris took the small carved charm and turned it around, his fuzzy brows drawn together in concentration. "What's a walrus?"

"We brought some books I'll show you later. If your mama isn't too busy."

"Show me now," he said with childish impatience.

Pasha glanced up at Trixi, his gaze studiously bland.

"As soon as we have the carriage unpacked, darling," Trixi declared, carefully focusing on Pasha's shoulder. "Let me show Mr. Duras the cottage first."

"And Merrycat," Chris excitedly said.

"Definitely Merrycat," Pasha agreed, standing.

Trixi introduced Pasha to her household, keeping the details of his relationship to the family suitably vague. Not that any Ripons two generations past would rise to take issue with her story, but the less said the better, Pasha had suggested.

Mrs. Orde took note of Trixi's happiness and didn't care what strange and foreign land the man had come from if he could bring such joy to her ladyship. Jane and Katy blushed and stammered when Pasha spoke to them, and Will, his criteria for judging a man simple, only asked, "Do you ride?"

"We breed thoroughbreds near Chantilly. I ride some," Pasha modestly added.

"Her ladyship managed to save her bloodstock from those Grosvenor scoundrels," Will muttered. "Come down to the stables later and I'll show you a promising youngster we have out of Myrobella."

"You passed the test," Trixi murmured with pleasure as Will walked away. Her old retainer's approval was not lightly given.

Pasha acknowledged her with a private wink and then offered to unload the luggage. Carrying in the few pieces of luggage from the carriage, he set them in the entrance hall. Returning a few minutes later with a large red box, he cast a questioning glance at Trixi. "Now?" At her approving nod, he set the box on a large oak table in the center of the wainscotted hall. "Your mama thought you might like these," he said to Chris, lifting him up on the table.

Ripping off the cover, wide-eyed, Chris squealed, "Presents!" and pulled out the first toy soldier. "A grenadier!" he cried, holding up the small cast-iron soldier in his hand. "With a real fur hat!" he shouted. "Mama! Look!" Then dropping the soldier, he plunged his hand into the box of silver tissue and reached for another.

Watching her son's delight as he uncovered each of his soldiers, Trixi felt an indelible sense of homecoming, joyous and pure, warm her heart. How good it was to be back, she thought, looking up for a second to smile at Pasha. Mouthing the words *thank you,* she blew him a kiss over the head of her son.

Thank *you,* he thought, smiling back at the captivating woman who had revealed to him a new and intimate meaning to the word happiness. He quickly glanced at his watch, gauging the time until evening. Such eagerness would have shocked any of his acquaintances; women waited for Pasha, but never he for them.

When at last each toy soldier stood unwrapped atop the oak table, when the gleaming tissue floated on the floor in great billows, when Trixi's small son was awed and speechless for the first time in his mother's memory, Pasha said, "Maybe later you and your mother would like to stand battle against me."

Sitting cross-legged on the table, Chris looked up, a small frown creasing his brows. "You need an army."

"I brought Napoleon's army along, but it's with the other toys," Pasha replied. "They should be here soon."

"Other toys!" The shriek brought Mrs. Orde racing out from the drawing room where she was setting a table for tea. Between Chris's clamorous declarations that he was getting *other* toys, she was assured no calamity had transpired and after suitable admiration for the young master's soldiers, she returned to her task.

"Show me the other toys, Mama!" Chris immediately demanded. "I want to see them!"

"He'll never wait," Trixi murmured, distracted by her son's renewed pleas.

"Why not go and meet the wagon," Pasha suggested. "Chris can ride with me."

His antenna alive to all the fascinating man who brought toys might say, Chris looked at Pasha. "I don't have to ride with you. I have my *own* pony," he proclaimed. Already scrambling from the table, he hung suspended for a moment, his legs dangling just short of the floor.

"You'll have to show me." Pasha leaned over to sweep Chris up into his arms.

"Will teached me," Chris declared, his boyish gaze earnest, his arms wrapped tightly around Pasha's neck, no shyness in his nature. "And he says I'm really, really good and *he* used to ride *real* racers, didn't he, Mama? Come see my pony, Petunia," he eagerly went on, not waiting for his mother's answer. "Is your name really Pasha?" he irrepressibly inquired, his dark eyes serious. "Do you have another name, like a regular name, like regular people have?"

"My real names are harder to say," Pasha said with a grin, moving toward the door. "That's why people call me Pasha."

"Is it Chinese?"

"I'm sorry," Trixi interposed, keeping pace with them, reaching to open the front door. "Chris has a favorite storybook about China."

"I'm not offended," Pasha assured her. "I'm sure I look slightly different from Kentish folk. Possibly your neighbors will notice as well."

"You can be sure they will." Trixi knew the parochial mentality of her neighbors. "Very pointedly, I might add."

"I'm inured to critical survey," he remarked. "My appearance often brings on a sudden silence."

Not only for his exotic looks, Trixi thought; his conspicuous beauty alone was quite capable of silencing a room.

"Petunia loves sugar lumps," Chris piped up, unconcerned with society's conduct. "Do you have a horse? Did you bring him with you? What's his name?" he finished in a rush, his excitement commensurate with the rarity of visitors at Burleigh House.

"I don't have my horse with me, but his name is Yakut."

"*All* your names are funny."

"Chris, mind your manners," Trixi cautioned, blushing at her son's candor.

"But I like them." Chris smiled up at Pasha with the same artless innocence as his mother's.

"He's allowed his opinions, darling," Pasha said. "I don't mind in the least."

"Good," Trixi said, relieved, "because he's impossible to stifle."

"Like his mother if I recall." Pasha's voice was a lush resonance meant for her ears only.

"What's stifle, Mama?" Chris inquired, catching the change of inflection in Pasha's tone.

"Nothing, darling." Trixi's face flamed cherry red, and her warning glance at Pasha was touched with a restless agitation. "Mr. Duras, would you prefer a barb or a thoroughbred to ride?"

"Neither as first choice," he softly said, wishing the sun in the sky was the moon, wishing he could hasten the next ten hours, hoping the inhabitants of Burleigh were early-to-bed types. "But as second choice," he went on in a conversational tone, as though he'd not undressed her with his eyes, "I'd take a barb."

"Jabar, Mama. Give Pasha Jabar."

She couldn't speak for a moment, lust flaring through her senses.

"Jabar would be fine," Pasha said, calm and composed, knowing all the while what he'd done to her. "Or whatever your mother wants."

When she spoke, a small tremor underlay her words. "Will can decide," she said, not capable of prolonged speech at the moment.

"You'll love Jabar," Chris enthusiastically declared.

"He's faster than fast, Will says. He can run like the wind."

Trixi took note of the stables, now within sight, and determined to stay well away from Pasha in Will's presence. The retainer was more discerning than a four-year-old child; the nature of her relationship with Pasha wouldn't be long a secret if she allowed him too close.

Will proudly showed Pasha their stable, the quality of the horses testament to his expertise as a breeder. "We had only five of our bloodstock left when them Grosvenors were done robbing us blind, and only because I hid the best of them. Damned farmers didn't know a thoroughbred from a hack so it weren't too hard to cull out the best for my lady. She's a right fine rider, too, if I do say so myself," he went on. "Taught her to ride when she were a tyke."

"Just like me," Chris pointed out, already mounted on Petunia. "I'm right fine, too."

Will smiled at his youngest charge. "Damned good seat, he has. Keep them hands up, now," the old man admonished. "And remember, Petunia don't like to run for too long at a time."

"We shouldn't have to backtrack far," Pasha said, sliding a bridle over Jabar's nose. "The wagon left before us and we passed it just before turning off the main road to London."

"Be ten miles back then," Will declared, tightening the cinch on Trixi's saddle. "She's ready, my lady." He patted the chestnut's flank. "I'll give you a hand up."

"Let me help," Pasha offered. The wiry old man was small in stature.

"No!" Trixi exclaimed, the vehemence in her voice so striking, even Chris paid notice. "I mean . . . Will is used to helping me," she quickly added, hoping she wasn't blushing too intensely.

"It don't matter to me, my lady, who you bring home to visit," Will bluntly said, "just so long as the gentleman knows his manners." His gray eyes drilled a hole through Pasha.

"Rest assured, Will," Pasha quietly replied, "Lady Grosvenor will be treated with respect."

"You overstep yourself, Will," Trixi murmured, a bite in her voice.

"Begging your pardon, my lady." Will's gaze remained hard on Pasha. "My mistake."

But there was no mistake, Pasha understood; he wasn't to cause harm to Will's lady.

The few minutes left before Pasha was mounted passed in an uneasy silence; even Chris was cognizant of the strained hush. But once they were out of the stable-yard, Chris perceived the altered mood and began chattering.

"Petunia knows the road all the way to the London turnoff, and once we even went as far as Geddinge," he said, cantering slightly ahead of the adults.

"That's quite a way," Pasha replied. "I'm sorry," he whispered, his quiet words for Trixi alone. "I won't be so obvious again. It was all my fault."

"Sometimes Will takes me with him when he goes to the horse fair at Denton," Chris jabbered on. "You'll have to go with us sometime."

"Whenever your mother likes," Pasha responded.

"It was just as much my fault." Trixi's gaze lay not on the road ahead but on Pasha riding alongside her. "I feel as though I'm on fire when I look at you and it shows. How could Will not notice?"

"While I'm looking at you or my watch like a giddy adolescent." Pasha grinned. "I'm appalled."

"The feeling's mutual, you luscious man," she cheerfully said, feeling gloriously free from prying eyes and scrutiny on the isolated country road. "And I seem to have absolutely no self-control."

"Then it's up to me to have enough for both of us."

"That would be marvelous."

He took a deep breath. "Although I'm not sure it's actually possible. Does Chris take naps anymore?"

"I'm afraid not."

He groaned.

She giggled and then immediately clapped her hand over her mouth, feeling much too giddy for a grown woman.

Casting her a sidelong glance, he grinned again. "This is going to be very bizarre—tiptoeing around."

"Perhaps I can make it worth your while," she flirtatiously murmured.

"Without a doubt you can. The question is when?"

"A mild headache might overcome me at teatime."

"Tea can do that to you, I've heard."

"Chris will be completely involved in his new toys, I'm sure."

"And long journeys always fatigue me," he lazily drawled.

"You'll have need of sleep then," she teased.

"Oh, yes."

The wagon was met, the riders and toys arrived back at Burleigh House, and as anticipated, Chris had eyes for nothing but his new playthings. The drawing room floor was awash with presents, wrappings, and boxes; Kate and Jane, even Mrs. Orde, came to admire the array while Chris showed off all his new playthings, moving from item to item, excited, glowing, bubbling with chatter.

After Pasha carried in the last of the boxes, he began assembling one of the buildings in a farm set, slipping small interlocking boards into place to make walls for a

barn. As the small building began taking shape, Chris
was drawn to the project, and with admirable patience,
Pasha helped the four-year-old manipulate the boards
into place. He quietly offered praise or suggestions,
lying beside Chris on the worn Tabriz carpet, the large
man and small boy working as a team.

Chris set the roof on himself, and clapping his hands
in excitement at the finished project, he immediately
cried, "Let's do another. You can unwrap the animals,
Mama," he said, suddenly remembering her presence.
"Us men will build the stables and farmhouse."

Trixi smiled, the four-year-old implying that there
were divisions of labor on gender lines amusing. "Can't
I help build?"

Her son looked up at her, then to Pasha.

"Your mama can do anything she wants." His gaze
was innocent.

"Thank you," she replied.

"You do the fences, Mama," Chris offered, scooping
up a handful of wooden sections.

Before long the entire farmyard was complete, the
animals in place, even the farmer's family arranged outside their sturdy house. The small construction crew sat
back and admired their handiwork. "Can I bring it to
my room tonight, Mama?" Chris asked. "I'll put all the
animals to sleep and—"

Mrs. Orde cleared her throat.

Unfamiliar with her housekeeper's unusual reticence,
Trixi didn't take notice until the second unobtrusive
cough, at which point, catching sight of Mrs. Orde's
expression, she said, "Oh, dear," and jumped up.
"Have we kept you waiting?"

"The tea will be a mite cool soon, my lady," Mrs.
Orde remarked, touching the pot with her palm.

"Of course. Forgive me. Chris, Mr. Duras, please join
me. And thank you, Ordie, for this wonderful array."

"Your favorites, Missy," she said, the childhood name accidently slipping out. "Scones, strawberry cakes, and those ham sandwiches on oatmeal bread. The poppy seed cake has a touch of orange for you and the lemon curd tarts are those heart-shaped ones you like. Would Mr. Duras prefer a whiskey, I'm wondering?"

"That won't be necessary." Pasha came to his feet. He recalled Trixi's suspicion of men who drank too much.

"Your papa *always* had a whiskey with tea." Mrs. Orde surveyed Trixi over the rims of her glasses. "Said it made tea drinking bearable."

"Don't look at me like that, Ordie," Trixi said, smiling. "*I'm* not keeping him from drinking."

"In that case, if Lady Grosvenor doesn't mind." Pasha cast a compliant glance her way.

"I'm sitting with *you*." Chris slipped his hand into Pasha's, a guest so generous with his presents and time a luxury in his young life.

"Should we fly to the table?" Pasha asked. Grasping both Chris's hands, he swung the boy up in a high arc, let him go, then caught him a second later in midair and midsqueal before gently setting him down.

"Do that *again*!" Chris jubilantly cried. "I was flying! Mama! Mama, did you see me? I was *flying*!"

Pasha repeated his glorious feat several more times to cries and screams of approval. On his feet once again, red-faced and gleeful, Chris exclaimed, "You're the bestest! Isn't he, Mama? Isn't he, Ordie?" he happily extolled, his little face beaming.

Mrs. Orde looked up from setting Pasha's filled whiskey glass in place. "Yes, indeed, Christopher," she agreed. "Mr. Duras is very kind."

Pasha's "best" had to do with other than kindnesses, Trixi heatedly thought, but her voice was temperate when she spoke as though tantalizing memory wasn't

bombarding her brain. "Do you want scones or strawberry cakes first?" she asked her son, opting for evasion
in lieu of personal commentary on Pasha's best.

"Cakes, cakes, cakes!"

And teatime commenced.

Conversation was child-driven in the presence of an
exuberant four-year-old, but neither adult minded. The
young boy's energy and loquaciousness were familiar to
Pasha, well experienced in the role of older brother. For
her part, Trixi viewed the occasion through a rose-
tinted haze; she was home again, returned to her beloved son and blissfully happy. That Pasha charmed her
entire household only added pleasure to pleasure.

The food was demolished in short order, gratifying
Mrs. Orde, who was never more pleased than when her
Missy and Chris ate heartily. "Her ladyship needs a
mite more meat on those bones," she whispered to Kate
from their vantage point in an adjoining room, both
their faces pressed to the narrow aperture between
doorjamb and door.

"She *has* lost weight," Kate murmured, careful to
keep her voice low. "I'm so pleased we have our Missy
back."

"And she brought herself home a right fine-looking
gentleman," Mrs. Orde declared, less concerned with
propriety than her mistress's happiness, "for all that he
looks like he just rode in with Genghis Khan."

"For heaven's sake, Mrs. Orde." Kate's original position as governess to Trixi placed her in a more exalted
social rank than her rustic companion. And while she
rarely exerted any undue privileges because of her
status, she felt duty-bound to warn the housekeeper
that such tactlessness would surely disturb their mistress. "Mr. Duras is obviously of importance to our lady
and wealthy, I'd surmise, from the extent of the gifts he
brought for Christopher. And if you don't think me too

mercenary—with our Missy's hapless marriage, may her husband rot in Hades, and Christopher's father, poor soul, taken so young—*and* considering her dire financial state, we should take *every* opportunity to see that Mr. Duras enjoys his visit at Burleigh House."

"I didn't mean any harm, Kate. Mr. Duras's a gorgeous man, make no mistake," Mrs. Orde said in atonement.

"I think his singular looks could be classified as Eurasian, Ordie. And very refined and splendid they are. Do you think," she went on in a worrying tone, "we should ask if they want more tea, or would that be perceived as interfering?"

"Good Lord, Kate, you'd think we never had company. I'll go and ask them." Mrs. Orde's busybody nature was never more invigorated than when she could interfere. "It looks to me as if that handsome young man could do with another whiskey, too."

Kate scurried for cover as Mrs. Orde shoved the door open, mortified she might be discovered eavesdropping. But we never *do* have company, the ex-governess breathed, pressed back against the wall, her heart palpitating wildly in her breast, the excitement as stimulating to her as it was to her young pupil.

A few moments later, however, her curiosity overcame her fear of detection because company *was* so rare. And *such* exciting company, she thought, her ideas of romance deeply influenced by Mrs. Burney's novels. Cautiously easing the door open a scant inch, she returned to her titillating observation.

After refilling Pasha's glass, Mrs. Orde set the decanter on the table beside him. "This here's his late lordship's favorite Irish spirits he kept for special occasions. Help yourself to more if you like." She gave an indulgent smile to the man who had brought such joy into the household. "Your papa would *want* someone to enjoy his special stock," she went on, casting a weighty glance in Trixi's direction, as if her charge didn't understand how to entertain a gentleman.

"I wasn't about to disagree, Ordie." Trixi was amused by the deference Pasha warranted from her housekeeper, who had kept the Irish whiskey hidden from her husband. And come to think of it, from Theo as well, she reflected with an odd start.

"I think Christopher should take some of his new farm animals out to show Will," the housekeeper suggested with a bland smile. "You know how Will would enjoy seeing that Percheron pair you have there, Christopher," she added, brushing some crumbs from the table into her apron. "And the matched bays, too. I'd say he might even have a taste to see those hunting dogs round that fine new stable you and Mr. Duras put together."

"Pasha and me builted it," Chris proudly declared, ensconced on his hero's lap, not inclined to move.

"You'll have to tell Will all about it. Come now with me," the housekeeper coaxed. "We'll find Kate and Janey and everyone will bring those fine animals out to show Will."

Not entirely convinced he cared to leave his new playmate, Chris looked to Pasha for guidance. "It's up to you, Chris," Pasha good-naturedly said, a philanthropic gesture considering his hugely selfish desires.

"You could bring Will that last strawberry cake," Mrs. Orde submitted, knowing the dessert was Will and Chris's favorite.

"Will really, *really* likes cake," Chris acknowledged, his indecision plain. Then a second later he reached for the sweet. "I won't be gone long." He slid from Pasha's lap, the cake balanced precariously on his small palm. "Don't play with any toys until I get back."

"Promise," Pasha said with a smile, his notions of

play moving in quite a different direction, with the possibility of a tête-à-tête imminent. "Tell Will I've a riding quirt from Obdorsk that I'll bring round later for him."

"Is Ob . . . dork," Chris struggled with the strange word, "far away?"

"A month of hard riding away."

"A month?" he breathed, awestruck.

"Give me that cake now, Christopher, and you bring along those Percherons," the housekeeper cajoled.

The horses were gathered up and the hunting pack and for good measure the farmer and his family. "Have you named them yet?" Mrs. Orde was saying as they left the room.

"She must like you," Trixi said into the sudden quiet. "Such blatant matchmaking, though. I apologize for Ordie's lack of finesse."

"I'm not complaining," Pasha said with a grin, the pernicious word matchmaking oddly tolerable in the drawing room at Burleigh House. "And Mrs. Orde's very skillful in persuading Chris."

"Thank you, too, for allowing him an option."

"I remember being young and in adult company. At times it was exciting."

"A roomful of new toys certainly inspires that kind of excitement. And you, of course. He adores you, I'm afraid. I hope you don't find him a nuisance."

"He's adorable, like his mother. And no, I don't find him a nuisance. I'm charmed."

"Thank you again. I find myself forever in your debt."

"You needn't. This is very much a mutual indebtedness. I've never enjoyed myself so much—having tea like this, playing with Chris, your housekeeper's sweet tyranny, Will . . . It's wonderfully bucolic. So thank you." Not prone to discerning insights from emotions, he didn't question his feelings beyond those general observations. "And," he said, surveying the sunny room, "to add to my gratification, we seem to be *alone*."

"By design, I perceive."

"Is it possible, then, that nap time has finally arrived?"

She hesitated, debating the options and possibilities with her household about. "I'm not sure." Actually put to the test, it was rather alarming to consider making love when any minute someone might appear.

"Anywhere will do," Pasha said, his voice unnaturally constrained, his libido in ramming speed ever since Mrs. Orde exited the room. His gaze swept the room. "That sofa?" he murmured.

Their eyes met across the debris of teatime.

Carnal urgency, heated and potent, struck Trixi like a blow.

"What if they come back soon?" she whispered, apprehensive even as desire flared at the sight of such naked lust.

"Then we'll have to hurry." Rising from his chair, he held out his hand.

"No, no . . . not here." Coming to her feet in a restless flurry, she abruptly said, "Follow me." She glanced back once as she entered the foyer and his lush smile impaired reason for a moment. Her body responded as if he'd entered her; a melting heat flared deep inside her. Flushed and breathless, she could feel his palpable energy as she swiftly crossed the marbled hall and moved up the stairway, a kind of insensate heat that propelled and roused, licked at her feet and senses, insinuated itself tantalizingly into every pulsing cell and nerve and tissue.

Halfway up the stairs, he scooped her into his arms with an effortless strength, his long-legged stride taking the steps two at a time even under her added weight. And when they reached the top of the stairs, he said, curt and low, "Which way?"

"Lord, Pasha," she equivocated, her nerves on edge, wondering where they would least likely be found and embarrassed. "All the rooms are so accessible."

Past problematical qualms, he moved toward the first doorway in sight. "This one, then."

"No!"

He stopped, his gaze insistent, flame in its depths.

"That's Chris's room."

"What about the third floor?"

"Janey and Kate's rooms."

He inhaled a deep, steadying breath that kept him marginally rational. "Where *were* you going?"

"I was thinking about . . . my father's room. No one uses it, but—"

Even in his present rut, such flagrant bad taste momentarily stopped him. "Where were you going to have me sleep tonight?"

"Under Janey's room."

"Show me."

It was decided.

5

Following her directions, he carried her down the hall to a room tucked under the third-floor stairway, eased two fingers free from under her legs to open the latch, then shoved the door with his foot. Two large-paned windows faced the orchard back of the house. Rows of gnarled fruit trees gleamed green in the sunlight, which bathed the small room in a golden glow as well. It had been a lady's room at one time, the decor faded now, but ruffled and pale in hue, with rosebud dimity-clad chairs and dressing table, the bed small. Too small, he instantly thought.

Although in his current frame of mind, a bed wasn't entirely necessary.

"Shut the door," she whispered, fear prominent in her voice.

Moving toward the bed, he seated her on its center and, returning to the door, quietly closed it. He attempted to turn the key in the rusted lock but it resisted his efforts.

"Put a chair in front," Trixi urged, fainthearted, yet feverish with need. "And hurry."

Glancing up from the chair he was about to lift from beside the dressing table, he saw her trembling, the sight so intensely erotic, all the jaded licentiousness in his past, so familiar and habitual, paled before such chaste longing.

Jamming the chair under the door latch, he was beside her almost instantly, holding her, gently stroking her shoulders, her back, the slender column of her throat. "I'm here," he whispered, soothing her as one might a frightened child. "I'm here."

"There's no time." Agitation, fear vibrated in her words.

"There's time." He lifted his head to glance out the window, rechecked that the chair was against the door, eased her back onto the bed and followed her down, pushing her skirt up so he could slide between her legs.

"I'm selfish." Part entreaty, part demand, her breathless declaration grazed his lips as he bent to kiss her. Her hand moved to his trouser buttons.

"I'm way ahead of you." His voice was rough, his carnal urgency barely under control. Brushing her fingers aside, he swiftly unfastened his riding pants. And a second later, the tip of his penis nuzzled her vulva, rubbed gently, and at her suppressed cry exhorting him to speed, he plunged in.

They both felt as though a long exile had ended.

The bed squeaked loudly under the heated rhythm of their ravenous passions. Speed, haste was in the forefront of their thoughts, all the pent-up longing from the hours past explosive within them.

"Pasha . . . the bed."

The alarm in her voice registered through the haze of his lust, and he heard the shrill creaking. The small bed was never intended to hold a man of his size. Instantly responding, he put his arms around her, lifted and rolled, landing on the floor on his back, cushioning her with his body. In his current libidinous state, he was immune to the jolt.

Another turn and he lay over her. He held her off the carpet, lifting her bottom to meet his down-thrust, his breath coming in low muffled grunts, intent only on

maintaining the rhythm of his strokes. Flushed, feverish, her skirts crumpled around her waist, she met his
violent plunging, welcomed it, craving the feel of him,
needing the rapturous pleasure he gave. And even as
she clung to him, frantically drew him deep inside, felt
herself reaching for her shuddering climax, she wondered how she'd survive his absence.

Peaking desire overwhelmed such impractical considerations and as she died away, as her last sighing
spasm fluttered through her senses, Pasha withdrew
with a practiced precision and came on the warmth of
her belly.

Braced on his hands, he hung suspended over her,
panting, his dark hair falling in a silken curtain, per-
spiration gleaming on his face. "Why am I still starved
for you?"

His query warmed her heart, even though she knew
better than to have romantic expectations. He was talking about sex, not love. In any event, he'd already dismissed the fleeting emotion. He'd reached for a pillow
on the bed, pulled the cover off with a jerk, and was
about to toss the pillow cover on her belly when she
squeaked, "No!"

In midthrow, his hand stopped, the lace-edged fabric
dangling from his fingertips.

"Mrs. Orde will notice."

His brows quirked.

"*You* . . . know."

He wasn't absolutely certain, but regardless her cau-
tionary fears, Mrs. Orde was a servant—which he
pointed out directly, adding, "How can it matter?"

"They're not servants, actually, or—well . . . Maybe
they are." She took the pillowcase from him, wiping
Pasha's semen off her stomach with a corner of her
petticoat instead, which she could handwash herself.
"They're more like family," she went on. "They've all

been at Burleigh House for years, even though I've not been able to pay them since—well, for a very long time."

"And Mrs. Orde is careful with her pillow covers?" Seated, leaning against the bed, he'd extracted his handkerchief to wipe himself dry.

"No, it's not that, but she starches and irons them all and—" Fascinated, she gazed at his erection.

He looked up when she paused and took note of her attention.

"I don't suppose . . ."

"No," she quickly replied, shaking her skirt down. "They could return any minute."

"Are you sure?" He glanced down at his rampant arousal and then at her. "You could just sit on me for a minute."

She opened her mouth, her refusal already formed on her lips, but found herself unable to utter the words with such lurid temptation before her.

"The door's shut. We can hear them come in," he gently murmured. "They might be out in the stables for a *very* long time." He took her hands and drew her to a seated position. He pulled her slippers off and she didn't stop him, so he leaned forward and lifted her into his arms. "Hold your skirt up," he said, moving her onto his lap.

"Pasha, no." The protest was so faint, he understood that she was willing, even if she didn't.

"Hold up your skirt," he softly repeated. And when she lifted the blue silk of one of Mme. Ormand's gowns after a certain degree of seductive coaxing, Pasha slid her down his erection. Her small, blissful sigh was another kind of acceptance.

Content, his carnal urges less frenzied now, Pasha considered the unblemished perfection of his current position. A woman of great beauty lay wide open to his libidinous urges and he had the leisure to pursue those desires in the days to come.

She was hot beyond the wildest fantasies. Perhaps even insatiable, he thought, smiling at the enticing, personal consequences of that word. And now, with his first lust assuaged, he was looking forward to the luxury of a more languid lovemaking. "I like your house," he murmured, kissing her cheek gently. "And this room . . ." Another kiss trailed down her neck. "And mostly this luscious lady riding me." His tongue traced the curve of her collarbone. "You're going to have to let me sleep with you tonight." He nibbled the lobe of her ear and she felt it in the usual place. No matter where he touched her, kissed or caressed her, the immediate carnal response spiked downward in a shimmering heat directly to her throbbing vagina. It wasn't fair what he could do to her. "Can we arrange that somehow?" he whispered. "Sleeping together," he softly added, thrusting upward as if emphasizing the advantages of his proposition, jolting her into a heated flurry of excitement.

She couldn't answer. She couldn't enunciate a single word, not with desire and pleasure seeping through her brain, dissolving her bones, shimmering in every taut nerve of her body. Stretched, filled, gorged, she was engulfed by longing.

A glutton, that's what she was, when she'd never even realized sex and gluttony went together.

Pasha Duras had enlightened her.

Her lashes lifted and she gazed at the sinfully beautiful man who held her lightly, his fingers splayed across her waist and hips. He smiled into her heated gaze, his lush mouth half curved, his dark, Tartar eyes wicked, tantalizing.

And then the ringing sound of her son's voice shat-

tered the hushed moment, followed a second later by
the hum of adult conversation. A door slammed shut.

"Will they come upstairs?" Pasha's voice was brisk,
as though he could separate emotion from reason.

Rigid in his arms, she nodded her head.

Groaning softly, he considered her household required some new rules concerning a servant's place. His
staff would never intrude. Taking a deep breath, he
lifted her away and swiftly began setting his clothes to
rights. That task accomplished with record speed, he
turned to help Trixi who, in her panicked state, was
retying a ribbon for the third time. More familiar with
in flagrante situations, he calmly retied her decorative
shoulder bows and smoothed out the worst wrinkles on
her skirt while she slipped out of her dampened petticoat and hid it under the mattress.

After handing her a brush and mirror from the dressing table, he put her slippers back. "It's not as though
Mrs. Orde wasn't hoping we'd spend some time together," he remarked, holding the mirror for her, handing her hairpins one at a time.

Trixi pursed her lips in the mirror. "I don't think
she had this in mind."

"Why couldn't we have been discussing our plans
for sightseeing tomorrow? Surely that's innocuous
enough."

"In the bedroom?"

"She won't ask, darling. Really." If ever he'd seen a
matchmaker, and he was a specialist at spotting them,
Mrs. Orde fell into that category. "Come now," he offered, holding out his hand as Trixi put the last hairpin
in place. "You look very presentable."

As they descended the stairs, Chris caught sight of
them and running from the drawing room, he cried,
"Where were you? I looked everywhere!" Mrs. Orde
had followed him to the doorway, and Trixi blushed

furiously while Pasha urbanely said, "Your mother was showing me the house."

"There's nothing to see up there."

"The views were nice," Pasha blandly replied. "Did Will like your farm set? I'll bet he's never seen dappled Percherons."

The segue set the tone of the conversation for the next interval, and before long Pasha and Chris were sprawled on the drawing room floor rearranging the barnyard.

"Would you like a cooling drink?" Mrs. Orde cordially inquired once Chris was occupied.

Trixi hesitated, reading numerous embarrassing interpretations to the inquiry.

Pasha simply looked up from his play activities and said, "Yes, please. Anything will do."

"A touch of that Irish whiskey?" Mrs. Orde inquired, her smile genial.

"You know the way to a man's heart, Mrs. Orde," Pasha cheerfully noted.

"Missy found herself a right fine figure of a man," Mrs. Orde pronounced as she entered the kitchen a short time later. "He brought a real glow to our darling girl's cheeks."

"Do you think it's love?" Kate dreamily inquired, prone to romantic sensibilities.

"I don't know about that, Kate." Mrs. Orde's more realistic appraisal had to do with Pasha's obvious sensual appeal. "But he's made her happy and that's all I care about. She deserves some happiness in her young life."

The following days were blissful, leisured, those entertainments most appealing to a four-year-old governing the schedule. They swam in the small lake Capability Brown had designed when the luxury of

wealth had allowed the Howards to indulge their tastes
for fine vistas and whimsical follies. They played tennis
and picnicked, fished in the river that ran through the
meadow, and gathered wild strawberries on its banks.
They often rode the country lanes and the perimeters of
Trixi's reduced estate in the cool spring mornings and
at twilight when birdsong and lavender skies serenely
eased day into evening. And at night when all was
quiet at Burleigh House the lovers were at last alone.
They made love in all its infinite variety—with tenderness, with impatient urgency and languid dissipation,
with teasing laughter, and one night when the moon
shone through the leaded panes with a snowy brilliance
they held each other close, their eyes filled with tears.

And if perfection were possible in this most imper-
fect of worlds, the young lovers at Burleigh House had
found it.

Their days passed apace, a week slipping by in this
Kentish paradise of play and ease and childish entertainments. And then a second week.

One dew-fresh morning, Will escorted them to the
horse fair at Denton where all the local folk had their
opportunity to finally see or meet the new guest at
Burleigh House who, rumor had it, was ten feet tall
and dark as the devil.

The progress of Trixi's small party through the village streets that day was exquisitely slow, checked at
every turn by the curious who wished to make their
bow to the tall foreigner at Lady Grosvenor's side.

Pasha smiled and answered the subtle, designing, or
artless queries with grace and civility. No, he was
French, yes, the restored Bourbon dynasty was interesting, although even politesse wouldn't concede more
than that from the son of a revolutionary general. Yes,
the weather *was* exceptional, the horses at the fair magnificent and no, actually Lady Grosvenor was a distant

relation—on his mother's side. Trixi would smile and nod at this point or add a comment or two about the Teeside Ripons on *her* mother's side. And bowing, they'd continue down the gauntlet of curiosity seekers, responding to fresh interrogations.

But the horses were, in fact, splendid enough that Pasha bought three racers for his stable. The day was sunshine-bright and balmy and the young lovers enjoyed being in each other's company so much, even the tactless and absorbed regard of so many of the local populace failed to alter their good spirits.

On the drive home in the open barouche, the spring sunlight bathing them in a lemony light, Chris asleep in Trixi's arms, she apologized for all the stares and prying questions.

"Don't be concerned," Pasha replied, thinking the picture of mother and child as fair and pleasing as the spring afternoon. "I'm inured. And all the tittle-tattle will keep your neighbors entertained for a time." Lounging across from her he bespoke a man at ease with the world's scrutiny. "As long as *you* don't mind the avid inquisitiveness my presence generates."

Her mouth quirked ruefully. "Born and raised here, I'm inured as well."

"I *do* think the deacon's wife might be calling soon," Pasha noted, amusement in his gaze. "Along with that chubby woman in blue."

"Your exotic allure might draw a good *many* visitors." Trixi had taken note of all the female glances, some conspicuously bold.

"Promise to have Ordie drive them off. I can't abide insipid people."

"Ordie will be more than pleased to accommodate you. She's developed quite a tendresse for you."

"And I for her. Anyone who can prepare beef so it melts in your mouth has my eternal devotion."

And Mrs. Orde gladly performed her duties of door custodian with crack efficiency, if not always with tact. Several of the more exalted visitors left Burleigh House with pursed lips and high tempers. Until one morning when even Mrs. Orde's curt rebuff failed to turn off three callers.

"She will see us this morning, Mrs. Orde, or the bailiff will accompany us on our return. Deliver that message to Lady Grosvenor," the small, wizened man crisply declared.

Moments later when Mrs. Orde entered the breakfast room Trixi immediately knew something was wrong. Ordie's grim, set mouth and high color were a sure sign of anger. "What is it?" she asked, setting her fork down.

"Them Grosvenors, damn their insolence," her housekeeper cursed, the pulse in her neck visible.

Trixi turned ashen.

"Threatening you again, they are," Ordie hotly asserted. "With the bailiff."

"I'll see that they leave," Pasha said, his voice curt. Brusquely pushing his plate aside, he swiftly rose from his chair.

"No, don't, please." Crumpling her napkin in her lap, Trixi schooled her voice to a moderate tone. "Chris, darling, go with Ordie and find Kate." She smiled at her son who, wide-eyed, was watching Pasha. "Mama has some visitors she must see. I think the playhouse would be more comfortable, Ordie," she cryptically added. "You could bring the kittens there, darling," Trixi went on, offering Chris an added lure. "Pasha, do sit down. This is nothing more than a misunderstanding. Chris, sweet, go with Ordie now and we'll be out shortly to see the kittens."

"Them kittens like you," Ordie said, taking her cue

from Trixi, smiling at Chris. "Let's bring them a bowl of cream from the dairy house."

"Will you and Pasha come out soon?" Chris inquired, his gaze traveling between his mother and Pasha.

"In just a few minutes, sweetheart," Trixi assured him. "Now go with Ordie."

A taut silence descended while Ordie and Chris exited the room, but the second the door closed behind them, Pasha said in a low growl, "What the hell did that mean—*comfortable*?"

"The Grosvenors have threatened to take Chris from me on several occasions, so I keep him out of sight when they visit." She exhaled a slow rush of air, her violet eyes direct. "They know he's not George's son. Although my husband was still alive when Chris was born, so—"

"Inheritance is an issue," Pasha murmured.

"I've told them repeatedly I want nothing from them."

"The law of course says otherwise."

"They're vicious—the whole family," she bitterly asserted. "I signed a release after George died, refusing an inheritance. That should have been sufficient, but with them nothing ever is. And they're very powerful here," she nervously finished. "Excuse me." She seemed to brace herself. "I must meet with them."

"Let me go with you."

"God, no. That would be worse. If you'd see that Chris is safe with Ordie and Kate, though, I'd feel better." Rising from her chair, she said, "This won't take long."

"You're sure now? Couldn't you use a little muscle here?" he lightly offered.

He made her smile despite the frightening circumstances. "I wish muscle alone would deter the Grosvenors. But," she added, shrugging slightly, "with the Duke of Buckingham so powerful a relative of theirs . . ."

Pasha's father had successfully defeated the combined forces of the Russian and Austrian armies several times, so "power" was a relative word in the Duras family. The Duke of Buckingham was more than manageable, Pasha thought. "I could be your solicitor," he suggested, "and keep you company in that capacity."

"Not after yesterday, darling. Everyone in the parish knows better. Really," she said with false bravado, "I'll be fine."

With her mind made up, Pasha acquiesced, but after swiftly checking to see that Chris was safe, he returned to the house, having no intention of leaving her unprotected. Following the sound of voices, he approached the small drawing room where tea was served every afternoon, moving with extreme quiet as he neared the door. If Trixi didn't require his help, he thought, positioning himself outside the doorway, he'd simply move behind the window draperies when the Grosvenors exited. If, on the other hand, they meant her harm, he would see that they suffered.

"Now that you've returned home, the Clouards wish to know your intentions," Harry Grosvenor was saying, his voice chill. "I'm here as their emissary to find out."

"They've contacted you?" Trixi's surprise showed. George's brother and his two unmarried, harpy sisters had queried her on Pasha first. To which she gave suitably vague answers. But this was unnerving—the speed with which the Clouard family had traced her.

"Your child is a disturbing issue for both families," Lady Lydia primly replied, looking down her sharp nose at Trixi. "Naturally we are interested in staying abreast of events."

"The Clouards *knew* I was coming to Paris?"

"We felt it our duty to inform them." The second sister smiled as she spoke, a hateful, rancorous tightening of her lips.

So Langelier hadn't accidentally appeared at the solicitor's that day, Trixi thought, a chill running down her spine. He had been playing both sides, appropriating money from the Clouards and from her as well, should she win her case. And if not for his murder, she might still be his prisoner. "You must be frustrated at my return," she softly said, forewarned now of her opponents' alliance.

"We *were* surprised," Harry coolly noted. "But since you have returned, we're here to inform you that the Clouards have taken action against you in the French courts. If you ever enter France again, you'll be arrested."

Astonished, she blurted out, "On what charge?"

"I have no idea." Harry Grosvenor's smile, so much like his brother's, was wickedly depraved. "Their solicitor no doubt has found a reasonable solution to your unwanted demands."

"Despite Theo's will?" Trixi contended, less frightened on discovering they carried no immediate threat to Chris. "It's legitimate."

"While your son is not," Cecilia Grosvenor snapped, bristling and testy, her scrawny form rigid with spleen.

"At least he's not George's son," Trixi ascerbically replied. "For which I'm grateful. Now if you'll excuse me, I prefer not exchanging insults." She turned to go.

"We can take the boy, you know," Harry coolly said, watching her like a viper.

Swiveling back, she paled before their eyes.

"He should be put in foster care," Lady Lydia purred, her gaze cold as the grave, "with other unwanted children. He should have been put there years ago."

"Why are you doing this?" Trixi breathed, her voice barely a whisper. "I've never harmed you, never asked for anything . . ."

"Your son represents a potential problem for us. More so after your foolish escapade in Paris." Harry Grosvenor sat on the sofa, a small gnomish man, his sisters lesser versions from the same mold, all three seated in a row, black-garbed as though for a funeral, naked hatred in their eyes.

They could take Chris from her if they chose to call him George's son, Trixi knew. The law was clear. She couldn't afford to challenge them. "You have my word," she murmured, her voice constrained by a suffocating fear. "I'll not contact you or the Clouards again."

"As if the word of a slut can be trusted," Lady Lydia sneered.

The drawing room door flew open, smashed against the wall, the tinkle of splintered plaster striking the floor suddenly loud in the hush. "This visit is over," Pasha barked, his large form filling the door frame. "*No one* will be taking Christopher from his mother," he decreed as the three Grosvenors stared bug-eyed at the huge apparition on the threshold. "Now leave," he growled, stepping into the room, "or I'll throw you out."

Assured of his importance in this small corner of Kent, Harry Grosvenor was not long overcome with shock. "How dare you," he blustered, coming to his feet. "Do you know who we are?"

"You're miserable scum trying to frighten a lady. Now get the hell out."

"Please, Pasha," Trixi intervened, fearful for her son's safety.

"Your newest swain is making a profound mistake," Lady Lydia warned, her cold gaze flickering from Pasha to Trixi. Rising to stand beside her brother, she briskly shook out her skirts. "We have consequence in this world!"

"Perhaps in Kent," Pasha coolly said, "but not in the *world,* I assure you. In the way of a personal warning, I *do* have consequence in the world, and you and your accomplices would be wise to heed me."

"Tell him he can't do this, Harry," Cecilia hotly said, jumping to her feet. She looked at her brother, a peevish pout twisting her thin lips. "Tell him we're Grosvenors!"

"I don't care if you're the King of Siam," Pasha snarled. Emperors trembled before his father's sword, and courage and boldness were a family trait. "I'm telling you to leave Lady Grosvenor and her son alone."

Pasha couldn't protect her from them. How *could* he? Trixi nervously reflected, charmed by his chivalry but realistic about the duration of his visit.

"You'll rue this day," Harry Grosvenor murmured, his gaze on Trixi. "Mark my words."

Pasha swiftly advanced, closing the distance between them in three long strides. Grabbing a handful of Harry's frock coat, he hoisted him off the floor as if he were weightless. Raising him to flinty eye level, Pasha said in the merest whisper, "Apologize to the lady."

Harry Grosvenor hesitated, his eyes flitting from left to right, searching for help.

"No one's going to save you. And I can crush your puny body without breaking a sweat," Pasha silkily murmured. "Now make that apology with feeling." Swinging the small man around to face Trixi, he nodded peremptorily.

"I apologize," Harry muttered.

Pasha shook him once with a hard snap of his wrist. "Louder. The lady can't hear you."

"I apologize," the dangling man rasped, his face

turning beet red, his frock coat and shirt collar a tightening ligature around his neck.

Pasha tipped his head in mild inquiry. "Is that the best you can do?"

Using the little remaining air in his lungs, Harry shrieked, "Forgive me!"

"That's better," Pasha murmured, dropping him as if he smelled. "Now get the hell out."

Gasping for breath, Harry scrambled up from the floor and stumbled from the room. Bonnets bobbing, his sisters scurried after him.

"You shouldn't have, but thank you," Trixi said, smiling broadly at the delicious retaliation. The Grosvenors' comeuppance was so long in coming. "I'll savor the moment."

"You're going to need more than my threats to keep them away." Pasha moved to the window, watching Trixi's odious neighbors clamber into their carriage.

"Eventually," she replied, joining him to watch the Grosvenors' retreat. "But let me bask in the present pleasure. You were wonderful."

"What will it take for them to leave you alone?"

"Fear certainly doesn't hurt." She smiled up at him, although her expression immediately sobered when she considered the crux of the issue. "Chris will always remain a problem for them."

"Do they have money? Is that what they're protecting?"

"Not a great deal. They're a cadet branch of the family, their fortune modest by London standards. Perhaps that's why they fear losing any of it. Although I've told them countless times I don't want their money."

"You do need some funds though."

"My problems aren't your problems, Pasha," she quietly said. "I'm fine. We can survive on the stipend my father left—it's not your concern. You're on holiday. Actually, *I'm* on holiday, if I recall, so the devil take the Grosvenors," she finished, grinning. "Now are you up to playing with kittens again? Because Chris will be waiting."

"Of course."

She searched his face, her brows faintly drawn. "What?"

"Nothing."

"I know that look."

"What look?" An innocent gaze suddenly met hers.

"The one that blatantly offers sex from under those ludicrously long lashes. Women would kill for those lashes, you know."

He lowered his desirable lashes marginally.

She cocked her head and grinned. "Are you asking?"

"If you think there's time."

"After the kittens," she murmured.

He smiled, a slow, luscious upturning of his mouth, no flash, just flagrant heat. "And then I'll have some sweet pussy of my own," he whispered.

But a messenger from Pasha's solicitor arrived when they were still at the playhouse, altering their schedule, and the courier and Pasha were closeted for some time in the library. When Pasha finally emerged, he found Trixi in the kitchen office and said only that Charles had sent some additional information on Gustave's condition.

"How is he?" she inquired, trying to read his expression as he stood in the doorway.

"As well as can be expected." His voice was cautious, controlled, and she knew.

"Will you be leaving?" she asked.

He shook his head, but a worry line creased his brows. "I came to see if you could have Ordie ready a room for the courier? He'll be staying overnight. And have her bring some food into the library when she has time. Come and join us if you like," he graciously offered. "It's taking longer than I thought."

When Ordie had been given instructions and Trixi returned to the library with a tray for the messenger, she found the two men deep in conversation, a map opened between them.

"Jean-Paul is updating me on the events in Greece," Pasha said, introducing the young man to Trixi. He turned out to be an assistant to Charles, further indication of the seriousness of his mission.

But Pasha turned the conversation to innocuous subjects while Jean-Paul ate his lunch, and then escorted the young man upstairs to his room for much-needed sleep. He'd been without rest for two days.

"Are you going to tell me?" Trixi inquired when Pasha returned to the library.

He sat down before he answered, stretched his trousered legs out before him, and contemplated the polished toes of his boots for a moment. "What do you want to know?"

"That man didn't travel this distance to simply update you on events."

He shrugged. "There's not a lot that can be done about the problem."

"Tell me anyway."

"Gustave's been moved to a prison in Preveza," he gruffly said.

"Will it be more difficult now to gain his freedom?"

Pasha sighed, ran his fingers through his thick hair, his discomfort obvious. "Fevers are rampant in those dungeons. Charles is trying to get him moved. But our information is at least ten days old by the time we receive it. *Merde,*" he swore. "God only knows if he's still alive."

"Does Charles want your help?"

"No," he muttered. "He can do as much as I. *More,* probably, with his diplomatic contacts. He was just letting me know."

But Pasha was restless the remainder of the day and evening, distracted, on edge, and when Jean-Paul woke at nine, Pasha closeted himself in the library with him again. He didn't come to bed until two.

"Is this really just about Gustave?" Trixi murmured, making room for him as he climbed into bed.

He gently kissed her and then rolled on his back, tucked his arms under his head, and stared at the ceiling, not sure he could sleep after hearing Jean-Paul's reports. "The Turks are on the offensive again," he said, his voice troubled. "They've landed thirty thousand troops since February. Modon fell two weeks ago, Jean-Paul tells me. Neokastron is sure to go next."

"And you feel a need to help?" The Greek struggle for independence had fired the imagination of much of Europe. She understood.

"A lot of my friends are there," Pasha quietly replied, "and—"

"You were planning on going again—until . . . the night at Langelier's," she softly finished.

"Yes." It was just a matter of time until he sailed for Greece again. Only the beautiful Trixi Grosvenor curtailed that impulse.

"And I'm keeping you."

He turned his head and smiled at her, the moonlight washing his fine-boned face and matchless beauty. "I'm keeping myself."

"I want you to stay forever, you know."

"And I want to stay forever."

Her own smile was winsome. "If reality didn't intrude."

His lashes lowered faintly in acknowledgment. "Except for that slight problem."

"I'll always remember these days with great fondness. When I'm old and gray and—"

"Hush." He touched her mouth with the pad of his finger, not wanting to think of the future, of tomorrow, of all the endless tomorrows without her. No more than he wanted to think of permanence in his life.

"Kiss me," she said, soft and low. "And hold me."

He did.

And she kissed him back and held him tightly. And told herself not to think of tomorrow. Only the soft warm bed existed tonight, and Pasha's strong arms and body pressed hard against hers.

"You're the best thing that ever happened to me," he whispered.

"I am damned wonderful," she impudently returned, nibbling at his lower lip.

She felt his chuckle.

"And modest, too," he teased.

It set the tone. She didn't want tears and sadness. She'd had enough of that in her life. But never with Pasha. And she meant to keep it that way—a glorious memory, pure and untarnished, full of joy. They made love with a special tenderness, both conscious of the brevity of their time together. She wanted to remember every sensation, each minute degree of emotion—the sound of his voice, the feel of his kisses, the exquisite heated passions he'd awakened in her. Her intense joy.

He'd not thought it possible to experience such sadness at leaving a woman, and he struggled to understand the unusual feelings she engendered. Although Trixi was beautiful, beautiful women were a constant in his life; something more than her physical comeliness affected him. But he couldn't stay, he knew, regardless his feelings; his commitment to his friends in Greece far outweighed any personal pleasures. He'd already stayed much longer than he should.

Emotion didn't so easily succumb to logic, though, and he held Trixi in his arms once she fell asleep, his thoughts in disarray. The word marriage entered his consciousness that night as he lay awake, her scent sweet in his nostrils, her warm body curled against his, the possibility of keeping her appealing. But his natural antipathy to the curbs of matrimony discouraged further contemplation, as did force of habit. Marriage had never been an option in his life.

Refusing to dwell on his curious sense of loss and the even more curious reflections on marriage, he kissed Trixi awake instead and distracted himself from the unpleasantness of parting by reminding them both of the exquisite pleasures they shared.

6

Jean-Paul left in the morning with a message for Charles and a further one for the Duras's solicitor in London. Taking a detour to Dover via London, the courier arrived in the city in time to speak to Mr. Woolcott before he closed his office for the day. The message he delivered was succinct and to the point.

Thomas Woolcott said, "That much?" when he read the note.

"Each month on the first," Jean-Paul declared. "Delivered in small bills. As for the Grosvenors, Mr. Duras would like you to see that the Prime Minister receives his note. Apparently his father and Lord Liverpool are friends. He would prefer the curbs on the Grosvenors' noxious behavior toward Lady Grosvenor be quietly applied. She's not to know of his intervention."

"The P.M. . . ." Woolcott murmured, thrusting out his bottom lip in concentration. "I'm not sure I'll be granted entrée."

"Pasha said you should mention Countess Wolletski from the Congress of Vienna. A charming friend. He said the earl would understand."

"The Lady Grosvenor has a powerful protector," the solicitor gently mused, his intensely blue eyes reflective.

"A very dangerous one," Jean-Paul corrected. "The

Grosvenors should be apprised of that fact in the plainest of terms."

Woolcott had been handling the Duras's business affairs in England for a decade. Well paid and competent, he nodded his balding head. "In the plainest of terms," he agreed.

"Then I'll bid you adieu." Jean-Paul rose to his feet, picking up his riding gloves from the table. "Events in Greece necessitate speed. I'm expected in Dover post-haste."

"Will Pasha be in Kent long?"

Jean-Paul shook his head. "A day or two. He finds the lady difficult to leave." The courier shrugged, a swift Gallic acknowledgment of female allure, and his mouth lifted in a half-smile. "I'd say three days at the most."

She'd known their time was limited since Jean-Paul left. Pasha wasn't the same; a shimmer of tension existed beneath the surface of his easy charm. He took care to speak in the present tense only; Chris garnered immeasurably more of his time and he and Will seemed to be in some conspiracy, their conversations soft-spoken, hurried, with much nodding of the head on Will's part.

Two mornings later, Pasha came up behind her as she stood before the dressing table in her nightgown. He was already fully dressed despite the early hour. "I'm leaving today," he murmured, sliding his arms around her waist, her body still warm from sleep. "I wish I didn't have to." Bending his dark head, he kissed her rosy cheek.

She leaned into him and his embrace tightened.

There were no words sufficient to describe their feelings, no easy phrases to mark the end of such gladsome

pleasure. Nothing that wouldn't sound trite and pointless.

"Thank you for everything," she simply said, shutting her eyes against the tears threatening to spill over.

"Do you want me to write?" He'd debated declaring
that he would write. Finally, uncertain of his own feelings, he thought she should decide.

She shook her head, incapable of speech, but sure at
least that she didn't want to prolong the good-byes.
Better to remember the joy he'd brought her than the
unhappiness of his forgetting.

He nuzzled her cheek, sweet as a young boy, and
then gently let her go. "I'm packed. Will's keeping my
horses for a few weeks before sending them on to Paris.
Do you mind?"

She should say something, she thought, deal with
this like an adult. Watching him in the mirror, she
forced herself to say in a temperate voice, "I don't mind
at all."

He turned her around then and took her hands in
his. "I'm terrible at good-byes, but for once I wish I
weren't."

She smiled faintly. "I despise them, too."

"We'll say au revoir instead."

"Yes," she agreed, thinking how smooth he was, how
accomplished to manage this all with suave gallantry,
as though they were parting after an evening together.
As if they'd meet the next day for tea.

"If you ever need anything, I've left addresses on
your desk where I can be reached—mine, my parents,
Charles's. If you ever need *anything* at all, let me know,"
he murmured, his gaze devouring her for a moment.

"Thank you." Mesmerized by the haunting depths of
his eyes, she wondered in some more rational part of
her brain whether he really meant what he said or if
this, too, was more of his consummate charm.

Touched by feelings he didn't understand, Pasha resisted being drawn into maudlin sentimentality. "Will and Chris are going to ride with me to the crossroad," he declared in a conversational tone that took some effort. "Would you like to come?"

"No, I couldn't," she whispered, her heart in her eyes.

"Jesus." His grip suddenly turned painful. And then he pulled her into his arms, crushing her. "I *have* to go," he finally whispered, sadness overwhelming him. Then his grasp loosened and he quickly stepped back, his arms spread wide, the pressure of constraint in every muscle in his body. A second passed, two, and his hands dropped to his sides. "Au revoir," he whispered, and spinning around, he strode from the room.

She heard his footsteps racing down the hall, taking the stairs in leaps, and then the outside door slammed. Running to the windows, she pressed her face against the glass so she could see the curve of the drive leading from the house.

There he was only moments later astride his new black, the long-legged thoroughbred prancing every few steps as though he could feel the agitation of its rider. Chris accompanied Pasha, riding Petunia, and they both laughed as she watched them, enjoying some mutual humor. Her mother's heart went out to the man who had shown such kindness to her son.

She watched them until they were out of sight, Pasha and Chris in front, Will following. When the forest finally obscured her view and she could no longer see, she sat down and allowed her tears to fall.

She hadn't felt such a sense of loss even when Theo left, and she wondered at her lack of loyalty to the father of her child. But Theo had always been wild, untamed, his talents more a part of the world than the province of a single person. Perhaps she'd always understood that no one would ever possess him completely. When he'd come to England to buy racehorses, to draw and paint them, he'd been as high-spirited a thoroughbred as any of his subjects. Drawn to the glittering light of his persona, she'd fallen under his spell, a country mouse on the world's stage for a brief engagement. He'd adored her and Chris with a zealous enthusiasm and passion she'd not completely understood. He'd be back in a month, he'd said, intense and ardent when he'd left.

The shocking news of his death had come via a notice in the London papers advertising an auction of the contents of his Paris studio. At least he'd died on one of his beloved racehorses, she thought as she read the brief description of his death.

How different Pasha was, she mused. Not a glittering comet, but a flesh and blood man, complex and subtle, like a dark warrior from a distant place at times, virile, powerful, yet tender . . . so tender. She smiled at the incongruous word. His gentleness was only one facet of a grossly material man, a wealthy, influential man who chose to bend the world to his will, a man raised to be contemptuous of authority by a father who had held the world at bay.

And yet he could be exquisitely compassionate, boyishly open, full of teasing laughter.

She'd miss him.

She'd miss the breadth of his worldly experience, his willingness to indulge her, the spectacular, shameless pleasure he gave. No one had simply held her before and provoked such flagrant feeling.

"Thank you," she whispered into the quiet of the room. "And Godspeed."

Pasha arrived in Paris the evening of the next day, early enough to join his family for dinner. "I invited

Charles, Maman," he said, strolling into the opulent dining room, looking point-device in black evening rig, his hair still damp from his bath. "I hope an extra guest won't disturb your chef."

"Everything disturbs Jallut, darling. I've learned not to worry. Did you have a pleasant holiday?"

"Yes, very," Pasha replied, smiling, taking in his parents and siblings ranged round the table. "I see the family is arrayed in force this evening."

"Odile has a reading this evening at the Comtesse Crozat's. She had a rehearsal earlier and we were her admiring audience," his father replied, bowing his head graciously in his oldest daughter's direction.

"Have you heard her Devil's Bridge poem?" his sister Honore inquired, her cat's eyes alive with emotion. "It's stupendous. Berri is going to let me do the illustrations for it."

"I *have* heard it, and congratulations, Rory," Pasha said, seating himself. "Berri has a good eye for talent." Honore had been studying with Guerin for five years and her talent had won her medals at two Royal Salons.

"You look tanned and fit, darling," his mother said. "And you bought yourself some more racehorses, I hear."

"From whom, pray tell?" Pasha murmured, his brows lifted. "I haven't been in town for more than three hours."

"Mansel, of course. He knows everything." Teo smiled at her eldest child and softly winked. "He counts your billets-doux as well."

Pasha groaned. "Don't remind me. It was a pleasure to escape the society belles for a time."

"Is the English lady safely home?" His father's inquiry was delivered in a bland tone, but his dark eyes held a quizzing note.

"Yes, safely, thank you."

"What kind of racehorses?" his youngest brother James inquired, a tremor of excitement in his voice.

"A chestnut, a black, and a bay, all from top-notch sires. I'm having them shipped over next month."

"Can I ride them?"

"If you think you can," Pasha teased.

"I can ride *anything*," his brother Eugene softly interposed, the only member of the family who knew every stud book from Kiev to Yorkshire. "Are any from Darley stock?"

"The bay."

"Will you race it this season?"

"*You* can. I'm off to Greece by week's end." And Pasha went on to explain the turn of events regarding Gustave. A political family, they discussed the full scope of current battles and naval engagements, their sources of information numerous and current.

"Take me with you this time," James pleaded. His older brother Eugene added his pleas.

Teo's gaze met that of her husband across the table.

"Not until you're eighteen," Duras said, understanding his wife's pointed glance.

"*You* were fighting when you were sixteen," Eugene declared. "Why can't we?"

"Because I won't let you," Teo interposed.

"Because your mother won't let you," Duras said with a smile.

"You outrank her, Papa," James exclaimed.

"You have to be eighteen," Duras quietly said, but everyone understood regardless the soft tone, the discussion was over.

Honore, a conciliatory middle child, stepped in with a question about the race schedule, and soon racehorses were the subject of debate. Pasha was too large to ride in any but amateur events, but Eugene at sixteen and fifteen-year-old James were still coltish enough to meet the weight standards for the track.

Charles arrived along with the second course and entertained the entire family with the newest gossip. Everyone was laughing by the time he'd dissected the dull court society, even Odile, who was much too serious of late. He brought a smile to her face, which was his intent. He didn't care to see her so morose.

Honore challenged him to a musical contest, and each of them tried to outdo the other in remembering the lyrics of the newest songs. Teo joined them, James and Eugene adding their voices to the race songs and music hall numbers. Duras never sang, not wishing to inflict his tuneless voice on the festivities, and Pasha sang an occasional bar when the others were struggling to remember the words. He was notoriously up-to-date on all the music hall ditties.

It was a joyous dinner *en famille,* like so many in the Duras household, and for a moment Pasha wished he could have Trixi and Chris at table with him. How they would have enjoyed the evening.

How he would have enjoyed having them.

He drank considerably more after that, wishing to obliterate such pointless yearnings. His mother noticed, as did Odile. She and Pasha had always been the closest. And Duras glanced once or twice at his oldest child, aware of a subtle constraint since his holiday abroad.

A woman did that to a man, he thought.

He recalled how beautiful the young lady they'd found that night at Langelier's had been.

And three weeks in England, he mused, was a very long time in one lady's company for Pasha.

The party broke up by nine when Teo, Odile, and Honore left for the Comtesse Crozat's literary soiree. James and Eugene were excused to ready their studies for school the next day, and Charles, Pasha, and Duras retired to the library.

Drinks were poured and the men drew up chairs to the map table.

"I wasn't sure you'd come back," Charles said, glancing at the red flags dotting the map of Greece spread out before them.

"I wasn't sure either," Pasha replied, leaning back in his chair, his expression shuttered.

"You liked the lady, I gather."

"Yes."

The liquor sloshed over the rim of Charles's glass at Pasha's unexpected answer. He'd anticipated some ribald, masculine comment, not a soulful, earnest response.

"You're wasting good cognac," Pasha said, his gaze amused.

"You shocked the hell out of me. Are you feverish?"

"No. She was just . . ." Pasha paused, considering an appropriate word for the indescribable Trixi Grosvenor. "She was unusual," he finally said. "Haven't you ever met a woman who seems different from all the rest?"

"No. Nor have you, as I recall," Charles sardonically retorted.

Pasha smiled faintly. "I recommend the experience."

"Does she have a friend?" Charles drolly inquired.

"No. Sorry. She lives in a small village away from the world."

"And no scandal ensued with your visit in this small village?" Charles was as au courant with convention as the next man.

"She's a widow."

Charles's brows rose and a slow smile graced his handsome face. "How convenient."

"Not that kind of a widow," Pasha remonstrated, a

rare fastidiousness in his tone. "She has a young son and lives in relative poverty."

"Which you were able to mitigate, I presume."

"I will, although I haven't yet. She wouldn't take any money."

"Good God, a veritable paragon of virtue."

"No comment, Papa?" Pasha quirked a brow at his father's amused countenance.

"If you enjoyed yourself and were able to do the lady a service in the bargain, I'd consider your holiday a success. As for virtue or its lack, I'm impartial. How old is the boy?" A young child was a consideration in any love affair.

"Four. He's the son of Theodore Gericault."

"So she's not completely a paragon of virtue," Charles coolly noted.

"Nor would such a woman interest me, Charles."

"With good reason. Pray tell how Gericault became involved with her?"

Pasha told them briefly, without undue detail, the mishaps and good fortune in Trixi's life. "The uncles Clouard have to be thwarted though," he added at the end. "Perhaps you could compose some suitable legal warning to them, Charles. I don't want Trixi harassed by either the Grosvenors or the Clouards. If they want to do battle with someone, I'll oblige them."

"I'd be more than pleased. Jerome Clouard tried to cheat one of my clients out of a property near Rheims. He's without scruple. Also, the judge Clouet is one of my close personal friends. So do you want to just scare them, or go for the jugular?"

"I'm inclined for the jugular. Chris deserves his inheritance."

"And if legal means don't bring results," Duras quietly added, "we could call on them and personally deliver a message they might better understand. Sometimes men of their stripe understand force. Death threats work wonders, I've found."

"There you have it," Charles cheerfully said. "If the judicial system fails you, your papa's suggestion will bring results. The Clouards are ours."

"When?" Pasha quietly inquired. "I'm pressed for time."

"I'll talk to Clouet in the morning and draw the papers up tomorrow. A messenger to the Clouards by, say, three, and none of them will enjoy their dinner tomorrow evening, I guarantee. I'll need some names and dates from you, Pasha, but if the will was registered, I'll find it somewhere. And we both know Theo had no love lost for his uncles. He would have registered it out of spite if nothing else."

"I think he cared for Trixi."

"The man was wild and unpredictable. He had ladies by the score."

Pasha nodded and exhaled softly. "*She* didn't know that, and he stayed with her for almost two years. She was different for him."

As well as for you, Charles thought. Pasha had never given more than a moment's consideration to any of the women in his life. And now he was savior to this young woman and her child. Charles wished he'd seen this wunderkind in person. He'd have to ask Jean-Paul tomorrow.

Charles asked several pertinent questions necessary for his conversation with Clouet, and then talk turned to the events surrounding Gustave. Meetings were planned with the ambassador and his attachés, and a list of supplies for Pasha's expedition to Greece was drawn up. Duras was of considerable help after decades in the military.

They agreed to meet for dinner the following eve-

ning to firm up further details on both the court case
and the journey to Greece.

The following afternoon Jerome Clouard slammed his
fist on the desktop with such force the inkwell jumped,
splattering ink. "The bitch has Charles Doudeau for a
lawyer now, damn her mercenary soul!"

"No need then to question who her protector is,"
Phillipe murmured. The Duras-Doudeau connection
was well known. "But they can't *force* us to pay her the
inheritance. Or not immediately at least. We can drag
this out in court for years." Trained in law, Phillipe
understood their dilatory prerogatives.

"Clouet was brought into this again," Jerome spat.
"Damn his righteous hide and Doudeau's connections."

"We'll see if we can get a postponement."

"From Clouet?" Jerome snorted. "With the Duras
family taking an interest in this. Not likely."

"We'll ask for a new prosecutor, too."

"Really, Phillipe. You're not that naive."

"Each request is simply a delaying tactic that re-
quires a response. We then challenge. They respond, et
cetera, et cetera." He smiled faintly from the depths of
a Moroccan leather chair, the ornate embossing ef-
feminizing his flabby plumpness. "Theodore's boy will
be full grown by the time the case is settled."

"I wish I had your optimism," his brother grumbled.

"You're too impulsive. You always want immediate
reprisals." Phillipe's voice was soft. "Delay will accomplish as much without violence."

"Violence works faster."

"Patience, brother."

"I've never acquired it, and this hearing has been
rescheduled for three days hence, in case you didn't
notice. An immediate reply is required."

"We'll send one requesting a postponement," Phillipe mildly replied.

"Do what you like," his brother snapped, "but if your method isn't effective, I'm having the boy seized." There was no softness in Jerome Clouard, his tall, gaunt form and relentless malice impassive to the gentler human emotions. "Without the brat, they have no case."

"What does this request for a postponement signify?" Pasha curtly inquired the succeeding morning, pacing the floor in Charles's office.

"Nothing more than an obstruction," Charles answered. "Clouet has already denied it."

"Next?"

"They'll attempt one or two more evasions—a day or so of these documents passing back and forth and then you'll see them at the hearing. By the way, Felix found Gericault's will in family documents in Evreux. It's also registered in the Minutier Central des Notaires Parisiens."[3] Charles leaned back in his chair with a self-satisfied expression on his face. "Felix is very thorough."

"Is Chris the heir?"

"Apparently Gericault was very ill when the will was made. It's one sentence, appointing his father the sole heir of all his possessions, dated November thirtieth, 1823. On December second, his father in turn willed their combined property to Chris. It was probably done this way for discretionary reasons. Champion de Villeneuve was appointed protector of Chris's interest."

"Then why didn't he protect him?"

"A good question. We should ask him. The Clouards may have gotten to him first."[4]

"It doesn't matter at this point," Pasha briskly said.

"If the will designates Chris as heir, the boy should have the estate."

"Clearly, yes."

While the various legalities continued to be debated in Paris prior to the hearing, Trixi returned to the familiar routines of her country life. She helped Will with the new foals and racers, an authority on breeding, a master hand with the horses, her expertise acquired from both Will and her late father. The summer crops were in full fledge and lush with the perfect weather, the fields maintained by day workers from the village. The Burleigh House women fed the field laborers lunch every day and busied themselves as well putting up strawberry preserves from the kitchen garden. Chris amused himself with boyish pursuits, his playroom an unending source of entertainment since Pasha had come·bearing gifts.

Chris asked for Pasha only on rare occasions, understanding his mother's explanation that Pasha had returned home after his holiday with them. When he asked if they'd ever go to Paris to see him, Trixi, respectful of his hopeful feelings, said, "Maybe we will someday."

She missed Pasha, too, although she was more able to rationalize away her wistful longings. But she missed him terribly at night when the activities of the day were no longer a means of distraction. She'd often wrap herself in the linen shirt he'd left behind and sit by the opened window remembering, the night sounds washing over her. The scent of him clung to the fabric, the soft linen warmed her body, and she thought of their shared pleasures with covetous yearning——but never with melancholy or grief. He'd brought unalloyed joy into her life.

But she wasn't completely unselfish, and at times she

wished with the benign fantasy of childhood that he'd suddenly materialize in the moonlight streaming through her window and take her into his arms.

Parisian nightlife seemed to have paled, Pasha noted, his comment not surprising to Charles after three days in his company. Their usual drinking companions were dull, he'd declared, the masked ball at Mme. Lafond's was monotonous, even the actresses from the Théâtre Français were insipid. He and Charles were now sitting alone in a quiet corner of the Jockey Club at four in the morning, drinking.

"The city seems humdrum and stale," Pasha grumbled. "Everyone's the same, the routines never change."

"The masked ball had a certain energy, I thought."

Pasha looked up from contemplation of the bottom of his brandy glass. "Did you think so?"

"It was a damnable crush."

"Unfortunately no one of interest was there."

Charles refrained from mentioning the score of women who had approached them at one time or another in their brief stay. "Perhaps we've attended too many," he said instead.

"My thought exactly." Pasha refilled his glass. "Although the Théâtre Français actresses weren't up to their usual standards either. Didn't they all seem cut from the same mold? Petite, perfumed, provocative."

Charles merely raised his eyebrows. Those qualities had always been more than sufficient to garner Pasha's interest.

"Don't give me that look, you know they were banal."

"Not blond enough?" Charles softly posed.

"No, as a matter of fact."

"A partiality for blondes has overtaken you?" Charles murmured.

"A not too subtle allusion to Lady Grosvenor, I presume?"

"You seem discontent with the usual wares tonight—not typical of your former scorched-earth policy with women. I don't recall your having a preference before for anything other than availability."

"Don't go there, Charles," Pasha said, surveying his friend through narrowed eyes. "I have no romantical sensibilities. Period."

"Your Trixi wasn't banal certainly."

Pasha's grip clenched on his glass at the possessive pronoun, but he gave away nothing when he mildly said, "No, she wasn't banal."

"You're allowed to miss her. It's perfectly normal."

Pasha inhaled, unclenched his fingers. "Not for me," he murmured, and emptied his glass into his mouth.

"Write her."

Pasha's piercing gaze held Charles's for a moment over the rim of his glass. "And say what, pray tell?"

"Tell her you miss her, tell her Paris has lost its charm, tell her you enjoyed your visit. Do you need a primer on letter writing?"

"Very funny," Pasha sardonically murmured, setting his glass down. "I have nothing to offer her. You know that."

"Maybe she doesn't want anything."

"They all do," Pasha muttered, slumping lower in his chair.

"So cynical."

"Realistic."

"You'll have to find someone someday."

Pasha's brows flicked up and down. "Someday is the operative word, my friend. I don't see you measuring any female for the marriage bed."

"But then, I'm not desolate in the midst of a feverish Parisian night."

"Nor am I," Pasha flatly denied.

"I've seen you more cheerful after losing twenty thousand at the races."

"I've a lot on my mind."

"That never stopped you from fucking before."

Pasha smiled. "So if I find someone to fuck tonight, you'll cease your harping?"

Charles grinned. "Maybe. But tell me about her first. Jean-Paul's descriptive powers are sadly lacking. He *thought* she might have blond hair."

"Golden blond, like sunflowers at high noon," Pasha softly murmured. "To be precise."

"And why did you stay so long?"

"She made me laugh. And cry once, too, come to think of it. Don't choke on your drink," Pasha said, grinning. "It shocked the hell out of me, too."

"I don't believe it. Too much hashish?"

"Not in Kent, Charles. Everyone goes to bed when the sun goes down."

"Unlike Paris."

"Oh, yes," he softly said. "But her father had put away a fabulous grade of Irish whiskey that added much to the pleasure of the evenings. That in itself would be worth a trip back."

"Take me with you when you go," Charles casually declared.

Pasha looked startled for a moment. "I didn't say I was going."

"It's just a thought," Charles offered. "Why not for the Epsom Derby?"

"If I wasn't in Greece."

"You're not obliged to go. Guillemont is moving heaven and earth."

"I'm going, Charles. I'm not staying for Trixi Grosvenor. At twenty-five, I'm not staying for any woman."

"In that case the Baroness Lacelles asked me to mention to you that she will be home tonight."

"It's four in the morning," Pasha reminded him.

"She particularly said *anytime,* in that luscious contralto of hers. I told her we'd think about it."

"We?" Pasha smiled.

"She enjoyed herself last time we were there." Charles glanced toward the curtained windows facing the street. "It's close enough to walk."

Pasha looked at the clock on the wall with the deliberate concentration of a man with several hours of drinking behind him. "What time do we have to be at the hearing?"

"Ten."

"And you're fully prepared for the Clouards?"

"There's nothing to prepare. Felix found the will. Clouet will take one look at it and tell them to pay up."

"We have until nine then."

"Five hours of Caroline's assiduous charm."

"Maybe I'll just watch," Pasha lightly surmised.

"And maybe the sun will fail to rise this morning."

"You're intent on this, aren't you?"

"It might curtail your moping."

"I don't mope."

"Well, then?" Charles softly challenged.

Pasha placed his hands on the chair arms and after the smallest hesitation, pushed himself to his feet. "She'd better be damned entertaining."

They were escorted to the baroness's boudoir by a tall, stalwart footman, the baroness's penchant for large men, including those on her staff, well known.

"Charles! Pasha! Do come in." Arrayed in a ruffled pink mousseline dressing gown that made her look resplendently female, she waved from a chaise. "Claude,

bring some more champagne." Her gaze flickered from
her footman back to her visitors. "Would you like a
late snack as well?" she inquired with the air of a gracious hostess.

Charles declined for both of them.

"Then come see my new pillow book," she offered, a
seductive undertone to her voice. She was the petite,
perfumed, provocative archetype much in vogue in
fashionable society. And pale blond like cool frost.
"Pouchat just delivered it today. The illustrations are
quite good." A young, childless widow, Caroline Lacelles was making up for lost time now that her elderly
husband had conveniently died. "When you didn't
come tonight, I thought the Princess Catulania may
have seduced you instead."

"Pasha was in the mood to drink. We've been at the
Jockey Club," Charles replied, walking toward her
across her rose carpet.

"How convenient," she cheerfully said. "But how
sullen you look, dear Pasha," she archly noted, her
downy brows delicately raised, her rosebud mouth
posed in a delicate moue. "I hear you're lovesick."

Pasha stopped midstride as though he'd been struck,
his gaze cool enough to put the fear of God in most
people. "You're an undeniable bitch, Caroline." His
voice was emotionless, little more than a whisper.

"Come, come, Pasha, it's not a cardinal sin," she
sweetly purred, unintimidated by any of her lovers.
"You're *allowed* to be lovesick."

"If you're looking for someone to whip you tonight,"
Pasha blandly declared, his composure restored, "I'd
oblige you without the goading." He moved toward
the large chair she'd had made especially for him.

"If you don't want to talk about the pretty Englishwoman you *rescued*," she murmured, her emphasis deliberate, "just say so."

"I don't, no more than you wish to discuss your husband."

Her expression instantly altered, the brittle gaiety wiped away. "Touché, darling," she quietly said. "We'll talk of more agreeable things." Married at sixteen to an aging libertine and roué with two deceased wives and grandchildren older than herself, she had not found the last eight years of her life pleasant.

"Pasha is off to Greece shortly to see to Gustave's rescue," Charles interposed, shifting the conversation.

"Poor Gustave," Caroline sympathetically responded. "Can you save him?"

"I can't, but Charles can," Pasha replied, dropping into the soft cushioned chair covered in an elegant rose du Barry leather.

"While you'll shoot Turks and save Greece," she said with a smile.

"I wish it were that easy. No matter how many you shoot, the sultan sends more. I don't suppose you have any cognac." Pasha slid down on his spine, disgruntled, discontent, his moodiness only adding to his sensual appeal. He looked elegant in evening rig, his diamond studs twinkling as he restlessly shifted his large body and recrossed his sprawled legs.

"Claude will bring you some. Should I read to you?" Caroline raised the small brocade-covered book. "It seems we all need some distraction."

Pasha didn't answer, his gaze focused on the toes of his evening shoes, but Charles obliged and Caroline began the story of a young man being instructed in the arts of love by his father's concubine.

Interrupted briefly by the footman with the champagne, Caroline directed him to bring Pasha cognac. Once their glasses were filled and the servant had departed, she resumed her narrative.

Charles, seated closest to the baroness, viewed the

salacious illustrations, making observations that occasionally drew Pasha's interest. But once his bottle of cognac had been delivered, Pasha spoke only when directly addressed. By the end of the first adventure in the pillow book, Caroline had discarded her dressing gown and, provocatively arrayed in a tightly laced pink satin corset, sheer black chemise, and black silk stockings, she read with a new huskiness in her voice.

When she reached the section in which fellatio was being performed on the young man in the story, she closed the book. "That's enough for a time," she murmured. "I prefer the real thing to these color prints. Should I see what I can do about bringing your fine cocks to attention?" Her heated gaze drifted over the men's groins.

"I can't imagine refusing such an offer," Charles softly replied.

"Are you awake, Pasha, or should Charles and I go on without you?"

Pasha looked up. "I'll wait."

Charles and the baroness exchanged a glance but Pasha had already closed his eyes, his thoughts distant from the silken boudoir.

Before long, however, he set his glass aside and rose from his chair, his gaze surveying the couple who had moved to the lady's bed to continue their amorous pursuits. The heated scene elicited no expression, his dark eyes blank; without a word, he turned away and exited the room.

The sun was rising as he left the house, the dawn stillness like the emptiness he felt inside. Drink didn't help, nor did the company of others. He recalled the sunrises at Burleigh House, the light shining through the second-floor windows, gilding Trixi's small room in a shimmering glow. Her waking smile putting the glorious beauty of the sun to shame.

He missed her.

When he shouldn't.

When he'd never missed any woman before.

Only her smile, the sound of her voice, her presence would cure his debilitating sense of loss. But that cure would entail marriage—how could he offer her less? And he wasn't prepared to sacrifice his independence regardless his misery.

He swore at his cheerless lack of choices.

Thank God he was leaving for Greece soon.

7

The hearing was brief—exceedingly brief. Clouet was furious when circumstances of the will's concealment were revealed. He said five minutes into the hearing, "Monsieurs Clouard, the young grandnephew of yours will be given his inheritance or you'll be spending time in prison." Glaring down the Clouards' lawyer, who attempted to speak, he went on. "And if these provisions aren't immediately executed, I shall institute a sizable fine. The court finds in favor of the plaintiff. Case dismissed. Good day, gentlemen."

Jerome Clouard stormed out of the chambers, Phillipe running to keep pace with him. "We leave for England tonight," the larger man snarled. "That boy will disappear and Clouet can go hang himself."[5]

"I'm not sure that's wise," Phillipe countered.

"But then I didn't ask for your advice," Jerome growled. "You stay here. If you're squeamish, I'd prefer you not come along."

"It's only money. Not worth a life."

"It's a helluva *lot* of money." Jerome's truculence would not be abated. "So the boy disappears. If he happens to die later in some foster home, we'll be none the wiser."

"Foster care, now that's better," Phillipe said with a modicum of relief. The number of unwanted children in foster care was legion, and condoned by a society that regarded illegitimacy as more wicked than the ruthless abandonment of young children to indifference and death. "What of the mother? Surely she'll have Duras on her side."

"The Grosvenors can take care of her. I'm not concerned what they do. Only the boy inherits. He's our problem."

Two days later, on the same morning Pasha embarked from Marseille for the Greek port of Nauplia, Ordie opened the door to a group of men. Harry Grosvenor, looking grim, had brought the bailiff with him and two other men, one tall and menacing, the other a pudding of a man who wouldn't meet her gaze.

"Tell your mistress we're here to see her," the bailiff Archie Prine said, a note of apology in his voice.

"Immediately!" Harry Grosvenor curtly added, pushing past Mrs. Orde.

Archie in turn was brushed aside by the taller man, who barged into the foyer behind Harry.

"I have me orders, Mrs. Orde," the bailiff murmured, showing the housekeeper an official-looking document. "From Judge Benson." His face flushed in embarrassment. "You'd best find Lady Grosvenor."

Mrs. Orde's heart skipped a beat as she stepped back; Judge Benson was known for his cruelty. He'd sent two poachers to the gallows last year, regardless that the men were taking game for their starving families. And he endorsed the use of mantraps by the gentry, even though the hue and cry against them was gaining increasing sympathy in parliament.

Leaving the men standing in the entrance hall, she hurried to warn Trixi. On entering the playroom, where Trixi and Chris were reading together, she said, "It's Lord Grosvenor, with Archie this time. I'll read to Chris while you talk to them." But despite her effort to conceal the danger from Chris, her expression mirrored her fear.

"Just two?" Trixi asked, keeping her tone moderate.

"Four. A shame Mr. Pasha is gone."

"He can't be here for every unexpected visitor in my life," Trixi casually said, not wishing to alarm her son. "I'll be back shortly, Chris. Show Ordie how well you can read the pages on the medieval knights in your new book."

"They could fight by the time they were twelve, Ordie," the young boy said, a level of awe in his voice. "And look at the size of their swords! It takes two hands to lift them!"

Relieved Chris had taken no notice of Ordie's apprehension, Trixi left her housekeeper and son in the playroom and, bracing herself with a multitude of maxims having to do with pluck and self-reliance, she squared her shoulders, shuttered her gaze, and descended the stairs to face the four men standing in her entrance hall.

"We've come for the boy," Harry Grosvenor said. His eyes gleamed with brutality, as did those of Jerome and Phillipe Clouard beside him.

She stopped in midstep, her grip on the railing turning her knuckles white. "He's mine. You can't take him." Her heart beat so hard, she could hear the echo through her chest wall.

"The Clouards have come to claim him," Harry repudiated, triumph in his assertion.

"I have a lawyer. You can't do this. I'll fight you."

"Judge Benson has signed the order. Bring us the boy," Harry viciously said, "or we'll go and get him."

She felt faint for a second. How could the law be so cruel? "He's only four."

"Get him," Jerome ordered.

The man's voice was so cold, it shocked her, brought

a fresh rush of adrenaline to her senses, and her mind began to race, sorting through options. "How can you bodily remove him from his home? I can't believe that's possible."

"Tell her, Prine," Harry Grosvenor commanded.

"Beggin' your pardon, ma'am," Archie said, regret in every syllable, "but I'm here to see that the judge's orders are followed."

She had to breathe deeply several times before she was able to speak, the horror of what was about to happen to her son overwhelming her. "Where are you taking him, Archie?"

"To Dover, ma'am, for the passage to France."

"I'll go with you." She needed time to think, time to find some way out of this frightful nightmare.

"Out of the question," Jerome Clouard snapped.

"Let me accompany Christopher to Dover at least," she pleaded. "He won't go with you quietly otherwise. Surely you'd prefer not being the cynosure of condemnatory gazes as you manhandle a screaming young boy aboard the packet boat," she pointed out. "I could make certain he goes without a disturbance."

"It might be a good idea," Phillipe suggested. "Once on board, we could procure a private room."

While Jerome Clouard considered his reply, Trixi prayed harder than she'd ever prayed in her life. She needed time; even the hour to Dover might allow her room to maneuver, to find some means of escape.

"A screaming boy *will* draw attention," Harry Grosvenor noted, interested only in seeing the boy out of England. Whatever it took to accomplish that task was acceptable to him. "Let the woman come along with her brat."

Archie Prine had had his share of unpleasant duties over the years; a bailiff was obliged to follow the law even when it didn't seem right. But watching the heart-stricken sorrow of a young boy taken from his mother, by men so cold-hearted they'd been joking about the seizure on the drive over, made him question whether the current task went beyond the bounds of justice.

"Very well," Jerome muttered. "If you can keep the brat quiet. You have ten minutes to pack his clothes."

"Thank you," Trixi murmured, feigning appeasement. Every minute she had with Chris was a minute more to find a way out. "We'll be right back."

"Go with her, Archie," Harry curtly ordered. "And don't try to evade us," he warned.

"Yes, sir." She pretended submissiveness even as she traced the route from Burleigh House to Dover in her mind: the two post stops, the descent down the cliff, the various docks and businesses, the streets leading up from the harbor. As Archie began ascending the stairs, she turned away and went to fetch her son.

She waited for Archie in the upstairs hallway, hoping he'd have some suggestions.

"I'm right sorry," he immediately said, his voice kept deliberately low. "They're a cutthroat crew, they are."

"Does Judge Benson understand Chris is only four?" Trixi inquired, her heart breaking at the thought of Chris's fear.

"He don't care none, ma'am," Archie replied, keeping pace with her down the corridor. "A heart of stone he has."

"You have children, Archie. What would you do?"

"I wish I could help, Lady Grosvenor, but he'd have my head in a noose next, if'n I did anything to help you."

"If you weren't actually *present,* though," Trixi suggested, watching the play of emotions on the bailiff's face. "Could they blame you then?"

"I reckon not. They're a nasty bunch though," he cautioned. "Colder than a witch's tit, ma'am, beggin' your pardon. That tall one's the divil himself."

"Do any of them carry a weapon?"

"Just me, ma'am."

She smiled for the first time since she'd received word of their presence. "I'm a very good shot myself."

"I knew your pa. Didn't think he'd raise a child who wasn't good with a gun. But don't kill no one, ma'am, or you'll be in worse trouble than you are already. And I don't want to know nuthin', your ladyship, so as to swear on a Bible in court if'n I have to."

"I'll just need you to look the other way for ten minutes, Archie, while I pack a few things."

"Reckon they only said go with you. Don't recall no more instructions than that."

"I don't suppose they'd be expecting a lady to carry an arsenal."

"Hard to tell with nasty folk like them. But I suspicion not."

"If you could stay in the playroom with Chris, I'll have Ordie pack for him and Janey run some errands for me. I'll be just next door should they follow us upstairs. Come for me."

"All you have is ten minutes, ma'am. I wish you luck. Them's some right wicked gentlemen."

Archie was introduced to Chris, and once Chris spied his pistol, the young boy's attention was fixed. He hardly noticed Ordie and his mother slipping from the room on their hasty missions.

Ordie went to see that Kate packed Chris's clothes. Janey was sent to bring Will from the stables while Trixi, panicked, terrified, raced to her father's room. The room had been unused since his death, an eerie sense of his presence still lingering in the air. For a fleeting moment of wishful thinking, she longed for her family again, the burden of taking on the Grosvenors and Clouards alone overwhelming. But wishes wouldn't help her now, she pragmatically reminded herself; only her own resoluteness would deliver them. Wrenching a valise from the bottom of the armoire, she ran to her father's gun cabinet. A collector, he'd kept his favorite guns in his room, where he could admire them. Lifting three pistols from the case, she swiftly loaded them with powder and shot and placed them in the valise. A handful of cartridges followed next and then two hunting knives. She briefly debated trying to fit the small rifle in the bag, but decided against it. She wanted only weapons that were easily concealed.

Swiftly moving to her room, she added a few of her garments to the valise. A gown, a change of underclothing, two pairs of stockings. She left room for some of Chris's clothing should the bag be opened. While without a plan as yet, she understood the necessity of fleeing Burleigh House, at least for a time.

When she pulled her desk drawer open to gather what money she had, her gaze fell on the addresses Pasha had left. Her hand stilled, poised in midair above them, the single sheet of paper with its scrawl of names and numbers holding her attention. Impulsively, she plucked it from the drawer, folded it twice, and tucked it into her valise. France was remote from her immediate thoughts, Pasha too casual a friend, the immediacy of her danger too intense to consider anything beyond escape before Dover.

It was imperative they elude their enemies before Dover; then she and Chris could disappear into the backwaters of England for however long it took to gain security again. She could hire herself out as a governess. Or perhaps a horse trainer, she more pleasantly thought, a flashing smile at such a glorious option momentarily pushing away her fear. But a second later, her terror was back in force, the men downstairs a stark reality. Snapping the valise shut, she ran from her room toward the playroom.

Will was waiting for her in the corridor along with the rest of her staff and, in a rapid staccato, she gave orders. They couldn't escape down the back stairs or Archie would be blamed, so Will was to follow the carriage as discreetly as possible with two of their best racers. What money and jewelry that could be scavenged should be brought along.

"And your pa's Roman coins," Will asserted.

Trixi looked hesitant.

"He'd have sold his soul for any child of yours, your ladyship," Will gruffly said. "He'd gladly have you sell them coins."

"Very well," Trixi agreed, the last of her parents' valuables finally sacrificed. "Bring them."

"If I were to ride cross-country," Will suggested, "I could take out a few of them planks on the bridge just above Closter vale."

"And when everyone gets out to inspect the damage . . ."

"You and Chris could stay near the carriage."

"Where you could bring up the horses. Maybe we should take to the roads as highwaymen, Will," Trixi cheerfully suggested, freedom beckoning. "It seems our minds are nefariously alike."

"Your pa always thought on his feet, too. Reckon that's how he survived all them travels to the hinterlands of the world."

"Take some pistols with you," Trixi coolly said.

"Already have."

"Archie can't help, but he won't stand in our way."

"He better damn well not. We've been friends for fifty years. Now go," Will ordered. "Ordie said you've only ten minutes."

Trixi nodded her head. "We'll be back as soon as we can," she briskly declared, not wishing to take leave of her surrogate family in tears.

Kate tried to be as valiant, her chin trembling with the effort, her role as governess to the young girl who had grown by necessity into a woman of strength both gratifying and sad. Janey visibly wept, her youth incapable of handling such trauma. Ordie gently said, "We'll take care of Burleigh House for you, Missy. God be with you."

Trixi quickly hugged them all, and then sending them off, entered the playroom. Telling Chris they were going to Dover on an excursion, she took his hand on their walk to the entrance hall and regaled him with stories of the sights they'd see. Trixi was careful to carry her own valise; Archie followed with Chris's bag.

Once they approached the men, Chris stayed close to his mother's side, half hiding behind her skirt, as if cognizant of their evil intent. With a curt nod, Jerome directed Trixi and Chris out of the house, the men following in silence. A moment later, they stood between the house and the carriage, a small knot of disparate people with only the life of a small boy in common. After a few hushed words with Jerome Clouard, Harry Grosvenor left, riding away without so much as a glance at the four-year-old boy he was sending away to a life of misery.

No one spoke in the carriage. The Clouards sat opposite Trixi and her son, seemingly oblivious to their presence. Phillipe dozed, Jerome stared out the window. Trixi watched the familiar landscape slip past, counting the minutes until they reached the bridge. Archie had placed their luggage in the rack at the back before mounting to sit beside the driver. Trixi hadn't dared ask that her valise be brought inside. So she visualized the distance from her seat to her luggage, silently counting the seconds, the number of steps, rehearsing what she'd say to Chris so he wouldn't be frightened.

Forcing herself to remain calm.

Who would think because of Theo, she ironically thought, she would be literally battling for her life? He had been solace to her in a time of deep despair, when she'd known only cruelty for three long years. He'd represented gaiety and joy when she'd given up hope that either existed in the world. And now, because of Theo's money, the men seated across from her wanted Chris's life.

She knew what a foster home meant, because scandals would periodically surface in the press and all the sordid details of some brutal home would be exposed. But before long the righteous indignation would die away and the business of disposing of unwanted children would continue, the published disclosures only transient ripples on the public consciousness.

One way or another, she had to find a way to reach her pistols.

The two small villages between Burleigh House and the London Road passed by the carriage windows, and as the road began the gradual descent into Closter vale, her pulse rate accelerated. Another half mile and they'd reach the slope plunging into the valley.

In short order, she heard the brakes being applied, the squeak and squeal of wheels resisting the pressure shrill inside the carriage. The vehicle lurched several times as it slowed, waking the dozing man.

His shiny bald head lifted and, flushed from sleep, he blinked against the glare of the sun. "Where are we?" he drowsily murmured.

"Still in this godforsaken country," his brother muttered, his habitual scowl deepening as he gazed out the window at the steep incline, the land to the left of the road falling away sharply. "The driver better keep this thing on the road."

His tone brought Phillipe to full wakefulness. Abruptly sitting up, he leaned across his companion and peered out the window. "Maybe we should walk down," he murmured, a touch of apprehension in his voice.

"For God's sake, show some courage!"

The sharp reply deepened the flush on Phillipe's face. "I should have stayed home," he pettishly said, "and you could have been *courageous* alone."

"For all the use you've been on this journey, you might as well have done so."

"I don't see you doing anything so damned significant. Anyone could have been sent over to take the boy to France."

"No, *anyone* couldn't. I had to do it, as I do everything that has to be done while you whimper and whine and complain. Shut up, dammit."

The swift journey had been too arduous for both of them, and Phillipe Clouard's temper was as frayed as that of his brother. He settled into a sullen brood, feeling like a small boy who had been unfairly reprimanded.

The Clouards appeared to be at each other's throat, Trixi reflected. Not precisely a united front. A trifling advantage perhaps, but a consideration.

The carriage finally reached the base of the hill after what seemed an excruciatingly long interval. Her palms sweating, her heart pounding, she understood this might be their only chance for freedom.

She had to succeed.

A string of oaths from the driver gave indication of trouble—she dearly hoped—and a moment later, the carriage came to a stop. Will had done his work, she suspected, her anxiety diminishing marginally. Now if only the next few minutes proceeded according to plan.

Snapping the window down, Jerome Clouard leaned out and shouted, "What the blazes is going on?"

"Part of the bridge is out," the driver cried.

Swearing, Jerome drew back in, pushed the door open, and climbed out.

Trixi waited, breath held, for Phillipe to follow his brother, but he didn't move. Nothing clever and artful to coax him out came to mind in her current state of high anxiety; all the cogs in her brain were jammed. He remained slumped in the corner, his arms crossed over his rotund stomach, his mouth pursed in resentment. Panicking, she frantically tried to think of some way to make him move so she could get out of the carriage.

"Would you mind if I went to see all the commotion?" she finally asked, not willing to simply sit and let her opportunity slip away. She was already opening the door. "Come, Chris," she went on in as bland a voice as she could manage, as though they were all friends on an afternoon drive. "Let's see what happened to the bridge."

"Better not go," Phillipe muttered.

"Your brother wouldn't let me, you mean?" she sweetly inquired, her jibe intentional.

"*I* won't let you," he gruffly said, sitting up to better assert his authority.

She paused, one hand on the door handle, debating whether she dared jump with Chris, whether Phillipe could stop her, whether the other brother was near enough to obstruct her escape.

"Watch the woman," Jerome shouted from the bridge, a sharp edge to his voice.

"Watch her yourself," Phillipe muttered, leaning his head back against the leather seat, shutting his eyes.

Saved by sibling rivalry, Trixi gratefully thought, shoving the door open. Glancing toward the bridge, she gauged her distance from Clouard. He was perhaps fifty yards away, facing the river. Turning back, she lifted Chris into her arms, jumped to the ground, and ran behind the carriage. Dear sweet Archie, she reflected, seeing he'd placed her valise on top. Lifting it out, she whispered, "Will's coming for us." Chris was clinging to her neck and she hugged him close. "Now don't say a word. Pretend we're soldiers on a mission."

"A spy mission?" He spoke in a four-year-old rendition of a whisper, his words part hiss, part murmur.

"A very important one. The king will reward us when we're through."

"I'll be quiet," he promised, tightening his grip around her neck.

Out of sight from those at the river, she opened her valise and took out her loaded pistol.

"I wouldn't do that if I were you."

She swung around, her heart in her throat. Looking aggrieved and pouty, Phillipe gazed at her. "Stay where you are or I'll shoot," she warned, hoping she sounded threatening.

"No, you won't."

So much for threatening.

"Women don't shoot guns," he said, a reproving inflection to his words.

Damn his stupidity. Anyone with brains would be wary of a gun no matter who held it. But perhaps she couldn't shoot at the moment, not because it was unacceptable to Phillipe's sense of propriety but because if she shot him, his brother would be warned. On the other hand, if she didn't, she and Chris would be captives again.

Merde. And Will was nowhere in sight.

"I mean it," she asserted, not about to docilely submit, hoping to buy some time. "Come any closer and I swear, I'll shoot."

"You don't even know how to shoot that big, heavy thing." Phillipe took a step forward. "Now be reasonable and put it down."

Recalling Archie's advice, she aimed not to kill but to maim and pulled the trigger. The pistol's percussion was overpowered by the howl Phillipe emitted that echoed down the vale, skyward, and halfway to London. But his shriek faded from Trixi's consciousness, for she was already running for the tree line.

Jerome spun around at the cry, took one look at the carriage, and leaped forward to give chase. Unfortunately, Archie's big booted foot became entangled with his and Jerome fell headlong onto the riverbank.

"Beggin' your pardon, sir," Archie apologized, putting a hand out to help him up, stumbling again in the process, falling heavily atop Jerome Clouard.

"You clumsy oaf!" Jerome screamed, his face so red Archie was sure he'd have an apoplexy right before his eyes. "Get the hell *off* me!"

Glancing up the hill, Archie caught sight of Will riding hard toward the carriage, and he allowed his full weight to rest on Jerome's chest.

"Damn you!" Jerome gasped.

In an apparent effort to rise, Archie dug his elbow into Jerome's sternum and leaned hard.

Jerome's scream of pain pricked the horses' ears, momentarily deafened Archie, and brought a faint smile to the face of the driver, who had borne the brunt of Jerome's spleen since being hired at Dover.

"Thank God," Trixi breathed, standing on the verge of the road watching Will spur the horses with such a feeling of thanksgiving, she considered the concept of miracles now truly revealed. "Hang on, darling," she whispered to Chris. "Will is almost here."

A moment later she lifted the boy to Will as he slowed his mount, and a second after, she swung herself up onto the racer he was leading behind him on a loose rein.

Will had been a championship jockey in his youth, and Trixi had learned everything he could teach her by the time she was ten. They raced away on the prime horseflesh born and bred at Burleigh House stables, putting the Clouards into the distance within minutes and out of their lives by the next crossroad. Pausing to decide which direction to take, Trixi said, "I'd feel more secure in the south, and we'd be closer to home."

"You won't be expected to ride north, though." Will spoke in the same conversational tone as his mistress, careful not to startle the boy in his arms, who viewed their race as simply another excitement in an exciting day.

After discussing their options briefly, they decided to travel north, and several hours later, the small party rode into Ramsgate. They took lodgings at an inn near the shore under assumed names, and while Chris played with a small hand-crafted sailboat left behind by some former occupant, Trixi and Will counted the resources available for Trixi's living expenses. It was a terrifyingly small amount, and the next payment from her father's stipend wouldn't be available for two months.

"The coins might fetch enough to last you til then," Will suggested. "We don't need anything at Burleigh House."

Her small farm was largely self-sufficient, for which she was grateful. But for the immediate future, even with the sale of the coins, she'd have to earn a living until such time as it was safe to return home. If that were ever possible with the Grosvenors as neighbors. "I'll have to find work," she resolved.

"Not such a simple task with a child," Will pointed out.

And everything seemed to stop for a second, the beat of her heart, the sound of the waves outside the window, the rhythm of the universe. "Why hadn't I thought of that?" she breathed. Rather blithely, she'd considered a young woman her age, well-educated, of genteel birth, could find employment in any one of the positions open to women of her class—governess, companion, nursemaid, housekeeper. Most of whom, she grimly noted with new, oppressive insight, rarely came into a household with a child in tow.

"I'll stay and find work," Will determinedly said.

"No, you can't. There's no one else to take charge of our horses." Her fledgling breeding program was the major source of her income. When one of their racers was sold, Burleigh House was in funds for almost six months.

"You could ask Pasha for help," Will quietly suggested.

"I couldn't, Will. I only knew him for so short a time. It would be humiliating."

"He wanted to help you before you left, he said."

"Did he now," she remarked. "And what else did he say?" she asked, recalling all the whispered conferences between Pasha and Will.

"He was concerned, that's all—about the Grosvenors and Clouards. And he was right," Will gruffly muttered. "He told me to send for him if you were ever in trouble. He meant it, Missy."

"He had the best intentions, I'm sure, but I prefer not going hat in hand to Pasha Duras. You wouldn't understand." He had women by the score asking for favors—sexual and otherwise. Her brief visit to the dressmaker had apprised her of that benevolent role. "I can manage by myself."

"The Grosvenors won't go away."

As if she needed reminding. That daunting thought weighed heavily on her mind. Even should the Clouards leave England, even should she somehow manage to eke out a living for herself and Chris away from Burleigh House, the possibility of her peacefully returning to her home was remote. "Why don't we see if we can sell the coins," she abruptly said. "After that, I'll consider the next hurdle." It was suddenly more than she could bear: the overwhelming crisis of her future, the Clouards and Grosvenors, the actual lethal threat to her son, the impossibility of existing without money away from home. "This was a godawful day, Will," she whispered, weariness suddenly washing over her. "I can't deal with anything more right now."

"I'll have supper brought up," he quickly said, "and in the morning, I'll see if I can find a buyer for the coins. Don't you worry none, Missy. We'll find a way out."

In the morning, Will not only found a buyer for the coins, but took it upon himself to send a letter to the address Pasha had left with him, describing the recent events and asking for his help. A captain of one of the vessels in port promised to see that the letter reached Calais the following day.

He convinced Trixi not to look for employment immediately, suggesting she wait at least until he returned to Burleigh House and reconnoitered the Grosvenors. He was hoping that meantime, Pasha would receive his letter and respond. So with a warning to remain as inconspicuous as possible in the event the Grosvenors or Clouards had mounted a search, he left, promising to return in a week.

The following days were a time of reflection and quiet, Trixi's only necessity that of entertaining Chris in a small lodging room. She bought them each a simple change of clothes, careful with her small reserve of money. She purchased a few toys as well, and several books that appealed to Chris. They took walks along the shore when the confining room drove them outside. Twice they bought apple tarts from the pie man and sat on the quay and ate them while watching the tide come in.

But their tranquility was brief, for when they returned to their lodgings the afternoon of the third day, the innkeeper took Trixi aside and told her a Bow Street runner had been asking for them. He was looking for a woman and four-year-old boy who met their descriptions. "For kidnapping, the runner said," the innkeeper added in an undertone. "You don't look like no kidnapper to me, ma'am," he kindly went on. "Thought you'd like to know." He winked. "The missus and me got a good eye for character after running this place for twenty-some years, and that boy ain't afeared of you. But there's others in town who might be willing to take the reward being offered."

Trixi blanched at the word reward. "How long has the runner been in Ramsgate?" She was already estimating the time remaining before she was identified.

"Not too long. He's inquiring at the lodgings in town first, he said. If you have need, ma'am, of passage to the Continent," he quietly offered, "I know a man who could help you."

She was shocked at first that he would suggest such a thing. Did she look like a criminal who needed to flee England? But saner counsel soon overcame her first reaction and she realized the extent of her danger. Bow Street runners had a reputation for capturing fugitives;

either the Grosvenors or Clouards had put them on her trail.

She was surprised at how coolly she was able to appraise her situation, as though she were viewing her circumstances from afar. She ticked off the liabilities with such detachment, she wondered if she was past hysteria and moving toward a catatonic lethargy. Will wouldn't return for days yet, so she had to face this alone. Could she make her way undetected to some other part of England? Or if she did flee to Europe, would the Clouards find her there more easily? "Where is your friend sailing to?" she asked, as if her dilemma would be resolved by his reply.

"Calais, ma'am. In two hours."

That was very close to Paris. To the Clouards as well. And to Pasha, she mused with a quiet need that startled her. She'd thought herself more pragmatic than to have expectations of a man of his repute. What would he say if she suddenly appeared on his doorstep? A vision of his shocked expression deterred her fleeting impulse. Impossible. She couldn't ask him to take care of her as if she were his personal charge. She and Chris would find refuge in England.

"There he is, ma'am," the innkeeper softly cried, pointing out the window at a tall, brawny man making for the inn.

"Tell me where to find your friend." Her decision was made instantly, expediency the ultimate arbiter.

"My wife will show you." He drew her away from the window. "Hurry," he urged, moving toward a door at the back of the parlor.

In a brief conference in the kitchen, it was agreed that the innkeeper would keep the Bow Street runner engaged in conversation while his wife guided Trixi and Chris through the backstreets to the ship. "I'll bring your belongings as soon as I can," the innkeeper vowed.

"Tell my man, Will, when he returns, I went to Pasha."

And moments later, the two women and Chris were running down the narrow alleyway behind the inn.

8

At the same time Trixi and Chris were sailing from Ramsgate, Pasha was coming ashore at Nauplia. The fast corvette from the Duras fleet at Marseille had made record time, news of the Greek defeat at Krommydi having reached him before he sailed. He carried two pieces of mountain artillery, six cannons, six hundred rifles, bayonets, and ammunition; also medical stores and two surgeons who would serve in the small infirmary Pasha funded in the Greek capital. And perhaps most important, he brought sixty thousand dollars in Spanish gold.[6]

The fortress of Nauplia was filled with troops. Military commands had been distributed with a bountiful hand once the English loans had reached Greece the past year. Every man of any consequence imagined himself at the head of a band of armed men, and hundreds of civilians paraded the streets with trains of kilted followers, like Scottish chieftains. The streets were crowded with thousands of gallant young men in picturesque dress and richly ornamented arms who ought to have been in the field against Ibrahim.

Pasha's factotum said as much when he greeted Pasha shortly after he'd embarked.

"We've quite a display of Fanariots, apothecaries, clerks, and barbers pretending to be soldiers," he said with a wave of his hand toward the passing parade outside the window of the Duras warehouse, his disgust plain. "The tailors have come flocking from Joannina and Saloniki to get rich."[7]

"Are any of those gloriously outfitted coxcombs going to leave town and fight?" Pasha sardonically inquired.

"Not when they can draw pay and rations for phantom troops and walk about with their grooms and pipe-bearers. The bazaars of Tripolitza, Nauplia, Missilonghi, and Athens are filled with gold-embroidered jackets, gilded yataghans—curved swords—and silver-mounted pistols for these opera soldiers."

"It's nice to see the London brokers aren't alone in getting rich from the English loans," Pasha cynically murmured.[8] "A shame Ibrahim brought disciplined troops this time."

"Trained by your French officers, effendi," the young Cypriot said.[9] "And not to be treated with contempt like the Arabs in the past who would run away at the sight of the armatoli, the Greek warriors. Although President Konduriottis and his Hydriotes haven't faced that fact yet. A month ago, he was hoisted onto his richly caparisoned Arab mare and, led by six grooms, set off like a conquering generalissimo. Followed by a train of secretaries, guards, pipe-bearers, and advisers, he was saluted with cannon from the ramparts, the fortress above, and the ships in the harbor. Of course he hung over the saddle like a sack of hay because he's so fat; two of the grooms had to hold him in place. He found the exercise trying. The ride to Tripolitza took him three days."

Pasha's brows rose; the city was only forty miles away. "What of his lieutenants?"

"The doctor Mavrocordatos, you mean, or perhaps Skourti, an old sailor he named lieutenant-general of the Greek army?"

"Jesus. Who the hell's fighting?"

"Not our president. After a fortnight away from Nauplia, he still hadn't gone anywhere near the enemy and, repenting of his boldness, he turned back to Nauplia."

"What of Navarino and Neokastron?" Pasha knew Ibrahim had landed south of the two forts at the end of February.

"They're still holding. Makriyannis is there with Bey Zade and Yatrakos."

Pasha smiled. "It looks as though I'll have to sail through the Egyptian fleet to bring in our rifles. Makriyannis should be needing some reinforcements by now." He and the young warrior were of an age and had been friends since the first campaigns in 1821.

"With the state of Turkish gunnery, even Ibrahim's fleet shouldn't be a problem. And Miaoulis is standing outside the bay with his thirty sail."[10]

"Good—a little backup. We leave tonight if the winds allow. Now, Nikos, take me to see Gustave." They'd received news at Zante that he'd been freed from prison. "His escape was a close thing, I hear."

"A month is a long time in a dungeon, effendi. He's alive only by the grace of God. The others with him were hanged in the bazaar at Preveza."

"Were you with Odysseus when he took Gustave out?"

"Ten of us went to make sure we could bring him back through the Turkish lines. Odysseus had sent word Gustave's body was so swelled up and inflamed from torture, he was at death's door. The filth and stink in the dungeons were abominable. The prisoners had to push their noses against the keyhole to get fresh air."[11]

Aware of Turkish methods of torture, Pasha frowned. "Will he live?"

Nikos nodded. "He's past the crisis and on the

mend. Thanks to you. The diplomats were too slow and timid, the consul afraid Ismail Bey would hang him up by his balls if he took Gustave out. But money always works with the Albanians and Turks. We brought five thousand groschen to convince Ismail Bey he wouldn't miss one prisoner."

"How soon can Gustave sail home?"

"Perhaps in a fortnight. The doctors at the infirmary disagree—he has a wound from leg irons that's deep."

But Gustave managed a credible smile when Pasha walked into the small hospital.

"Marie will be pleased to see you're mostly in one piece," Pasha said, smiling. "She's the one who made sure you were rescued."

"Along with your men and money. Thank you." Gustave's voice was faint, his body visibly wasted now that the swelling had subsided. His eyes, sunk deep into their sockets, held a wariness Pasha hadn't seen before.

"Nikos will make arrangements for your journey home just as soon as the doctors release you," Pasha declared, sitting down beside the bed, understanding what torture could do to a man. "It's good to see you alive. Marie will be pleased."

A warmth momentarily displaced the apprehension in Gustave's gaze. "Her memory kept me alive in that hellhole," he whispered.

But he was the one who'd not succumbed to the torture, Pasha thought, nor given up. "I told her we'd teach her how to sail when you came home. Do you think it's possible?"

Gustave emitted a croak of laughter. "Probably not in our lifetime. She'll put us in the river sure enough."

"Tell her when you see her, I've not forgotten my promise. I'm off to Navarino soon. I'll give your regards to Makriyannis."

"You've heard, I expect, that Ibrahim's troops aren't like the sultan's army. They could pose a real threat," he warned.

"Thanks to Ibrahim's French officers. It gives one pause to be aiming at a countryman."

Gustave moved his head on the pillow in negation. "Not so long as they're fighting for the Turks—just pull the trigger. Be careful, Pasha," he murmured. "Don't let them do this to you." A sheen of tears gleamed in his eyes. He remained a prisoner to horrific memory, his dead friends haunting his dreams.

"I'm caution itself," Pasha assured him, this man who was about to put himself within range of Ibrahim's artillery and troops. "Don't worry about me. Nikos has orders to see that you follow all the doctor's orders," he went on with a smile. "Marie is impatient for your return."

"I'm marrying her when I get back to Paris, despite my family."

"Good. She deserves you. Now wish me luck. I'm off to see if Makriyannis can use my help."

"Tell him to kill a few Turks for me," Gustave whispered.

"I'm sure he'll be happy to. Do you want their ears?"

Gustave's eyes sparkled for a moment. "I'm supposed to be civilized, so I'll say no."

Pasha shrugged. "If you change your mind, Makriyannis always has a few." He touched his friend's gaunt hand lying atop the blanket. "Get well, *mon ami*, and Godspeed on your journey home."

A tear spilled over and ran down Gustave's cheek, sliding into his growth of dark beard. "I owe you my life."

"No," Pasha softly murmured. "You were strong enough to survive in there. Not many men do." Patting his friend's hand, he stood. "Invite me to the wedding," he said with a smile.

"Stay alive."

"I intend to." And with a salute, he left.

Fifty Egyptian warships were in the bay at Navarino when Pasha's vessel came within sight the next morning, the rifles and ammunition having been transferred to a lighter Greek craft. With the breeze up and its white sails spread, the cutter wove through the huge frigates at anchor, under fire from the Egyptian fleet for a mile or more. But the ship bore no crippling damage when she reached the Greek defenses—a measure of the state of Turkish naval gunnery.

Makriyannis came out of the entrenchments and welcomed him, his hug genuine, his smile broad. "If the Turks ever learn how to aim their cannon, it'll be time for all of us to go back to our villages. It's been almost a year, Pasha Bey, since you left, and we're both still alive. God is gracious to his sinners."

"Even Koletis and Gouras haven't been able to see you hanged in the civil war this year, I see," Pasha noted jokingly.

"A curse on them," Makriyannis muttered. "They both chill my heart with their greed. But someone has to fight the Arabs while they fight each other."

"I've brought you some rifles to help even the odds."

The young warrior grinned. "Look around you, Pasha Bey. It's going to take more than rifles to win this battle. The walls are in ruins, we have no water, Ibrahim is close up, ready to make another assault. And he has ten thousand troops."

"How many are here?"

"Sixteen hundred. And stay here they will. I had their caiques sunk so they can't get away."

"And they didn't murder you?" Pasha drawled.

"My Roumeliots gathered round me and they changed their mind." His mouth quirked in a grin.

The only true fighting force the Greeks had were their warrior bands, each commanded by a leader the men elected to follow. The guerrilla-style war had been successful in the preceding four years, against the incompetent commanders and troops sent out from Constantinople.

But Ibrahim and his troops from Egypt were very different from the sultan's army. The Egyptians had been trained by disciplined French officers. They advanced in Napoleonic ranks, fired in volleys on words of command, and charged with bayonets, while their cavalry waited the moment to charge and complete the rout of the enemy.

Since Ibrahim had landed in February, he'd twice met a large Greek force in the field and vanquished them.

And the men in the following days and nights at Navarino fared little better. Ibrahim's cannons, bombards, and mortars gave them no peace. Ibrahim's gunners and engineers, Frenchmen too, laid the fort in ruins. Those within the walls worked to patch the damaged walls as they crumbled, and fought as well day and night. Water was rationed out at seventy drams a day, and destroyed by thirst, the exhausted defenders waited for the sixteen thousand Greek troops at Chorae to come to their assistance.

But the leading commanders, at odds and jealous of one another, sat on the high ground at Chorae, watching the fort at Navarino through their glasses, not stirring a finger. The lagoon was full of drowned men like frogs in a marsh, floating in the water; the island and fort were full of corpses. But no help came.

When Ibrahim had taken all the outlying positions, he set up cannons from the ships and storehouses and crowded guns above the fort only a pistol shot away. At dawn, he attacked. The defenders held their ground, and the battle continued all day and evening until even the Turks grew tired and stopped firing at midnight.

Ibrahim sent two men to parley and negotiate a surrender, but the Greeks refused his offer, determined to fight to the last man.

In the following days of fighting, he sent envoys twice more to ask for surrender, only to be refused—which caused him a dilemma. Desirous of winning the Greeks to his government, he wished to treat this garrison honorably and by doing so facilitate his future conquests. So he needed a surrender. And had not the English doctor, Julius Millingen, betrayed the fort to Ibrahim, telling him of the lack of water and provisions in order to save his own life, those inside the fort might have been able to deceive Ibrahim as to their strength.[12]

Upon learning of their desperate straits, Ibrahim brought up more guns and placed them all round the fort, while Makriyannis's men tried to ready the weakened structure for the next assault. At daybreak a last messenger was sent, asking if the defenders wished to parley.

With Millingen's betrayal, many had lost hope. There was no food or water left and very little ammunition. A vote was taken and it was agreed Makriyannis and Pasha would go to make terms.

When they presented themselves at Ibrahim's splendid tent, they were shown to an inner chamber where Ibrahim received them. He had two officers with him who supported his two hands with much ceremony so that his greatness might be acknowledged. Unfortunately, he was fat as a porpoise and pockmarked, diminishing any air of distinction.

"Where did you come from?" he asked.

"From the Roumeli," Makriyannis replied.

"From Nauplia," Pasha answered in Greek.

"My agents tell me you're a Frenchman," Ibrahim countered, "although you look as much a brigand as the others. Work for me instead of these klephts who are bound to lose and I'll pay you one hundred piastres a month. I've two hundred French officers in my pay."

"Your Highness is too kind," Pasha gently said, "but I've taken a liking to Makriyannis and his amusements."

"Have you been amused during the past week, Giaour?" Ibrahim ironically queried, taking in Pasha's clothing, skin, and hair filthy from gunpowder and dirt, his lean form and unshaven face gaunt from hunger.

"There's a certain degree of excitement," Pasha drolly said.

"Have you had enough excitement that you're here now to talk?"

"We're under constraints from others," Makriyannis interposed. "Some aren't prepared to die just yet. Although Pasha Bey and I are more than willing to lay powder mines and blow your Turkish force and ourselves into the sky."

"What do you want?" Ibrahim said, knowing unflinching men like those before him were capable of causing him a great deal of harm.

"We ask for European ships to take us out."

It took another two days of wrangling before satisfactory terms were arranged. Ibrahim wanted to use his own ships. An unacceptable premise to the Greeks, who distrusted the word of a Turk.

Who would pay to charter the ships? Ibrahim contended. And what of the weapons? Also, he'd heard there were two beautiful women inside the fort; he wanted them.

Makriyannis and Pasha negotiated each item at
length, and even when all the controversial items were
settled, Ibrahim tried at the last moment to revoke the
entire agreement by holding two groups of Greeks on-
shore, rather than allowing them to embark as negotiated.

Makriyannis immediately countered by having his
troops surround the Turks who had come to take over
the fort. He shut the gates and held them hostage,
vowing to eat them before he surrendered.

Ibrahim himself rode up to the gates and made good
on his promises.

The embarkation proceeded.[13]

No sooner had the English ships carrying the defenders of Navarino arrived in Nauplia than Makriyannis and his men were ordered to occupy and fortify
Lerna. After lifting the siege on Navarino, Ibrahim had
wasted no time beginning his campaign to subdue the
Peloponnisos.

Commander Kolokotronis had been appointed to
bring Ibrahim to battle at the Leondari pass, and all the
troops from the Peloponnisos had gone with him along
with country folk moving up supplies and ammunition
for the battle.

"As usual Kolokotronis abandoned his posts and took
to the mountains when he saw an Arab," Makriyannis
said with disgust, dropping into a chair in Pasha's bedroom after returning from his meeting with the Minister of War. "Ibrahim moved into the pass without a
fight. Our commander, Kolokotronis, is a specialist in
stirring up civil wars and factions, but he won't bring
his ass within range of the Turks. What are you drinking?"

Pasha was resting on his bed, a tall frosty glass in his
hand. "Lemonade and vodka. Nikos had a new ship-

ment of spirits from Odessa this week. Help yourself." He indicated a pitcher of lemonade and a liquor bottle on a bedside table. "Can you reach Lerna in time?" Pasha asked as Makriyannis came to his feet and crossed to the table. Nikos had a host of well-paid informers, and Pasha had just interviewed several of them. "Word has it Ibrahim is nearing the site already."

"We leave within the hour. Which only gives me time for several much needed drinks." It was hot out and both men were near exhaustion.

"And some food, I think," Pasha remarked.

"That would be a pleasant change after a month at Navarino. I'm not sure my relatives would recognize me now. Have you frightened your lady friends?"

Both men had the lean, hard look of hungry wolves.

"I haven't had time for any ladies," Pasha lazily replied, lifting his glass to his mouth.

Makriyannis looked up from pouring the lemonade. "We've been in Nauplia for what—twenty hours?" His brows rose in query. "Surely the Pasha Bey I knew wouldn't have waited so long."

"Nor would you," Pasha countered, not inclined to scrutinize his disinterest in women since leaving Kent.

"I'm too weak from hunger," his friend retorted. "Feed me for a week and I'll think about it."

"We might be dead in a week if Ibrahim has his way."

"Then I'll go to heaven virtuous," Makriyannis said with a grin.

"A convenient time to go, between profligate scandals."

"Who the hell has time for scandal? We barely had a day to rest. Are you in the mood to see the Mills at Lerna with us?"

"After dinner. I'd like one more of Tula's fabulous meals before I meet the angel of death."

"So little faith, Pasha Bey." Makriyannis pulled a chair up to the foot of the bed.

"I'm just a realist. How many men can you even muster on short notice?"

The Greek warrior shrugged. "Two hundred."

Pasha laughed. "Jesus, Ibrahim's hordes will run right over us."

"But then, there's no one else," Makriyannis softly said, sitting down and propping his feet on the bed.

Pasha's mouth quirked in a rueful smile. "True. We are the forlorn hope. I think I'll see that my yataghan is extra sharp for this picnic."

When Trixi and Chris arrived in Paris and found their way to Pasha's apartment, Hippolyte opened the door and smiled in recognition. "Master Pasha is away from home, but please come in."

Glancing over her shoulder as she'd done with great frequency since sailing from Ramsgate, Trixi saw no one untoward in the street outside, and breathing a small sigh of relief at having reached safe haven, entered the house.

"Although the master is away," Hippolyte explained, "he left orders to welcome you should you arrive in Paris."

"Will he be back soon?"

"I'm afraid not, my lady," Hippolyte replied, taking Trixi's small valise. "He sailed for Greece."

"Oh, no." A wave of hopelessness washed over her. In the course of her flight, she'd had time to consider all her lessening choices, and Pasha had loomed large as crucial to her salvation.

"He left instructions for your accommodations, my lady," Hippolyte quickly intervened, her distress obvious. "Let me show you into the Watteau drawing room and I'll send for Jules. He's in charge of the household when the master's away."

"Is Pasha gone far?" Chris piped up, tugging on his mother's hand.

"I'm afraid so, darling." Trixi struggled to maintain her composure when the world was crumbling away beneath her feet.

"Let's go see him, Mama. Let's go. I like Pasha and he always gives me toys."

It helped to hear her son's casual response to calamity; it gave her pause to reassess the possibilities still available to her. "I'm afraid Pasha is too far away, and I don't think we can travel so far." Certainly not with her limited funds, she reflected, her resources further depleted by her hasty passage to France. "Come, darling," Trixi suggested, moving toward Hippolyte, who stood at the opened door of the drawing room. "We'll see what Jules knows."

As soon as he entered the room, Jules kindly said, "Welcome to Monsieur Duras's home. Please make yourself completely at home with us. Could we have some food prepared for you and your son?"

"Thank you, yes. Chris is hungry. We've not had time for more than a snatched meal since we left England. Will Pasha be gone long?" she asked, the length of his absence the overriding question in her mind.

"One never knows, my lady, but presumably he will be involved in the rebellion for several months at least. But we're pleased to have you stay with us until he returns."

How could she, she immediately thought, a virtual stranger to these people? "I'm not sure," she murmured, "that is, I don't know if—"

"Why not wait until you've eaten, and then we could discuss the reasons bringing you to Paris. The master's collection of sailing ships might interest your son," he offered with courtesy. "Giving us an opportunity to talk."

"Thank you . . . thank you very much," she gratefully replied. She smiled at the small man with spectacles and gray hair. "Chris is very interested in sailing ships."

After they'd eaten and Chris was intently playing with the collection of ships in Pasha's library, Jules came in with tea for Trixi. Asking her permission to sit down with the well-bred courtesy of a man fastidiously aware of social rank, he bowed to her stammered acknowledgment and sat. He politely refused her offer of tea, however, such familiarity too great a breach of etiquette.

"Master Pasha would like to extend the hospitality of his home and staff for as long as you wish, my lady," he began, pouring her tea, putting in two lumps of sugar as though Pasha had left those directions as well. "And if we can be of service in any other way, you need only ask." Infinitely polite, he didn't immediately bring up her flight or Will's letter, which had arrived the previous day. Already Doudeau's office had been consulted.

"I'm . . . that is . . . I don't know how much, er, Pasha has told you."

"As majordomo, my lady, my concern is the master's life down to the smallest detail. My function and duty, my orders are to offer his resources to you. We are completely at your disposal."

"How very kind of him," she said on a suffocated breath, awed by both Jules's lofty consequence and his punctilious benevolence. "At the moment—I'm not sure how to say this—but—actually . . . I'm in fear for my son's life," she finished in a rushing tumble of words. "Although with Pasha gone, perhaps—that is

. . . I was wondering if you could summon Charles Doudeau for me."

"I took it upon myself to contact his office immediately upon your arrival." He did not mention he was aware of her peril from Will's letter. "I'm sorry to say we were informed Monsieur Doudeau is away in Copenhagen for a holiday."

"Copenhagen?" Trixi softly exclaimed, astonishment in her tone.

"My feelings exactly, my lady. A most unusual destination. Apparently an acquaintance of Mr. Doudeau desires his company for her spring fête. He'll be back in a fortnight, we're told."

"That may be too long to wait," she anxiously replied. "Would Pasha think me forward if I contacted his parents? He'd left their address for me should I need it."

"I wish I were the bearer of better tidings, my lady, but the elder Durases are now in transit to their summer home in Siberia."

"Oh, dear." She felt abjectly alone, just when she'd hoped her fearful journey over.

"Allow me to say, my lady, our staff is fully capable of keeping your son safe. You needn't fear in this home."

"I'm afraid there's more, Jules," she said, nervously touching the rim of the saucer, her teaspoon, the tablecloth. "It's possible the people who wish to harm my son have instituted some legal action against me in France." She clasped her hands tightly to quell her fingers' nervous flutter. Could she be arrested by the police, even while in Pasha's home? she wondered. Could Pasha's staff deter the police? What would happen to Chris then? Her head was swimming with unanswered questions.

"I'm sure Mr. Doudeau's office could serve as advocate," Jules calmly replied. "I'll summon one of his associates to speak with you. In the meantime, might I suggest a bath, a change of clothes, and some rest. You must be exhausted."

She was suddenly overwhelmed, ghastly fears pressing her from every side. The Clouards and Grosvenors were like raptors waiting for her to falter, make a mistake, come out into the open where they could tear her apart and take her son from her. "I *am* very tired," she softly agreed.

"Rest always helps make every dilemma more manageable," Jules soothed. "And I'll see that someone from Mr. Doudeau's office is here when you wake. Do you think your son might like to take some ships upstairs with him for his nap?"

The room she was shown to was light and airy, the Seine directly outside her windows, the rococo decor and furnishings delicate and pale-hued. A beautiful room with a view. But once Chris was put to sleep in the adjoining chamber and Jules and the servant girls had left, she curled up on the painted bed, stared at the joyous, cavorting putti dancing amidst rose garlands on the headboard and gave in to her despair.

Why me? she thought, self-pity inundating her senses, tears streaming down her face. Why should the few months of happiness she shared with Theo put her son in jeopardy? Wasn't she allowed any normalcy or peace? Was she required to live in misery under the Grosvenors her entire life? She hadn't asked to be sold away for the price of a few thousand acres, nor had she ever wished to be married to her monster of a husband.

But before long her tears of misery gave way to a heated resentment. Why should she give up her life, her son's life, to them or to anyone? she furiously thought. Wiping away her tears, she sat up and left the bed. Walking to the washstand, she splashed water on her face, toweled it off, and decided she'd see that she survived this assault as she had all the previous ones. Hadn't she always refused to live as the Grosvenors' poverty-stricken pensioner, turning to her horses as a means of livelihood, however uncertain and modest? Why couldn't she succeed with this as well? But how exactly could she contend with this new allied force? The Clouards and Grosvenors together had made living in England or France nearly impossible.

For the first time the notion of actually going to Greece appeared in her consciousness. She pondered the possibility briefly—at least she'd be out of the Clouards' jurisdiction there. And the flower of romantic youth throughout Europe had been making the pil- grimage to those distant shores for years.

But as quickly as the idea appeared, she rejected it. Traveling to Greece would be outrageously expensive, and she didn't have the funds. A continual problem. Jules had offered her safe haven and she would have to be content with that; when Charles returned, she would speak to him about the Clouards and keeping them at bay during her stay in Paris. In the meantime, she felt a modicum more relaxed, less troubled. A partial di- lemma had been resolved—she and Chris would avail themselves of Pasha's hospitality. He'd offered it in friendship and at the moment, she couldn't afford to let pride stand in the way of her son's safety.

"Eureka," the man hired by Jerome Clouard softly murmured, his gaze falling on the citation in the records of incoming travelers to France.[14] The frontier post outside of Calais had been the most likely spot, but he was pleased he'd found it and not his colleagues who'd been sent to Le Havre and Dieppe. An extra five thousand francs had been promised to the man who found evidence of Beatrix Grosvenor's entry into France.

Jerome Clouard was suitably pleased when he received the news. Equally gratified, Paul Scheffler pocketed his bonus. But the necessity of discovering Lady Grosvenor's precise location in Paris was the next item on Clouard's agenda, and possible sites were discussed for some time.

At the end, Jerome said, "Once we locate her, would you be adverse to—ah, abducting a child if necessary? Or perhaps if not you, you might know someone who could accomplish the task."

Paul Scheffler steepled his fingers under his chin and gazed across the desk at his present employer. "How much are you willing to pay?" Price determined interest.

"Fifty thousand francs."

The Parisian tough had no trouble reaching a decision. "Half now," he said, "half when I hand the child over to you."

"No," Jerome brusquely returned. "I don't want the child. I want him taken to the country. I'll pay you one third now, a third when you have the child, a final third when the child is deposited in the country. But time is critical. This must be accomplished with all speed." Magistrate Clouet had required surety that the money would be paid to Gericault's son within the month.

"Then I'll be taking that third and be on my way." Scheffler rose from his chair. His suit fit his large body superbly. He could have passed as a member of the Bourse.

"You'll get the initial installment only when you've located the child."

"Fair enough. I'll be back tomorrow afternoon at the

latest." The ruffian put out his hand. "It's a pleasure doing business with you, Monsieur Clouard."

Jerome hesitated briefly, but thought better of antagonizing a man of Scheffler's profession. He clasped his hand. "The pleasure will be mutual once the boy is abducted, Mr. Scheffler," he gruffly said.

Jean-Paul was waiting for Trixi in the Watteau drawing room when she woke. "We meet again, my lady," he said with a cordial smile. "I hear the Clouards have disrupted your life."

"Very seriously, I'm afraid. They tried to abduct my son. I was hoping Pasha would be here . . . or Charles."

"We should be able to deal satisfactorily with the Clouards despite Charles's absence. Pasha spoke to him before he left." Jean-Paul went on to detail the legal procedures that could be used to stop the Clouards. "In the meantime, I'd suggest you not venture outside the grounds. Until we see the Clouards imprisoned or adequately censured, you'll be safest within the walls. But don't be alarmed," he hastily added when he saw her expression. "Pasha's staff is large and very capable."

Trixi tried to smile, but managed only a tight grimace. "I keep telling myself it's impossible that people are out to harm my son. I try not to be alarmed, but the memory of their attempt is too fresh in my mind, and the Bow Street runner they hired indicates their continued pursuit. I've even considered carrying a pistol."

"There's no need for that, my lady. But as added insurance, I'll have Jules give orders that no strangers, no unfamiliar tradesmen, be allowed on the premises."

"Can they actually be stopped?" she fearfully asked, wanting an end to the ghastly terror.

"Yes, of course. I'm on my way to see Judge Clouet

immediately after I leave you. We will stop them, madame, I assure you."

"Thank you so much. I hope some day I can repay all your kindness." She felt terribly beholden.

"Please, everyone is more than eager to help. Your concern for repayment is unnecessary. Pasha's a friend and you're a friend of his." He smiled, gracious and charming. "Leave this to me."

How wonderful, she thought after he'd gone; all one had to do was be Pasha's friend and the world was at one's disposal. She winced slightly at her role as Pasha's *friend* but she couldn't deny it, nor did she wish to take back the glorious days of his visit. So if she was paramour to him in the eyes of the world, so be it. He would bring her safety now even in his absence.

The evening was relaxed and homey, if such a state existed in a city residence of forty rooms with a staff of sixty. But the petite dining room with the painted birds and butterflies and small fire in the fireplace was as near to cozy as Richelieu's architect could conceive. Over dinner, Chris described in detail all the rooms and servants, already on a first-name basis with most of the staff. Pasha's housekeeper had immediately taken Chris under her wing and during the meal he kept up a steady chatter, filling his mother in on the below-stairs lives. He'd adapted to his new environment with the ease of childhood, lightening Trixi's worries.

She slept peacefully that night for the first time in days, as if the cares of the world were lifted from her shoulders. And when she woke, no sudden fear sprang into her consciousness. Jules had seen to her new tranquility, and Jean-Paul. And Pasha from afar.

"I talked to a young servant girl from Duras's household at the greengrocer's this morning. She was buying strawberries for their new guests. Young servant girls are blissfully naive," Paul Scheffler informed Jerome Clouard. "Apparently their guests arrived yesterday. Is the boy's name Christopher?"

"Well done," Jerome muttered, already begrudging the money he'd have to spend for such an easy task. He should pay the ruffian by the hour. "I suppose I could have located her myself."

"But you didn't, now, did you? And you were in a hurry if I recall."

"Yes, yes, you want your money I suppose."

"And I suppose you want the boy out of your way. Which is why we're partners, monsieur," Scheffler silkily replied. "Sixteen thousand, six hundred sixty-six francs if you please."

"You can *do* this now?" Jerome leaned forward across his desk, his brows beetled.

"Better than you, I expect, or you wouldn't be out looking for an accomplice in this dirty deed," Scheffler lightly returned, sure of his abilities. "Tell me where you want the boy taken."

"There's a lady near Arles. I'll give you the address."

"That's a long way."

"She's discreet."

"I'll have to drug the lad to transport him that distance, or he'll bring the gendarmes with his screams."

"Do what you have to do," Jerome curtly said. "I'm not interested in your mode of operation. Just take care of it with dispatch. Today, preferably." He'd received a message from Clouet earlier, disturbingly early in the morning. He wondered how much Lady Grosvenor's appearance in Paris had to do with Clouet's timing. The magistrate was giving him until Friday afternoon to give evidence the transfer of funds had been accomplished.

Scheffler recognized nerves. In his profession one became a specialist in discerning degrees of panic. And while Jerome Clouard was too iniquitous to have a conscience, something else was causing him a high degree of consternation. Money, he supposed, for a man of his stripe. Taking advantage of the situation, another of his specialties, Scheffler said, "If you want the boy snatched today, it'll cost you more."

"Impossible."

"Sorry, then."

"I'll find someone else."

"Be my guest." He'd be hard pressed to find someone else on such short notice.

"Damn your extortion!"

"Now if we're going to trade insults," Scheffler smoothly murmured, "I could think of a few choice words for a man who pays to have young lads snatched and sold away."

"This is a business matter."

"So is mine."

"How much, damn you?"

"A hundred thousand francs, half now. I'm not sure you're a trustworthy man. The other half before I leave Paris. I'll have a friend come and pick it up—in case you get any ideas that don't appeal to me. Just remember I have the boy and he could turn up again at his mum's as easy as not."

When Jerome had resentfully counted out the money and pushed it across the table toward him, Paul softly said, "This boy must be worth a fortune to you. Sure you don't want the mum, too? I could give you a sale price on two."

"Just the boy, thank you," Jerome ground out, fury in every syllable. "Now get out of here and do your work."

The walled garden that opened from the drawing room offered fresh air and sunshine after a morning of indoor activities for Trixi and Chris, and soon Chris was helping the old gardener plant begonia starts in the shade of the stone wall. Trixi admired her son's handiwork a dozen times, each new planting requiring additional words of praise and encouragement. How pleasant all the staff were, she thought, watching the elderly man guide Chris's awkward attempts at horticulture. And the housekeeper let Chris eat in the below-stairs dining room that morning—a thrill he was still bubbling about hours later. His world had greatly expanded in a house with such a large staff, and he was thoroughly enjoying the liveliness.

"Mama, Mama, we're going to plant new roses back *here,*" he shouted a short time later, waving his dirt-covered hand in the direction of the small toolshed tucked into a corner of the garden wall. Seated under a flowering apple tree, Trixi looked up from the book she was reading, smiled, and waved back. It would be very easy, she thought, to let herself be taken care of by Pasha's retinue. Every need or wish was anticipated and taken care of by one of the numerous staff; she couldn't even open a door for herself.

Jean-Paul had stopped by again that morning and given her news on Judge Clouet's message to the Clouards. Jules had offered her carte blanche in running the household, if she wished. Staggered, she wondered if all Pasha's paramours were treated so lavishly. But she'd declined Jules's offer, which brought a smile to his reserved face. He was obviously relieved. And she'd wondered for a moment exactly what instructions Pasha had left.

Thoughts of Pasha brought back sweet memories of their enchanted time together and, lost in her reverie, she didn't at first notice the absence of childish chatter. When she became aware of the curious silence, a moment more passed before she became fully alert and looked around.

An ominous quiet hung over the garden; even the trilling birdsong had stopped.

A sudden wave of panic engulfed her, the faces of her enemies flooding her mind. "Chris!" she screamed, tossing her book aside. Scrambling to her feet, she raced toward the toolshed. Her shrieks for help, for Jules, for Hippolyte, echoed from wall to wall to wall in the small enclosed garden, shattering the afternoon calm. Her heart thudded in her chest, and the most terrible fear ate at her soul. Praying she wasn't too late, she turned the corner of the small shed and suddenly came upon a large man in a gardener's smock hauling Chris's limp body up the garden wall. Even in the horrifying circumstances a wave of relief washed over her.

He'd not yet taken her son from her.

With Chris slung over his shoulder, the man was standing on a rain barrel, reaching for the top of the wall to pull himself up. Trixi leaped at him, attacking like a maddened lioness, clawing at him to bring him down, knowing once he scaled the wall he'd disappear. She clutched at his trouser leg, found a grip, and yanking with all her might, she screamed for help.

The kidnapper struggled to free himself but she held on with the superhuman strength of extremity, jerking hard on his leg, trying to tumble him down.

Tottering for a split second, he almost lost his balance, but regaining his equilibrium, he savagely kicked back, slamming his heel into her chest.

A crushing blur of pain eclipsed her consciousness, radiating outward from the point of impact, briefly swamping her hold on reality. But she maintained her grip, some subconscious level of instinct still operating beneath the corrosive agony, directing the signal from her brain to her fingers. Hold on, don't let go, the primal message commanded—no matter what, don't let go. If she let go, she understood, her son would be gone.

She clung to his leg with all her strength, waves of nausea washing up her throat, lights dancing before her eyes, her knuckles white with the strain. You'll have to kill me to get my son, she thought, a gut-level, stubborn tenacity holding her upright. Or carry us both up that wall.

She drew a shallow breath through the raw, excruciating pain. Keep breathing, hold on, keep breathing, hold on, she silently intoned in a singsong rhythm that seemed to come from a great distance. She no longer had the strength or capacity to scream, nor the mental acuity to gauge the length of time since she'd last cried for help.

Was it a second, a minute, five? Had anyone heard her in the immense house? Had her cries penetrated through the stone walls, up the long staircases, through the labyrinth of corridors?

"Damn it all, let me go."

She looked up toward the sound, and she met the cool gaze of her son's kidnapper. "Here, lady," he gruffly said, easing Chris from his shoulder and sliding the boy to the ground. "Take my advice. Find a better hiding place. You've some determined enemies."

She didn't release her grip until Chris was free and then, falling to the ground, she gathered him close and cradled him in her arms, not even noticing the kidnapper disappearing over the wall. Chris was too still, she frantically thought. Pale, motionless like the dead.

"He's not breathing," she whispered, as Jules suddenly appeared at her side. Heart-stricken, she stroked Chris's ashen cheeks, desperately searching for some sign of life.

"He's alive," Jules assured her, his fingers on Chris's pulse. Gently searching through Chris's hair a moment later, he found the swelling node where he'd been struck. "He was knocked out." Leaning forward, he lifted the boy's eyelids, surveyed his pupils. "Let's get him inside," he said, rolling back on his knees, "and call the doctors."

Trixi didn't let Chris out of her sight, staying at his side as he was transported into the house and up the stairs to his bedroom. Three doctors were brought in and they confirmed Jules's diagnosis. Refusing help for her injuries, Trixi sat beside Chris's bed, keeping watch over him, offering silent prayers of thanksgiving for having him safe. And when his eyelids first fluttered, she leaned forward and whispered in his ear. A faint smile formed on his mouth, although his eyes remained closed. But she was reassured. He recognized his pony's name.

A short time later, his eyes opened and he said, "My head hurts."

"We'll put ice on it, darling," Trixi said, touching his cheek with her fingertips.

"Why are so many people in here?" he asked, his gaze taking in the array of servants and doctors ranged around his bed.

"We were afraid you were hurt."

"That new gardener wasn't very nice. I like Louis better."

"You can talk to Louis tomorrow," Trixi promised, the old man a victim of the kidnapper as well. He'd been found tied and gagged in the toolshed.

"Could I have some chocolate cake?"

Ten servants jumped at his request and Trixi smiled, relief flooding her. Her son was on the mend.

•   •   •

That evening she consulted with Jean-Paul and Jules. Or more accurately informed them of her decision. "I've decided to try to find Pasha, or at least sail to Nauplia. The capital has been in Greek hands for three years now. It should be safer than Paris."

At the expected protest, she firmly declared, "The Clouards are willing to do anything to save their inheritance." And she related what the kidnapper had said. "Even such a man warned me against them. I *can't* stay here." She took a deep breath because in order to say what she was about to say, she would have to deal with the fact she was perhaps a woman of a certain class. "Pasha offered me his protection should I ever need it, and I'm desperate enough to do whatever's necessary to see that Chris is safe." It wasn't easy to take advantage of the brief relationship she'd had with Pasha, but he'd offered. Had his family been in Paris she would have petitioned them for help, but they were more difficult to reach than Pasha. And she couldn't trust legal means to stop the Clouards; they operated outside the law. So if it required fleeing to Greece to put her son out of harm's way, she intended to make that journey.

"We could put guards on the house," Jean-Paul suggested.

"The Clouards could bribe one of them. They're willing to use any means and any amount of money."

"Greece is in the throes of Ibrahim's invasion. The war is very uncertain," Jules warned.

"As is my life in civilized Paris or the quiet of Kent," Trixi countered. "I won't be deterred, gentlemen, so if you'd please arrange for an escort to Marseille, I'd appreciate it. Are there any restrictions on Pasha's orders concerning me?" She should be more polite, she thought, listening to her clipped voice. Pasha's household was exceedingly gracious to her, but she felt besieged by the Clouards, attacked in the very heart of a secure home. She'd been in fear for her son too long; she refused to remain a docile target. "Or if there are restrictions," she went on, "perhaps you could advance me funds which I'd repay from the sale of my horses, and I'd be happy to make the journey myself."

She refused to simply wait for the next attack.

Pasha's orders were explicit—Lady Grosvenor was to be accommodated, so it was agreed Jules would accompany her. Intent on seeing Pasha's orders followed to the letter, he immediately began arrangements for the journey. He understood as well that his employer's instructions hadn't been lightly given, even though Pasha had relayed his directions with an apparent casualness. But Pasha had never gone out of his way for any woman before. Jules suspected something more than friendship in his master's carte blanche generosity.

Now Lady Grosvenor had expressed her wishes, and it was up to him to see that the plans for their journey to Greece advanced with dispatch.

His first act was to send a message to Pasha informing him of Lady Grosvenor's intentions. He had one of the grooms ride with it in all haste to Marseille. He hoped it would precede their arrival.

One never knew the particular female company with whom Pasha was involved. He would prefer not walking into an embarrassing scene.

9

The only embarrassing thing about the scene in Greece at the moment was that two hundred twenty-seven Greek guerrilla fighters were facing twelve thousand of Ibrahim's Frank-trained troops, four hundred of his cavalry, and ten large-scale artillery pieces purchased in England.

"Even as a nonreligious man," Pasha sardonically murmured, surveying the force arrayed against them from behind the ruined garden wall at the Mills of Lerna, "I'm seriously thinking of having your priest give me a last blessing."

"You've plenty of time, my friend," Makriyannis lazily replied, sprawled with his back against the wall. "The Turks won't move in this hot sun. But take the priest's blessing anyway for good luck. And if his prayers don't protect you, his sharpshooting might. He's a crack shot."

The small force had been working for two days to ready the ground for the Turkish attack. The mill was crammed with supplies and ammunition the Greek ships had taken as prizes from the Turks, and Ibrahim was here now to take back their supplies. Also, unknown to Ibrahim, the chief part of the grain stores for Greece were at the mill, making it a crucial site to defend.

The Greeks had thrown a ring of redoubts round the

mills and built up the wall right into the sea. The watchtower near the mill had been augmented with firing holes above the first floor and in the basement, and the water had been cut off from the millrace and made to flow underground to the tower, so there would be no lack of water as there'd been at Navarino. A sniper's nest had been built on the tiles of the tower; the area around the mills had been made so strong that they could fight there until they were shot to pieces. Which was the intent of the small guerrilla force. For if that ground was taken, Nauplia would go, too. There wasn't a drop of water in town, or any defensive artillery.

"Ibrahim hasn't moved from the sunshades they rigged up for him," Pasha murmured, gazing across the sloping ground. "Convenient way to fight a war."

"He won't move even when the sun goes down," Makriyannis noted. "The coward has others to fight for him."

"I wouldn't mind having some of Kolokotronis's army in the trenches with us."

"His army wore out their shoe leather running up to the safety of the mountains. We'll have to be the ones to save our country."

Pasha surveyed the millpond and garden, the azure sea behind them. "I suppose it's as good a place as any to die."

"When one is resolved to die," Makriyannis said, shutting his eyes, "seldom does one lose."

"A pleasant thought." Pasha made himself comfortable in the shade of the wall. "I hope you're right. Wake me when they attack."

Not til the shimmering haze of heat had subsided did the shout, "The Turks, the Turks!" wake everyone with a start. The defenders leaped into position, training their rifles on an attacking column coming up the hill at a run. The first Greek volley tore through the enemy ranks and the Turkish line faltered. Taking advantage of that small hesitation, the guerrillas poured over the walls like fiends from hell and fell upon the wavering line, slashing with their knives and swords, driving the Turks back down the hill.

The rashness of the Greek attack, its ferocity, unsettled the Turkish troops, and while they rallied their line, they didn't advance again. They waited for Ibrahim.

After a lengthy interval, he came up with six or seven more columns, deployed his mounted troops and infantry on every side, had his cavalry ring the mills ready at the charge, and set more artillery in position.

Everyone in the small defending force, knowing there was little chance against such odds, took their posts.

Dusk was approaching before the Turkish columns finally began moving in ranks of disciplined order. In his pride, Ibrahim had set up his heavy cannon and brought up two additional columns. In the first charge, the Turks overran the enclosure, the tower of the enclosure, and all the ground surrounding it—pushing the Greek forces back to the walls facing the sea.

There they dug in, picked their targets, sighted in, and prepared to die.

At the next assault a desperate hand-to-hand battle ensued, the heat still oppressive, not a breath of wind, the smoke from the muskets and rifles like a mist, a fog, the Turks slowly overwhelming the small force by their sheer numbers.

"Fire on the officers!" Pasha suddenly shouted, taking aim at a captain in gold braid. Through the smoke and din, the call passed from Greek to Greek. By this point, hundreds of Turks had been killed and wounded, the Greeks being accomplished marksmen, and the officers were forcing the columns up now against their will. One by one, the Greeks began picking off the officers, killing them with such precision it wasn't long before the spirit went out of the attack. The lines began to slow, falter, and break. Drawing his yataghan, Makriyannis shouted, "Up and over!" and leaped the wall with a bloodcurdling yell. The guerrilla fighters drew their swords and followed him, falling upon the wavering lines with a vengeance.

The Turks broke and ran.

But Ibrahim had his officers beat them back, and they charged once again, breaking the fragile Greek line, routing it. Retreating to their posts, the Greeks held against another attack.

Suddenly, a stillness fell over the field of battle. The Turks were bringing in their dead and wounded. Taking advantage of the lull, Pasha and Makriyannis handed out the last of the cartridges. As each man pocketed his twenty rounds, the guerrilla fighters understood the coming advance would be their last. "And now we try our luck against the tyranny of the Turks," Makriyannis said to the men with their backs to the sea. "And if we die, we die for our country and faith."

The Greeks took the offensive this time, vaulting over the wall, charging at the startled Turks, firing volley after volley until their weapons were empty, then drawing their yataghans because there wasn't time to reload. The unexpected, appalling slaughter was terrifying to the invaders, every Greek cartridge finding its mark, and against such wild, fierce attackers Ibrahim's forces turned fainthearted and ran.

A cheer went up all along the thin Greek line as the Turks abandoned their positions and took flight. The small, outnumbered force was triumphant, its enemies routed. Pasha's glance met Makriyannis's across the dead bodies and slaughter, the breeze lifting the smoke away into the twilight sky. He raised his sword in salute to the klepht *kapetan*. "To independence," he said, smiling broadly through the blood and grime of battle.

"To fine marksmanship," Makriyannis replied, his grin white against his powder-blackened face. "And good friends."

Trixi's flight began the following day, the journey to Marseille accomplished with speed, fresh horses ready at each post stop, the logistics smoothly managed by Jules. He was accomplished at his task, the run from Paris to the Duras shipping line at Marseille a matter of routine.

A small, fast schooner was at the ready when they arrived, and without delay they set sail. Safe at last, Trixi thought, watching the shoreline recede into a gray misty sky, feeling a tangible relief. Whatever faced her in the days ahead, at least she was free from the Clouards.

"Let her go," Phillipe was arguing, about the time the sails on the Duras's schooner filled and the ship picked up speed. "Even if we turn over the money as ordered by the magistrate, if she doesn't claim it, it reverts to our family. You're a fool to take this vendetta so far." Information on Trixi and Chris had finally been gleaned after two frenzied days of activity by Jerome's agents.

"It's three million francs, damn you. And it may or may not revert to us. She's not an innocent maid from Kent if she's sleeping with Pasha Duras. And he hasn't been within shooting distance of innocence his entire life. I'm telling you, the boy must be found and silenced. Or we lose three million."

"You're demented. Who will you find to scud off to

Greece in the hopes of tracking her down? All your paid informers are no more than gossip-collectors from the streets of Paris. Just give up, you fool. She's gone and good riddance."

"I'll find someone," Jerome growled.

"Like the last thug you found, who took your money and ran."

Jerome's glare fell on his brother. "Eat your damned mousse or pudding or whatever it is you're stuffing down your face and I'll think for both of us. As I always have."

"You're up against the Duras family this time," Phillipe warned, lifting a spoon of crème brûlée to his mouth, "not some milquetoast business colleague who's intimidated by your threats. General Duras defeated entire armies. Rumor has it the boy has killed any number of men in duels, not to mention his leisure sport of fighting the Turks. Are you mad to take on a family like that? They'll kill you and you'll never enjoy the money."

"I'll do as I please."

"You'll lose on this one."

"I never lose," Jerome Clouard growled.

The seas were calm, the winter storms long gone, even the spring rains delicate as summer neared. The eleven-day run to Nauplia was a time of peace and solitude for Trixi, the days and nights without care, the rhythm of the sea tranquil, its enduring pulse a measure of the harmony of life. As they entered Greek waters the sea became a luminous turquoise, sometimes the deepest cobalt blue, and it was so clean and clear the bottom was visible at forty feet. The Mediterranean scent came off the land, the hills covered with spiky aromatic bushes, olive groves, stands of lemon and orange trees. An excitement strummed through her

senses at the sight of the stark white houses, the sound
of the goat bells on the air, and when they sailed into
the crowded harbor at Nauplia, she felt as though she
were on a great adventure.

She was also a lifetime away from Kent, she thought,
surveying the feluccas and caiques, the schooners and
cruisers, French frigates, English brigs, Austrian cor-
vettes, German merchantmen.

The whole world was in port.

Jules had a guide take them through the bustling
docks to the Duras warehouse where Nikos greeted
them effusively. "But Pasha Bey is away fighting," he
explained. "I'll see that a message is sent to him immediately."

"We'll go to the house," Jules declared, "and wait
there."

But the message never reached Pasha in the disarray
of the war-torn country, nor had the earlier one Jules
sent, and when he and Makriyannis returned two
nights later from a successful sortie near Argos they
were in high spirits. Hussein Djeritl, Ibrahim's
brother-in-law, had been defeated and his train captured by Makriyannis's troops. By klepht tradition, half
the spoils of war were divided among the men, and
much rich booty had been collected from the battlefield: silver-mounted pistols; gilded yataghans; richly
ornamented long guns; gold embroidered jackets; and
large sums of money—English sovereigns, Venetian se-
quins, Austrian groschen. But the most splendid booty
was Hussein Djeritl's harem, fifty beautiful women ex-
cessively grateful to be free. Makriyannis had promised
them all passage back to their homes, additional reason
for gratitude, and the ladies of Hussein's harem had
insisted on showing their appreciation personally. They
rode into Nauplia with Makriyannis's troops, a num-

ber of them accompanying Pasha's party back to his house.

The sky glittered with stars, the bay below Pasha's house was gilded by moonlight, and the air was fragrant with heliotrope from the gardens round the house when the troop clattered noisily into the courtyard. Men's voices, raucous, joking, rose in a jovial cacophony, the jingle of harness delicately counterpointed the harsh masculine tones, and the silvery laughter of women was a sweet sounding trill above the bass rumble and guffaws.

The hubbub drifted up through the main floor windows, opened to the dulcet evening and the twinkling lights of the port. Pasha's voice was heard occasionally above the dissonance below, giving orders in a crisp, clear voice.

The clatter of footsteps rolled up the stairway to the reception rooms, to the dining room where Trixi, after putting Chris to bed, was having a late supper in the company of Jules. Informality was allowed, she'd declared, in the holiday circumstances, and the majordomo had succumbed to her arguments rather than offend her.

Jules recognized the distinctive sounds of revel first, familiar with his master's entertainments, and coming to his feet, began moving toward the din—to warn Pasha or deter him.

The enfilade of rooms opened one upon another, the first reception room at the head of the stairs, followed in turn by several more, the dining room midway.

Pasha's voice was recognizable to those in the dining room, familiar in the roar of voices, even though the language he spoke was unfamiliar. He laughed suddenly, a roguish sound, followed immediately by several female giggles and titters. Another man interjected a comment, his tone lighthearted, too, and several male voices suddenly broke into song, the merrymaking jubilant and noisy.

Trixi froze in her chair. How naive of her to forget that Pasha was never without company—more pertinently, without women in his life. How embarrassing. Now he'd discover she followed him all the way to Greece, and he'd wonder why.

"Please Lord," she prayed, "let the floor open up and swallow me."

But the sharp rap of boot heels and the jingle of spurs echoed from the adjacent room, advancing toward them, and a moment later Pasha stood in the archway, his gaze sweeping the room. He looked as much a *kapetan* as any of the klephts in the streets of Nauplia, his dark hair loose on his shoulders, his skin more deeply bronzed from the summer sun, his hybrid uniform part Greek, part western, the sheer physicality of a warrior returned filling the doorway. His white shirt was opened at his neck. A vest decorated with double rows of silver buttons gave him the look of an Oriental potentate, as did his richly embroidered jacket. Two silver-mounted pistols and a dagger were thrust into a red braided cord wound several times around his waist, the grips well worn. No evidence remained of the Parisian gentleman.

"I'm so sorry to bother you," she whispered, thinking how wrong she'd been to come. He looked a stranger.

Pasha had had a moment to suppress his shock after his few words with Jules. "How nice to see you again," he pleasantly replied. "I trust Jules saw to your comfort on your journey. You'll have to tell me what brought you to Greece." With the merest flicker of query in his gaze, he glanced at his majordomo, who'd followed him.

"You have company now," she said, flushing pink at being de trop. "I'll tell you in the morning."

"We're leaving early." That thought apparently reminded him of his companions. "If you'll excuse me for a minute," he said, "I'll be right back. Set me a place, Jules."

The voices in the adjacent rooms flared high for a short span of time, in interrogation and query. After a few brief sentences from Pasha the clamor subsided. Shortly after, footsteps and conversation echoed in diminishing volume as the throng moved back down the staircase to the lower level. By the time Pasha returned, nothing remained of their presence save a distant hum drifting up through the windows.

"Forgive my grime," he said, unstrapping his curved yataghan. "We've been out on campaign for a fortnight and the opportunities to bathe are rare. Tell me now to what I owe this pleasure," he went on, slipping the pistols and dagger from his waist and placing them on the table. "I must say, after the first shock, it's wonderful to see you again." Pulling out a chair, he sat across the small table from her, his smile delicious as she remembered.

"I'm afraid I came out of necessity, and I apologize."

"Whatever the reason, there's no need for apologies. Tell me what necessity drove you and we'll do what we can to alleviate it." He leaned back in his chair and his weariness suddenly showed, his eyes heavy-lidded, the shadows beneath them conspicuous as he settled into a sprawl. A servant brought him a small cup of coffee as if knowing he needed sustenance. Glancing up, Pasha smiled. "I hope a spoon can stand up in it."

"It's half sugar, Pasha Bey, as you prefer."

"It's good to be back," Pasha casually returned. "The service isn't as fine out country."

The young man grinned. "But the booty is much better."

"They're only here temporarily, Christos. They're going home," Pasha noted, his tone deliberately neutral. "Have the cook send me up something to eat, and then if you and Jules will see to my guests downstairs?"

"Yes, sir, of course, my pleasure, sir," the youth cheerfully declared.

"And another coffee. I haven't slept for days." When Christos left, his attention returned to Trixi. "Now then. I want to hear everything."

She told him, briefly and succinctly, all that had transpired before she'd fled Paris, and he forgot to drink his coffee as she recited her harrowing tale.

"Good Lord," he murmured when she finished. "The man's deranged."

"I don't even want the money. I was quite clear about that to the Grosvenors."

"Maybe I should have them shot." He spoke casually, his voice without inflection. After surviving weeks of human slaughter, he found the existence of a Clouard or two incidental. Taking note of Trixi's shock, he immediately said, "Forgive me. One forgets, when the Turks send sacks of ears back to Constantinople every week. Humanity is at a premium here."[15]

"I was hoping to simply distance myself from them, put Chris out of danger if I could. Greece seemed far enough away . . . and you'd offered," she self-consciously added.

"I meant it." The reply was gracious even though in the past he'd developed the art of avoidance to a virtuoso degree. "We'll have to find someplace safe for you, though." He sighed faintly. "Although safety's at a premium here, too. Ibrahim has twenty-eight thousand troops marching back and forth across the Peloponnisos, burning everything in sight, taking women and children for slaves, killing every man they capture."

"Isn't Nauplia safe?"

"For the moment. But Reshid Pasha is currently besieging Athens and should the city fall, he'll march south and converge with Ibrahim's army. Also, I'm not sure Jerome Clouard won't appear in one guise or another. The man is clearly depraved, without conscience if he'll try to murder a small boy. Would you be averse to going up into the mountains?"

"I'll rely entirely on your judgment. I'm just so pleased to be away from Paris, from England."

"Good. We'll settle the logistics later. Ah, food," he gratefully murmured, at the approach of two servants bearing platters. "Had you finished eating? Would you like to join me? Tula is the most splendid cook. I stole her from Ali Pasha years ago, before the sultan sent an army to bring his head back to the Porte." He laughed at her sudden dismay. "You haven't been here long enough to know the Turks have refined depravity to a fine art. I'm numbed to it—a necessity in this war, I'm afraid. But talk to me of something else instead. Something to do with joy and good cheer, like those days in Kent." His gaze held hers for a long, intense time. "God, it's good to see you."

He'd just returned from killing people, she thought, and she was experiencing this wonderful frisson of pleasure that he was pleased to see her. Was she so perverse as to casually forget the brutality and savagery of his deeds? Or was the cause of Greek freedom excuse enough?

"Do you know how many times I've thought of that small bedroom at Burleigh House?" he whispered, leaning forward, his elbows on the table so he was closer to her, intent perhaps on forgetting the slaughter as well.

She nodded, that room etched on her memory.

"I don't have to leave until daybreak," he said, reaching to take her hands in his.

"You should *eat*," she murmured, clinging to his hands.

He smiled and shook his head. "Later."

"We could bring some food with us."

She wasn't coy. She'd never been coy. He liked that. "I'll take the *melomakarona*—honey cookies," he said, standing, moving around the table to pull her upright, lifting the platter of food. "I'll feed them to you." He leaned over in exquisite slow motion to brush her lips with his. "And then you can feed them to me."

She'd forgotten how he could make her flame hot with the merest word or touch, how just standing beside him could make her tremble, how she longed for him inside her, deep, deep inside her. She'd forgotten perhaps because she didn't want to remember how much she craved him.

"This way." He nudged her arm with his elbow, tipping his head toward the darkened room behind them. "I haven't been with a woman since you."

Her eyes flared wide.

He grinned. "What do you think of that?"

She thought there was a fairy godmother somewhere that answered wishes. "Really?" she asked, because she was a skeptic at heart about fairy godmothers.

"Really."

"You please me greatly," she whispered.

"I haven't even started yet—*pleasing* you," he whispered back.

She could feel the heat race up inside her, feel the pulsing begin, the streak of pleasure coursing though her so intense she felt the hair on the back of her neck rise. "I may just come right here," she murmured, clasping her hands together to still her shivering.

"Wait for me instead." He bent low to gently bite the lobe of her ear. "You'll like it better."

"I'm not sure I can wait." Her voice was breathless. It had been too long, she thought, or she wanted him too much.

He recognized the taut edge to her voice, and quickly placing the platter down, he lifted her into his arms and strode into the darkened room, through it with long strides, his boot heels a staccato rhythm like her peaking desire.

He kicked open his bedroom door, left it open in the interest of speed, and placed her on his moonlit bed. He swiftly unbuttoned his riding pants and, brushing her skirts aside, climbed on top of her, boots and all. When he entered her she gasped, her breath rising into a sigh as he plunged deep inside her.

It was a ravishment, fierce and wild, mutual, the intensity sensational, a mating of wills and spirits and bodies.

And swiftly over.

Their breathing ragged, panting, they existed in a shimmering limbo, their bodies still strumming with feeling, their minds bereft of all but the trailing vestiges of ecstasy.

Head bowed, his hair light on her face, he lay above her, braced on his elbows, thinking, now that his rutting frenzy had passed, he shouldn't touch her with the clothes he'd worn in battle.

As he began to pull away, her hands tightened on him.

"My clothes," he said. "The dirt—"

"I don't care."

"Let me just take them off," he whispered, bending his head to kiss her lightly. "A second, that's all."

"A second?"

He smiled. "Watch me."

She chuckled. "Now that's incentive."

"I should bathe." He slid away, careful now of his boots on the coverlet.

"If I could wait, you could bathe."

"Or you could bathe with me." Standing beside the bed, he quickly stripped off his embroidered jacket and dropped it to the floor.

"Afterward."

"I'd forgotten how impatient you are."

"So you should hurry." She was slipping her gown off.

A sudden disconcerting thought arrested his fingers on the buttons of his vest. "How many other men have you said that to since I left?"

"None, if you must know."

"A woman of your appetites?" he suspiciously queried.

"A man of your propensities?" she countered, pulling her chemise over her head. "You've been celibate, you tell me. Why shouldn't I?"

"I'm not sure I believe you." Always indifferent to the concept of fidelity in the past, he found it suddenly mattered, and her frankness eased some of his apprehensions. He continued his undressing.

"Then we're both equally distrustful," she remarked, "because you celibate—of all people—is difficult to conceive. Especially with the harem women in your entourage tonight. I don't suppose you were planning on discussing Plato with them?" She dropped her slippers on the floor.

"Makriyannis brought them," he said, his casual flirtation with the harem ladies more habit than impulse; his interest in them had been minimal. Unlike his fascination with Trixi Grosvenor, he realized. "I find myself possessive about you. Now that you're here, now that I think about it."

"As I find myself. I'm glad you didn't sleep with the harem ladies. Really, really glad," she softly said.

"*I'm* glad you traveled so far to see me."

"Good. Now if we're both agreed on this mutual attraction, I'd like you back in bed." Her silk stockings sailed through the air.

"Don't be coy," he said, grinning, pulling off his shirt.

"Do you like coy women?" She stretched luxuriously in the moonlight, all gilded femaleness.

"I like you."

It wasn't an extravagant sentiment but she liked the sound of his simple admission because *she* liked *him* very much. And if she'd dared consider a future with a man like Pasha, she might have allowed herself to love him. But she mollified her susceptibility to sentiments he could more readily accept. "And I love to make love to you. Do you need help?"

"Restrain yourself, darling, for a second more." Nude now, he picked up the pitcher of water from the washstand, walked out to the balcony, and poured it over his head. After wiping his hair and body swiftly, he climbed back into bed. "A marginal improvement," he noted, sprawling on his back beside her.

"You're absolutely perfect," she murmured, half rolling on her side, sliding her palms over his sleek torso.

"This is damn near paradise, isn't it. Why didn't you come sooner?" he added, turning his head to smile at her.

"Had I known of your gracious welcome, I may have."

"I should have written." And for an odd moment it seemed strange that he hadn't. He was deeply content, seriously happy with her soft, warm body against his. He pulled her close.

"Now there's no need to write." Her tone was deliberately playful; she preferred not to consider the alarming degree of her attachment.

"This is much better, I agree."

"For us both," she whispered, sliding onto his chest, lying atop him. "Would you think me forward if I—"

"Need another climax, do you?" he lazily drawled, smiling.

"I don't, I suppose, precisely *need* one, although I would dearly *love* one. And seeing how you seem to be . . . ready," she murmured, rubbing his arousal with her thigh. "As usual . . ."

"Why not put it to good use?" he pleasantly finished, watching her move up into a seated position straddling his legs.

She grinned down at him. "Exactly."

They made love that night with a rare and special awareness, feeling a tangible physical accord—and more. Both were impatient, not Trixi alone, both heart-touched, hypersensitive to a raw, primitive need, their responses keenly felt, sharpened by their long privation.

The warfare and slaughter made Pasha more conscious, perhaps, of his own mortality, of their special nearness.

Trixi hadn't realized how truly important he was to her, how vulnerable her feelings were, how extravagant a joy he brought to her life. It was both terrifying and wonderful to feel what she felt; the pleasure layered nuances of bliss and trepidation.

But pleasure overwhelmed all else as the night progressed and she experienced rapture so sweet, so profound, that all the constraints that warned her against love disappeared.

And she allowed herself to acknowledge her love for him.

Hours later, bewitched, enchanted, reckless with

feelings he could no more describe than acknowledge, Pasha murmured, "Would you like another baby?"

Her body immediately opened to receive him, the words triggered to a deep, unspoken longing. "Yes," she whispered, languorous after hours of making love. "Yes, yes . . ." she breathed with such feeling he felt her words strike his heart.

Yet he hesitated, the concept once voiced so utterly heedless of all his former pragmatic principles and assessments, alarm bells went off in his brain.

But she was lying beneath him, warm, hot, receptive, and the inescapable specter of death ever present in his thoughts gave warning he could be killed tomorrow. Today, he corrected himself, with the moon on the wane, their marching orders assigned. "Are you sure?" he said, his voice taut with indecision.

She reached up to kiss him, her breath warm on his lips. "I'm sure."

"It might not happen anyway." A sop to his conscience, to the indecision and demur.

"Or it might." She felt afraid suddenly for his life, afraid she might never see him after tonight.

"I have to leave very soon." Time seemed to be ticking away, and his whole life was in the balance.

"Come back to me," she whispered, stroking his cheek, smoothing his hair behind his ear.

"God willing," he softly replied. Moonlight washed the room in a silvery glow, the cool night air carrying the scent of the sea. "If there's a child," Pasha said, kissing her cheek, knowing he was making a commitment however tenuous, knowing there was one thing more he must say, "and I don't come back—"

"Hush." The word came heated and low as alarm flared in her eyes.

"Everyone's time comes," he gently declared. "I

want you to see that my family knows. I'll leave a note, but tell them—"

"Please, please . . . don't talk that way."

"Not another word." He smiled. "Kiss me instead, and we'll pick out baby names in the morning."

10

Waking while it was still dark, Pasha eased himself from the bed, careful not to disturb Trixi. He had to make arrangements for her safety before leaving. Their troop had orders to guard the supply train coming from Tripolitza to Nauplia, the transfer of the new harvest to a more secure location critical to the maintenance of the army. He had only a few hours before their scheduled departure at first light.

Jules materialized as he entered his dressing room, a cup of coffee in his hand.

"You're a lifesaver," Pasha murmured, taking the offered cup.

"Your clothes are laid out, sir," Jules quietly said. "And your bath is ready."

Pasha grinned. "You're worth a fortune, Jules. Give yourself a raise."

"You pay me sufficiently, sir." Jules's bank account, in fact, was adequate to support his entire family residing in Normandy. "I took the liberty of having your saddlebags packed."

"Did you happen to find any brandy?"

"I brought a case from your cellar, sir. You have three full silver flasks in your saddlebags."

"Enough to take the edge off the rough ride. We're to make all speed to Tripolitza this morning." He drained his coffee cup and set it down. "Lady Grosvenor will be moving to the Monastery of St. Elijah before I leave, so see that her things are packed," Pasha instructed, stepping into the white marble bath. Taking the soap Jules held out to him, he sank into the warm water with a sigh. "Damned Turks are keeping us on the move. I wouldn't mind a day or so of rest sometime soon."

"Nikos tells me of your success at Lerna. Perhaps Kolokotronis's army will give you some respite now."

Pasha was cynical. "And maybe he'll restore all the money he stole from the Greek treasury while he's at it."

"The factions are as corrupt as ever, then?"

"Worse, since the English loans have given them larger prizes to fight over. Loyalties are everywhere for sale. Except for Makriyannis. His troop's accomplished damn near miracles this summer. Now if we can get the supplies out of Tripolitza in time, Ibrahim won't have the advantage of starving out Nauplia this winter."

"When do you anticipate returning?"

"Three or four days," Pasha said. "I'd like you to watch over Lady Grosvenor while I'm gone," he added, coming to his feet in a sluice of water. "And stay armed," he cautioned, taking a towel from Jules. "If she wakes before I return, tell her I'll be right back."

"Will you have time for breakfast when you return?"

"No."

He dressed swiftly in the clothes Jules handed to him, his weapons added at the last. Even in Nauplia one never traveled unarmed. Minutes later, he was riding through the courtyard gate.

On entering his bedroom an hour later, he silently moved to the foot of the bed and stood utterly still for a moment, captivated by the delectable sight. It still didn't seem completely real—that she was here in Nauplia, sleeping in his bed. She lay uncovered in the summer warmth, curvaceous, lush, the image of fecund womanhood, perhaps fertile motherhood, he thought, beguiled again by the possibility, although in perverse contrast, her arms were thrown over her head in the sleeping pose of an exhausted child. He momentarily chastised himself for selfishly keeping her up all night. But she'd been silken flesh and playful eagerness and wild and demanding and tearful at the very last, the precariousness of life in wartime terrifying to her, only too well known to him. And now he had to see that she was kept safe until his return—from the spies in town, from the thieves and cutthroats, from the entrepreneurs who viewed a golden-haired beauty such as she with an eye to her price on the slave block. It was dangerous for a beautiful woman in this hotbed of intrigue and rivalries, in this city that was living in the shadow of war. But he'd found the most secure residence possible.

Moving to the side of the bed, he sat down beside her, the dip of the bed under his weight bringing her half awake. Her eyelids fluttered open briefly before falling shut again.

He delicately touched the curve of her ankle, his calloused finger sliding over her silken skin, and she murmured, eyes closed, "Where have you been?"

"Did you miss me?"

"I missed your warm body," she softly breathed, languidly stretching, her lashes lifting. "And your gifted talents . . ."

"You'll have to miss them both for a few days," he playfully retorted. "Duty calls."

Her mouth formed into a moue. "For how long?"

"Three or four days." He delicately ran his finger up the length of her body, leaving a heated path in his wake and reaching her chin, he lifted it a fraction.

Leaning over, he gently kissed her pouty mouth. "Then I'm taking you up into the mountains."

"For a holiday?" She knew better but preferred to ignore reality.

In the light of day neither mentioned their talk of babies and baby names, the irrevocable timetable of war once more in control of their lives.

"A holiday from the Turks," he replied, glancing at the clock on the bedside table as he straightened. "They don't venture off the main roads."

"Are you late?"

"Soon I will be. But first I have to see you and Chris to the monastery. Pappas Gregorios and his well-armed brotherhood will watch over you."

"Nauplia seems so beautiful and bustling, the sense of danger eludes one." The sun was just rising, bathing the room in lemony light, the morning air wafting through the open windows fresh, scented, the summer day fresh and new.

"Unfortunately, the Turks have their spies everywhere. You're safe only with an army at your back. Now get up, darling," he gently charged, offering her his hands. "Jules is packing for you."

A short time later, the small party reached the picturesque monastery on the hill overlooking the bay, and after being vetted by the armed monks at the gates, solid-looking, studded oak doors swung open and they rode into a paved court. As Jules led Chris to the fish in the courtyard pool, the Archbishop Gregorios came out to greet them, his long beard and flowing robe, his sandaled feet an image from the Old Testament—with the exception of the pistol and dagger thrust into the roped tie at his waist.

"Welcome, welcome," he boomed, his warmth obvious. "We're pleased to offer you sanctuary, Pasha Bey.

Would that the infidel Turk were driven from our land and we could live in peace."

"Ibrahim hasn't won yet, Pappas," Pasha replied, dismounting, handing his reins to a monk.

"And he'll never win this spot of ground as long as we've ammunition." The prelate patted the pistol at his waist. "Your lady will be safe with us."

Moving to Trixi's mount, Pasha lifted his hands to her and she slid from her saddle into his arms. Setting her on her feet, he introduced her to the archbishop. "Pappas Gregorios, I'd like you to meet Lady Grosvenor. Lady Grosvenor, our militant Pappas, the first prelate in Greece to take arms against the Turks."

"Our Lord spoke to me, Lady Grosvenor, and I couldn't deny him. Welcome to our order."

"Thank you for having us. Pasha tells me despite Nauplia's idyllic charm, danger lurks everywhere."

"I'm afraid so, my lady." A gravity entered his voice. "I wish I could say it was only the Turks we need guard ourselves against. But our country has divided loyalties and dozens of warlords, each greedy for power. One never knows from day to day whom to trust. But we trust in our Lord and these," he added, his hand on his sword hilt.

"Their daily target practice never hurts either," Pasha noted, grinning. "Along with the ammunition cache in the monastery cellars."

"The Lord helps those who help themselves, Pasha Bey. He can't be everywhere at once."

"As long as He's keeping Lady Grosvenor safe, I'll be more than willing to build Him a new chapel after the war."

"Your generosity to our order has always found favor in His eyes, my friend," the archbishop cordially declared. "He'll view your jaded soul with kindness when your time comes to meet Him. I light candles for you, too."

"I'm depending on that, Pappas. Especially with Ibrahim bringing up more troops from Crete. Put extra guards on at night now, if you will," he warned. "Word has it, Hussein Djeritl is looking to take his harem back."

"*My* spies tell me he's taking this personally. Beware of strangers in your midst, my friend. The ransom on your head has reached enticing proportions."

"I sleep with my eyes open, Pappas, and have since this war began. A few more groschen one way or another doesn't concern me."

"Take Brother Zaimes with you. He can smell a traitor in a slaughterhouse."

Trixi had been listening to the conversation with growing alarm. A ransom, she nervously thought. As if there weren't peril enough. "Please, Pasha," she urged, "do as he suggests. Take the brother with you."

"Don't worry, darling," Pasha soothed, not overly concerned with nuances of risk in the constant battlefield of his existence. "I've survived so far regardless of Hussein's enmity." Pasha had outbid Hussein at a slave auction in Constantinople some years ago and taken a woman away from him—as an act of kindness—and sent her back to her home in Georgia. Their bad blood wasn't exclusively of recent origin.

"Did I say Brother Zaimes has two new Berenger rifles?" Pappas murmured.

Pasha grinned. "No, you didn't. Send him along by all means. Those Berengers are like having an extra trooper." He turned back to Trixi then, because time was at a premium and he should have ridden out of Nauplia half an hour ago. "Now listen to Pappas and do as he says, even if it seems ridiculous in this sanctuary." He took her hands in his and squeezed them gently. "I'll be back as soon as I can."

"Be careful, please . . . please." How awful it was to see him go.

"I ask the same of you," he gravely said.

"Can you kiss me one last time?" she whispered. "I mean here . . ." She cast a glance at the archbishop.

"I'll kiss you in front of the pope if you want." He drew her near and, dipping his head, he lightly brushed her lips with his. His mouth lifted and he looked at her, wondering how he could go off and risk his life when she was waiting for him. When he might have responsibility for a child, when his world had altered in a thousand ways since last night. Pulling her closer, he kissed her again, a different kiss this time, a long, deep, necessitous kiss, feverish, fierce, touched with despair. She clung to him as if she could keep him with her by sheer force, tears sliding down her cheeks.

He felt the wetness and, raising his head, gently brushed her tears away with his gloved knuckles. "Don't cry, darling. I'll be back."

"Don't get hurt—for me," she whispered, her heart in her eyes.

"I can't," he replied, teasing her. "Brother Zaimes is guarding me." It pleased him to see the fear leave her eyes.

"And I'll have Pappas." She was trying to put on a brave front.

"God is on our side," he murmured, a mischievous light in his eyes. "Now, listen to Jules, listen to Pappas, don't take any chances." He spoke briskly, a new level of detachment in his voice. "I'll be back in three or four days."

"Do you have to go?" A last rash plea.

"You know better," he quietly said, motioning for Pappas. "Take Lady Grosvenor inside," he told the prelate, unwrapping her arms from around his waist. He turned without another word and walked toward Jules and Chris. His good-byes to them were brief, a few words, no more. Mounting quickly, he rode through the guarded gate.

Jerome Clouard was no longer completely rational. His need to assure himself of the Gericault millions had become an obsession. Never before thwarted in an enterprise of this magnitude, he intended to triumph at all costs. Greed drove him, and an irrational need for mastery. He had to win.

He set his affairs in order, instructing Phillipe with a vast array of orders for the weeks he'd be gone. Phillipe had given up trying to dissuade him and calmly listened to his brother's commands, exempt from the avarice that drove his brother, content to be left peacefully in Paris.

Jerome brought along an arsenal on his journey south and hired an assassin at Marseille, the docks of the port city home to criminals of every persuasion. Marcel spoke all the languages of the Mediterranean, a requirement for a man in his line of work. The necessary money changed hands and a week after Trixi set sail, Jerome embarked from Marseille. Immune to the beauty of the summer seas, he spent the entire journey grumbling, irritated at the tedium and slowness of the voyage. Driven, impatient, he wished only to set foot in Greece and begin stalking his prey.

Another man with a similar mission sat in his silk tent under a hot sun on a hill near Navarino, his lieutenants silent before his wrath. Hussein Djeritl had been haranguing his officers without mercy since their defeat at the hands of Makriyannis and Pasha Bey. And while he would be able to explain the lost battle to the

Porte with a suitable aggrandizement of the forces against him, the loss of his harem was a personal scourge. Worse, it had been inflicted by his old enemy Pasha Bey.

"You have two days to remedy this affront to my honor," he raged, his fingers white as they clenched the arms of his ivory-inlaid camp chair. "I want my harem back, and Pasha Bey's head on a pike outside my tent." A cold light gleamed in his eyes and he shifted forward in his chair, his hard, trim soldier's body taut as a wire. Unlike his brother-in-law, Ibrahim, a coarse, corpulent sybarite who had his position by the vagaries of birth, Hussein had earned his rank by dint of military successes before his marriage to Mehmet Ali's daughter. "If," he softly said, his voice trembling with the violence of his feelings, "you fail to accomplish this task, each of you will be sent back to the Porte in chains."

Everyone understood what was left unsaid. At the Porte, they would be found guilty of cowardice and impaled. With that form of torture, it took agonizing days to die, and Hussein's officers visibly paled under the threat.

"Do we understand each other?" He leaned back marginally, his chill gaze surveying his subordinates.

A moment of silence ensued before one of the men had the courage to reply.

"Very well," Hussein growled. "I'll expect my revenge will be complete in two days."

11

Cautious of Hussein's spies and informers, his officers conferred on their plan of action in an olive grove well out of sight of the camp—open in all directions so no one could approach without being seen. Even within their ranks, the possibility of betrayal existed, but in their present circumstances they had to work together—or die together.

Such vital, common cause transiently obliterated individual agendas.

"The harem had to have been taken to Nauplia," one of them said.

"The question is where in Nauplia?" another declared.

"I have an uncle who still lives there," a third man noted. "Let me go and talk to him." Hadji's family had fled to Constantinople when the rebellion began, but he'd lived in Nauplia most of his life. And even within the Greek community there were those still loyal to the Porte. Lavish fortunes had been made by the Greek primates and Fanariots collecting taxes for the sultan. A time-honored association, the rebellion had at times disrupted the efficiency of that partnership but not severed it. So a Greek was not always a Greek.

Nor was a Turk always what he seemed in this country where the two races had lived together in various stages of ease and dispute since the fifteenth century.

"We'll need transport for the women once they're found," Hadji remarked.

"And enough trusted men to bring them back to camp," a colleague added.

"Pasha Bey will be—"

"Difficult to take," a young officer declared, his brows drawn together in a scowl. "He rides with Makriyannis's troops, who have the best marksmen and more luck than infidels deserve."

"We locate him first," Hadji brusquely said. "Then we send him a message that we've recaptured the harem. He'll walk into our trap."

"If we can find him," an officer countered.

"We'd better or we die by slow degrees."

"Will he come?"

"Of course. He and Makriyannis are men of honor," an officer sardonically replied.

Trixi spent a restless night at the monastery. The armed monks stood guard throughout the night, the first relief at midnight, another at dawn. She could hear the murmur of voices, the patrols passing by on the circuit of the grounds, such vigilance eerie in a house of God. She finally rose when the first light muted the brilliance of the starlit sky and, dressing quickly, went outside. She wished to inspect her stronghold, the walls, the grounds, buildings, and sheltered gardens; she needed to satisfy herself that she was indeed secure.

After the past weeks of pursuit and personal jeopardy, she was no longer comfortable leaving her safety completely to others. She'd ask for a pistol this morning when she saw Pappas Gregorios, she decided, following the path that led to the courtyard. It would be wise to examine the stables as well, should she and Chris require a horse quickly. She'd heeded Pasha's warning. How could she not, with the degree of military readiness displayed at the monastery?

Chris would have to be forewarned in some ambiguous way that flight might be necessary. Fortunately, he was still of an age where such conduct could be couched in terms of adventure and fantasy. She'd talk to Jules and decide on a suitable story.

A glint of sunlight glistened off the barrel of a rifle high in the tower of the chapel, where a monk perched as lookout. The monastery was well positioned, she reflected, to defend against attack. Later, she'd ask permission to climb the tower and survey the approaches to the monastery.

Day one, with two or three more to go before Pasha returned, she mused, crossing the courtyard. How strange that she was contemplating methods of defense on a guarded hillside in Greece. All because fate had dragooned her into a despicable marriage and Gericault had appeared to save her soul.

As for Pasha, she benevolently thought, he'd given her the will and the spirit to take charge of her future and for that, she realized after the events of last night, she not only loved him, she owed him her life.

An unnerving thought for a woman so recently come into a modicum of independence. Perhaps, she thought with a faint smile, she could owe him a *portion* of her life.

And that portion, she thought, smiling broadly as she mounted the stairway to the archbishop's quarters, wouldn't be in question. The reflection seemed scandalously salacious in such a setting and suppressing the delectable images from their passionate hours together, she returned to matters of a more immediate and pragmatic nature.

Knocking on the priest's door, she waited in the dawn of a summer day to be bid enter. That she was or would soon be the target of men determined to do her harm seemed remote in the calm stillness of morning.

Pasha had no such illusions. He knew anyone connected to him was in danger. He had a host of enemies in Greece, any of whom would take whatever means possible to bring him down—to defeat Makriyannis and his troops and thus eliminate the most threatening force currently at war with the sultan.

He and Makriyannis rode at the head of the troops, their horses lathered, the pace an all-out gallop, the necessity of reaching Tripolitza with all speed spurring them. Their barb steeds were bred to maintain a steady gallop for long distances; with luck, they should reach Tripolitza before noon. But once the supply train began the journey to Nauplia, their snail's pace would make them a prime target for any Turkish attack.

"Do you expect Hussein to reappear?" Makriyannis inquired, turning to cast a searching glance at Pasha.

"As soon as he can put some courage back into his troops," Pasha replied, his eyes heavy-lidded, lounging half asleep in his padded saddle.

"Will he want the women back?"

Pasha's dark brows rose in sardonic inquiry. "Do fish swim?"

"A shame the ladies sail home today."

"A fucking shame." Pasha smiled faintly. "If we had the time, I'd like to go in some night and slit his throat while he sleeps in that great silk tent of his."

"And put an end to his vendetta."

"The world would be a finer place."

"Maybe after this trip back to Nauplia."

Pasha shrugged. "Not likely, with Ibrahim on the move north again and Athens still under siege. Hussein will have to wait."

·   ·   ·

Hadji entered Nauplia that afternoon wearing Greek dress, appearing like any other guerrilla fighter in the city. Waiting in the square across the street from his uncle's tobacco shop until it was empty of customers, he cautiously approached the entrance and opening the door, quietly walked in.

His uncle looked up from behind the counter, his shock visible. Hurrying around the counter, he put his finger to his mouth and motioning with his hand led his nephew down a corridor, through a doorway into a small office without windows. "Stay here. I have to find Ali to take over."

He returned within minutes and sat down behind a table strewn with papers and tobacco containers. He lifted a bottle of *raki* from a nearby shelf, uncorked it, poured himself a glass, and drank it down in one gulp. Pushing the bottle across the table toward Hadji, he gazed at his nephew. "What do you want?" he coolly said. "I hope it's only information, because I'm not interested in putting my life in jeopardy for that stupid Albanian Ibrahim."[16]

"I have similar reservations, uncle, but at the moment, my life is at stake." He went on to explain the necessity of carrying out Hussein Djeritl's orders. "If you could discover where the women of his harem have been taken, as well as the location of Pasha Bey, my mother, your sister, would be as grateful as I. Otherwise my colleagues and I will be sent to the Porte in cages to die."

His uncle grimaced, shifted in his chair, reached for the liquor bottle again. "You understand my life would be forfeit as well as my family's if my treachery were revealed."

"Hire an informer."

"Worse. None of them can be trusted."

"Simply give me some possible locations then. I'll reconnoiter them myself."

"Pasha Bey's residence is no secret. I'll direct you there. And for the sake of my sister, I'll ask two sources I trust what they know of the harem ladies. But I won't do more. I'm sorry, my family would die by the hands of the Greeks if I were implicated in your plot."

Hadji nodded his agreement. The two men shared a drink, shook hands, and agreed to meet after the store had closed for the night. Hadji left to survey Pasha's house and warehouse, while his uncle went in search of his friends and any information they might have on Hussein's harem.

Later that evening, his uncle related the news that the harem had left Nauplia that day in English ships.

Hadji listened to the information with mixed feelings. Hussein's reactions were unpredictable, and his harem was definitely gone. On the other hand, he and his colleagues couldn't be expected to return the harem once the women had been placed on English ships beyond their reach. A modicum of relief invaded his senses.

For his part, he'd discovered possible recompense for the loss of Hussein's harem. A worker in Pasha Bey's warehouse had been loquacious after several drinks in the café, and Hadji had learned that Pasha Bey's newest paramour had been placed for safekeeping in the armed monastery of St. Elijah. Perhaps Hussein would settle for an alternative prize in lieu of his lost harem. And with his English paramour Hussein's captive, Pasha Bey was sure to come calling.

At which point his head could be placed on the pike outside of Hussein's tent with a minimum of effort.

Hadji smiled and extended his hand to his uncle. "Thank you. I'll be gone from Nauplia before morning. You and your family can rest easy."

"I never saw you, should anyone ask. I'll deny you in public. You understand?"

"Certainly." Hadji stood and bowed. "You won't see me again."

A moment later, alone in his office, the uncle of Hadji poured himself a large *raki,* the tremor in his hands visible. It was over and he'd survived. Short of torture, he'd never tell anyone of this visit.

When Hadji returned to the small camp north of the city where his colleagues waited, his news was greeted with cheerful smiles. England and Turkey were allies. International repercussions would ensue should they attempt to recapture the harem.

"Thank Allah for the women's swift departure," one of the officers rejoiced.

"One less obstacle in our bid for life," another declared.

"But we still need Pasha Bey," Hadji reminded them, "and he's a formidable opponent. I suggest we take his woman, and . . ." He went on to explain.

He'd spent considerable time reconnoitering the monastery site that day and he outlined the stronghold's defenses. "We have to go in tonight in order to return to Hussein in time. The steep rise above the monastery offers the best ingress."

Each man had responsibility for maintaining watch on the dozen patrolling guards Hadji had estimated were on at night. Their routine had to remain unbroken, for they reported in sequence at ten-minute intervals. It would be up to two of them to slip between the patrols, pass through the north gardens, and enter the building where the Englishwoman slept. "I talked to the guard at the front gate this afternoon. I told him I'd brought a message to the government from the siege at Athens and had half a day leave before returning. By good fortune, he had relatives near Athens. He gave me a letter to deliver to them. The English-woman is of supreme importance to Pasha Bey. He left orders for no one to be admitted into the monastery for any reason. The gates are sealed until his return."

"Hussein should be pleased to have her if she's so prized by Pasha Bey."

"But more pleased to have Pasha Bey's head," Hadji tersely said.

Weapons were checked, yataghans and daggers the weapon of choice tonight. Only in extremity would their guns be fired. They hoped to take the woman out noiselessly so they could be well on their way to Nava-rino before her loss was discovered.

The cloudly night aided their movements, their approach undetected. Everyone counted under their breath, watching the armed monks pass under the wall, knowing another would soon follow. "Now," Hadji whispered after the guard disappeared, and the two men jumped, landing in the soft dirt of the garden. Clothed in monk's garb, Hadji and his companion moved through the shadowed garden on bare feet, care-ful to make no sound in the silent night. Keeping to the shadowed wall, they approached the doorway into the wing housing the Englishwoman. The door hinge squeaked as they pulled it open and both men froze, their hands on their daggers. Taut seconds passed while they waited to see if the noise had wakened anyone. After several breath-held moments, the stillness re-mained unbroken, and they continued their course, eas-ing themselves through the door. On alert for any movement in the darkened corridor, they advanced toward the stairway. The woman was on the second floor, Hadji had deduced from his conversation with the guard at the gate. She'd been given the room with the best view of the bay.

Like muffled wraiths, they ascended the narrow staircase, crossed the landing at the top of the stairs, and stood in the doorway of a large room dominated by a bed and an elaborate prie-dieu. The woman lay asleep, her golden hair pale in the darkness, her skin alabaster, her white sleeping gown drawing the eye in the shadowed room.

Both men stood transfixed for a moment by the glorious female confined within the walls of the monastery. A delectable enchantress their master was sure to appreciate.

At a signal from Hadji, they moved swiftly. A dark hand clamped hard over the woman's mouth, her eyes were covered before she could completely open them, and seconds later she was secured with bonds, hand and foot. A gag replaced the unyielding hand and she was tossed over Hadji's shoulder.

Who were her captors? Trixi wondered, surprised at her lack of hysteria. Alarm was useless in any event, at this stage, she decided. Instead her mind raced with possible enemies—such capable enemies. Were the Grosvenors so far from England? Or the Clouards? Who else could it be? Where were the monks on guard? And then a jolt of terror chilled her to the core. Had Chris been taken? Please, God, no, she silently pleaded. He was too young to be frightened from his sleep, too young to be torn from his mother. As if propelled by a sudden madness, she kicked and twisted and turned, trying to break free, her panic giving her strength.

Quickly coming to a stop, Hadji whispered briefly to his companion and immediately a hand covered her mouth and nose, cutting off her air supply.

She lost consciousness within moments, and Hadji ran from the building. Racing through the garden, he lifted her to the men on the wall. Pulling Trixi's limp body up, two officers bundled her into a plain dark cloak and handed her down to a horseman outside the monastery wall. Settling his burden across his lap, he walked his horse away from the monastery wall as quietly as possible.

It was three-thirty in the morning, two hours before sunrise.

Two hours before the guard at the monastery would change.

When Pasha first saw the monk riding hard toward them, the horse and rider were barely visible on the horizon. But the black flaring robe was distinctive enough to send an immediate danger signal to his brain. Whipping his mount away from the supply train plodding down the road to Nauplia, he raced toward the oncoming rider, praying his instincts were wrong.

Trixi and Chris were well guarded, their presence in Nauplia relatively unknown. He'd been gone only a day. But the monk was riding low over his horse's neck, forcing the pace, and fear gripped him.

When he was close enough to see the man's expression, he expected the worst. As both men drew their mounts to a plunging stop, Pasha's heart was drumming in his chest, panic suffocated his ability to think. "Is she alive?" he shouted, all else insignificant.

"She was kidnapped by Hussein Djeritl's men. A message was left for you," the rider gasped, pulling a crumpled note from his bandoleer.

Pasha unfolded it and read the few words written in Arabic: *If you want the Englishwoman, come and get her.*

He glanced up at the sun, estimating the time. "When was she taken?"

"Shortly before dawn."

"And the boy?"

"Unharmed."

If it were possible for him to feel relief in his current state of numbness, Chris's safety offered brief solace. He should have taken mother and son with him, he thought, or better yet, sent them back the minute he'd discovered her in Nauplia. Neither option without danger in itself, he understood, safety and security problematical on several counts. But *merde*!

He'd have to kill Hussein.

"I can't take this supply train to Nauplia," he said to Makriyannis as he rode up a second later, deadly purpose having calmed his thoughts. "Hussein has Trixi. I have to get her back."

"The general's in the center of his army at Navarino. You'll need help."

Pasha shook his head. "I'm better alone."

"It's suicide alone."

"Unless we can match his army, which is an impossibility, less is better." Pasha was checking his water supply, gauging the amount he'd need to take him that far.

"Then just you and me and someone to wait with the horses while we go into his camp," Makriyannis proposed. "We'll slit Hussein's throat while he sleeps."

Pasha looked up. "You don't have to do this."

"And you haven't needed to fight my war. Hell, with luck," Makriyannis cheerfully went on, "we can walk in and out of there with no one noticing."

Both men knew better; both men knew Hussein was as closely guarded as the sultan's favorite wife.

"This will cash in all my markers," Pasha quietly said.

"You've saved my life three times, my friend. Don't talk to me of payment. Are you ready?"

"I'm killing him this time," Pasha coldly murmured, testing the sharpness of his dagger blade before placing it back in his belt.

"Since you don't collect trophies, I'll take his ears."

"Be my guest," Pasha grimly replied.

Cautious of informers, they left the supply train with a spurious explanation of another government mission and rode off in the direction of Nauplia. Only after they were out of sight of the supply train did they change course and travel west.

Once away from Nauplia, Trixi was freed from her bonds and given a mount. She couldn't escape surrounded by Hussein's officers, her reins firmly in their grasp. And while she was fearful, the fact that they'd not taken Chris offered her comfort. She was treated with courtesy; one man spoke a few words of English. She was being taken to Navarino to their superior, Hussein Djeritl, he said, alternating English, Arabic, and hand signals.

She recognized Hussein's name although she was careful to show no recognition. But her abduction had an explanation now. It had something to do with Pasha and the harem he'd brought to Nauplia. If this Hussein had her kidnapped because of Pasha, her life wasn't in immediate danger. She was being transported to his camp at Navarino for a purpose.

A kind of serenity overcame her, as though she were aloof from this mounted troop, as if she were independent of their mission. Perhaps having traveled so far from Kent and overcome such hazards during the past months, she'd become hardened to danger. She no longer took instant fright when threatened, but thought instead of contingency plans. Surveying the country around her, she took note of landmarks, wanting to recognize this area again should she return. The Turks weren't likely to kill her; she would be viewed as a valuable item for sale if nothing else. Not exactly a comforting thought. But death wasn't imminent.

And she had enormous faith in Pasha.

Perhaps she was naive, but she was confident he'd come for her, the phrase like a mantra in her mind. Lulled by that hope, comforted, she was able to control her anxieties.

The Turks rode at a steady canter, broken only once when they came to a village where they watered and fed their horses. She was offered a handful of dates and water, but not allowed to dismount. It seemed they were driven by a schedule of some importance, a note of concern in their voices. She was under the impression they had to reach Navarino by a certain time.

Pasha and Makriyannis were four hours behind, riding full out, traveling cross-country to save precious time, taking a dangerous mountain trail that would cut two hours from their ride. No one spoke, neither the mood nor the pace conducive to conversation. Trained to kill, proficient at the task after years of fighting the Turks, they understood what had to be done.

The precise fashion in which they'd accomplish their mission would depend on circumstances once they reached Navarino.

Trixi's level of alarm rose as they rode through the army camped around Navarino, and hundreds of men's eyes followed her progress through the tented city surrounding Hussein Djeritl's flamboyant red silk pavilion. What lay in store for her? Did Turkish generals meet with females, or would she be dealt with by some functionary? How would they treat her? A degree of fatigue after hours in the saddle marginally blunted her concerns; a haze of weariness dulled her senses.

Coming to a halt at last before the elegant lodging, two men dismounted and went inside. The conversa-

tion was impossible to hear, hopeless to translate in any
event, but a harsh angry voice exploded on several occasions, followed immediately by a rapid flow of placating words.

And after a lengthy interval, the sound of laughter.
A chilling, evil laugh.

A man emerged a few moments later and spoke rapidly. One of her captors jumped to the ground and,
striding to Trixi's horse, abruptly pulled her from the
saddle.

She stumbled briefly as he set her down, his hands
rough, his gruff, curt order unintelligible. When she
didn't respond, he brusquely pushed her toward the
entrance to the tent.

Clutching the black cloak around her, she moved
forward, a sense of unreality pervading her mind. How
did one conduct oneself when a captive of a Turkish
general? What ultimately did he want of her? The obvious answer was unpalatable. Lifting her chin, she
straightened her spine, determined to face her captor
with courage. But such resolve was quickly put to the
test when she entered the large tent and came under
the scrutiny of a dozen hard-eyed men.

She stood at the entrance on soft carpets piled one
atop another so the ground was entirely covered and
cushioned. "Does anyone speak English?" she said
into the silence, addressing the men leaning forward,
staring.

With the exception of one man who lounged on a
chair set on a small dais, gazing at her from under half-
lowered lashes. He snapped his fingers, spoke a few
short words in a low, harsh voice, and one of the men
rose and walked from the tent.

Pasha Bey hadn't lost his admirable taste in women,
Hussein reflected. The golden-haired beauty dazzled

even covered in that common black cloak. She might indeed be recompense for losing his harem. Turning his head, he said as much to his dinner guests and everyone laughed heartily.

The humor was at her expense, Trixi thought, surveying the amused faces. The man on the gilded camp chair who drew such sycophantic laughter must be Hussein Djeritl. Oddly, he was dressed in a western uniform, reminiscent of a Napoleonic cavalry officer.

"Parlez-vous français?" she inquired.

He answered in a Parisian accent, his tone constrained. And then he gruffly spoke to the men in his own language, that same short, staccato delivery—an order, she presumed from his tone.

It was. They all rose like puppets on strings and exited through a flap held up by a servant at the rear of the tent.

"Come here," he said in a less gruff tone, beckoning her forward with a wave of his hand. "Pasha Bey brought you a long way for his pleasure. I want to see what he found in England."

The smallest hint of a Marseillaise patois underlay the more cultured French of Paris, she incongruously thought as she obeyed his order to approach. It mitigated the authority marginally, reminding her that at one time he was learning this foreign tongue like any other human being might. He'd not always been a supreme commander with the power of life and death in his hands. Also, she reflected, on a more personal note, he'd not wanted to share her company. A male phenomenon she understood. "He didn't bring me. I sailed here myself."

He almost smiled. "The adventuresome English female. Take your cloak off. Pasha Bey and I enjoy similar tastes in women. I want to see more of you."

"And if I refuse?"

"That would be very foolish under the circumstances," he mildly replied. "My men have brought you here for my pleasure."

"I prefer not staying, of course."

"Women in my world have no autonomy. And you are now a resident of that world. Kindly remove your cloak."

Even as she did, she was contemplating the extent and limitations of her current situation, weighing her chances for escape, making the necessary decision to appear compliant against some future hope of liberation. She dropped the black wool cloak at her feet and stood before him in her night shift.

A man of rare hedonistic impulse, Hussein was actually moved by the fresh innocence of the woman before him. So pale and golden, so bountiful and lush. "Take that off too," he murmured, indicating her night shift with a sweeping gesture.

"I prefer leaving it on."

"I can have two of my officers come in and take it off. They'll appreciate the duty. I could offer them your body once I've finished with you, if you choose not to cooperate."

"Should I call them in?" Her brows rose in query, as capable of a bluff as he.

He smiled, an actual smile that briefly warmed his eyes. "Tell me your name."

"Beatrix."

"Blessed indeed. Now be sensible. Take it off or I'll take it off for you." He uncrossed his legs and sat upright. "This can be pleasant or unpleasant. You decide." His dark gaze had turned chill, his voice held a frightening note of indifference, and he shifted in his seat as if ready to rise.

"Would it be possible to have a bath?" A means of putting off the inevitable, of buying herself some time.

"Everything's possible with an army at my command, the Peloponnisos under my control, the booty of conquest in my hands," he pleasantly declared. "But I'm not naive, Beatrix. Nor have I been for a great many years. Take off your shift so I may observe the prize my officers have brought me as partial surety for their lives. Your lover is the other requirement should they wish to live. You understand how limited your choices."

"I'm here as bait?" Her abduction was suddenly clarified.

"The very prettiest. And unless I mistake Pasha Bey's sense of chivalry, we should expect him in the near future. Did you know he took a woman I prized away from me at the slave market in Constantinople and sent her home to Georgia so I couldn't have her? A most irritating memory. As is his trying opposition in this war. Come now. Indulge me and you'll have your bath. Indulge me," he went on in a placating murmur, "and I may not kill your lover right away."

Her instant alarm brought a knowing smile to his lips; a cunning man, he'd survived the scramble for power in the sultan's army by understanding human weakness better than most. "If you cooperate I may let him live—for a time."

Her hands came up to undo the small buttons at the neckline of her nightgown, a faint tremble in her fingers the only indication of her dismay. Her gaze was unflinching, her posture straight and tall; she was stronger than most of the women he'd captured or purchased, and that strength intrigued him. What an indomitable woman with which to begin rebuilding his harem, he thought. A woman like her could give him many fine sons. He'd have to thank Pasha Bey before he killed him.

In utter silence she unfastened the small pearl buttons at her neckline and cuffs, slid the fine linen off her shoulders, down her arms, and let the nightgown fall to the carpeted floor. Stepping over it, she kicked it aside, gazed up at Hussein Djeritl, and said, "I could use a bath now."

He chuckled. "A woman of mettle. I look forward to the challenge. You shall have your bath and then we'll meet in my bed and see who will ultimately prevail." His gaze slowly traveled down her body and then up, coming to rest on the plump fullness of her breasts. "Men will envy me after tonight, my English Beatrix. If you please me in bed as much as you please my senses, I may take you as one of my wives."

"I killed my first husband."

"You'll not kill me." He didn't hesitate at her comment or his reply. Hussein Djeritl was insensible to death after a lifetime of war. And so utterly ruthless he feared no one. He spoke three gruff Turkic words and a servant materialized from the depths of the tent. "I'll see you after your bath," he pleasantly said, as though she'd not threatened him. "If you require anything, Jamil speaks French." He rose and stepped down from the dais.

She stiffened at his approach.

"Ah, a modicum of fear after all." He brushed a fingertip over one nipple and she stepped away. He didn't speak, but he followed her that half step and, taking the nipple between his thumb and forefinger, squeezed it until a small suffocated gasp escaped her. "There now," he whispered, releasing the stinging crest. "Just so we understand who's in charge here." With a nod of his head, he beckoned his servant forward, speaking to him in a low temperate tone. Then he addressed her once more. "If you'd follow Jamil, he'll see that you have all you desire," he pleasantly

said. And he walked away, moving toward the entrance
to the tent, calling out a name.

Reaching down, Trixi quickly snatched up the cloak
and slipped it around her shoulders before following
the servant who waited for her, his gaze dispassionate.
Her heart was beating in double time. She understood
Hussein Djeritl wasn't a man who could be put off or
cajoled or placated, and she had only a brief interval
before she would be placed in his bed.

But much worse than what might transpire there
was his threat to Pasha's life. Could she do anything to
save him or thwart the execution of Djeritl's plans?
With that stark horror prevalent in her mind, she followed the servant through an opening into an adjacent
room as resplendent as the one she left.

"Please, madame," Jamil offered, showing her to a
silk-covered chaise. "Your bath will be brought in.
Would you like any refreshments?"

She shouldn't be hungry in a crisis like this. How
could anyone of principle think of food at such a time?
But a few dates and a drink of water hardly satisfied a
day's hunger. "I'd appreciate something to eat, please,"
she replied. "Anything at all."

"The general's commissary is extensive. You have
but to express your wishes."

"Then I would like beef and potatoes. With a cup of
chocolate."

Jamil contained his astonishment with difficulty.
The lady didn't have a ladylike appetite; Hussein's
harem preferred sweetmeats and sorbets. Bowing himself out, he left to see to the lady's bath and odd menu.

Trixi surveyed the silken chamber from the chaise for
a moment and then rose to more closely search the
premises. It was an antechamber of some kind, luxurious but small, the furniture consisting of the chaise, a
chair, and a low table. A hookah sat on the table, re-

splendent in gold. She'd once seen such an instrument in an illustrated book of travel in the East. Three covered doorways were draped with red silk. The first she'd come through, the second Jamil had exited through. She moved toward the third one and gently lifted one corner of the silk drape.

The back of an armed guard came into view at very close range, and past him an enormous divan strewn with pillows. Hussein's bedchamber, she surmised, dropping the drapery. Would the guard remain later, when she was scheduled to become Hussein's entertainment? If crying would have done the smallest bit of good, she would have readily broken into a torrent of tears.

This is too much, she dismally thought, falling onto the chaise in despair. How was she equipped to deal with this awful crisis? Worse, how was she ever going to find a way to warn Pasha or help him or save him from Hussein's ruthless plans? Would it be possible to actually kill Hussein, make her way past the armed guard, find a pathway through the labyrinth of the tented city, retrace the route back to Nauplia? How impossible each stage of that wishful scenario, the entirety beyond even a miracle.

But in the next second she reminded herself that she was alive. Pasha was still alive. And the very worst she had to consider at the moment was sharing Hussein's bed. She wouldn't die from having intercourse with Hussein. That was survivable. And if even a remote possibility existed that she could somehow warn Pasha of his danger, she must remain alert for that possibility.

So . . . a bath first. Or eat first. The need for food was more pressing than the bath, if she hoped to remain vital. She should have asked for more, she thought, deciding she needed all the strength she could muster to get through a night with the Turkish general.

It helped, she found, to silently discuss the alternatives as if another person were bolstering her nerve. Pushing herself upright, she straightened the cloak around her and looked about with a more resolute gaze. How long could she take to eat and bathe? she wondered. Would it be possible to linger over each activity for a lengthy time? She was of a mind to try, at least.

When the servant returned, he brought a tray of sweets and a bowl of sorbets. "Your beef will take some time to prepare," he politely explained. "In the interval, the chef thought you might like some savories. Your bath will be brought in shortly."

"I prefer eating first. Bring my bath after dinner." She wished she had a timepiece, but delay was delay even if she couldn't precisely define it. The sweets were tempting, small cakes and candies, glazed dates and figs, a small carafe of liquor in the center of the arrangement. A chased gold cup with which to drink the saffron-colored liquor. The colorful sorbets in delicate white porcelain dishes lay atop a mound of shaved ice. Ice in the heat of summer, in the midst of an armed camp. Hussein traveled in style.

With his harem as well, she recalled, or at least until recently. The comforts of home at the front. A role she was to single-handedly fill tonight. On that daunting note, she reached for the carafe of liquor. Perhaps a drink would blunt the harsh edges of her coming ordeal.

The scented liquor tasted of peaches, its fragrance augmented by a flower perfume she didn't recognize. But it was sweet to the palate, slightly chilled, and it almost instantly soothed her nerves. A small heat warmed her. The weight of the wool cloak on her skin suddenly pronounced, she unwrapped the doubled folds of material slightly to allow a modest circulation of air. The sorbet looked enticing, she decided, reaching for a dish filled with pink ice.

Jamil dropped the drapery back in place, his mission accomplished. The woman had drunk some of the nectar. The general would be pleased. Soon she'd need a lighter robe.

Her first impulse on seeing Jamil enter with the magenta silk robe was constraint. She was fine, she said, thank you, no, her cloak was adequate. He didn't argue; no servant of Hussein's ever contemplated such a breach of etiquette.

But he left the silk robe.

The sorbet was delicious, pomegranate ice, soothing and cool. She loosened the wool cloak slightly more and reached for a jellied sweet coated with sugar. Why wouldn't she be hungry after almost a day without food, she reflected, plucking a small iced cake from the platter. It was filled with almond paste, a favorite of hers. She ate two more. Which required another drink of the chilled liquor.

Shortly after the silky liquor slid down her throat, the magenta robe took on a more demanding presence in her consciousness. Light and diaphanous, with loose sleeves and delicate gem-encrusted closures, it lay beside her on the chaise—close enough to touch.

It wouldn't hurt to touch it—would it? Considering the very real peril she was in, a silk robe was the least of her worries. The fabric was lush, almost sensual, the word disturbing even as it came to her. She pushed the robe away.

But her appetite was acute, as was her thirst, and she continued to assuage them with the refreshments before her. Her anxiety dissipated, melted away, her surroundings no longer seemed ominous. Perhaps it was the succulent sweets, the lush richness of the interior

that made her forget she was in an armed camp at war.
Perhaps nourishment and drink were consoling comforts.

Whatever the reasons, she welcomed the tranquility.
If she were to face the general soon, surely this prelude
was more agreeable than terror. With each sweet consumed, images from her former world dimmed, and all
memory of the past seemed to drift further away.

When Jamil brought in her dinner, she ate it all, her
appetite undiminished. The chocolate was exquisite,
silken dark splendor, and at the end, she drank another
small cup of the chilled peach nectar.

She was visibly sweating at this point, the heavy
cloak a burden, and when her bath was brought in, the
water lured her senses. The servants carrying the filled
cloisonné bath departed once the tub was placed in the
center of the room, as did Jamil.

She glanced around and, finding herself alone, shed
the heavy cloak with relief. She tested the water with
her fingers, found it wonderfully tepid—perfect, as if
someone understood how heated her body was. Feeling
oddly dissolute that she should be so looking forward
to a cooling bath under the grievous circumstances, she
stepped into the tub and as if mesmerized slid into the
water. Attar of roses wafted into her nostrils, the
scented oil lying in droplets on the surface of the water.
A single drop glistened on her upper arm and she
rubbed the sleek oil with her fingertips.

Her skin tingled briefly and then felt blissfully
warm, charged with sensation as if it were glowing
inside. How curiously enticing that she could be cool
and yet warm, serene yet infused with excitement, how
the noise from outside had faded away and only the
silk-hung tent, silent and perfumed, surrounded her.

Lying back against the resplendent cloisonné depic-
tion of a desert hunting scene, she shut her eyes. The

fragrant water enfolded her, and the boundary between reality and dream blurred.

She heard voices from a great distance, several, too many to decipher, and her lashes languidly lifted for a fraction of a second before they dropped shut once again. A new scent invaded her nostrils, faintly acrid, pungent, unfamiliar. But she felt too relaxed to force her mind into logical deduction; it was much easier to do nothing.

Hussein Djeritl, kneeling beside the bath, smiled. Without turning his head, he spoke in a low tone to Jamil; Jamil, in turn, spoke to the servants who had come in with Hussein. They placed the objects they held on the low table and left the chamber. "Stay," Hussein said to the slender young man who was more adjunct than servant. "I'll need your help."

"You'll find her pleasing, master. She's a woman of appetites."

"She drank the peach nectar?"

"As you see, master," Jamil answered with a faint smile. "The heat is coursing through her."

Hussein's dark gaze grew speculative as he surveyed Trixi. "How much did she drink?"

"The whole carafe, master."

Momentarily startled, Hussein glanced at Jamil. "All of it?"

Jamil smiled again. "In spite of that heavy wool cloak. The opium and mandrake will see that she's eager for three thousand thrusts, master."

"We must see that she's well used then." Hussein rose, his arousal blatant in the form-fitting cavalry breeches. "Cancel my meetings for two days."

"Should the Frank come for his woman during that interval?"

"Cage him until I'm done. I'll bring her out to see him before he dies."

"Gratifying sport, effendi."

"But not on a par with this," Hussein softly said, beginning to unbutton his breeches. "Bring me a robe."

When Jamil returned moments later, having left instructions with Hussein's staff, Hussein had already discarded his western uniform. He slipped his arms into the colorful silk caftan Jamil held for him. "Light my hookah," he ordered, moving toward the divan. "We can set a leisurely pace tonight, with no new campaigns until supplies reach us from Crete. Dry her and bring her over here." Dropping into a comfortable sprawl on the silk divan, he reached for his hookah, raised the gold-tipped tube to his mouth, and inhaled deeply.

Jamil lifted Trixi from the water and placed her on the plush carpet. As he toweled her dry, she stood docile, flushed, her mind operating within a warm, opalescent haze. And yet every tactile impression, every movement was taking on a sensual glow, a heated glory of wanting, and images of Pasha saturated her mind.

"She seems ready," Hussein observed.

"The poppy brings relaxation and dreams, the mandrake visions. She's feeling the bliss."

"Soon she'll be feeling something more," Hussein sportively murmured. "Do English women have orgasms, or are they too cold in that country with no sun?"

"With the amount of mandrake she ingested, this one will."

He reached for a jar from the silver tray. When he opened the container of ambergris and musk, the pungent fragrance seemed to color the air.

Trixi's nostrils flared, the aromatic vapors redolent of heated passion, and she inhaled deeply, recalling tantalizing memory, sweet desire, lush, torrid sex with Pasha.

When her legs were eased apart and the first dollop of perfumed unguent slid over her mons, the stroke was so light, Trixi felt only the mildest of sensations like a flutter of wings. The touch instantly transmuted the incipient throbbing within her to a new captivating level. But when those smooth, silken strokes invaded her vagina, fierce, uncurbed lust struck her like a blow, and she groaned deep in her throat. The coolness bathed her hot, pulsing tissue in a drenching decadence, the exquisite chill was piquant bewitchment to her heated body. Wanting more, she took a step forward as though reaching for the tempting pleasure, but unsteady under the influence of the drugs, she stumbled.

Jamil swiftly caught her, bracing his shoulder against the curve of her hip.

"She's roused to fever pitch, effendi," Jamil murmured.

"Then we must entertain her, must we not," Hussein softly replied. "Ease that burning hot cunt. Give her one of those." He gestured toward the sex toys on the tray and drew in another draught of hashish smoke. "Have you ever had an Englishwoman?" he casually asked.

"Once in a Paris brothel," Jamil replied, selecting an object from the tray.

The shocking words *Paris brothel* registered in Trixi's consciousness, but a second later they disappeared into the nebulous warm cloud that surrounded her. She made an effort to open her eyes but her lashes seemed extravagantly heavy and the transient impulse vanished into the same golden haze. Her feverish senses seethed and simmered, a frantic pulsing centered in the liquid core of her body, a wild driving need for consummation overwhelmed her brain. "Pasha," she whispered, needy, yearning, carnal passion synonymous with his name.

Jamil glanced at his master. "She speaks of him."

Hussein shrugged. "She'll accept anyone. Bring her here," he said, indicating the table before him.

Lifting her into his arms, Jamil carried Trixi the few steps to the table and placed her on its polished length.

"Can she hear me with so much liquor?"

"If you speak slowly."

"Spread . . . your . . . legs . . . my dear." Hussein gently nudged her thighs apart and obedient, she complied. She writhed at the feverish need coursing through her vagina, lifted her hips, searching for surcease, and the liquified ambergris undulated within her like a tidal wave, further goading her lascivious flesh. A cry of longing escaped her.

"She's becoming impatient, Jamil. See if that new machine will temporarily quench her desires."

The turquoise-colored apparatus was made of lustrous Florentine leather, the dildo and attached gold buckled harness tinkling as Jamil moved toward her. The size of the leather device required introduction by slow degrees and even feverishly aroused and well lubricated, she stirred fitfully under the delicate thrusts. By the time the enormous shaft was partially lodged, she was whimpering, her tissue stretched taut.

Pressing the shaft home, Jamil stroked, pushed, massaged, penetrated a small distance at a time until the last invading portion of turquoise leather disappeared inside her. Completely glutted, throbbing so pervasively the feverish ache stretched through her entire body, insensible to all but images of Pasha and a voracious sexual craving, Trixi was so near orgasm she could scarcely breathe.

"Now," Hussein quietly commanded, watching her with a sharpened concentration.

Jamil exerted a delicate pressure and Trixi gasped, agonizing pleasure tearing through her senses. She screamed as her climax broke, her cry swelling, rising, lasting, lasting, the drugs inducing a feverish level of raw, unbridled feeling. Her orgasm was so prolonged, Hussein abruptly reached for the bottle of cantharides and swallowed a double dose.

"She's undeniably a woman of sexual appetites," he murmured. "But then I should have known, with Pasha Bey having her service him." Reaching for his pipe and inhaling, he debated what pleasures his newest acquisition held in store for him. Then exhaling, he lazily commanded, "Have her walk before me so I can admire the pale English beauty from all sides."

"She may not be able to walk, master, with this huge instrument inside her."

A slow, salacious smile formed on the general's mouth. "Why don't we see."

Jamil clasped the turquoise leather belt around Trixi's waist as she lay in an incandescence of carnal lust, the aphrodisiacs coursing through her blood, voracious desire still raging in every pulsing nerve and cell and tissue. When Jamil slipped two straps into fasteners, front and back, she shifted at the slight movement inside her. But moments later, she drew in a gasping inhalation as he tugged the first buckle tight, forcing the dildo deeper, the padded collar at the base squeezing her engorged vulva and clitoris. After the second clasp was firmly buckled, the pressure intensified, the friction on her clitoris so sensational she instantly climaxed again in a long, shuddering orgasm.

Hussein shook another dose of cantharides into his palm. Indeed, three thousand thrusts *might* be required before the Englishwoman was sated.

Jamil wiped Trixi's heated body with a damp perfumed cloth, offered her a drink to cool her, made her comfortable with pillows under her head. "When she's somewhat more calm," Hussein directed, "set her on her feet. I want to see her promenade in her pretty harness."

After a moderate interval, Hussein had Jamil lift Trixi to her feet. But even the slightest movement stirred the dildo inside her, stimulated her overstimulated flesh, rendered her immobile, and standing utterly still, eyes shut and panting, she shivered under the heated delirium flaring through her senses.

But Hussein motioned for her to walk and Jamil gently tugged on her hands. Submissive under the effects of the drugs, she took a step and instantly reeled from the shocking pressure of the tightly fastened dildo. Catching her around her waist as she fell, Jamil carried her back and placed her beside the general. "We'll have to let her rest for a longer time," Hussein noted, caressing her plump breast, gratified by her wanton passions. "After an hour or so, she'll feel less agitated. Pour us some wine, Jamil, while we wait and tell me, how long do you think it will be before Pasha Bey is captured?"

12

Pasha stood arrested in the doorway of Hussein's tented bedchamber, Jamil's blood on his dagger, his breath momentarily in abeyance. Could you kill someone more than once? he wondered, watching the man and woman on the divan. His need for vengeance was so great, he forgot he had only seconds to accomplish what he'd come to do. He put his hand out, to restrain Makriyannis, who was about to move forward.

His blood-lust was so acute, he could taste it.

His hand came up, fingers spread.

Makriyannis pushed it down, shook his head, and held up one finger.

Fuck you, Pasha mouthed. The silence in the tented chamber was broken only by the sounds of carnal arousal, a woman's soft moaning, the harsher breathing of Hussein.

Damn her.

Damn him.

Damn the whole world of shameless cunts.

He'd cut off Hussein's balls first, Pasha vowed, silently moving forward. And if there was time, he'd watch him bleed to death. But Makriyannis was thinking with more than his gonads and his dagger sailed through the air past Pasha, striking its target with precision a flashing millisecond later. Hussein fell forward with a muffled gurgle, the dagger blade piercing his neck and throat.

"I'm not dying for him," Makriyannis whispered, racing forward to execute a coup de grace with his yataghan. Pasha dove to cover Trixi's mouth with his hand, her eyes wide, frantic, patently unfocused.

Already wrapping her in the sheet, Pasha forced a portion of the fabric in her mouth. She was obviously drugged, in an unstable state, her eyes vacant. Pulling a cord from his pocket, he tied the gag in place. They had five hundred yards of armed camp to traverse in complete silence; he couldn't take any chances. His mind was clear again, his judgment restored.

Makriyannis rolled Hussein's head in the magenta robe and, slinging it over his shoulder, pointed at the door with his yataghan.[17] Pasha nodded, his dagger between his teeth, Trixi in his arms. Both men carried loaded pistols.[18]

The dead guards in the antechamber lay where they died; the two outside guards had been dragged into the tent out of sight, the men's throats slit in a silent death. Dressed as Turkish noncommissioned officers— their apparel requisitioned from two of Hussein's sentry posts—Pasha and Makriyannis hoped to make their way back through the city of tents, past the campfires that blazed in the night.

The first two hundred yards they passed unmolested, the men walking at a stroll through the shadowed passages between the tents, careful not to call attention to themselves by undue speed. Most of the army slept at that time of night. They skirted a soldier relieving himself outside his tent and avoided another drunkenly weaving his way back to his quarters. But as they moved into the sector adjacent to their escape route, they came within sight of a group of soldiers sitting around a fire drinking.

The sea was to their right, the armed camp to their left. They had no choice but to continue forward. Makriyannis moved between Pasha and the fire, hoping to shield Trixi. Both men checked to see that their weapons were primed.

When they came within twenty feet of the firelit scene, one of the soldiers called out to them, the man's voice thick with drink. "Is that a lady I see?" he shouted, adding a ribald comment on ladies of the night.

"We're taking her to our sentry company," Makriyannis blandly replied in an Alexandrian dialect.

"I was born in Alexandria, too." The Egyptian soldier jumped to his feet, striding toward them, and moments later he was hugging Makriyannis like a long-lost brother. Offering him a drink from his cup, he spoke in the inebriated fulsome tones of an intimate. "Come, come, join us . . . bring the lady. We've plenty of rum. Rumor has it Hussein won't be moving for days, so we've plenty of time."

He didn't know how true his words were, and although Makriyannis tried to beg off, each of his excuses was resisted with the single-minded purpose of a man well into his cups. Once the soldier's companions joined in the chorus of invitation, Pasha and Makriyannis had little choice but to join them.

Pasha had slid his knife and pistol out of sight when the soldier first approached, but his weapons were at the ready beneath the draped sheet enfolding Trixi. Both men approached the firelit group with caution.

"Just one drink," Makriyannis declared, taking the bottle offered him and sitting down. "We have to go on first patrol in the morning."

"Leave the lady with us, then," a sprawled soldier replied, leering. "We'll see that she's well taken care of."

"Sorry, we paid too much for her," Makriyannis genially replied. "She represents all our booty from Choura, so she comes with us."[19]

"But there's only two of you and four of us," another drunken trooper crudely threatened, patting his hip where his sword should have been.

The lack had already been noted by Pasha and Makriyannis. None of the men were armed, their muskets stacked beside the tent; the surrounding tents stood silent, without campfires. "Let's not argue over a woman," Makriyannis jovially remarked, "when there's plenty of rum. When do you think we can finally finish this damned war?" he went on, passing the bottle to the man beside him. And the conversation turned to the quick and speedy subjugation of Greece.

Positioning himself in the shadows beyond the glow of the fire, Pasha sat with Trixi on his lap, her face against his chest. That she was gagged didn't pique their interest; women were a commodity to be bought and sold in their culture.

The rum bottle made the rounds several more times. A fifth man wandered out from the labyrinth of passageways between tents and joined them, lengthening their odds.

With the possibility that the slaughter in Hussein's tent might be discovered at any moment, Pasha carefully kept watch on the moon moving across the sky, his tension rising with each quashing of Makriyannis's attempts to leave. After what seemed an interminable time, unable to endure any further delay, Pasha abruptly rose and said in Turkic, "I'm taking the lady to my quarters."

"That's not very friendly," one of the men replied in broken Turkish.

"But then I'm not in a friendly mood," Pasha softly growled.

"If we don't show up for patrol," Makriyannis interjected, quickly coming to his feet, "they'll give us the lash. Thanks for the rum."

"I want a turn with the cunt," a brawny soldier muttered, beginning to rise, drunken menace in his tone.

"I don't share," Pasha calmly said, moving back a step.

"Maybe you don't have a choice," the contentious soldier snarled, standing unsteadily.

"I always have choices," Pasha murmured, his finger resting on his pistol trigger.

A tense silence fell, hostility palpable.

"We want the woman—right?" Pasha's opponent surveyed his compatriots, his gaze flickering over his friends, poised now in varying states of readiness.

"Why not?" one of the soldiers agreed. "We deserve some booty, too."

"Come and get the woman tomorrow when we're done with her," Makriyannis proposed. "Our sentry post is just over that hill." He indicated the closest rise.

"I don't want to wait," the brawny soldier brusquely retorted. "We'll keep her tonight and *you* can come and get her in the morning." He pulled a dagger from his boot. "What do you think of that?" he challenged, touching the tip of his blade with his finger.

"Not much," Pasha softly said. "You've two seconds to change your mind."

The man lunged.

Pasha fired, flame burning through the draped sheet concealing his pistol, a neat hole tinged with powder burns appearing in the man's forehead. The Egyptian soldier hung in space for a split second, his arms flung out, his eyes wide with shock.

Makriyannis had already discharged his firearm into the man on his right, and whipping his pistol around he shot the man on his left. His weapon empty, he reached for his yataghan. Pasha's pistol blazed again, taking down a fourth soldier racing for his musket. The fifth man, deciding no woman was worth his life, ran. Pasha and Makriyannis exchanged a considering glance, but before the decision had to be made whether to pursue and silence the fleeing soldier, a trumpet blast blared out across the hills running down to the sea, echoing over the sleeping camp—a shrill, piercing call to arms.

The men recognized the alarm signal and instantly broke into a run. Hussein had been found. Racing alongside Pasha, Makriyannis reloaded his pistol, tipping two percussion caps into the chamber with a much-practiced deftness.

"If I'm hit, take Trixi out of here," Pasha cried, sprinting over the rough ground. Soldiers were spilling out of the tents, half-dressed, groggy, their weapons in their hands.

"We're all getting out," Makriyannis muttered, sliding his loaded weapon into his belt. "Two hundred yards more and we're safe." He put his hand out for Pasha's pistol.

"I don't want her taken again." Pasha panted, Trixi's weight telling at a sprint. The crest of the next hill was their goal, Demetrius hidden there with their horses.

"Don't worry. One of us . . . will get her out," Makriyannis puffed, quickly reloading Pasha's pistol and tossing it back. "Oh, fuck," he muttered a second later. "Watch out."

A Turkish officer had careened out of the shadows. "Stop!" he cried, holding up his hand, his gaze raking the men, a look of astonishment coming over his face when he caught sight of Trixi's flowing blond hair. "The camp is under full security," he barked, striding toward them. "No one leaves." He was close enough now to see the gag in Trixi's mouth, the insignia of Hussein's rank embroidered on the sheet wrapping her. His mouth set in a grim line and he reached for his sword. "Don't move," he commanded, drawing his weapon out, looking away for a split second to call for help.

His shout died in his throat, Makriyannis's yataghan slicing through to his spinal column. "Run!" Makriyannis cried, jerking his sword from the man's spine. Shifting Trixi's weight onto one arm in a blur of motion, Pasha whipped the dagger from his teeth and threw it with a slashing downstroke at a man roaring out of the shadows of the tent, burying his blade in the man's heart. For a moment he debated going back for his dagger, the weapon having served him well, but saner counsel deterred him. He'd lose it tonight gladly if they got out of this camp alive.

Turning, they raced for the crest of the hill. With fifty yards to go, the outcry behind them rose to the sky. "Greeks! Greeks! Kill them!"

Seconds later a shot skimmed by, then another and another, their pursuers in full cry. The moon was partially obscured by clouds, they were moving fast, and the sultan's troops weren't marksmen, advantages to the two men racing up the hill. But perhaps still not sufficient advantage with an armed camp behind them in hot pursuit. Pasha was already making contingency plans—wondering if they could conceal themselves rather than flee. Then a rifle report cracked above their head; a scream quickly followed. A second and third shot, then several more exploded in the pale moonlight, striking home, agonized shrieks behind them evidence of Demetrius's superb marksmanship.

Twenty yards to go now . . . Ten . . . Both men were conscious of the critical distance and every crucial second. Six more rounds in quick succession discharged over their heads, taking a toll on their pursuers, an immediate barrage of conflicting orders breaking out in their wake. Most in Hussein's army were unwilling to face lethal gunfire.

Pasha's mouth curved in a faint smile; the Turkish soldiers' lack of courage was advantageous. "While they're arguing," he gasped, "we'll get the fuck out."

"They don't take . . . the offensive . . . well," Makriyannis cheerfully panted.

Seconds later they reached the top of the hill where Demetrius was speedily reloading one of three rifles laid out on a limestone ledge.

"I'll stay and slow them down for another few rounds," Demetrius offered, calmly sighting in on a soldier racing up the hill.

"I'll stay . . . with you," Makriyannis breathlessly replied. "As soon . . . as I see Pasha and his woman off."

"There are too many to hold off," Pasha warned.

"Just a few more rounds to change their minds about pursuit and we're off," Makriyannis replied, gathering the reins for Pasha's horse.

Pasha was up and mounted a second later despite Trixi's added weight. With shots ringing out around them, he pulled the gag from her mouth and took the reins from Makriyannis.

"Ride!" Makriyannis shouted, slapping the black's rump.

But Pasha's barb didn't move, recognizing only his master's commands. "I'm not leaving you here," Pasha shouted above the din, pulling a rifle from his saddle scabbard.

"Demetrius!" Makriyannis cried, understanding Pasha's partisan feelings. They'd fought back-to-back too long.

Seconds later the small troop galloped away through

a rain of gunfire, lashing their horses to speed, melting into the shadowed night within moments. They stopped briefly over the next rise to assess the damage, but no one had been seriously hit and, well acquainted with the countryside, they were soon on a little-used trail to Leondari and freedom.

They rode fast for nearly two hours, needing to put distance between themselves and Navarino. The repercussions of Hussein's death would be far-reaching, pursuit a dead certainty. Still in a deep sleep, Trixi was oblivious to the grueling pace until, a few miles short of Leondari, her lashes fluttered open slowly as though she knew she was safely in Pasha's arms. The air was cool on her face and gazing up, she saw a canopy of brilliant stars. "We're in the mountains," she murmured, smiling up at Pasha, her eyes still heavy-lidded. "You found me."

"Not soon enough." His voice was low, gruff.

"Are we safe? Is Chris safe?" She was still dazed, so the distaste in his tone eluded her. But her instincts as a horsewoman were intuitive; she could tell they were riding fast.

"We will be soon. We'll be coming into Leondari in a few miles. Chris is with Jules in Nauplia and well."

Pulling aside the sheet that held her, she slipped her arms around his neck. "How nice to hear that everyone is safe. How wonderful to have you back."

Jerking the sheet up again, he covered her exposed shoulders, the curve of her breast. "You're going to get cold," he muttered, constraint in every word.

"Why am I wrapped in this?" She slid her hand from his shoulder, plucking at the embroidered silk sheet.

"It was handy. We left in a hurry."

"We?"

"Makriyannis came with me."

"Was I at Navarino?" Her memory still clouded, she spoke hesitantly.

"With Hussein Djeritl," Pasha curtly muttered.

"Now I remember." She paused as if clarifying that memory. "He wore a French cavalry uniform."

"Not when I saw him."

She gazed up at him, query in her eyes; his words had been muffled, indistinct.

"He views himself as another Napoleon," he remarked, not about to reveal his anger before an audience. "We're almost at Leondari. We'll stay there tonight." He turned to Makriyannis, riding beside him. "I'll meet you in Nauplia tomorrow. We're stopping at Grivas's."

"Sure you don't want company?" his friend inquired, concerned with the undercurrent of violence in Pasha's voice.

"No."

"We have his head if it's any consolation," Makriyannis quietly said, understanding Pasha's resentment.

Pasha shrugged. "Maybe in a thousand years."

There was nothing more to be said, no condolence or sympathy that would change what they'd seen. No words that could erase the dishonor.

Trixi had fallen back to sleep, weariness and fatigue augmenting the drugs she'd been given. And the men rode through the night without speaking, parting at the outskirts of Leondari where the road to Nauplia turned east.

Pasha had been through the city on numerous occasions in the past four years, and when he rode into the courtyard of Grivas's inn, the stable boys recognized the wealthy Frank and his splendid black. Crowding around him, they held his horse while he dismounted with the woman, and before Pasha could carry Trixi more than a few steps, the landlord came out of the door. "Welcome, Pasha Bey! I hear you've found some fine booty in this war." He gazed at Trixi, his glance sweeping over her with discernment, taking note of the embroidered insignia on the silk sheet. "Hussein Djeritl gave you another of his harem, I see," he jovially said. "I thought you cleaned him out last time."

"I left one behind."

"She's worth going back for, I'd say. You'll want my best room for her."

"Yes, and bathwater for us both, immediately," Pasha brusquely said, his expression shuttered.

"Something to eat as well?" the landlord inquired, although his voice had altered. The wealthy Frank who fought with Makriyannis didn't have the look of a man celebrating his good fortune. Moody, too quiet, his impatience showing. "Right this way," Grivas quickly offered. "I'll see you to your rooms."

Pasha Bey hardly spoke, the innkeeper later told his wife, and the woman he carried in his arms had been drugged. She slept too deeply. Had Pasha Bey drugged her? Or Hussein Djeritl? There were drops of blood on the sheet, he went on, lowering his voice. They'd best not inquire too closely into their newest guest's business. Although in wartime, such prudence always prevailed.

Bathwater was carried in, two tubs set up; servants brought up food and arranged it on a small table, the activities overseen by a silent Pasha. The lady still dozed on the bed.

"Thank you," Pasha politely said when all was in place, showing the landlord out last, offering him a generous gratuity. "I don't wish to be disturbed tonight. Under any circumstances." The emphasis on the last words was unutterably clear.

"Of course, sir." The landlord cast a last glance at Trixi. "I understand."

"Good."

That single word was so emotionless and cold, the landlord mentioned with a small shudder, detailing Pasha's last instructions to his wife. It might be safer if they slept above the stables tonight.

The moment the door closed on the landlord, Pasha walked over to the table laden with food and drink, picked up a bottle of ouzo, pulled out the cork, and poured half the contents down his throat. After that precipitate dose of narcotic, he pulled a chair into the center of the room where he'd have an unobstructed view of the bed, dropped into it, and proceeded to systematically empty the bottle, his rage and temper becoming more implacable with each drink—tortured memory, despicable images, betrayal, and dishonor a bitter poison in his brain. Two bottles soon lay on the floor beside the chair, a third rested on his chest, his sprawled pose incongruously taut, as if he were waiting for an enemy attack.

Midway through the third bottle, Trixi came awake with a start. Abruptly sitting up, startled, she quickly glanced around, fear prominent in her eyes. At the sight of Pasha, she visibly sighed, fell back on the bed, and shut her eyes again.

Another few minutes passed, punctuated only with the occasional gurgling sound of liquor flowing from the bottle into Pasha's mouth. When she opened her eyes again, she stared at the ceiling, her mind at ease, recognizing the room, the fact that Pasha was near. Pushing herself up on one elbow, she sleepily inquired, "Have I slept long?"

"The critical question," he murmured, his voice flat and low, condemnation in his gaze.

Her lashes rose at his response, her violet eyes suddenly attentive. "Is something wrong?"

"Several things, I'd say." His eyes narrowed as he took in her tousled, golden hair and rosy cheeks, her buxom nakedness barely concealed by the sheet. "A great multitude of things."

Following his brutal gaze, she looked down and realized she was nude beneath her silken wrap. Wide-eyed, she gazed at him. "Where did you find me like this?"

"In Hussein Djeritl's bed." Ill-temper in his eyes and voice, in every lounging inch of his body.

"No!"

"Yes. You were having a very good time," he churlishly added.

A chill ran through her. "Are you sure?"

He didn't answer for a long time, his jaw clenched tight, a tick fluttering over his cheekbone, his eyes like ice. "I'm real sure," he murmured, his grasp on the liquor bottle tightening.

"I get the impression," she slowly said, "you perceive those circumstances as *my* fault."

His dark brow quirked in mocking rebuttal. "Let's just say you weren't complaining."

He seemed so certain, so caustically sure; how could she disclaim it? "I don't remember anything," she said. "*Nothing* at all. How can that be?"

"It can be damned convenient, I'd say." He lifted the bottle to his mouth, his gaze pitiless. "Unfortunately I recall your moans of pleasure—vividly."

"Impossible!" She sat upright, clutching the sheet to her throat, the thought sending a shudder down her spine. "You're lying. He never touched me!"

"He touched you, my little bitch-in-heat," Pasha growled, each word acrid with censure, "every way a man can touch a woman."

She went still. Her eyes wouldn't meet his for a moment, the scenario he intimated too excruciating to conceive. "Could you have been mistaken?" she whispered.

"No mistake, Lady Grosvenor," he brutally returned, lifting the bottle to her in mocking disdain.

"The food must have been drugged." She shook her head as if trying to clear her mind. "The peach nectar . . . tasted odd. Like a strange perfumed—"

"But you drank it." Condemnation in every word.

"I didn't know. I hadn't eaten or drunk all day. How was I supposed to know?" She felt shamed and defiled, mortified.

"Fine. You didn't know," he disgustedly retorted. "Let's just say it was all a fucking dream. Now if you'll just wash his come off you, we can end this discussion. Get into the tub."

"How dare you be angry at me." Her brows rose and she surveyed him, challenge in her gaze. "Are you accusing me of complicity?"

"Maybe you were just being sociable. We both know how friendly you can be," he acidly finished. "But we can argue the finer points of hospitality later. I'm tired. Let's get this over with. I want his come off you," he said in a low, savage murmur. "Either you do it or I will."

Her temper flared. "I'm not yours to command."

His mouth lifted in a tight, brutal smile. "If Hussein can have authority over you," he silkily breathed, "so can I."

"I am not arguing about this." She sat up straighter, lifting her chin defiantly. She'd come too far, both in spirit and distance, to take orders from any man. "Nor do I care to be the target of your cynical reproach."

He gently shook his head as if in disbelief. "Amazing. First convenient amnesia and now what? Outrage?" His voice went flat. "Just fucking get into the tub."

"While you saved me and I thank you," she said with stinging ire, "you don't own me. *No one* owns me."

"Hussein Djeritl owned every little inch of your flesh, Lady Grosvenor," he savagely growled. "Are you sore from that big gold dildo he was ramming up your cunt?"

"Stop!" she cried, horrified, shamed afresh by the humiliating image. Taking a deep calming breath, she spoke, her voice slightly shaking. "I don't know what Hussein did or didn't do." Another steadying breath was required to displace further contemplation of what vile things he may have done to her. "But I'm very grateful to be alive, and if your masculine sense of honor was somehow offended, I'm sorry. I wasn't a participant in whatever happened. I don't even *know* what happened." Her hand had turned white-knuckled as she clutched the sheet to her throat. "I have no memory of the events—none. And if a gold dildo was involved or anything else that gives you displeasure, listen to me," she said, leaning forward, her voice no more than a whisper, "fuck your righteous indignation. *I don't care!*"

"But I do," he ground out.

"Too damn bad." Each word was icy.

"For you," he brusquely muttered.

She gazed at him for a moment, at his scowling wrath and arrogant lounging pose. "Are you threatening me?"

"Just making you aware of my feelings."

"In that case, let me clarify the state of *my* feelings. You can go screw yourself."

"I've an alternative," he malevolently drawled.

"Just so long as it doesn't involve me."

"Sorry." He set the bottle down very gently, his motions that careful precision of three bottles imbibed.

"What are you doing?" Bristling with anger, she stared at him.

He looked up. "I'm putting these bottles under the chair."

"Why?" Contentious, accusatory, she was on the offensive.

"I'm very neat." He rose from the chair, a faint smile registering his uncharitable wit. "And then again I wouldn't want you to cut your feet on any glass." He wasn't smiling now, standing in the center of the room, still booted and spurred, his clothes bloody from the butchery in Hussein's tent, his eyes burning with affront. "Your bathwater is getting cold."

"Arrogant bastard. I don't want a bath." Offended, indignant, she retreated into the far corner of the bed.

"I'll help you," he said, as if she'd not spoken.

"Stay away from me."

"It's only a bath, not the guillotine."

"Then let it go." Each word was pronounced with stiletto precision.

"I wish I could. But I have this aversion to fucking someone through the last man's come."

"Will I be pure enough for you after a bath?" she insolently inquired.

"Clean enough, anyway. Let's not have undue expectations."

"You hypocrite," she snapped. "As if you're morally guiltless."

"This conversation is getting off track, darling," he silkily countered. "I just want you to take a bath so I can fuck you."

"How romantic. Do you get good results with that line?"

"You'll have to tell me sometime how you charm Turkish generals," he acerbically retorted, moving forward.

"Don't you dare touch me."

It was the worst possible thing to say to a man who'd

witnessed what he'd witnessed in Hussein Djeritl's tent. "I'll touch you where I wish, when I wish, as often as I wish," he said, his voice no more than a whisper.

Pressed against the headboard, she gauged the distance to the door as he approached and when he reached for her, she leaped from the bed. She'd almost reached the door when his fingers closed on her arm. "Don't be so foolish as to run again," he softly said. "It's only a fuck."

"You're as bad as Hussein." She tried to shake his hand away.

"Was," he corrected, his grip crushing as he turned her around. "Makriyannis has his head in his saddlebag."

"His head?" she whispered, shock widening her eyes.

He towered over her, his fingers like a vise on her arm. "His or ours—it was an easy choice."

"Oh, my God," she breathed.

"If you're feeling sorry for Hussein, consider he died happy, with his hand in your cunt."

"You're vicious," she bitterly accused.

"I saved your life."

She shut her eyes briefly, reality suddenly too harsh and uncompromising. Against the larger issues of life and death, her cavil and censure seemed woefully insignificant. Pasha had come through an army to save her, after all, undaunted by the insuperable odds against him. "What do you want me to do?" she said on a quiet exhalation of breath, no longer able to decipher good from bad, right from wrong, salvation from vengeance. "Just tell me and I'll do it." He was hating her for reasons she couldn't control, couldn't recall, and she was tired of fighting over issues that didn't make sense, that didn't matter in a country where people were dying every minute.

"I want you to take a bath."

"Fine." She shook his hand from her arm and turned away, walking toward the tub. A hush fell, the room suddenly alive with summer night sounds, the scent of oleander invading the air. Reaching the battered copper tub, she unwrapped the sheet, let it fall to the floor, and stepped into the water.

Pasha forgot for a moment that he was standing in a room in the mountains of Morea with war minutes, seconds away. Her lush form momentarily arrested time, his breathing stopped, and as he watched her, hatred for Hussein Djeritl rose like bile in his throat.

He flexed his fingers, jealousy choking him, the image on the divan playing over and over again in his mind, the possibility of a pregnancy too repulsive to consider.

"Tell me when I'm clean enough for you," she said, the acerbic edge back in her voice. Sainthood had always eluded her.

"When I can't smell him anymore," he coolly replied, beginning to unbutton his jacket. "I'll let you know."

She wouldn't look at him, washing herself with a concentration that shut out everything but the simple act of bathing. All else was too complicated and awful, rife with rancor, shame. A nightmare she didn't want to remember.

Stripped to his breeches, Pasha sat and drank, watching her, his fury barely under control because the exquisite nude woman before him was only recently under Hussein—the memory so cursed and foul, he wasn't sure he could contain his need for vengeance.

When she finished, he didn't move to help her from the tub. She shot him a glance as heated as his, stepped from the bath, reached for a towel, and dried herself. "Would you like a smell?" she rudely inquired, standing nude and resentful, not sure she could continue to be grateful against such overt rancor.

"Later. Get into bed." He could have been saying pistols at dawn, his voice was that chill.

"And if I don't?"

"I'll fuck you on the floor."

"I'd forgotten the full degree of your charm."

"Yours of course is always amenable to a man with a hard-on."

"I'm not going to apologize for being alive, if that's what you want," she said with a quiet defiance. "What should I have done? Killed myself to save your honor?"

There was no answer of course. Nor did he give one, save a deepening scowl.

"That's what I thought," she said, tossing her towel aside. "So while you sulk and carry on like some pure-as-a-virgin cleric"—her brows rose in sardonic mockery—"definitely a new role for you, I'm going to have something to eat. I'd appreciate it, though, if you'd bathe. You've blood on your hands," she coolly noted, moving toward the table.

Glancing down, Pasha saw the stains on his hands, and he remembered Hussein's severed head spraying blood, and then the image of the Turk's body poised over Trixi. He forcibly shook away the reprehensible picture in his mind. But a renewed anger infused his brain, so hot and wrathful it brought him to his feet in a surge of power that toppled the chair.

Spinning around at the explosive crash of chair and bottles, Trixi saw Pasha bearing down on her in great furious strides.

Backing away, she snatched up one of the liquor bottles on the table and raised it like a club. "Stay away from me," she cried.

He came to a sudden stop, the high-pitched tremor in her voice infiltrating his mindless rage.

Infiltrating but not assuaging.

"You don't really think that's going to stop me, do

you?" he scoffed. He lifted his hand negligently in the direction of the bottle.

"Whatever you want, you're not going to get," she heatedly replied.

"Perhaps we differ on that point."

"What are you going to do? Make me pay in some way for your damned resentment?"

"You seemed to like fucking Hussein so much," he retorted, outrage in every syllable, "I thought I'd fuck you until you can't move. And then I'll fuck you some more."

"Because I'm to blame," she murmured, bitterness dripping from every word.

"Something like that."

"And you're my judge and jury."

"You get the picture." Nothing was clear save the violence of his feelings. "What if you're pregnant by him? Have you thought of that?"

She turned white. She hadn't, not in the remotest part of her brain. But she couldn't change what had happened. Nor could she have stopped the abduction or any of the ensuing events—so what the hell did he want her to do, grovel basely at his feet? "Or I could be pregnant by you," she said instead, plain and cool and caustic as he.

"You bitch," he whispered so softly only his lips moved.

"Have we reached an impasse?" She cast him an oblique glance, rude and impudent.

"Get the fuck into bed." Curt, hard, uncompromising words.

In an abrupt, furious downswing, she struck the bottle on the table edge with such force shattered glass flew across the room. "Come and get me," she malevolently purred, holding up the jagged bottle neck, hotspur temper in her eyes.

"Jesus," he breathed, shocked out of his black rage by the incongruous image. He held his hands out in a propitiatory gesture. "Relax," he murmured, his voice deliberately calm. "Just relax now."

"I don't *feel* like relaxing," she caustically noted. "I wonder if it has something to do with being abducted *again* by some man who thinks he can make me a prisoner *again*." She spat the last word. "I wonder if being threatened with the same *ridiculous* masculine possessiveness I just escaped might make me *uninterested* in relaxing. Actually," she hotly declared, "I'm thinking about making *you* pay for offending me. Just for a bloody change of pace."

His mouth had begun twitching midway through her tirade and when she finished, he was smiling faintly, the malevolence vanished from his eyes. "Did I say something wrong?"

"How astute," she whispered, her gaze narrowed.

"And you don't think I should be angry."

"Not at me." Her weapon was still poised.

"And if I yield," he softly proposed, concerned she might actually attempt to use the lethal weapon and hurt herself, "will you put that down?"

"You must apologize." The words were softly put, but her tone was uncompromising.

"For what?" A flash of frustration illuminated his eyes.

"For insulting me."

"You were the one in bed with him." Willful, his jaw obstinately set, he glared at her.

"Apologize." As headstrong, she glared back.

"And if I do?" A mixture of moodiness and restraint was in his voice.

"I won't have to kill you," she sardonically replied.

His laughter erupted, a deep-throated guffaw that bent him over double, brought him staggering and chuckling to the bed, where he collapsed in a fit of muffled mirth.

"It wasn't *that* funny," she testily remarked, setting the broken bottle down with a twinge of embarrassment.

Lying on his back, he opened his arms wide and smiled at her. "Yes, it was. Come here."

"You still haven't apologized." She wasn't so easily appeased.

"Do I have to?"

She nodded.

He grimaced briefly. "It's that important?"

Her nostrils flared and she nodded again.

"Then I apologize," he quietly said, this man who had never apologized to a woman before, "for intent and misjudgment, for my rudeness." And Hussein's dead, he thought, his own partial indemnity for the muddied, violent disorder of his emotions. "Did I say it right?" he went on, his gaze traveling down the voluptuous, bewitching woman standing nude and barefoot amidst glistening glass shards.

"Yes, thank you." She required recompense for his slurs and aspersions. "I am what I am, you know. Take it or leave it."

"I'll take it," he said, not moving, not sure he'd answered properly, not completely sure any more of this woman who had threatened to kill him for his insults. But he had no intention of leaving her. None at all. "You probably shouldn't move with all that glass," he added, sitting up. "Let me lift you away."

She looked down, suddenly aware that she was standing naked in a bedchamber in an inn in Greece surrounded by broken glass, but more happy than sad, more pleased than angry, and all because of the man seated on the bed across the room smiling at her with a rare, tentative smile. "You're barefoot, too," she said as though all the recent turmoil had been about glass and bare feet.

"Don't worry," he murmured, sliding from the bed.

"Because you can walk on glass and I can't?" But the acid was gone from her voice this time.

"Because I can reach across that mess and pick you up," he prosaically replied.

"Oh." It was a very small sound.

"I don't have an agenda," he murmured, arms open, palms up, like a prisoner surrendering.

She looked at him for a moment, his strength and power in repose, his temper extinguished, the heat in his eyes bereft of animosity, just warmly tempting. "I haven't thanked you properly for rescuing me."

"You haven't thanked me at all." But he spoke very softly, the intimation that she could thank him if she cared to, hushed.

"You're too far away."

"Better?" he said a second later, having picked her up, and swung her over the shards. Holding her in his arms, he now viewed her with a sweetly quizzical look that had nothing to do with a war in Greece or male possession. That reminded her instead of a wickedly unbridled, indulgent young man she'd entertained in her bedroom at Burleigh House. "Damn, you're loveable," she whispered.

He grinned. "Does that mean I should bathe in a hurry?"

"Oh, yes."

When she asked, he said, "No, don't help me. That won't help at all," and he proceeded to wash swiftly in the now cool water.

She stood and waited, shifting impatiently from foot to foot like a child waiting for a prize until he finally said, grinning, "Come here." But he didn't let her in the tub. "This water has a hundred miles of dirt in it while you're squeaky clean." Reaching out with the hand not shampooing his hair, he pulled her up against the rim of the copper tub, slipped his hand between her legs, and slid two fingers inside her.

She caught her breath at the tremulous flurry of pleasure seeping upward from the point of contact. The intensity of the drugs in her body had diminished from the raging, torrid peak, but the residue still exerted considerable libidinous ferment. And she found herself strangely restless, overwrought, a simple touch keenly felt, feverish beyond her memories of fevered need.

"More," she said, leaning into his hand.

And he obliged, dexterous in not losing the rhythm even when he briefly submerged to rinse the soap from his hair. "That will do now," he murmured, coming out of the water, rising to his knees. "This level of cleanliness will have to suffice." And leaning over, he gently spread her legs, placed his tongue on the pulsing tissue of her clitoris, and licked with such delicacy, she fervently whispered, "Oh, my God . . ."

The heated pleasure pulsed in a widening effervescence, spreading outward from the expert ministrations of his tongue and fingers, intensifying with provocative subtlety, the glow moving by minute degrees to tinder point, the feeling so deliriously fine, she cried, "No, no, no," as her climax washed over her, not wanting it to end.

Her eyes opened after a languorous time.

"Welcome back." Pasha smiled up at her, and rising to his feet a moment later, he stepped from the tub.

"I'd forgotten—" she softly breathed, not moving, the heat still fluttering through her senses.

He cast her a small incredulous look as he reached for a towel. She was no novice to orgasms.

"—how good you are."

The cynical taint vanished from his gaze. "Well,

thank you, ma'am," he murmured, amusement rife in his tone. "Allow me to refresh your memory tonight."

"You bring me such joy, Pasha." She was touched by feelings that transcended all the poetic, poignant, most zealous sentiments of love and affection. She gazed at him, his smile so generous, lighthearted, roguish, and blissfully hers at the moment.

"I'd ride to the ends of the earth for what you bring me," he said, tossing the towel aside, closing the distance between them.

"I'm very grateful you came for me. Words can't adequately convey how deep-felt my feelings."

"I know." He pulled her into his arms, experiencing the same profound gratitude. He would have killed a hundred men to have her back, although he was careful to make no mention of his bloodthirsty thoughts.

"But I don't want to waste time talking."

His brows rose. That was his line.

Her arms twined around his waist, she gazed up at him. "Just hold me and love me," she gently said.

"With pleasure," he smoothly replied, but the smallest niggling unease crept into his mind. Had he met a woman like himself, interested in transient pleasure, in living only for the moment? She was certainly unconventional, sailing to Greece to find him, and so irrepressibly seductive he found himself contemplating the idea of a harem without complete repugnance.

"I don't want to think about anything tonight," Trixi whispered, having been too recently traumatized to begin sorting out the disarray of her emotions. "I want only to feel."

The too-familiar words struck him oddly, as if he were listening and speaking simultaneously.

"Kiss me," she whispered, rising on tiptoe.

Disturbed by her frankness, he almost said no. But

ultimately not *that* disturbed, his libido reminded him. A monk he was not.

He kissed her.

And then she kissed him.

Everywhere as it turned out.

Very quickly he decided he preferred the bed. "You taste lemony," she murmured, moments later, trailing kisses down his stomach.

"It's the soap." No longer concerned with unresolved issues, his mind was as focused on feeling as hers.

"Does everything taste lemony?" she seductively purred, touching the crest of his erection quivering just short of his navel.

"Let me know." His voice was rough-soft, a smile beneath the words.

She forced his arousal upright and licked the engorged head like a lollipop, wetting it completely with her tongue, watching it swell larger, her body responding to the tempting sight. The ache between her legs intensified, the throbbing accelerated as she drew the crest into her mouth and softly sucked.

There was never a time in his life that he'd wanted a woman with such pressing urgency, and only seconds later, lifting her head away, he abruptly said, "That's enough."

Pulling her down beside him, he immediately rolled over her, forced her legs apart, and drove into her. "There," he murmured, half under his breath, plunging in with a savage thrust, yielding to the most selfish of impulses. He felt an overwhelming need to possess her in the most elemental way—dominant male to submissive female. No games, no seduction, no motive beyond the inexcusable one of ownership. "I'm sorry," he whispered, penetrating deeper, as if the words absolved his brute, primal urges.

"I want you more," she breathed, understanding, clinging to him. "Let me feel you . . ."

She offered him all he wished, because she wished it, too, perhaps more. He was like water to her parched soul, joy to her deprivation, the lodestone of her desire.

They made love that night like two people who had almost lost each other, whose lives had been in mortal peril.

Who had survived.

Toward morning, when carnal passion had been slaked and languor had overcome desire, they lay in each other's arms content. "Stay with me," Pasha said, lightly stroking her back, "so I can always feel you."

"How can I refuse?" she whispered, half asleep in his arms.

"Good." He shut his eyes, tightening his grip.

Paradise was within reach.

13

The ride to Nauplia the next morning was dew fresh, sparkling, a new day, a new beginning, and as they rode side by side, they discussed staying together— "permanently," Pasha said. An evasion of sorts for a man who had not to date considered any permanence in his life, the word just short of the fearful word, marriage.

But Trixi was content with any nuance of the word permanent, feeling blissfully happy. She smiled across at him.

He smiled back, all the memories of the previous night joyfully filling his mind, happiness oddly tangible, alive as he gazed at her. It also helped that Hussein Djeritl was dead.

They stopped for lunch at a friend's house outside Tripolitza, a poet who fought for the Greek cause because he had a wife and young children who needed to be free, he said. As they were leaving, he gave them a poem he'd written, for a wedding present, he jovially declared.

Riding away from the small house, Pasha looked at Trixi and smiled. "Well, what do you think?"

"About the price of currants or something more personal?"

"Something more personal."

"Are you capable of saying the word?" she teased, in tune with his thoughts.

"Certainly. Are you?"

A small silence fell, only the sound of hoofbeats echoing on the summer air. "I can say the word marriage," she slowly replied, "but the concept brings up demons I'm not sure I can deal with."

"We don't *have* to get married," he casually remarked, but rather than relieved, he felt disgruntled. Perhaps he'd always had women say yes, perhaps he'd gotten what he wanted too long. Or maybe he was finding he couldn't live without Trixi Grosvenor.

"We certainly don't have to get married today," she pleasantly remarked, cowardly, evading all her demons.

"What if I want to marry you today?" The grievance over Hussein reasserted itself in his mind as did the unanswered question of a pregnancy. She seemed immune to both; did she prefer her freedom?

"You're joking."

"Answer the question."

"It's too sudden."

"Do you love me or don't you? That's simple enough." A small truculence colored his words.

"I do love you." She had for a very long time.

"Marry me, then."

"My Lord, we're riding another three hours to Nauplia. You've had too much sun. Why so insistent?"

Leaning over, he grabbed her reins and drew them both to a halt near a small grove of olive trees. Dismounting, he tied the horses, walked around her mount, and put his hands up to her. "Get down."

"I thought we settled all the tyrannical behavior last night."

"Please dismount, Lady Grosvenor," he said, punc-

tiliously courteous. "I have a matter of some importance to discuss with you."

"You *have* had too much sun," she playfully said,
sliding into his arms, her heart suddenly beating
wildly.

He set her on her feet and taking her hand, drew her
under the shade of an olive tree. "There's a possibility I
may have lost my mind," he said with a faint smile,
knowing he was jettisoning Hussein together with all
the corollary emotional baggage. "Certainly, I've lost
my seat at the Libertine Bachelor's Club, for which I'll
have to forfeit a hefty sum for their next revel—if you
say yes," he softly finished.

"Seriously?"

"I've never been more serious," he gravely said, all
levity gone from his face. "This is a long way to come
to find love."

"You didn't see it in Kent?"

"No, nor did you." He glanced around as if searching for some esoteric sign. "Am I right?" he softly
inquired, his dark gaze frank, direct.

She nodded.

"I hope you don't need all the gracious phrases," he
went on, tipping his head marginally by way of apology. "I'm not capable of that. But I want you to marry
me."

"Why?" She should be sensible and just say yes, but
this was too sudden and he was more emphatic than
romantic.

"Damned if I know. You'll have to show me in the
next hundred years."

How much did hearts and flowers matter? she wondered, trying to understand his blunt sentiments.
"You're sure, now?" she offered.

"Please, just say yes."

"Well, yes, then," she softly said. "If you don't faint from sunstroke in the next few minutes."

"I don't want a yes, then. I want a yes now."

"Yes. Satisfied?"

He smiled. "Apparently you haven't read the etiquette books that explain how to accept a marriage proposal with grace and compliments."

"I could change my mind."

"No, you can't."

"You're not in charge."

"Neither are you."

"We're partners, then."

"On the ship of love, on the road of life, til all the seas run dry," he went on, grinning. "We'll get married at the monastery."

"Do *I* have anything to say about it?"

"You can pick the hour tomorrow."

"Tomorrow!"

"Morning or evening," he offered, teasing laughter in his eyes. "You decide."

"We'll *discuss* it tonight."

"Excellent." He was very good at persuasion in bed.

While the newly betrothed couple continued their journey to Nauplia, two men carried their luggage into rented rooms near the monastery of St. Elijah. Once their gear was stowed, the younger man stood at the window, his gaze scrutinizing the narrow street below, his glance sweeping upward at the last toward the monastery gate. "This will do," he softly said, pushing the shutters open wider, leaning out past the sill. "An easy shot from the south." He swiveled his head to look uphill again and calculated briefly. "Even at night," he noted, easing back into the room. "We should be able to cover anyone coming or going into the monastery."

Turning to his companion, he asked, "Is the ship captain ready?"

"A boat is waiting on shore to take us out," Jerome replied, seated at a small table, loading his rifle.

"With Makriyannis returned and the Turk Hussein's head on display in the town square, we just have to wait for the lady and Duras to show up. Once she's reunited with her son, the boy should be taken out from under his heavy guard at the monastery." With enough money, information was for sale. Jerome's accomplice had been scrupulous in his research.

"I'm not impatient," Jerome said, sliding in another cartridge. "Now that we're in position, we'll stay here however long it takes for them to ride out from that monastery."

When Pasha and Trixi rode past the house late that afternoon, the man from Marseille on watch at the windows called Jerome over. "Just to confirm," he murmured, indicating with a nod the two figures on horseback traveling up the narrow street.

"Lady Grosvenor in the flesh," Jerome whispered, a slow smile creasing his gaunt face.

"She might be worth saving," the man who answered only to Marcel quietly breathed. Even dressed in male attire, Lady Grosvenor would fetch a tidy sum in the slave market, her bosom straining the fabric of the military jacket she wore, her shapely legs discernible beneath her linen trousers. The pistol at her waist only enhanced its narrow span, the gun belt pulled tight to keep the jacket closed. And such pale hair and sumptuous beauty. He might keep her himself for a time. Which complicated his plans slightly. Shooting three people and escaping was easy enough, but if he wanted to take her alive, an added risk factor had to be considered.

"Don't get any ideas," Jerome warned, moving away from the window. "I want her dead."

"You could get your expenses back if we sold her in Constantinople. The sultan has a penchant for golden-haired women," he pointed out, quietly closing the shutters, his shoulder muscles rippling under the shirt he wore.

With money Jerome's first priority, Marcel had chosen a judicious approach. But Marcel knew a number of men like Jerome Clouard who prided themselves on value for their money; he wasn't a novice when it came to the avarice of wealthy men.

"How much?" Jerome had the look of a vulture, cautious but clearly interested.

The husky young man shrugged. "With her extravagant charms and the ear of the sultan's minister, probably two hundred thousand francs."

"Is it possible, though," Jerome charily inquired, "to capture her? She's sure to be guarded."

"Anything's possible," Marcel flatly said. He picked up his jacket from a chair. "I'll go and snoop around, see if I can acquire any new gossip."

"What if they should come out while you're gone?"

"They won't. She'll take time with her son. But if they do," he added with a half-smile, "shoot them yourself. You'll save part of my fee."

"You're back!" Chris exclaimed when his mother walked into the small dining room where he was having supper with a monk and two young boys who had been brought in from Nauplia as playmates. "You found Pasha!" he cried, catching sight of the tall man entering the room behind her. His mother had gone to visit Pasha for a few days, he'd been told. Jumping from his chair, he raced toward them.

Trixi scooped him up, lifted him into her arms, and

hugged him hard, deeply grateful to be back with him, thankful he was safe and healthy and in good spirits. "Have they kept you busy while I was gone?" she murmured, squeezing him tight.

"I've been playing war with Michael and George." Pushing away, he gazed up at her. "Pappas shows us the maps,"—his head swiveled toward Pasha—"so we know where you're at! Mama," he whispered, casting a glance at his friends, "put me down. They'll think I'm a baby."

Pasha smiled at Trixi over her son's head. "Would you like to show your friends the yataghans we collected on our last campaign?" he asked.

"Would I!" Chris renewed his efforts to escape his mother's hold. Relinquishing her much-too-grown-up son, Trixi put him down.

"The swords are in my room," Pasha said. "Jules has them."

The boys were gone a second later.

"So much for being desperately missed," Trixi murmured with a rueful smile.

"Jules tells me Pappas took special pains to see that Chris had companions to play with while we were gone. He didn't want him concerned for our absence." The men had had a brief conversation in the courtyard, Jules detailing the pertinent activities at the monastery, Pasha leaving Jules with a small commission to perform.

"I appreciate Pappas's efforts," Trixi said. "But Chris is growing up too fast. I'm losing my baby."

Pasha laughed. "You lost that baby quite awhile ago, you haven't been paying attention. Although," he murmured low so the monk at the table couldn't hear, "I'd be happy to give you another baby if you'd like."

She blushed, her gaze flicking toward the table in warning.

"We could talk about it later," he went on in a conversational tone.

"How sensible, Mr. Duras," she crisply replied. "Since we're supposed to eat now." The table was covered with a variety of dishes.

"Are you *hungry?*" His voice held the faintest innuendo, his dark eyes more explicit in their message. "Because we could eat later . . ."

"We might be expected—"

"I'll take care of that. Brother Konstantinos," he said, approaching the young monk at the table, "the lady is fatigued from travel. Could we have her dinner brought to her room? I'll send my man."

The young man stammered slightly in awe. Pasha Bey, who had taken so many enemy heads, was a renowned figure. "Of . . . of course. She need . . . only ask."

"Thank you, too, for caring for Christopher. He seems in excellent spirits."

"He's a cheerful young boy and very good at the war maps," the cleric replied, on more comfortable ground with talk of war. The friars of St. Elijah had been one of the first brotherhoods to rise against the Turks. "We kept apprised of your movements with the daily reports Makriyannis sent back. Hussein Djeritl was a grand trophy. Pappas said a thanksgiving mass when we heard the news."

"He deserved to die," Pasha curtly said, a flare of anger in his eyes.

"For the thousands of lives he's cost the Greeks."

"For one transgression in particular," Pasha softly murmured.

"He made a mistake taking your lady," the man said, understanding.

"Yes, that was a mistake." A second passed before the shuttered look vanished from Pasha's eyes, and when he spoke again, his tone was deliberately mild. "If you'll send the boys to Lady Grosvenor's room when they return, we'd appreciate it. She missed her son."

"Yes, sir," the monk replied with deference. His God was a militant God, and men like Pasha Bey with their bravery and courage, were his Lord's disciples on earth. "Will Ibrahim attack Nauplia?" he abruptly interjected, wanting his hero's expert opinion before he walked away.

"He's been ordered to Missilonghi by the Porte, so fortunately he won't return this year. He'll be in winter quarters soon."

"Are you staying through the winter?"

"It depends on the lady." Pasha's voice was casual.

"Greece needs you." The young monk's boldness brought a visible flush to his tanned skin.

Pasha glanced at Trixi waiting by the door, his indecision plain. He exhaled softly. "That's what I have to talk to her about."

But the remainder of the evening was taken with boyish conversation and play, Chris and his companions filling the rooms of Trixi's apartment with careening charges and noisy attacks against imaginary Turks. It was late before the boys were put to sleep, their bedtime extended on this special occasion.

After dozens of final questions, four delaying drinks of water, and a multitude of promises given for more play tomorrow, Chris and his playmates fell asleep at last. "Are you tired?" Pasha murmured, brushing Trixi's fingers as they exited the boys' room.

"I should be but I'm not." Slipping her fingers in his, she smiled up at him. "Too much excitement."

"You didn't tell Chris about our marriage plans."

"There never seemed an appropriate opening. He was more engaged in battles and weapons."

"Do you mind, all this talk of war?" he softly inquired, drawing her down the corridor.

"I wish there wasn't a war, of course. But there is and it's not going away."

"Until the Turks are gone."

She nodded.

"I have a serious question." He came to a stop.

"Please, Pasha, not now," she pleaded, "not when everything is so pleasant again. If you're going to say you don't wish to marry, I understand. You've lived such a different kind—"

He stopped her words with a lightly placed finger on her mouth. "It's not that," he murmured, smiling down at her. "I'm marrying you. My feelings for you are unequivocal."

"Love, you mean?" A mischievous grin suddenly appeared.

"My *love* for you is unequivocal," he silkily rephrased. "Is that better?"

"I should make you go down on your knees and ask me," she teased.

"Not likely, and you've already agreed. So I'm absolved from that humiliation." His expression turned serious again. "If you want me to wait with my question, I will . . . If you—"

"No . . . ask." Her eyes held his. "This world we're in won't wait for very much."

"I'm afraid not. So would you mind," he slowly began, "staying in Greece after we're married, through the winter perhaps—maybe a little longer if necessary? I *should* send you home. Any man of principle would. But I can keep you safe." His brows rose in brief disparagement. "At least I'll try. With the current status of the campaign, the fighting could be over in a matter of months. Since I can't leave, selfishly, I want you with me."

"Is that all?" she replied with a great sigh of relief. "Good God, Pasha, you couldn't have *made* me leave. Do you think I could sail away not knowing from day to day where you were, whether you were alive or dead? Actually, you might have to take me with you on campaign. I'm equally selfish about *your* company."

His smile could have melted the glaciers at the poles. "That must be why I love you. Your bloodthirsty nature intrigues me."

"And I'm a damned good shot."

"Always my highest priority in selecting female companionship." His voice was playful.

"While I've always been drawn to your virtuoso ability to keep me shall we say, happy, all through the night."

"A plain-speaking woman," he said with a grin.

"If I'm not mistaken," she seductively purred, "night has fallen."

"Do we have time to reach your room or would you prefer"—he glanced up and down the darkened hall—"a prelude here?"

"I'm not so rash," she said, tugging on his hand. "This is a monastery, after all. If a monk should come . . ."

He smiled. "I'm much less impatient than you, darling. If you can wait, I certainly can."

"You've had more practice." She glanced up at him walking beside her. "This is all very new and exciting to me."

Exciting. The word startled him for a moment. "You mean traveling to Greece?"

"No, I mean having sex with you. It's irrepressibly, heedlessly exciting, Pasha Bey," she finished with a seductive purr.

He chuckled. "I'll see if I can live up to your expectations."

"Oh, I'm sure you can."

"Perhaps I can think of something memorable on our betrothal night."

"That in itself is memorable," she facetiously noted. "Did you realize you must be faithful now?"

He hadn't of course. Men of his class rarely were. "Really," he ambiguously said.

"Absolutely. You've turned pale, darling," she mischievously replied. "Was it something I said?"

He had no intention of discussing fidelity. "I have a surprise for you," he said instead, moving up the stairs to her room overlooking the bay. "Tell me if you like it."

A moment later he opened the door and stood aside so Trixi could enter first. Arrested on the threshold, breath held, she gazed on the splendor of hundreds of twinkling candles. Votive candles lined the windowsills, were massed on the table and bureau tops, illuminated the bedside tables and magnificent icons on the walls. Four large *torchères* stood at the head and foot posts of the large bed. And the prie-dieu held a huge bouquet of white lilies that scented the room.

"Go inside," Pasha murmured, pushing her lightly. "I want you to pick out your betrothal gifts."

When she moved into the room, the twinkle of candles on the windowsills and tabletops turned out to be not only the flame and sparkle of lighted wicks. Amidst the colored votive glasses were scattered a sultan's ransom in precious jewels. Some stones were unset—diamonds, rubies, emeralds, sapphires strewn like glowing embers on the stone and wood surfaces. Strings of pearls draped on the prie-dieu caught her eye; they cascaded over the velvet prayer rail, hung from the silver vase, coiled in gleaming ropes around the icon of Saint George above the lilies.

"Come see the diamonds," Pasha softly said, turning her toward the bed.

She gasped, this young woman from Kent who had lived a quiet, frugal life for so long. A silver salver had been placed in the center of the bed. Piled high with diamond jewelry, it blazed in the candlelight.

"Take whatever you want—or all of it. I didn't know your taste in jewelry."

"How . . . where . . ."

"Jules did it," Pasha noted. He smiled. "I said candles. He's very creative."

"There's so much," she whispered, almost struck dumb by the display.

"Part of my booty from Hussein's harem and entourage—they travel in style. My percentage supports the hospital, but there's more than enough funds for the hospital. Take it all if you wish."

"That would be terribly greedy."

"You're allowed, darling," he indulgently said. "Try some on."

"Really?" The heap of luminescent jewels had the look of fantasy, overwhelming her.

"Try on what appeals to you. There's a mirror on the bed and more baubles on the tables. I'm going to have a drink." And while he lounged on the bed and drank brandy, Trixi sat beside him and draped herself in jewelry.

"It seems like playing dress-up," she blithely said, adding another bracelet to her wrist. "Do you like me in emeralds?" she sportively inquired, holding out her arm for Pasha to admire.

"I like you in anything or nothing at all. Preferably nothing, but I can wait," he genially replied, her pleasure so obvious he was more than willing to oblige her.

"Should I take my robe off?" She touched the silk

skirt of the dressing gown she'd changed into before dinner. "Why didn't you say so?"

"I was being courteous and tactful and in general accommodating."

She glanced at the array of jewels spread over the bed. "Oh, yes, this is definitely accommodating." But her voice had changed at the end and when she said with narrowed gaze, "Have you—"

"No, I haven't. You needn't ask." He knew that calculating look.

"Never?"

"Only for you."

"I'm enormously jealous."

He thought of Hussein; he'd never be able to forget Hussein if he lived ten thousand years. But he kept his voice moderate by sheer dint of will. "I know what you mean."

"I'm so desperately in love with you, it's frightening."

He gazed at her draped and dripping with colorful necklaces and bracelets, brooches and rings—and two sets of earrings, one hooked to the other. How young she looked, how vulnerable in the white moiré gown, and beautiful. Even beneath that gaudy excess of jewelry. "I'm frightened, too," he softly agreed. "It's terrifying to contemplate love in the midst of a war, but I believe in luck and good fortune. How do you suppose I found you? So no more dismal talk. Pick out a wedding ring now. Good God," he went on, grinning, "we're actually getting married."

"I can see I'm going to have to take your mind off such disconcerting thoughts."

"I've an idea."

"I thought you might. But you'll have to indulge me first."

"Of course." It was his most charming trait with women. He never said no—to anything.

"How do you know what I want?"

"It doesn't matter." Long ago he'd learned to decipher the nuances of female propositions. A nun had asked him once in an inn parlor in Zante whether he believed in God, when she'd been asking something else entirely. His responses to the more conventional inquiries were second nature. "Are we doing this clothed or unclothed?"

"Ummm," Trixi facetiously murmured, her finger to her chin in mock consideration.

"You're such a sweet ingenue, darling, in all your ostentatious glitter."

"But I don't want to be an ingenue," she said, her pout delicious. "I feel more like a courtesan in all these glittering jewels."

"Real courtesans are very modish and fashionable."

"I could be a tart, then."

He laughed. "And who would I be?"

"The man with the enormous cock."

His grin flashed white. "An irresistible role. What must I do?"

"You must audition for me."

"Audition?"

"I'm a very demanding tart."

"I see," he murmured, sitting up, shrugging out of his jacket.

"You don't have any questions?"

"The role seems self-explanatory. Will I be performing with you?" His vest came off next and joined his jacket on the floor.

"Of course. I do all the auditioning personally."

"Do you now?" he said, his fingers arrested on his shirt sleeve button, the merest contention in his voice.

"Is that a problem?"

"It depends." He unbuttoned the cuff.

"On?"

"The degree of fantasy in this production." The other cuff was opened.

"We'll have to see, won't we."

"Without a doubt." He stripped his shirt off. "Do you undress?"

"Not usually," she replied with a sweet insolence that set his teeth on edge. "Would you like me to?"

His dark eyes traveled slowly from her face to her crotch and back again. "Suit yourself," he brusquely said, tossing his shirt aside.

He rose from the bed, and his boots and trousers came off with a swiftness that both irritated and excited her. He was much too adept at undressing, Trixi thought with her own heated temper.

And he was aroused.

Splendidly aroused.

As usual, she petulantly thought. "What if I said this role required abstinence? Could you do that?"

He stood very still for a moment. "Why would I want to?"

"That's not the right answer from a man marrying in the morning."

"Nor is your interest in personal auditions," he curtly retorted.

"You must be faithful to me."

"I'll keep you locked up," he growled.

"Oh, dear," she said, very, very softly—all the terrors of her past marriage flooding back. "I can't do this."

"What?" he gruffly muttered, but a wary caution revealed itself in his gaze.

"I'm not walking into another vile marriage," she whispered. "I'm sorry." She began stripping the jewelry away. "This was all a terrible mistake."

He watched her slide three rings off and a string of
pearls, his own uncertainties and resentments con-
founding. But beneath the flash and iridescence of the
sparkling gems was Trixi Grosvenor, who'd suffered too
much already in her young life, he thought.

A tear slid down her cheek and she quickly turned
her head away, her fingers fumbling at a bracelet clasp.

"I can't stand to see you cry," he murmured, her
misery woeful, his conscience pricking him.

She brushed her cheek with her fingertips and turned
back to him, her expression tremulous, her eyes shiny
wet. "I'm *not* crying."

"I apologize for everything," he said, not sure it was
enough, not sure he was capable of obliterating any of
the horrors from her past. "Marry me." He moved a
step closer to the bed, smiling. "Don't leave me standing at the altar."

"It's not funny, Pasha." Sniffling, she slid a diamond
bracelet back and forth on her wrist.

"I know. Forgive me." He placed his hands on the
bed, bending low so their faces were level.

She looked at him through her half-lowered lashes.
"It's scary."

"Let me show you it doesn't have to be that way."

Her chin came up a fraction. "You're going to
change?"

"Yes." He sat down beside her.

"You can't."

"Yes, I can. The same way I know enough to take my
hand off a hot stove. I'm capable of making that decision."

"For how long?"

"Forever."

Utter silence hung suspended in the candlelit room,
the distance separating them mere inches.

"I have a son, too."

He began breathing again. "I know. He likes me."

"It's really hard to trust someone again." She nervously plucked at the skirt of her dressing gown.

"Let me change your mind."

"Like this?" She swept her hand over the jewelry heaped on the bed.

"No, like this." In a flashing second he'd leaned over and lifted her into his lap in a rustle of watered silk. "I love you," he whispered, tenderly holding her.

"Do you know what that means?"

"We'll learn together."

"Because I'm no specialist in the field."

He smiled. "I was being polite."

Her mouth twitched into a grin.

"That's better," he murmured, bending to kiss one corner of her smile. "Have you picked out an engagement ring? Because I'm determined to do this properly this time and get down on my knees and ask you to marry me."

"On your knees?" Her expression brightened.

"Don't look so gratified. How about this ruby?" He held up a heart-shaped stone framed with diamonds.

"I like it." The gems were all magnificent.

"In that case . . ." He slid her from his lap, seating her on the edge of the bed in her billowing angel-white gown. Going down on one knee, he gazed up at her and gravely said, "I love you with all my heart." His smile was full of grace. "I've loved you from the first time I saw you. I should have known . . . I should have paid attention." He wondered how he could have overlooked the truth so long. Humbled by the timely opportunity for redemption now that he'd found her again, he softly asked, "Would you do me the great honor of becoming my wife?"

Trixi's eyes filled with tears.

"You have to say yes." He wasn't a man to be completely humbled.

She nodded, her throat too full to speak.

It was enough; he wasn't going to tempt fate or her irresolute emotions. Sliding the ring on her finger, he swiftly rose and swept her up into his arms. "I'll make you happy, I promise," he whispered, moving to the windows overlooking the bay, the white sweep of her skirt trailing over his arm, brushing his bronzed leg. "Look, Orion is giving us his blessing."

"Like the first night I met you." She gazed at him, her eyes huge with hope. "You were very good to me that night."

"And you were the most irresistible temptation. Like now."

"It must be my jewels," she teased.

"I don't think so." His smile was affectionate. "Much too parvenu."

"Maybe you should take them off," she murmured in a tone that immediately caught his attention.

"It would be my distinct pleasure," he whispered back.

The jewelry was removed between teasing kisses and playful repartee, and by the time the bride-to-be was stripped of all but her engagement ring neither could conceive of ever having another disagreement.

The glow of candlelight lent a magical radiance to the room, gilding their twined bodies, warming their senses, Pasha's bronzed skin taking on a sepia hue in the shimmering flame. His long dark hair gleaming blue-black, scented, lightly brushed her face, his strength and power engulfed her, his wickedly sensual eyes heated inches away, raked her with a smoldering gaze.

And she could only purr in gratification. He was enormous, filling her, gorging her, bestowing resplendent pleasure with unbridled stamina and finesse. When she gazed up at him and said as much in sighing bliss, he dipped his head and lightly bit her earlobe. "I'll stand stud for you anytime, my insatiable nymph," he whispered. "Did I find you sleeping in a meadow, flushed from the summer sun? See how pink you are as though the sun has warmed you. Look." He reached for the mirror she'd preened before while admiring her jewelry. "See how dark my cock is sliding into you," he softly said. "How pale your skin." Lifting the mirror from beneath folds of embroidered coverlet, he held it out to her.

She shook her head and bit her lower lip, struggling against the shameful excitement his words incited.

"You still blush, my darling nymph, when I've already fucked you a hundred times. You can look, sweet. It's allowed. There's no one to see your wantonness. Look how long my cock is." He pulled a pillow down, propping the silver-framed mirror at a convenient level. "How can you take it all? Does it hurt when you whimper?" His lower body was moving as he spoke in a slow, exquisite rhythm, tantalizing now rather than satisfying, teasing.

She whimpered, entreating him to deepen his thrust.

"That can't hurt, I'm only halfway in," he whispered, pretending to misunderstand her appeal. "You can see how much more is left."

Clutching his lower back, she tried to draw him in.

"You have to look." He took her chin lightly between his thumb and forefinger and turned her head.

His enormous erection was only partially submerged, the portion visible in the mirror engorged, pulsing, his swarthy skin in riveting contrast to her creamy flesh. Enticed by such stark, unrestrained maleness, her vagina fluttered, as if cajoling the instrument of its pleasure into closer contact.

He felt the heated shimmer. "You must be ready," he breathed, slipping his hands under her bottom, lifting her, continuing his penetration by minute degrees.

She watched his long, hard length slide in, felt the tremors of pleasure, the feverish rapture overwhelming reason, and she drifted away into a sensual nirvana.

"Open your eyes or I'll stop."

His voice seemed distant but she assimilated the pertinent words, her covetous needs sensitive to his threat. Her lashes lifted.

"That's better," he whispered. "Tell me when I'm all the way in."

The image in the mirror was tantalizing, terrifying, a prodigious length still flagrantly visible.

"Can a nymph fully absorb a satyr's cock?" he softly queried.

The core of her body pulsed in response and she nodded, breathless, every nerve quivering with longing.

"I can't hear you."

"Yes," she whispered, shuddering with need.

"You can take all that?"

His erection seemed to swell before her eyes and inside her in an explosive melding of feeling and vision. She gasped at the rarefied ecstasy.

"You have to tell me."

"I'd like it all," she breathed, naked entreaty in her voice, on the very brink of orgasm, the wanting so ravenous she trembled in anticipation.

"Watch," he softly ordered, his thigh muscles flexing. And when she did, he swung forward, his dark-skinned erection slowly disappearing, her tissue reluctantly yielding to his engorged size. She melted around him. He could feel her sleek, fiery heat, her tightness surrendering to his entry until he was completely embedded and she was quivering irrepressibly.

"Tell me you're mine." It was the softest whisper, but jurisdictional, possessive, his need for ownership acute.

"When you do," she murmured, breathless, saturated, flooded with pleasure, but her sense of autonomy still operating under the deluge.

"I'm yours." Unguarded, he opened his heart.

"You have me body and soul, every breath and touch and feeling." Speaking in a sultry purr, she languidly moved her hips so the searing rapture heightened to a raw, indelibly sweet profusion that glowed through her body, sparked an answering heat in his.

"You're so damned luscious," he breathed.

"And you're just perfect for me." Her smile was flirtatious, coquettish, filled with love.

"I know."

14

They were married by Archbishop Gregorios the next morning in a small ceremony attended by Makriyannis and his troop, the brotherhood of St. Elijah and, for reasons of legality, a French and English counsel.

Young Chris gave his mother away with boyish pride in a chapel gilded by the light of hundreds of candles, bouquets from the monastery garden perfuming the air.

As Trixi slowly walked down the nave, her small son's hand in hers, Pasha waited for his bride at the altar, love and pride in his gaze, a feeling of heartfelt gratitude in his soul. She wore a simple dress Makriyannis had purchased in Nauplia, pink silk with a white-ribboned waist, a nosegay of white roses in her hand. A chaplet of the same white roses wreathed her brow and she looked an angel, golden-haired, ethereal, breathtaking. And his.

The Greek marriage ceremony was abbreviated for the sake of a four-year-old boy, and perhaps for Pasha as well, who had an aversion to ceremony. When they were pronounced husband and wife, he presented Trixi to the small audience with a graceful bow and a broad smile. "My wife, ladies and gentlemen. I consider myself the luckiest man in the world today," he cheerfully proclaimed.

Trixi cried at the sweetness of his words and smile

and he immediately kissed her because it was the only
way he knew to silence female tears. Their audience
cheered and clapped their approval, Trixi stopped crying, and Pappas had to cough loudly after a lengthy
time to remind Pasha Bey he was in church.

The reception took place in the walled lily garden and
everyone made merry, the war ignored for a time. The
newlyweds had made plans to spend two honeymoon
days at a villa outside Nauplia. Not precisely alone, for
Chris would accompany them with his friends and
Makriyannis and his troop would stand guard. But it
would be a honeymoon, no matter its brevity and the
entourage in attendance. Pasha had promised himself to
give Trixi those two days at least before he left on campaign again.

He wouldn't tell her until absolutely necessary that
she wouldn't be accompanying him.

He didn't wish to mar the sweetness of their time
together, perhaps the last they would ever have with
the war once again taking center stage. Makriyannis and his men had been ordered to break through the
Turkish lines at the siege of Missilonghi.

The troop was noisy as they left the monastery late
that afternoon, wine having flowed freely all day. But
the soldiers formed a guard around Trixi and the boys,
a matter of habit in this war-torn land. Weapons were
at the ready, the men in battle formation, Pasha and
Makriyannis in the lead.

News of Pasha Bey's wedding couldn't be concealed
in a town where informers fed informers, where a dozen
countries had spies, where the exact whereabouts of a
troop like Makriyannis's could make the difference between life and death to a Turkish battalion.

Marcel and Jerome Clouard had been waiting since
morning; there was only one road to and from the
monastery.

Positioned at the open window of their apartment, Jerome had six loaded weapons beside him on a table, his best rifle in his hand. A tremor of excitement ran through him when he first heard the sound of men's voices drifting down the hillside from the road above.

They were coming.

Personal reasons now impinged on Marcel's objectives and purpose. Since he'd seen Lady Grosvenor, he'd not been able to stop dreaming about her. He could almost feel her pale, silken hair, see her eyes raised to him in surrender, feel himself penetrate her lush body. Soon, he thought, sitting perfectly still in a tree that overhung the road. Trained to the inch, he intended to drop onto her mount as she rode beneath and make off with her.

Jerome was to shoot the boy—the easiest task. Marcel would take on Pasha Bey, who he assumed would escort his wife. A professional killer, Marcel had every confidence in his abilities. And then he heard the men's voices, too.

His adrenaline began pumping.

As the troop passed down the roadway on the outskirts of the city, a number of people lined the verges of the road, offering flowers and congratulations to Pasha, wishing him good fortune on his marriage. News of his nuptials was abroad; a soldier of glorious exploits and renown, he was a hero in this small country at war. Leaning over in the saddle, he acknowledged his well-wishers, accepting the flowers, shaking their hands, or simply smiling at the shouted felicitations.

"So much for secrecy," he said to Makriyannis, riding at his side, tucking a small bouquet under his barb's bridle. But he was grinning, in high good spirits on his wedding day.

"The news is already on its way to Constantinople,

Pasha Bey," Makriyannis cheerfully noted. "Secrets don't last long in a city seething with spies."

A woman ran out with flowers and Pasha bent low to take the proffered bouquet. "May you have a long life, Pasha Bey," she sang out, "and many babies."

Pasha laughed. "I'll do my best."

"Babies, Pasha Bey?" Makriyannis sardonically queried. "A new concept for the standing stud of the western world."

"I like babies," Pasha serenely replied, adding the flowers to the others in his saddlebags, sheer happiness purging Hussein from his thoughts.

"Really. Last I recall, you prided yourself on your discretion in that regard."

"Trixi likes babies."

"Ah . . . and you're willing to comply."

"More than willing," Pasha said, his smile broad, "so I don't need any of your—" A gleam of metal caught his eye and his glance swung back to it. Even before the image fully registered in his brain and his gaze came to rest on the gun barrel, his instincts had come alert to danger. "Sniper!" he screamed. Whipping up the rifle resting across his lap, he twisted around and fired from the hip at the figure in the window. Swearing at his negligence in not having scouted the road, he jerked his horse sharply to the left and plunged back up the hill, racing for Trixi and Chris. "Back!" he cried. "Go back!" as the crack of rifle fire burst around them. His gaze swung up to the window. The man was wounded, but still firing into the troop. Galloping hard, he snapped his rifle butt to his shoulder, taking that extra second to carefully sight on target.

He squeezed the trigger.

And Jerome Clouard's head exploded.

But an unnatural silence had descended around him,

and when his gaze swiveled around, he hastily reined his black to a stop.

A man was mounted behind Trixi, his muscular arm around her waist, his pistol barrel pressed against her temple.

And he had the icy, hard look of a man who knew how to use his weapon.

Chris, mounted beside his mother, was white, paralyzed with fear, the troopers surrounding Trixi and her son, utterly still.

"I'll pay you any price," Pasha shouted. "Let her go."

"Now if only I trusted you, Pasha Bey," Marcel returned, his voice taunting. "I want you to all move out of my way . . . slowly, very slowly, or this pretty lady gets a bullet in her head. And I know none of you want that."

"Take Christopher away," Trixi urged, her greatest fear for her son. "Do what he says."

"Drop your weapons, first, or I'll shoot the boy, too."

"No!" Trixi pleaded.

"You heard the nice lady. She doesn't want to see her son killed. Drop them."

Pasha dropped his rifle first and everyone followed suit, their weapons quickly discarded.

"I like to see that kind of cooperation," Marcel said, his voice bland, dispassionate. "Now, if everyone will ride back to the monastery, the lady and her son will live—at least for a time," he brutally added.

Makriyannis looked to Pasha and he nodded his assent, kicking his horse into a walk. He and the troop complied with the man's instructions; he couldn't take any chances with Trixi and Chris. Swiftly returning to the monastery as directed, Pasha rode into the courtyard and once the gates were shut, he jumped from his mount and called for Jules. "The Clouards have taken Trixi and Chris," he brusquely told him. "Get rid of

these flowers and find us some less conspicuous dress."
Turning to Makriyannis, dismounted and at his side, he
went on, "What do you think—workingmen's clothes,
peasant dress?" Jules was already relaying instructions
to two monks. "I want to be back on his trail in five
minutes," Pasha murmured. "We'll go out the back
gate. The kidnapper doesn't have any choice but to
leave Nauplia instantly. Otherwise he knows we'll find
him."

"The harbor, then," Makriyannis noted, stripping off
his embroidered coat.

Pasha nodded. "Our first search area." While they
waited for the garments, Pasha quickly outlined the
direction of their pursuit, indicating to the men the
direct routes to the docks, possible hiding places, by-
ways that would serve a man attempting to conceal
himself. "Talk to anyone who might have seen them,
scour the alleys and backstreets in case he's gone to
ground. I'll take two patrols to the docks. We have
three hours, gentlemen, until dark." He paced then,
taut and silent until the clothing arrived. Throwing on
a coarse linen smock over his shirt, he leaped into his
saddle, wheeled his mount, and galloped toward the
rear gate.

Everyone understood the necessity for speed. With
nightfall, the abductor could easily slip by them and
sail away to any distant shore. The harbor was filled
with ships from around the world, the slave markets of
Constantinople only a few hours away.

"Now that was almost too easy," Marcel softly murmured, his breath warm on Trixi's cheek, his pistol
concealed under her hair at the base of her ear. He held
her and Chris's reins in the hand pressed tightly against
her stomach, easing the two mounts down another side
street on his cautious journey to the harbor. Chris sat

his pony in silence, his frightened gaze on his mother, knowing she was in danger with the man's gun to her head. "Your new husband wasn't as brave as I expected," Marcel mocked, "although he's a damned good shot. Clouard's head virtually disappeared."

"Clouard?" she blurted out, unable to contain her astonishment.

"He was obsessed. All he could think of was killing your son." Marcel spoke casually, no more emotion in his voice than if he'd been remarking on the weather. "That's pretty stupid when the kid will fetch a pretty sum in the slave market. Young boys are favorites there."

His words struck terror in her soul. She knew of the demand for young boys in the Levant. The thought of her small son alone and in fear, bartered away on the slave block, was so ghastly, so sad and awful she wanted to cry and scream and swear vengeance against all the torments that had befallen her because of Theo's inheritance. She felt besieged, beleaguered, attacked at every turn by the Clouards, the Grosvenors, Hussein Djeritl, and now this unknown man, his pistol barrel millimeters from her brain.

This was hardly the time for anger and yet she felt an inexplicable fury beginning to pervade her mind, a simmering resentment against the greedy, rapacious men who felt they could impose their will on her and her son.

How dare they do this to her again? she hotly reflected.

Her pistol was in her saddle scabbard hidden under her thigh, and she knew how to use it. Hotspur temper drove her, as well as the fear they might be taken away where no one would ever find them again. Her right hand came up in a blur of motion, knocking the pistol barrel away from her head, at the same time driving her left elbow into the man's stomach with such force it felt as though she'd dislocated her shoulder. Already reaching for her weapon, she closed her fingers around the grip and jerking the handgun out, half-twisting, she fired under her arm—once, twice, emptying both barrels.

Her horse reared at the sound of gunshots and clutching the pommel, she screamed, "Ride, Chris! Ride away!" But the arm around her waist only tightened, the reins were jerked hard to control the horse, and Marcel snarled, "I should kill you." Blood was discoloring his jacket but her shots hadn't been mortal. "Call your son back right now," he growled, bringing the mount to a halt, "or I'll shoot the brat."

Although Chris had ridden a few dozen yards away, he'd pulled his pony to a halt and waited, fearful of leaving his mother. At Trixi's request, he slowly returned, fear written across his young face.

"Now take his reins," Marcel ordered, prodding her head with the pistol barrel, "and see that we get down to the harbor without further incident or I'll kill you both. If it comes to your lives or mine, you understand who lives and who doesn't."

Trixi didn't dare call out to the few people they passed, not wishing to put Chris at risk, and when they came to the harbor, a boat crew was waiting for them. She and Chris were placed beside her abductor, his pistol hard against her ribs. None of the crew spoke as they rowed them out to a vessel flying a Cypriot ensign. A privateering ship for hire, she didn't doubt, the role of the Cypriots in the war of independence flexible—their only concern which side best paid their fees. Once on board the brig, Trixi and Chris were escorted to a small cabin and locked in.

The sound of receding footsteps left Trixi feeling utterly defeated. On an unknown ship, in a horde of anchored vessels in the harbor, she and Chris were completely hidden away. And once the vessel sailed, they might as well give up any hope of freedom.

Chris was mute. Huddled on his mother's lap, his normal chatter stilled, he seemed to understand the extent of their danger even without explanation.

She rocked him, singing a familiar lullaby, hoping to calm his fears. But her own heart was beating in double time, and panic filled her brain.

"Pasha will shoot them."

Startled, she abruptly stopped her song.

"I been thinking," her son calmly went on, the contrast of his childish voice and grave assurance oddly whimsical. "Pasha will shoot them dead for sure, so you don't have to worry no more, Mama."

Tears came to her eyes at his solemn announcement, his utterance so hopelessly impossible she didn't know how to respond. He didn't understand they were going to be sold into slavery, and she dared not even contemplate what lay before them then. "We'll pray very hard that he comes to save us," she quietly said, tightening her hold on her precious boy.

"He will, Mama. He's strong."

How simple Chris made everything sound; how elemental. As though strength and bravery always prevailed and the villains of the world received their just punishments. "Maybe we should see if we can find some way to help Pasha when he comes," she suggested, wanting to engage his interest beyond the dilemma of their abduction. It helped her own depressed sensibilities as well to at least search for some possibility of escape.

The room held two bunks, a table, a chair, and little else. But a small portal offered light and a view of the sea. Chris had already pulled a chair up to it and, standing on tiptoe, was peering out. "It doesn't open,

Mama," he said, hitting the glass with the palm of his hand. "We need to smash it and jump into the water."

Swinging around, he looked at her quizzically for a moment. "Maybe you won't fit." He glanced at the small portal again. "I'll stay with you til Pasha comes," he decisively went on, taking on the role of protector with such seriousness, it brought a lump to her throat. "He'll be here quick, I know."

"Then we'll just wait," she softly said, wishing and hoping her son was right, because the room had been stripped of everything, including the mattresses on the bunks. And they were bereft of all resources save their wits.

"I'm telling you again, even if I had the fiends of hell on my heels, we can't set sail until the wind comes up," the Cypriot captain firmly said, his French rough but recognizable. "Look for yourself." He gestured in the direction of the main mast. "There's not a breath of air in the sails."

"Dammit!" Marcel angrily jabbed the weapon he held at the captain's chest. "When the hell will that happen? You're being paid a damned fortune to see that we sail!"

The old, grizzled captain mistrustfully eyed the wounded man brandishing the pistol. Regardless the sizeable fee he'd been paid—and not by this man—it wasn't worth his life. "One never knows," he cautiously replied, "but the horizon has the look of storm clouds. Possibly within hours."

"Hours!" Marcel exploded. "I don't have hours!"

"You should have your wound dressed," the captain suggested, hoping to divert the conversation. He couldn't command the wind no matter how loudly the man screamed.

"It can wait," Marcel snapped. His flesh wound

wouldn't kill him. "Send another lookout up, dammit. I want to know the second the wind comes up."

"Do the woman and child require anything?" the captain inquired. He'd been paid to sail to Constantinople, and understood without saying that his passengers were intended for the slave market. "You probably want them in good health."

"Have them fed something, I suppose," Marcel gruffly noted, his mind totally consumed with setting sail. "And bring me a bottle of rum."

Pasha and Makriyannis's men spread out across the harbor, interviewing scores of people, searching every dwelling and business, discovering at last when a young boy came forward, that a small dinghy had left shore some time ago from the docks of an untenanted warehouse. A woman and small child were aboard. But the boy hadn't taken note of the dinghy's course for he'd not lingered at the docks. After rewarding the youngster, Pasha stood looking across the harbor, his gaze sweeping the multitude of anchored craft, knowing Trixi and Chris could be on any one of the ships. "We have to get to every damn vessel."

"We've enough men," Makriyannis noted, sympathy in his gaze, understanding how narrow their window of opportunity.

"I want a messenger sent to each vessel," Pasha declared. "Have the captains informed that I'm offering a million groschen reward for the return of Trixi and Chris."

"That should be enough to bring out the Judas in Clouard's minions."

"We hope," Pasha gruffly replied. "It'll be dark soon, and should the wind come up . . ." His voice trailed off, his jaw taut. Abruptly turning from the sea, Pasha waved Makriyannis along, and the two men strode briskly to the seaside inn where their troops had been left. In short order the men were given instructions, and after enough boats were procured, the troops dispersed on their mission, rowing out to every vessel in the harbor with Pasha's extraordinary offer. The peasant garb no longer necessary, their military uniforms lent them an air of authority.

When the messenger climbed aboard the Cypriot ship and asked for a private meeting with the captain, Marcel watched from a discreet distance, his gaze wary. But the Greek returned almost immediately from the captain's quarters, reentered his dinghy, and was rowed back toward shore.

Entering the captain's cabin without knocking, Marcel stared suspiciously at the Cypriot sitting behind his desk. "What did the Greek soldier want?"

"The harbormaster has imposed some new fees," the captain smoothly countered, placing some papers he held in his hand in a box on his desk. "They're informing everyone."

"He looked like a soldier to me." His brows drew together in a scowl. "What are those papers?"

"The government employs the men not on campaign for shore duty. And these are bills of lading for part of my cargo," he went on, much preferring to discuss his cargo rather than the messenger's visit.

"Show me."

When the captain handed over the few papers, Marcel surveyed them but he didn't recognize the language, with the script so crabbed and small. "You wouldn't be lying to me now, would you?"

For a million groschen, the Cypriot captain would have lied straight-faced to God himself. "You can see the columns of items and prices. We're carrying dried currants and wine, that's all."

Marcel's gaze bored into him for several tense moments. "We *have* to sail tonight." It was an order.

Relieved he'd accepted his explanation of cargo fees,
the captain felt a modicum of tension drain from his
body. "The wind should be up soon. Look over there."
He pointed through the stern windows at a faint
shadow on the horizon. "That cloud should blow up a
breeze. Would you like more rum?"

Marcel seemed to be examining him again, each
word, each nuance.

The captain took care to keep his expression bland,
his tanned, weathered face a mask.

Several more moments of silence passed.

"Why not," Marcel muttered.

The captain's lean face creased into a smile. With a
million groschen, he could give up his privateering.
"Use my cabin if you wish," he offered, rising from
behind his desk. "I'm going to stay on deck and watch
for the coming storm."

That examining stare again, and then a nod of acceptance.

It would take a half hour or more for the troops to
return, the captain reflected, shutting the door behind
him, striding out onto the deck. Once at the port rail,
he scanned the shore rather than the horizon, his glass
coming to rest on a portion of the docks where a large
troop of soldiers was assembling.

The sun was low on the horizon when the boats filled
with soldiers put off from shore. Their direction wasn't
clear at first but within fifteen minutes, as the long
shadows of sunset stretched over the harbor, it was obvious the boats were making for the Cypriot vessel.

"Strange," a voice behind the captain softly murmured, "that we'd be having guests so late."

The captain spun around and came up against the
barrel of Marcel's pistol.

"Perhaps they're coming out to discuss more harbor fees," the Marseillaise killer sardonically said. "Send them away." His voice was suddenly curt. "Or you die where you stand."

"They won't listen. They don't care if you shoot me." The captain had survived three decades of privateering because he never underestimated his opponents. "They're going to attack and board us."

"In that case, I don't need you." Marcel fired point-blank, and as the old captain staggered backward, he turned and ran toward Trixi's cabin.

At the sound of the shot, Pasha shouted to the oarsmen for more speed. In brief moments, his troops were throwing up grappling hooks and swarming up the sides, the crew of the Cypriot vessel knowing better than to oppose the boarding.

The shot hadn't been audible below decks, but the sound of running footsteps alerted Trixi, and she and Chris were standing when the cabin door was thrown open.

"Get over here!" Marcel barked, gesturing with his pistol.

Could Pasha be near? Her abductor was obviously agitated. She didn't move.

"Get over here or I'll shoot that useless pup!" He directed his weapon at Chris.

Trixi swiftly moved, trying to shield Chris with her body, holding him close to her side.

"Up on deck and fast!" Marcel ordered, jerking them through the door, shoving them into the narrow passageway. The sounds of men's voices drifted down the companionway, the intonations strident, loud, a clamorous hubbub of shouted orders resonating in their ears. Until they appeared on deck, Marcel's hand hard on Trixi's shoulder.

Every voice and movement abruptly ceased. The

men could have been statues in the glow of the setting sun, mute, utterly still.

Marcel's pistol was at Trixi's head, her body clasped to his, she and Chris his shield. "The captain turned out to be expendable," he announced into the hush. "I'm sure we can come to some agreement before these two become useless to me as well. I want everyone but the crew off this vessel."

"There's no wind," Pasha declared, his voice bland. "Let me charter an oared felucca and you can leave immediately."

"That must be why you're so rich, Pasha Bey," Marcel sneered. "You're smart."

"As are you, I'm sure," Pasha returned, moving toward them. "I'm willing to pay you whatever you want, do whatever you want, to bring this to a satisfactory conclusion."

"We'll talk satisfaction once you get the felucca," Marcel curtly replied. "And keep your distance." He held Trixi firmly around the waist.

Pasha turned to speak briefly to Makriyannis, who left with two men. "It shouldn't take long," Pasha explained, his voice deliberately polite, "with so many vessels in port. In the meantime though, why not let the boy go? He's so young."

"Why don't you just row back to shore and leave me alone," Marcel silkily argued.

"If you didn't have my wife and son, I would." Pasha stood very still, his voice unruffled, like an island of sanity in the terror.

"Get the oared boat," Marcel brusquely noted, "and we'll talk."

"Fair enough." Pasha remained where he was; no more than twenty feet away, bristling with weapons, Makriyannis's troop ranged along both rails. The crew had retreated out of gun range.

Everyone waited.

"Hi, Pasha," Chris said into the lengthening silence.

Pasha smiled at Chris.

Trixi squeezed her son's hand in warning and tugged him closer, as if she could protect him with her body.

Looking up at his mother, Chris said in a clear, piping voice, "I told you Pasha would come."

"Shut the brat up," Marcel growled.

"Hush, darling," Trixi quietly warned. "Just for now."

"For how long, Mama?" Four-year-olds didn't stand still or silent willingly.

"Not too long, darling," she murmured, tightening her grip on his hand.

"But I don't want to." Chris struggled to pull free.

"Darling, please." Trixi fought his resistance.

"You're hurting my fingers!" Squirming and jerking free, he leaped away.

Heedless of her own danger, her only thought to save her son, she lunged forward to pull him back, but all she caught was a wisp of his shirt on her fingertips.

Her frantic gesture left Clouard's hired killer an open target.

"Stay down!" Pasha shouted.

As she dove for the deck, the deafening roar of gunfire exploded above her head, a hundred klephts firing at her abductor. Bending low, Pasha sprinted forward, scooped up Chris under one arm, and raced toward Trixi. Seconds later he lifted her from the deck and, carrying mother and son, strode away from the sudden quiet at the scene of carnage. The klephts were superb marksmen, and in order to protect Trixi and Chris, their target had been high and tight. Only bloody gore marked the remains of Marcel's head.

Her face buried in Pasha's shoulder, Trixi clung to him while he took them far down the deck, well away from the killing. Setting Chris atop a large coil of rope, he gently placed Trixi on her feet and held her close. "You were very brave," he said to Chris, patting him on the shoulder. "You're going to grow up into a fearless warrior."

"Mama needs us men to be strong for her," Chris proudly declared, his pink-cheeked countenance breaking into a wide smile. "You sure shot him deader than dead. Show *me* how to shoot like that! Look! Here comes the rowboat."

Trixi slanted a startled glance at her exuberant son.

"No trauma, darling," Pasha whispered, taking note of Makriyannis at the bow of the fast-moving vessel.

She gazed up at him, her brows quirked faintly in disbelief. "I'm beginning to think this is all a normal life."

He shook his head. "Not for you, it isn't." His voice was suddenly weighty with concern. "It's too dangerous."

"It is for you as well."

"That's different," he gruffly muttered.

"Really."

"Don't become difficult, sweetheart," he quietly said. "You can't stay in this war zone."

"Paris or Kent are safer?"

"Yes, after I cower or kill every last Grosvenor and Clouard. You can't stay here, and that's that."

"Excuse me. Is that an order?"

They were both speaking in an undertone, Chris's attention fortunately distracted by the imminent arrival of the felucca.

"I'm absolutely firm on that point," Pasha tersely said. "You could have been killed today."

She shot him a determined look. "I'm not going to live my life in fear. I'll just have to carry a better weapon, a larger calibre."

"You can't control the course of events with one weapon."

"You do."

"Along with a small army at my back."

"Then that plan should work for me as well," she sweetly maintained.

Jumping down to the deck, Chris ran toward the men throwing ropes to the felucca coming alongside.

"He's not frightened, as you see," she noted. "And I can deal with my apprehensions. If you're staying, we will, too."

His brows arched. "Even if I disagree?"

"Even then," she pleasantly affirmed. "Did I tell you I'm seriously thinking about having a baby?"

"No." His mouth immediately set in a firm, hard line. "No," he harshly repeated. "That's the last thing I need right now—a pregnant wife. It's bad enough when you can ride or run or shoot your way out of danger. But if you're pregnant or with a very young baby—no," he growled. "Absolutely not."

"But then you don't have much to say about it," she serenely returned, not willing to be separated from the man she loved.

"Damn right I do."

"You're not going to touch me, you mean."

"Well, I wouldn't go that far, but I'll manage not to get you pregnant."

"Maybe you have already. Have you thought of that? And if you haven't, I might be able to *see* that you do," she murmured, her smile dulcet innocence.

"Is that a challenge?" he silkily inquired.

"It could be."

"You don't stand a chance," he drawled.

But very late that night, in their honeymoon bed at the villa north of Nauplia when she gazed up at him and said, "Please, please, please," firm principles were less easy to maintain. Her face was bathed in moonlight, her eyes gleaming with tears and entreaty. "What if I never see you again?" she whispered, her voice breaking at the end. "Please, Pasha . . . I love you so much. Don't tell me no again."

He briefly shut his eyes. Would he lose her in this war more readily, put her at greater risk if he gave in to her pleas? Was it a moot point, already beyond decision-making? How could he live with himself if something happened to her—if she died?

"I'll be careful, Pasha, I won't get in harm's way," she whispered as though she could read his mind. Reaching up, she touched the grim line of his mouth.

He took her hand in his and gently kissed her fingers, his mind in tumult. "If I agree," he slowly murmured, wondering if this conversation was irrelevant, if she was already pregnant with his or Hussein's child, "you'd have to stay here under guard."

"Yes, yes. You'll come to see me?" His hand enfolded hers and she wished with all her heart that the war wouldn't harm them, that they'd have the chance to grow old together, touching, close like this.

He exhaled slowly, still debating all the precarious unknowns, the three-year siege of Missilonghi about to come to a bloody climax. "I'll come to see you when I can," he softly said.

She couldn't ask for more; she knew better than to insist on riding with Makriyannis's troops. "Thank you," she breathed. "I hope we do make a baby tonight, or we already have made a baby. *Our* baby," she wistfully murmured.

Her words gave him new pause, fatherhood a responsibility he'd avoided for so long. Nor had he forgotten Hussein. But the words "our baby" held such joyful promise and like her, he hoped a future existed for them all. And, too, he realized, love mercifully forgave everything. He loved her that way—purely, simply, without reservation. "I really hope so, too," he gently said, and taking her face between his hands, he dipped his head to kiss the woman who made life so dear to him.

EPILOGUE

Nine months later

Pasha Duras held his wife's hand while she cursed him and her own stupidity for not remembering the incredible agony of childbirth. He turned pale watching her suffer, wincing at each labor pain, deciding, as the ordeal continued for what seemed endless hours, that he would see that she never had another child.

But when their daughter was born and the memories of labor had faded—the body's way of ensuring the survival of the species—they both agreed their pink-and-white and golden-haired daughter was perfection beyond all standards of perfection.

Pasha and Trixi named their daughter Venus, for obvious reasons. For her beauty, for the affection they held for Greece, because she was the unmistakable manifestation of their love.

The war came to an end for a time when Britain, France, and Russia intervened and defeated the Turkish navy at Navarino, their own interests at last helpful to the Greeks. Their decision had nothing to do with freedom or democracy or the liberation of Greek culture from the sultan. It had to do instead with the balance of power.

But Greece regained a modicum of freedom in the peace treaty, the bloodshed diminished, and Pasha and his family sailed home to show off the newest member of their family to all the Durases and to Trixi's surrogate family at Burleigh Hall.

Andre and Teo met them in Zante, where they spent a fortnight getting to know their son's new family. Andre became Chris's favorite. A really, *real* general who had fought whole, *big* armies—in Chris's infectious, glowing syntax—was as close to any medieval knight as he could imagine. They became fast friends.

Holding her first grandchild in her arms, Teo felt an irrepressible contentment. The years had barely dimmed her exotic beauty, and at fifty-four she was still striking to behold. As was the plump, golden-haired baby in her arms. She and Trixi became dear friends, their independent personalities instantly kindred spirits. And too, they'd both survived cruel first marriages. It made one appreciate such darling men, Teo said to her daughter-in-law one day.

Trixi smiled her agreement. "Although I'm not so sure they need the flattery, considering the legions of adoring women in their wake."

"Don't worry about that," Teo replied, smiling. "They both know how lucky they are."

Father and son agreed, although with the kind of masculine brevity that didn't elaborate unduly on emotion.

"I like Trixi," Andre had said shortly after meeting Pasha's wife. The men were having a drink before dinner while waiting for their wives to join them.

"I can't live without her," Pasha simply said.

"I know what you mean."

Father and son smiled at each other and Pasha lifted his glass to his father. "To happiness," he saluted.

"And family," Andre Duras added. "The rest doesn't matter."

NOTES

Byron's interest in the Greek War of Independence is well known, as is his death in Missilonghi at the age of thirty-seven. While not the originator of the romantic attitude toward ancient Greece—many others had said the same things before him—he made the romance of Greece a bestseller. Enormous numbers of people read his poetry, not only in Britain and America, but throughout Europe, and the famous stanzas from *The Giaour* were inspirational to all who sympathized with those oppressed.

> Clime of the unforgotten brave!
> Whose land from plain to mountain-cave
> Was Freedom's home or Glory's grave!
> Shrine of the mighty! can it be,
> That this is all remains of thee?
> Approach, thou craven crouching slave:
>   Say, is not this Thermopylae?
> These waters blue that round you lave,
>   Oh, servile offspring of the free—
> Pronounce what sea, what shore is this?
> The gulf, the rock of Salamis!
> These scenes, their story not unknown,
> Arise, and make again your own.

The story of his journey to Greece inspired me as well. And as I researched his participation in the Greek War of Independence, his motives were both admirable and realistic; he detested what he called "enthusymusy."

His renewed interest in Greece (he'd spent seven months in Greece as a young man) was stimulated by the London Greek Committee, who approached him in Genoa to represent them as one of the three commissioners administering the loan they would send to Greece. His letters show an uncomfortable awareness that he was expected to play a role that he still could not quite comprehend. To be useful was his aim, but how was still uncertain. In his letter to Augusta Leigh in October 1823, he says:

"You ask why I came up amongst the Greeks? It was stated to me that my doing so might tend to their advantage in some measure in their present struggle for independence, both as an individual and as a member for the Committee now in England. How far this may be realised I cannot pretend to anticipate, but I am willing to do what I can."

He arrived at Missilonghi after an adventurous journey on January 4, 1824, and his last three and a half months are a deeply moving story of tragedy and disillusion, courage and glory. "I believed myself on a fool's errand from the outset," Byron wrote from Missilonghi, but he also wrote: "I must see this Greek business out (or it me)."

Always consistent through pain and disappointment, he continued the quest to be practical, useful, and constructive. "I am not come here in search of adventures," he told the romantic Stanhope, "but to assist in the regeneration of a nation." To his banker in Zante he wrote: "I still hope better things, and will stand by the cause so long as my health and circumstances will permit me to be supposed useful." Again he wrote: "I cannot quit Greece while there is a chance of my being of (even supposed) utility; there is a stake worth millions such as I am; and while I can stand at all, I must stand by the cause. While I say this, I am aware of the difficulties and dissensions and defects of the Greeks themselves; but allowances must be made for them by all reasonable people.

My future intentions as to Greece may be explained in a few words: I will remain here till she is secure against the Turks, or till she has fallen under their power. Whatever I can accomplish with my income, and my personal exertions, shall be cheerfully done. When Greece is secure against external enemies, I will leave the Greeks to settle their government as they like."

He was determined to do something after years of dissipation and ennui. "If I live ten years longer," he had said three years previously to his old friend Thomas Moore, "you will see that it is not over with me. I don't mean in literature, for that is nothing; and—it may seem odd enough to say it—I do not think it was my vocation. But you will see that I shall do something— the times and Fortune permitting . . ."

Nothing showed the character of Byron in a better light than his noble and humane conduct in Greece.

1. See page 16. Antonin Careme, born in 1783, was probably the greatest cook of all time. His work reflects the freedom of thought and action that flooded France after the revolution. Like Napoleon, he combined a classic sense of order with romantic ambitions and a flare for drama. At age nineteen he attracted the attention of the most famous statesman of the time, the Prince de Talleyrand, who kept one of the best tables in Paris. After leaving Talleyrand in 1815, Careme worked for the Prince Regent of England, Tsar Alexan-

der of Russia, and the British ambassador in Vienna before returning to Paris in 1823, where he enjoyed an Olympian fame.

One of his many inventions was the classic soufflé. As Anne Willan points out in her book *Great Cooks and Their Recipes* (Boston: Bulfinch Press, 1992), "Puddings made fluffy with meringue had been known for many years. It was thanks to new ovens heated by air draft instead of the old method of filling with hot coals that the constant heat needed for a true soufflé could be maintained. The *croustade*, or pastry case, was not eaten; it was made with the same straight sides as our soufflé dishes, and in fact inspired them."

2. See page 49. Years ago, I first read that Gericault had had a love affair and child with his young aunt. It was no more than a rumor, a line or two in a monograph of his life. Wildly handsome, talented, filled with angst, fire, and melancholy, dead at thirty-two, Gericault epitomized all the drama and pathos of the romantic movement in France. Since the illicit liaison with his aunt had always intrigued me, the role of Trixi evolved from that bit of gossip.

In my research for this book, I discovered that many new details of Gericault's affair had been unearthed in recent years. In the summer of 1815, Gericault (his signature appears in contemporary documents without the accent on the "e") entered into a clandestine, stormy love affair with his maternal aunt, Alexandrine-Modeste Caruel, the wife of Jean-Baptiste Caruel, the head of the family business. Barely thirty years old in 1815—Gericault was twenty-four—she was married to a man of fifty-eight to whom she had borne two sons, then six and seven years old. Gericault was godfather to her younger child, Paul, born in 1809. Their shared youth and tastes in art drew aunt and nephew into an

increasing intimacy that soon altered into a passionate
sexual attraction from which neither would ever re-
cover.

Disgraced by the birth of their child, Alexandrine-
Modeste was exiled to her estate of Chesnay near Ver-
sailles, where she survived her lover by fifty-one years,
dying in 1875 at age ninety. His memory remained
with her always, and she mourned his death to the end
of her life. Gericault's biographer, Clement, notes in a
letter to a friend, "She had gathered in her bedroom all
the relics, the sketches, watercolours, etc., that she had
from him, and never allowed strangers to enter, so that,
much as I tried, I could never see these works."

Although Alexandrine-Modeste submitted to her exile, there were many contemporary women who would
not have so docilely complied. Trixi is a composite of
the legion of early nineteenth-century women who not
only survived but prospered despite love affairs.

On his deathbed on November 30, 1823, Gericault
made a one-sentence will, appointing his father the sole
heir of all his possessions. On December 2, his father in
his turn willed their combined property to Georges-
Hippolyte, Gericault's son, then five years old and still
living nameless and obscure with foster parents. The
thought of his child must have weighed on Gericault's
mind as his health deteriorated. He knew that his father, aged eighty and rapidly declining into senility,
would not be able to provide for his son and that the
rest of the family, still unforgiving of his liaison with
his aunt, would be hostile to his boy.

3. See page 152. The secret of Gericault's love affair
remained closely guarded by his family and friends.
Clement merely hinted at it in his 1867 biography,
although he knew the identity of Gericault's mistress.
The sculptor Etex (see note 5) was the first to publish,

in 1885, the fact that Gericault had fathered a son. A chance find of family documents in Evreux in 1976 and subsequent searches in the *Minutier Central des Notaires Parisiens* finally enabled Michel Le Pesant, of the Archives Nationales in Paris, to unravel the true story and to shed some light on this unhappy, passionate episode in Gericault's life.

4. See page 152. I wrote a good deal of *A Touch of Sin* before going back to check my facts on Gericault. As I was developing the villainous uncles, I said to my daughter one day, "Maybe I'm making this too melodramatic. These men are not only trying to disinherit Chris, but intend to put his life in jeopardy as well." Then I read Eitner's definitive biography on Gericault—including the forty-one pages of footnotes, always the most interesting part of a book—and on page forty I came across this citation referring to Michel Le Pesant's research of 1976: "After Gericault's death, the elder Gericault, feeble in mind, was persuaded to sign a substitute will (dated July 24, 1824) which largely disinherited Gericault's child to the profit of various Clouard and Bonnesoeur relatives. With a touch of malicious humor, the drafters of the new will awarded the gold medal of the *Medusa* (a salon prize for Gericault's painting of that name) to Gericault's godson, Paul Caruel, one of the legitimate children of Alexandrine-Modeste." So I needn't have worried about melodrama after all—the truth was stranger than fiction.

5. See page 162. The only mention Eitner makes of Gericault's son, other than that he was nameless and in foster care when Gericault died, is the story related by Antoine Etex. Etex was a young sculptor who designed a monument for Gericault's grave, the model exhibited

at the Salon of 1841. Later that year, Etex tells of the evening when a shy young man of undistinguished appearance called at his studio. It was Georges-Hippolyte, Gericault's son, age 23, who had come to thank him on his father's behalf. Etex never saw him again.

After living in Paris for some years, pursuing architectural studies, Georges-Hippolyte settled in Bayeux, where he spent the remainder of his life—nearly forty years—living in the cheapest room of a small seaside hotel. After Georges-Hippolyte's death in 1882, his will, dated 1841, was discovered; besides various bequests to friends of his father, he'd left 2,000 francs to Etex and 50,000 francs for the completion and embellishment of the monument, next to which he wished to be buried. Etex, now forty years older, sculpted a monument to Gericault, which still stands on his grave at Père-Lachaise.

6. See page 182. Hundreds of Philhellenes of wealth funded expeditions of their own to Greece. I appropriated the cargo and money amounts for Pasha's expedition from those of Byron when he set out on his impulsive journey to Greece from Genoa on July 16, 1823. Byron took along chests of medicine to provide for a thousand men for a year, ten thousand Spanish dollars, and bills of exchange for forty thousand more. Also, when Thomas Gordon of Cairness sailed for Greece during the war, he chartered a ship and freighted it at Marseille and Genoa with six cannons, six hundred muskets, bayonets, and much ammunition—all at his own expense.

7. See page 183. Since the sword alone commanded respect and political influence in the Ottoman empire,

the power of the Albanians steadily increased as the strength of the Turks declined. Every pasha enrolled a guard of Albanian mercenaries, and a striking mark of the high position the Albanians had gained was exhibited by the general adoption of their dress. Turks and young Greeks of rank assumed this dress, particularly when traveling as it afforded them an opportunity of wearing arms. The Albanian kilt, as well as the dramatic, rich, and splendid garb, was imitated by everyone with pretensions to the military: gold-embroidered jackets and vests adorned with rows of gold or silver buttons, gilded swords, silver-mounted pistols. The arms and dress of an ordinary *pallikar* (warrior), made in imitation of the garb of the Tosks of southern Albania, often cost fifty pounds (two hundred fifty dollars). Those of an officer with the showy trappings for his horse generally exceeded three hundred pounds (fifteen hundred dollars). A warrior's arms were the pride of his heart, so every dollar he could get he expended in ornamenting and beautifying them. The stock of the pistol, the handle and scabbard of the yataghan, should be massive silver washed with gold. To obtain these, soldiers would endure for months and years the want of a shirt and all the comforts of life.

8. See page 183. In need of funds to continue the war, Greece approached several organizations interested in a financial alliance: The Knights of Malta, the French House of Lafitte, a retired Russian officer acting for the East India Company. The London Greek Committee were able to convince the Greek deputies Orlandos and Louriotis to accept their loan instead of the others'. At that time, England had an enormous surplus of capital. Huge sums were already invested in foreign government bonds and loans to poorer nations. If the

members of the London Greek Committee could raise a loan on the London Stock Exchange to finance the war for the Greeks and set the country on its feet, they and their friends would also profit. These businessmen, also interested in trade, were convinced they could exploit the valuable markets in the Levant. In January 1824, when the Greek deputies Orlandos and Louriotis arrived in London, accompanied by Hamilton Brown, they were given a grand reception by the London Greek Committee at the Guildhall. The banquet was graced by the presence of Canning, the British foreign secretary, a tacit sign of government approval. The Greeks accepted a loan from Loughman and Son and O'Brien, with the nominal value of the loan set at 800,000 pounds. The rate of interest was five percent or 40,000 pounds annually. Two years' interest was reserved, and a sinking fund of 8,000 pounds was placed under the control of Joseph Hume, Edward Ellice, and Andrew Loughman. The loan was floated at 59 pounds and the net sum raised was 472,000 pounds. But after various expenses had been deducted, the total sum available to Greece was 315,000 pounds. (In a Greek account the sum is noted as 280,000 pounds and called a very disadvantageous loan.) The difference translated into 157,000 pounds (or 192,000 by Greek accounts) for the use of the London brokers. William Cobbett, a celebrated journalist of *The Weekly Register,* made the London Greek Committee's mismanagement of the loans one of his favorite targets. None of the principals of the committee came out of the story with much credit; most of them made large personal profits.

A year later, another loan, for 2,000,000 pounds, was arranged in London. The actual sum realized was 1,100,000 pounds after deductions for a sinking fund, for contracting expenses, and for a fund to purchase script of the previous loan in order to rejuvenate it. So the London brokers made a very tidy profit on this transaction as well.

9. See page 183. At the time of the Greek War of Independence, so soon after the end of the Napoleonic Wars, Europe was full of disbanded army officers, men unqualified either by training or by temperament for any other trade. Many were drifting around the continent as mercenaries, participating in any revolutionary plot that offered employment; many also were in political disgrace or under suspicion in their own countries, so they could never go home. The scent of war attracted them, and rumors of the happenings in Greece aroused their wildest hopes for glory and promotion. In this flooded marketplace for mercenaries, Mehemet Ali, the sultan's Viceroy of Egypt, who recognized that European methods of warfare were more effective than any in the Moslem world, built up his army and navy with European instructors. And to all who would apostatize, he gave commands. The majority of his instructors were French, and the most senior was a romantic colonel called Seve. He was one of the very few men who claimed to have fought both at Trafalgar and Waterloo; a man of talent and few principles, he embraced Muhamet and was raised to high command under the title of Suleyman Bey. When Mehemet Ali's adopted son, Ibrahim, set sail from Alexandria to conquer Greece, many of the European officers who had long been employed in disciplining the troops accompanied him. And the medical staff was filled up by young surgeons, principally from Italy, who had been intrigued by the munificent promises of Mehemet Ali. Many French officers served on the Greek side as well, hoping their success in Greece might show that the Bonapartist party was still a living force and the French nation would do well to abolish the Bourbons and re-

vive the glories of the Empire. Other Bonapartist Philhellenes like Persat, Fabvier, and Jourdain felt a need to wipe out the stain of Waterloo, and Greece offered them that hope of victory.

10. See page 184. In Finlay's *History of Greece,* Lord Byron, who witnessed the firing of two Turkish men-of-war endeavoring to prevent the Greeks from taking possession of a stranded brig, quaintly observed, "These Turks would prove dangerous enemies if they fired without taking aim."

11. See page 184. I used *The Memoirs of General Makriyannis* extensively, since his account was less tainted with personal aggrandizement than some of the other military memoirs of the time. Also, he was born in 1797, which put him very close in age to Pasha. A survivor of the dungeon fictionalized in Gustave's character, he describes the events of March 1821: "At night, as Easter Sunday came in, I went to Arta, met my confederates, and told them the news. The heads of the leading men of Patras had been brought there, to be sent on to Khursit Pasha. Then I too was arrested as an unreliable subject of the sultan, since I had been over to the Morea. They put irons on my legs and inflicted other hardships on me to make me betray the mystery. I endured seventy-five days of ill-treatment.

"They were going to take twenty-six of us for the gallows, and, by the grace of God, I alone escaped. The others came from Vonitsa and other parts, and they hanged all of them in the bazaar. They wanted to question me again and make me declare my means of livelihood, so they brought me back from the place of execution before the pasha, who examined me on my means of livelihood and that of my fellow countrymen. They took me back to the castle to torture me for a second time and threw me into a dungeon.

"There were one hundred and eighty of us there. The place was full of rotten loaves of bread and we had to empty our bowels on them because there was nowhere else. The filth and the stink were abominable, none worse in the whole world. We pushed our noses against the keyhole of the door to get fresh air. And they beat me and inflicted innumerable tortures on me and almost finished me off. As a result of the beating, my body swelled up and became inflamed and I was at death's door. I offered a fair sum to a certain Albanian to let me out, so that I could see a doctor and get medicine and the money I had offered him. He detailed a Turk to go with me to my house. As we went along I was limping and groaning. The Turk was a stupid blockhead and he thought that I'd take leave of my life—he didn't know how firmly set it was inside me. When we got home, I lay down like one dying. Then the doctor came and I began to plan how I should escape from the Turk. I got out the money to give him, and I said to him, to the Turk, 'Take that. The Albanian told me you should give it to him so that there should be no one else in the plot.' I added about a hundred groschen for him. When he took it I said, 'Take the money back to the camp and come back for me when the doctor has mixed my medicine, so we can go back to the castle together, because I am not going out alone. I am too afraid of the Turks who live here.' He took the money, and as soon as he was out of the door I got myself away."

12. See page 189. In his memoirs, Makriyannis recounts that Dr. Julius Millingen betrayed the fort to

the Frenchman Suleyman Bey (Colonel Seve) when
Suleyman was sent with two others by Ibrahim to negotiate a surrender. "We had an English doctor with
us; he was paid five hundred groschen a month by both
myself and the Bey Zade. The government had made
terms with him but were not giving him his pay, so he
was paid by the pair of us. This man must answer for
the death of our comrades. He betrayed all the lack of
provisions we suffered in the fort: He told this to the
Frenchman in his own language when he came with
Hadjichristos. I would have killed the bastard but they
would not let me."

Millingen went over to Ibrahim's service and survived to go to Constantinople, where he lived for fifty
years as physician to five sultans and was the husband
of four wives.

As an aside, Millingen was one of the numerous doctors around Byron in the days before he died in April
1824, and contributed a good deal toward aggravating
his suffering. Millingen left his own account of the
treatment inflicted on Byron. It included bleeding, lu-
nar caustic, purgatives, and a solution of cream of tartar
known as "imperial lemonade." Millingen and Byron's
Italian doctor then disputed the merits of leeches on
the temples, behind the ears, and along the jugular
vein, as against antispasmodic potions of valerian,
ether, et cetera, but both agreed on yet more bleeding.
When all was over, Millingen sent in a bill for two
hundred guineas, on the argument that "Lords do not
die every day."

13. See page 191. As embarkation actually took place,
Ibrahim reneged on his agreement and Makriyannis
was told that Ibrahim was keeping some men behind.
The English, French, and Austrian ships taking the
survivors of Navarino away had no power to stop

Ibrahim, and sixty-three Greeks were kidnapped just as they were moving to the boats. They were seen carried off by Ibrahim's columns, and they were slaughtered in the fort as a Moslem sacrifice to Allah.

14. See page 198. It had been generally conceded that Gericault spent a continuous sojourn in England covering the better part of the two years 1820–21, until research by Donald Rosenthal in 1980 placed him in Paris in the summer and autumn of 1820. Further clarification by Christopher Sells was found in the archival source the *Enregistrement Chronologique de la Correspondance Reçue par le Ministère de l'Intérieur,* which records the issue of passports and visas during the years of the Restoration. The *Enregistrement* records the daily run of information received from the offices that dealt with the issue of passports, and from the frontier posts that checked or collected those of incoming travelers. It is a valuable source but not a comprehensive one: The registers do not list exits from ports and frontier posts, and apparently not all entries. A typical day's *enregistrement* contains lists of passports collected at frontier posts (registration occurring a few days after the report was made, depending on distance from Paris), a list of passports retrieved from the Prefecture of Police by travelers—foreigners and French nationals—arriving in Paris, a list of applications made for passports at the Prefecture of Police, a list of passports issued by the Ministry of the Interior to foreigners leaving the country, and a list of those issued to diplomatic personnel by the Ministry of Foreign Affairs. Names are carried onto an index at the end of each register.

In researching the records, it was discovered that Gericault traveled back and forth between France and England several times in that period. In terms of Trixi, evidence of her entry into France was available to the Clouards.

15. See page 220. It was customary, in true Oriental tradition, to exhibit the heads of important outlaws or enemies at the outer gate of the imperial palace at Constantinople. The same was done with the ears or noses of lesser rebels, especially when they were killed in large numbers in outlying provinces. The trophies were packed in salt to make the journey to Constantinople. The Greeks collected the heads of their enemies as well, and often pyramids of heads were erected on the sites of battles.

16. See page 242. The Albanians, raised to be warriors, fought for the Turks throughout the Levant. Mehemet Ali, the Viceroy of Egypt, had originally been sent to Egypt with three hundred Albanians under the command of a Turkish governor's son to fight the French in the Napoleonic Wars. Distinguishing himself for bravery, artful by nature, sure of the loyalty of his Albanians, he soon made himself superior in power to all the commanders of the sultan. Yet he was illiterate. He never learned to read or write, and only began to learn to speak Arabic when he was old. In 1824, when Egyptian forces were ready to fall upon Greece, the President of Greece, Konduriottis, and the Pasha of Egypt were both Albanians. The president of Greece did not speak Greek and the Pasha of Egypt did not speak Arabic.

The power of the Albanians in Greece was greatly increased in 1770 by the employment of a large force to suppress the insurrection excited by the Russians. Fresh bands of Albanians were again poured into the Morea by the sultan during the Russian war in 1787 to contain any rebellion, for the Greeks regarded these rapacious mountaineers with far greater terror than Turkish troops. About this same time, all the pashas in European Turkey greatly augmented the number of Albanian mercenaries in their service, and the military authority of Albanians spread across the empire.

17. See page 268. Both the Greeks and the Turks cut off the heads of their enemies. In addition, when any Greek warrior was seriously wounded in battle and could not be carried away, his comrades all kissed him and then cut off his head to take home to his village. It was thought a great dishonor to have the Turks bear away one's head.

18. See page 268. When I was planning this scene I needed a pistol that could fire more than once and be reloaded on the run. Luckily, the new developments in percussion caps were just becoming available in 1825. Multibarreled pistols firing single shots weren't a new innovation, but percussion powder was. In 1805 the Scottish clergyman Alexander Forsyth made a lock that used the detonating powers of fulminate, or percussion powder, to ignite the charge in a gun barrel. He patented it in 1807. It was a great improvement over the flintlock that was susceptible to damp or a broken flint, not to mention the obscuring of the target by the smoke from the priming pan. The successful introduction of percussion locks encouraged gun makers all over Europe to design new locks or actions. The Swiss inventor Samuel Johannes Pauly patented in Paris, in 1812, a revolutionary breech-loading system employing a metal-based cartridge with a central percussion primer. He came to London and patented, in 1814, another type of lock for his breechloader, which used the heat of compressed air to ignite the cartridge. The

manufacture of anticorrosive percussion caps was perfected by the London chemist Frederick Joyce, and they were soon readily available in their distinctive bags and tins.

19. See page 270. In the course of the war, women were sold in great numbers. Slaves were taken from Greece for the slave markets in Constantinople, while in Greece, the one purchase most men seemed able to afford was a Turkish woman, or several. They were being sold at thirty to forty piastres, according to age and beauty. Thirty piastres equalled one English pound or five American dollars, which meant a woman cost next to nothing. But at that time and place it seemed a perfectly moral transaction because it often saved the women's lives—although the men made the most of this aspect when they wrote about it afterward.

Oddly enough, it was in women that the Greek government made its only recorded profit. By some unaccountable chance, the only part of the booty of Tripolitza that fell to the government was the pasha's harem, forty ladies in all. The pasha was away commanding the attack on Joannina when the town was sacked, and a British ship came in to ask the price of the forty ladies' ransom. Presumably the ship came from the Ionian Islands, but nobody recorded and possibly nobody knew whether the message came from the pasha himself or from an enterprising tradesman who wanted to make a profit. Mavrocordatos or his spokesman asked a large sum of money, and the ship went away and soon came back with the cash. It was paid to the Minister of War and the forty women were placed on board.

Among them was the pasha's principal wife—said to be the sultan's sister—who went unwillingly. She'd not expected to see her husband again, and during her months of captivity she'd fallen in love with one of the handsome sons of Petrobey (a Greek warlord). Now the poor woman expected her husband would find out and she would be tied in a sack and dropped in the sea. She disappeared from history when she boarded the ship at Corinth. As you can see, the price for women varied greatly from next to nothing to very large sums—depending on circumstances.

ABOUT THE AUTHOR

SUSAN JOHNSON, award-winning author of nationally bestselling novels, lives in the country near North Branch, Minnesota. A former art historian, she considers the life of a writer the best of all possible worlds.

Researching her novels takes her to past and distant places, and bringing characters to life allows her imagination full rein, while the creative process offers occasional fascinating glimpses into complicated machinery of the mind.

But perhaps most important . . . writing stories is fun.

ROBBIE CARRE IS BACK!

You met him in Susan Johnson's sensational bestseller *Outlaw*. Driven from Scotland, he now returns home to reclaim everything he'd been forced to leave behind— including the beautiful Roxane.

Don't miss this new spectacular romance from Susan Johnson, coming soon from Bantam Books.

Don't miss any of the sensuous historical romances of

Susan Johnson

___29957-3	*Blaze*	$5.99/$7.99 Canada
___57213-X	*Brazen*	$5.99/$7.99
___29125-4	*Forbidden*	$5.99/$7.99
___56328-9	*Love Storm*	$5.99/$7.99
___29955-7	*Outlaw*	$5.99/$7.99
___29956-5	*Pure Sin*	$5.99/$7.99
___56327-0	*Seized by Love*	$5.99/$7.99
___29959-X	*Silver Flame*	$5.99/$7.99
___29312-5	*Sinful*	$5.99/$7.99
___56329-7	*Sweet Love, Survive*	$5.99/$7.99
___57215-6	*Taboo*	$5.99/$7.99
___57214-8	*Wicked*	$5.99/$7.99
___57865-0	*A Touch of Sin*	$5.99/$8.99

From *The New York Times* bestselling author

Amanda Quick

stories of passion and romance
that will stir your heart

Teresa Medeiros

Breath of Magic
___56334-3 $5.99/$7.99 in Canada

Fairest of Them All
___56333-5 $5.99/$7.50 in Canada

Thief of Hearts
___56332-7 $5.50/$6.99 in Canada

A Whisper of Roses
___29408-3 $5.99/$7.99

Once an Angel
___29409-1 $5.99/$7.99

Heather and Velvet
___29407-5 $5.99/$7.50

Shadows and Lace
___57623-2 $5.99/$7.99

Touch of Enchantment
___57500-7 $5.99/$7.99

Nobody's Darling
___57501-5 $5.99/$7.99

Ask for these books at your local bookstore or use this page to order.

Please send me the books I have checked above. I am enclosing $_____ (add $2.50 to cover postage and handling). Send check or money order, no cash or C.O.D.'s, please.

Name _____

Address _____

City/State/Zip _____

Send order to: Bantam Books, Dept. FN116, 2451 S. Wolf Rd., Des Plaines, IL 60018
Allow four to six weeks for delivery.

Prices and availability subject to change without notice.   FN 116 12/98